a parable of regret, and those stories are truest when the protagonists are people like us, ordinary people who are neither excessively virtuous nor intrinsically evil."
—*American Book Review*

"…vividly-realized, bringing both past and present to life."
—*Prick of the Spindle*

"This story is so believable and well-told that I felt I had an insider's knowledge of what it would have been like to live through the protests on college campuses during the Vietnam War era."
—*Whistling Shade*

"… a masterful job of evoking memories of the halcyon days of political activism."
—*The Baby Boomer Brief*

ALSO BY BOB SOMMER

Where the Wind Blew

"In this sensitive and heart-felt novel, Bob Sommer examines the impact of shattering violence on three generations of an American family. While rooted in the landscape of eastern Kansas in the late twentieth century, the story opens itself to all of us, tracing with care and insight the struggle to overcome loss and to forge new bonds of love and trust in the face of all the challenges that life presents."
—Kimball Smith, author of *Missing Persons* and *Nothing Disappears*

PRAISE FOR BOB SOMMER'S *WHERE THE WIND BLEW*

"*Where the Wind Blew* is a story of the past and an allegory of the present.... Bob Sommer hears the music and voices of the past and gives you what America has become today."
—Mason Williams

"Emotionally taut and historically intriguing, this novel explores the psyche of a man whose past finally catches him. Although set in the past, its themes transcend time."
—Ron Jacobs, author of *The Way the Wind Blew: A History of the Weather Underground*, writing for *Counterpunch*

"This blistering, fast-paced tale of a man whose radical past catches up with him... cross-examines our culture, then and now."
—*Chronogram*

"I had a hard time putting *Where the Wind Blew* down."
—Robert Pardun, author of *Prairie Radical: A Journey through the Sixties*

"*Where the Wind Blew* is not intended to be a story about a hero but

A GREAT FULLNESS

BOB SOMMER

Fomite
Burlington, VT

Cover Painting
Artist Edward Hopper
Rooms for Tourists
1945
Oil on canvas
Yale University Art Gallery
Bequest of Stephen Carlton Clark, B.A. 1903

ISBN-13: 978-1-942515-33-3
Library of Congress Control Number: 2015958602

Fomite
58 Peru Street
Burlington, VT 05401
www.fomitepress.com

*Erin, Alex, and Francis have ever been a source
of inspiration, encouragement, and infinite love.*

"Cool!" Francis would have said.

For Heather,

lover, muse, friend

CONTENTS

I have been in a place where
nothing is, it is not
silence, for there are voices, not
emptiness, for there is
a great fullness…

> —Robert Penn Warren,
> "A Place Where Nothing Is"

Strawberry Ice Cream

PINK RIVULETS TRICKLED DOWN Kim's knuckles and onto her T-shirt and shorts as she swirled her tongue over the mound of strawberry ice cream atop her cone. She sat on the curb by the pick-up, arms draped on her splayed knees like Daddy when he sat on the back steps in the afternoon heat. Nearby, a gleaming SUV rocked into the curb. People climbed out and hurried by, edging past others also headed for the counter window.

She sculpted the ice cream into a creamy precipice with a morsel of frozen strawberry embedded in the summit. She licked deeply beneath the summit, plowing all the way around until it resembled a snowman's head, a pink Cyclops snowman, like the monster in the book Mommy read to her, with the strawberry morsel for its eye. And then, in one gulp, with her lips pulled back over her teeth – the ice cream was so cold! – she decapitated him, took his head right off and worked it around her mouth, savoring the sweet, smooth lump as it oozed down her throat. Then she studied her next approach to the shortened summit.

—Kimmy, you done yet? Daddy said.

He sat nearby at a concrete patio table with a watery Coke.

A klatch from the Dairy Queen window paused, ice cream cones in hand, wondering if he was about to leave. All the other tables were taken. They looked expectantly at Kim, who pursed her lips in a thoughtful scowl, shook her head no, and took another layer off the cone.

Ross Oden hadn't noticed them, nor their sniffs of irritation as they drifted past. It was the kind of thing he did notice. On another day, he would have stared down the fat man in shorts and sandals who frowned at Kim and sent him skulking off. All it would've taken – a look. Even more than his size and thick tattooed arms and calloused, grimy hands, the reckless anger in Ross's eyes would have served notice that he was ready in an instant to turn a peaceful outing for ice cream on a warm Kansas evening into whatever the man wanted.

But Ross ignored him, and the man in shorts and sandals wandered off never knowing what might have happened.

Ross clawed ice from his cup and rubbed it over the fresh scratches on his hands and neck. The ones on his neck irritated him most, as if he'd been stung by wasps.

Daddy shook his cup, rattling the ice, raising it to his open lips and allowing shards to slide into his mouth, now crunching them and staring off vacantly as more customers passed. All that remained of Kim's pink ice cream was at the bottom of the cone. She nibbled at its crunchy edge.

His key ring dangled from his belt like a shiny spider. Sometimes Mommy tied Kim's bright plastic keys on a string around her waist, just like his, kneeling as she tightened the bow, settling back on her heels so she was no taller than Kim. Big people mostly bent over at the waist – they felt big and shadowy – but Mommy always knelt or sat on the floor. She smelled of bathroom soap and shampoo from the bottle with the peaches on it, but beneath those smells was a musty thick scent that was always there, like damp, freshly turned soil, like apples that sat too long in the basket on the counter. Kim knew her smell, knew it in the dark when she awoke between Mommy and Daddy in their bed when she had a bad dream or the night the power went out and it was so cold that they all huddled together, and she slept and then awoke and knew by the smell which side was Mommy and which was Daddy. He smelled oily, like inside the truck, and sometimes another smell, foul and bitter, of cigarettes and something else, something rotten; no other smell was like it. She would turn toward Mommy while Daddy snored behind her. Mommy took long deep breaths. Kim would listen to her breathe as sleet rattled against the window, and she'd pull the blanket up to keep Daddy's mouth stink off her neck.

He lifted her into the seat still clutching her cone and slammed the door, which banged with a hollow echo. She knew to sit straight when he shut it, that if it didn't catch right he'd slam it again: he'd say *Fuck!* and slam it again, and if Mommy was there, she'd say *Ross!* but he'd just wink at Kim and bang the door shut, grinning. Mommy would sit in the middle, one hand resting inside his leg while he drove, and Kim would have the window, where hot wind blew into her hair and purple thistles and sunflowers and black-eyed susans whisked past below her as she watched the white line and the concrete stream along like the current of the river.

The truck lurched to a stop at the parking lot exit.

Daddy hissed, —Shit!

She slid into the dash and wiggled back, clutching her cone. Daddy waited for a car to pull into the lot. He followed it with his eyes, a predatory glare, watching to see if the driver glared back, but he didn't. Kim studied the red welts on his neck, still fresh and raw, but not seeping blood as they were earlier when he came out the front door and scooped her up from the grass without a word and carried her to the truck. She'd got a close-up look then, and they shivered her.

She bumped against the car door as he swung onto the road and zoomed away fast and rolled through the gears.

—Just toss it, Kimmy, he said.

All that remained was a soggy, pink nub.

—Go ahead! he said over the wind and the engine's roar.

Mommy never would have said throw it out the window. Sometimes when Mommy wasn't there he let Kim ride in back of the truck, or he'd take her on the motorbike in the fields behind the house. He surrounded her in his big arms as the bike went airborne. She shrieked with joy at every bounce, and then, before she could breathe, they were up in the air again, bumping and jostling through the field's ridges and gullies.

She tossed the cone away, but the wind blew it back onto the seat. He grabbed it and flicked it out like a cigarette butt.

—Was it good?

—Yah.

He nodded, but it didn't seem like it really mattered if it was good.

—We're gonna see Gammie now, he said.

—Kay.

—⁓—

—Pitching, Phil hissed. His lips curled around the word, edging it toward the light whistle that would have graced it if there'd been a sibilant in it. —No pitching, no team.

Nancy wasn't always sure he was talking to her, like right now, if the rustle of her jeans and her light step on the carpet, just her quiet presence in the room, which most people would have felt more than heard, had jarred the words loose or if he was talking to the TV again.

She squinted to read the bug at the corner of the screen. The

4

Royals were hopelessly behind. The tiny rhombus of yellow-lit bases meant they were loaded with Yankees, who just seemed to queue up before they inevitably scored. The next pitch surfed through the dirt, past catcher and umpire, leaving puffs of dust as if Roadrunner had just blown through, as the Yankee on third trotted easily home.

Phil pulled his chin back into the folds of putty that made up his throat and blew an exasperated breath.

Wouldn't enjoy the games if the team won, Nancy always said. But anger just seemed to moil inside him. How could Ross and Phil have shared this trait, this bitterness, she often wondered, when Ross wasn't even his?

The batter fouled off the next pitch, and she went back down the hall and peered into the darkened bedroom. A tangled shock of corn-silk hair drifted across the pillow. She stepped softly inside, gathered the filthy clothes up from the floor, and brought them back to the laundry room, where she tossed them in with a few of her own things to make up a load.

Ross looked ashen when he dropped Kimmy off. Just showed up. No call. Just pulled in and brought her up to the door. Didn't even come in either. Nancy heard the truck before he made the turn. They got so little traffic out here in the evening that she knew its rhythms. A car slowing for their place couldn't be anything else. And she knew the heavy, pulsing rumble of his truck too. It might look like salvage but he kept that engine tuned. From the living room window, she'd watched through the gray dusk as he pulled in. The rose-pink swirls and ribbons of sunset out beyond the break of trees across the road had mostly dissolved, leaving a charcoal wash across the sky. His headlights were just two pale beacons bouncing up the long driveway, a couple of football fields from the road to the house. She waited on the porch as they climbed out. First Ross. Then he strutted around and jerked the door open for Kimmy. It squealed, the door did, a sharp, hollow moan. A calf in pain. He hadn't put her seatbelt on. Nancy was about to let him hear about it too, but something wasn't right – about them being here, about him not calling, about the sullen way he carried Kimmy and set her on the steps and stayed in the half-light on the walk.

Without a greeting and barely a look, he said, —She just needs to stay here tonight is all.

Kimmy climbed the steps one at a time. Nancy bent down as she reached the top.

—Hi honey! Oh my, what happened to you?

Kim looked down at her pink-smudged shirt and shorts.

—Nothin. Ice cream.

—Was it good?

Kim's eyes widened, and she bounced her head a quick nod.

—We have to get you cleaned up, Nancy said.

Ross hooked his thumbs on his jean pockets.

Nancy waited for an explanation. She didn't expect much. She could figure the gist of it – he'd argued with Anna and she'd stormed off to her sister's for the night and now he was going down to Hawkings to fetch her. It galled Nancy how Anna would just stalk off like that. Wasn't the first time. Nancy wondered if she'd be so quick to walk out on her family if her sister didn't have a comfy B&B, where they probably drank white wine and said god-knows-what smug things about all of them up here in Bueller County. She always had a tightly wound kind of superiority, Anna did. Most people down Hawkings way did.

Nancy took Kimmy's sticky cheeks in her hands and kissed her on the forehead and then asked Ross if he was all right.

He didn't look all right. His face seemed swollen. He was sweaty and unshaven and still in his work clothes. He looked distant, as if he was trying to remember where he was.

Probably been drinking too. They both probably had.

Maybe it was just as well they hadn't married, though here was this child, turning five, starting school soon, and then what? Anna acted as if it was no business of Nancy's when she brought it up, and Ross, he'd just shrug, couldn't see the point of worrying about it, especially that far off, a year away. School was just something you got through. Wouldn't be any different for Kimmy than for him, she supposed he thought.

His eyes were shadowy. He could treat a question as if it hadn't even been asked and somehow make you believe his silence was the answer.

She asked again, louder, —You okay, Ross? What's going on? Why don't you come in? I'll fix you something.

—Yeah, 'm all right… sorry. Gotta leave her tonight.

—You pack her a bag?

—Didn't have time.

—Time? What happened?

—Just gotta go.

Nancy shook her head and asked sharply, —You gonna call?

—Yeah, I'll call later.

He perched one of his thick boots on the edge of the first step and leaned forward.

—C'mere, baby.

His broad hands engulfed her shoulders and he put his nose up to hers and said, —You be good for Gammie.

—Kay.

Then he kissed her long on the cheek with a tenderness that left

Nancy feeling guilty for her sharp tone. Why didn't she see more of this side of him? She sometimes thought Kimmy was more like a puppy to him, that he could just roll around on the floor with her when the mood suited him and then ignore her when it didn't. And she knew Anna thought the same thing, though she'd hate to admit they'd agree on anything.

—Bye-bye, Kimmy, he whispered and stepped away.

—Can't you come in a minute? Nancy asked, almost pleading, as he started down the walk.

But he just shook his head and went to the truck, and she watched him turn around and pull away, the red tail lights quivering on the gravel. She took Kimmy's sticky hand in her own as the truck revved past the rail fence that separated the lawn from the gully and disappeared.

Phil was standing at the door when she turned.

—She needs a bath, was all Nancy said.

The short cycle ended. The white neon glow of the laundry room, off on the far side of the kitchen from the living room, felt like its own galaxy. Without a window, it could be day or night in here. The ballgame's hum resurfaced in the abrupt silence after the rinse cycle. Buttons and snaps echoed like the first smatterings of hail on the deck as she tossed the clothes into the hollow drum of the dryer. She checked Kimmy's shirt to see if the ice cream came out. All she had to wear fit into Nancy's palm, shorts, T-shirt, panties. No socks – she'd worn flip-flops. They'd have to go to Walmart in the morning. Nancy wondered if Ross would call. It'd been hours. She didn't think he would now. The Kansas Speedway logo on the tiny shirt was cracked and faded from scores of washings and dryings, but she tossed it in for one more. She'd buy Kimmy some new things tomorrow.

By now the urgent voices of the ten o'clock news had replaced the game announcers. She startled Phil as she took up the remote from where it'd gotten wedged in the cushion and muted the sound.

—Everything all right? he asked.

She perched herself at the edge of the sofa cushion.

—No, she was filthy. I gave her a bath and then… I don't know what's going on. She was covered with ice cream, her clothes, face, hands, but she said she was hungry. I made her a sandwich. Said she hadn't eaten dinner.

—What'd Rosss ssay?

S's swirled through his lips.

—Nothing. You know how he is, she shrugged. Said he'd call but he hasn't.

The muted TV emitted a high-pitched whine. The silent news anchor looked plastic and surreal. His pancake and eyebrow makeup were so heavy and flat that he might have been a cartoon character. There wasn't a shadow or wrinkle or blemish on his face. She found its perfection disturbing, like being too close to a clown.

—I put her clothes in the washer. He didn't even bring a bag. She has nothing else to wear. We'll have to go to the store in the morning.

Phil looked back at the TV. A lone car streaked along a snowy mountain road through lush forests. The road was wet even though the day was bright. A beautiful woman held the wheel, smiling with erotic pleasure and making you worry that she might drive over the mountain side. The dryer thumped and rattled as they watched the car disappear into the forest and Phil lifted the remote.

IN THE MORNING, EVERYTHING smelled fresh, even her. Gammie gave her a bath last night and she slept in one of Daddy's T-shirts from when he was little. It smelled of inside the closet, a warm, woody scent you only smelled at Gammie's house. Daylight's glow framed the window shade. She savored the clean white sheets but missed her own blanket with the silky edge, and Snuffy, her yellow stuffed dog that grinned like he was always glad to see you.

On the dresser and shelves stood framed pictures in glass so shiny her reflection engulfed the faces when Gammie held her up to look – Poppa in his Army uniform, Gammie and Poppa in their wedding clothes, Daddy playing Little League, Mommy and Daddy squeezed together on the sofa with Kim as she opened a birthday present, which turned out to be her new truck. Daddy was glancing at Gammie, who you couldn't see, and Mommy looked like the camera caught her by surprise. She said she didn't like that picture, but there it was in a shiny frame on the dresser top.

The voices down the hall first seemed regular. (That was Poppa's word for okay. *Regular*, he'd say.) Gammie said she'd make pancakes today, like she always did when Kim visited. But the voices weren't from the kitchen. Kim knew from how they echoed in the hall. They were closer, in the living room, and there was another voice, a man's, but she couldn't tell the words.

The man said things, then Gammie said things, then the door shut, and Gammie and Poppa both talked at once, and Gammie laughed… no, she wasn't laughing… she was crying. Outside a car started and crunched over the gravel and whished down the road.

—How could this happen! Gammie burbled.

Poppa mumbled, and she cried louder now.

—How?!

She let out a terrifying wail, like a dog howling, and then whimpered and sobbed.

Kim shivered and pulled her knees up tight against her chest and tucked her head under the covers. She tried to shut out daylight and the awful sound of Gammie's crying. She'd never heard them talk like this or Gammie cry.

She shook with terror as harsh footsteps passed in the hallway. Mommy had told her about strangers. Maybe it wasn't Gammie and Poppa! Maybe they were gone and bad people had come – strangers!

Water ran in the bathroom. The front door opened and slammed shut. She couldn't tell where anyone was, or who it was.

Maybe they'd take away and no one would know where she'd gone.

Where was Mommy? She wanted Mommy. Where was she?!

Kim cried aloud into the blankets, into the empty room. Her voice echoed back to her. She couldn't stop and couldn't make words come. She couldn't say the words she wanted to say.

She sobbed and whimpered and called Mommy. She could hear the word but it didn't come out right.

She called again. She called Mommy.

Footsteps returned. The door opened. The blanket was pulled back and hands grabbed at her. She screamed as she was snatched from her warm blanket. And now she felt herself wrapped inside Gammie's arms. Kim quaked with terror. She didn't know what she feared, only that fear had sucked the air and sounds from the room. She gasped and sobbed and pushed herself into the quivering softness of Gammie's belly.

Stuffed Mushrooms and Dead Fish

Two years later

Jo curled her fingertips back, away from the knife edge, like Emeril, as she chopped mushroom stems. Guests often said they came here just for her crab and parmesan stuffed mushrooms. That was the thing, to have a signature item, something people would talk about after they stayed at Monarch House. Chop chop chop. She turned to the stove, put on the gas, sprinkled olive oil into the pan. When the oil was heated, turning runny, starting to smoke, she added the chopped stems, brushing the last bits off her dampened palms into the smoldering heap, which she salted and prodded with a wood spoon. Guests raved about her pies and chocolate chip-walnut cookies, but the stuffed mushrooms were to die for, so they wrote in the guest-room journals – *"to die for"* – so that's what she put in her brochure, in quotes.

Jo Pugh was a nervous woman, always in motion, always two tasks ahead of the one she was doing. When she made up beds, her mind was busy working through shopping lists and calculating the likely net for next weekend's reservations. In her early forties now, Jo might have been called frumpy in an earlier time. Her floral house dresses and aprons left that impression with guests. Guests much older than Jo would settle into their rooms with a vague sense that they'd just been told by their mothers to put the dirty towels in the hamper and which doorway to use after ten p.m. She could negotiate firmly over a bill yet leave guests feeling as if they'd just spent the weekend visiting relatives – a mixed feeling for sure, but a visit they were likely to repeat.

She glanced out the back window to check on the rehearsal in the courtyard. The children could never stay out of the koi pond. The flower girl leaned over it now, dipping her fingers, tracing circles in the water. A postcard image, Jo thought. Perfect for the brochure. The girl's little brother now escaped from a corral of grown-ups and dashed for the water, but one of the ushers snagged him from behind and the boy shrieked with laughter.

—He'd've gone in headlong for sure, Elliot said, pulling the back-door curtains aside for a better look.

Jo startled. —Oh! I didn't hear you. That fan's so loud.

She returned to the stove and prodded the sizzling mushrooms.

Elliot watched outside. Most of the wedding party had scattered across the lawn and veranda while the minister and bride and groom remained in the gazebo. The minister moved them about like actors in a play.

—You should keep track of these people, Elliot snorted, find out if the marriages last. You could advertise it! Ninety-eight percent of all ceremonies in our gazebo still going strong five years later, and eight-two percent after ten! Like a guarantee.

—You're a very sick man, Elliot.

Jo looked out once more.

The minister was wrapping the bride and groom's hands in his stole.

—Where's Nick and Kimmy? he asked.

—Store. Plus he had to stop at Home Depot, too. Number eight needs a new flusher. Least it's the children's room. They can go in their mother's for now.

The wedding party lined up again and marched down the aisle, or where it would be once the chairs were set up, and slapped high-fives in the clearing.

—What's the plan for rain? Elliot asked.

—Rain?

—Sixty-percent chance.

—I didn't see that. She drew a breath. —Elliot, I think you enjoy delivering news like that.

—I do, but I take no pleasure in admitting it.

Clatter erupted in the breezeway.

—Must be them, Elliot said, as he headed that way.

—Make sure nobody's parked in the church lot or we'll hear about it, Jo called, and then muttered into the kitchen noise, —good Christians that they are.

———∞———

KIM PUSHED THE CAR door shut and scampered around back to check out who was there, but she stopped short at the sight so many people, especially the flower girl squatting at the edge of the pond. Kim watched her like a cat who'd just spotted another of its own kind.

A couple of heads turned, idle glances at someone new. One man cracked a joke to his group and they all laughed. The man waved. —Not you, honey!

He looked away but glanced back as he realized she was still watching him.

The flower girl touched the water and jerked her hand up as a fish splashed to the surface.

—They think you're gonna feed them, Kim said. —They don't bite.

14

The girl looked up. —I know, she said, turning back to the water.

—They don't.

—I know.

Kim knelt down and plunged a hand in. The fish scattered. She swooped her hand through the water and sent waves plashing against the rocks. The girl seemed delicate and fearful. She backed away as water rippled up on the slate stones at the pool's edge. Her white slip-on sneakers looked new. Everything did – her pleated pink blouse and cargo knee pants, which had so many straps and pockets and snaps. Kim noticed that her mother wore almost the same outfit. What were all the pockets for?

The girl had taken Kim's window seat on the stairway landing this morning, where Kim sat when she read a picture book with Boxer curled up against her. His purring hummed all through her and felt as if it came from inside her. But the girl sat there like it was *her* seat and stared when Kim passed by with Uncle Nick, helping him with chores. He carried his toolbox, and Kim wore his tape measure clipped on her waist and stared back.

Kim wasn't allowed to play in the pond. Aunt Jo was probably watching from behind the glare of the kitchen window. One splash, two, and the door would open. She'd step up to the railing as if she'd just remembered something outside, but it'd be Kim she was checking on.

The girl brushed flecks of dirt from her knees.

—What grade you in? she asked.

Carp glided through the water, curling this way and that for no reason, seemed like.

—What grade you in? the girl repeated.

Kim stared at the water. —Second.

—Last year or next?

—Next.

—Me too. I'm in the wedding tomorrow. My mom's getting married.

The bride and groom and a few others lingered in the gazebo. The groom was shorter than the girl's mother and wore his hair buzz-cut, military style, with a whisk-broom tuft on top.

—He your dad? Kim asked.

The girl screwed up her face like Kim had just said something dumb.

—No, they got divorced. My bathroom don't work. Your mom said they'd fix it soon. You think it's fixed yet?

Kim shrugged and looked back at the fish. —She's not my mom.

—She's not?

—No.

—Then where's your mom?

—She's dead.

The effect was satisfying. The two words swallowed up the bright new clothes, second grade, and the broken toilet. They were much more fearsome than hungry fish.

The girl was smaller than Kim, but more than her size, it was her white shoes and stupid shorts and curled hair and most of all her need to have someone fix her toilet that made her seem weak and vulnerable, as if she just didn't deserve mercy.

Just then the ring bearer came striding up to the water and knelt at the edge.

The flower girl stared at Kim. —What about that man, that your dad?

A fish splashed at the surface, and the boy laughed and flicked water at it. Kim splashed water too, ignoring the girl, who now stepped closer. —I asked you what about that man, he your dad?

Kim slapped a hand down on the water, splattering the boy, who laughed again. Kim noticed the tight pink stitching on the girl's white shoes. Then one foot levered up at the heel and the toe came down sharply on the slate stone as if demanding a response, and with that Kim scooped up a handful of water and splattered the shoes, and as the girl sputtered in shock, Kim doused her again, soaking her blouse and shorts. The boy howled and splashed her too. She let out a fierce wail. Heads turned. Then she darted across the lawn to her mother, who called the boy sharply, certain he was the culprit.

Jo wasn't watching just then, so she missed seeing the bride scold the boy and the flower girl pointing at Kim and then her mother staring crossly, also at Kim, before she marched the children upstairs to change. She also missed Kim shrugging at the yellow streak in the window as if to say what could I do before she disappeared around the side of the house.

When Jo finally did check again, the children were gone. Maybe out back to play in the field behind the barn. She hoped Kimmy and the little girl would make friends. Kimmy had so few.

The breezeway door swung open and banged into the counter. Nick scanned the kitchen for somewhere to park the water. Jo cleared space at the corner of the island.

—So, back to the point, Elliot continued, what'd that be for this whole place? You got what, twelve bedrooms with eight bathrooms upstairs, plus your apartment, plus the two on the main floor, plus the two rooms over the barn. That's thirteen. Good God, imagine that! Thirteen bathrooms in one house! So, times how many flushes a day? Let's see. Everyone's gonna pee at least five, six times. (Maybe some of us a few times more!) Then, you got...

—Enough! Jo exclaimed. I clean every one of them, so I'm sure I know how many there are.

—Doesn't matter, Nick said. Those toilets're four-five hundred each, plus the installation, which I can't do. Oh, maybe I could, probably take a whole day or more just to learn how, but it'd still be thousands to do this place.

He snorted at the absurdity of spending so much money.

Elliot had come to live with them about a year before Kimmy.

Straight out of rehab. Wasted and gray – the gray of cigarette ashes, and this after six weeks at a treatment center in upstate New York and another two months in a halfway house in Albany, a grim sight for a man approaching seventy. He joked darkly, though they hadn't said a word about his appearance (though what he must have looked like was written on their faces), that they should have seen him before. Probably be dead if he hadn't gone in, he said, and then added, might have been just as well – and then didn't utter another word on the drive home from the airport.

Nick and Elliot were studying the new flusher box, heads tilted back for their bifocals, noses scrunched. No doubt about the bloodlines.

—Elliot, Jo said, Kimmy's outside somewhere. Might be around back with that little girl. Can you go see what she's up to? Nick's got to fix that toilet.

—Hah! She been in the pond yet? Elliot laughed.

—Not so far.

Nick looked outside and asked, —Flann back?

—Unh-uh.

—I'll do the lawn when I finish this.

—No! Jo said. That's his job. You just go fix that.

Nick took the breezeway stairs down to the basement to fetch his toolbox and then wove through the maze of dressers and bedposts and side tables and pictures that Jo accumulated at yard sales and antique shops, then took the butler's stairway up to the second floor.

That led to a door that blended so well into the walnut paneling and wainscoting on the hallway that few guests even realized it was there. The door knob was nearly invisible, just a slender oval of darkened brass that looked like another leaf in the floral wallpaper.

Nick startled the little flower girl when he emerged in the hallway. The child's eyes widened, and she scuttled into her mother's room. Nick tapped on the door, and when the bride opened it, he said, —Shouldn't take but fifteen, twenty minutes. To which the bride pursed her lips and nodded approval, and then shut her door with the flower girl inside.

As he let himself into the children's room, Nick wondered what had put her out of sorts. Probably a lot on her mind with the wedding tomorrow.

⁓

A HEDGEROW OF BOXWOODS separated the lawn from the fields out back where the horseshoe pits and badminton court got the late afternoon shade from the barn. Wildflowers bloomed in beds filled with goldenrod, aster, bishop's weed, painted cup, persimmon, and many more that Jo had seeded to bring the butterflies each year.

Kim spotted a garter snake. Maybe she'd catch it and slip it under the flower girl's door. That'd be something.

But then Uncle Elliot appeared in the driveway, looking for her, she figured, scanning the yard like it was a big checkerboard and the next move was his.

She ducked behind the boxwoods and slipped into the barn. The oily smells reminded her of Daddy's garage behind the house where the motorbike was and all his tools. She didn't know where he'd

19

gone. Aunt Jo said he lived far away out west now and they'd probably never see him again. Kim wondered what probably meant.

When Uncle Elliot passed the barn window, she scooted out the
door and across the berm of pine trees behind the gazebo. The two mutts
next door woofed lamely through the fence. Aunt Jo always worried
they'd bark at guests, or worse, during a wedding ceremony, like tomorrow. Kim growled. That riled them up. Next thing they were barking
and howling at the fence as she whisked around front and dashed onto
the porch, where the bride's mother was posing for a picture.

At just that moment, in the middle of the street, the bride's father
snapped a blurry photo of the bride's mother on the front porch,
looking as if *she*'d just seen a snake as Kim charged up the steps and
smacked one of the porch columns like home base in hide-and-seek.

The man hurried to the curb and waited for traffic to pass and
then tried again, but his wife wasn't sure what to do, with Kim there
and the light about to release another fleet of cars on her husband.

—Just stay there, he barked, … and smile!

He clicked and captured his wife grinning stiffly at Kimmy, who
was leaning on the handrail and staring blankly at him.

—Sorry about that, Elliot huffed, as he rounded the corner. I'm
supposed keep her out of trouble.

—No matter, the woman said, waving a hand. Most of his pictures don't come out anyway. Turning to Kim, she asked, —And
who's this?

—That's Kimmy, and I'm Elliot.

Before the woman could say another word, her husband called as
he came up the front walk, —Haven't I seen you somewhere before?
From somewhere… from TV?… were you on TV? Thought I recognized you when we arrived. Said so to Alice too, didn't I?

Alice nodded dryly.

—Was a long time ago, Elliot said.

The man brightened. —Ah, so I was right! Hey, Alice, take my picture with… mister…

—Just Elliot, no mister.

—But now I can't remember, right on the tip of my tongue, too.

—That's my fate, Elliot snorted. To be immortalized on the tips of a generation of tongues. When they die off, I'll fade into history with their drying saliva.

Alice shuddered.

—Elliot Pugh, he added. Nick's my nephew, who runs this place, and Kimmy's my great-grand niece, I think.

—Ah! I remember now! Elliot Pugh! I'm Jim and this is Alice.

—I think I knew that, Elliot said.

The man shook hands with him and ignored Kim. —Let's see, you were in…? a sit-com, right?

—*Better Think Twice!* Alice said.

—What? he snapped.

—*Better Think Twice!* That was the name of the show, she said.

Elliot realized she'd already made the connection, probably yesterday when he took their bags upstairs. Jim had offered him five dollars, which he refused.

—Here, Jim said, let's stand in front of the flowers.

—Oh, Alice said, brightening, wait till we tell everyone!

Her husband ignored the sarcasm and smiled widely as Alice squinted into the viewfinder at the two men, side-by-side, Elliot in his bib overalls (decidedly not the outfit Jo wanted to appear in anyone's photo album) and Jim with an arm around Elliot's shoulders like his long-lost brother. Then… nothing. Alice fumbled with the camera until her husband huffed and snatched it from her hands. Then it snapped a picture of the grass and she laughed as he stood beside Uncle E again, who slipped a grin Kim's way and smiled as if he'd just pulled a smiley face from his pocket and smacked it on his own face.

Shadows passed in the front window. The flower girl pulled aside the curtains and glared at Kim, who sneered back.

Elliot noticed the two sizing each other up. —Aunt Jo's probably wondering what happened to us, he said.

Jim was checking to see what damage Alice had done to the camera, while she thanked Elliot apologetically, as if mortified that he'd had even this brief exposure to the radioactive aura of their lives.

—⁓—

UPSTAIRS, SHE PULLED HER shoes off, stretched on the bed, and closed her eyes while Jim lingered in the doorway.

Across the hall, Mattie's door thrummed with chatter, children's voices, the halting fragments of a phone conversation.

—Who could she find to talk to? he asked. Everyone's here.

—Probably Glenn, Alice sniffed.

—But he's just across the driveway in the barn.

—Exactly.

Jim shook his head in wonder and shut the door. —Guess it's fixed.

Alice released a breath, like air hissing from a tire valve. She remained still, sinking into rest, her arms and legs draining into blissful limpness.

From the edge of bliss, she whispered, —What's fixed?

—That toilet.

—Mmm.

In the bathroom Jim peed. His stream splattered in spurts, echoing off the tiling. The noise found new life in Alice's tingling nerves – the

22

energy of sound transmuted into silent irritation, a thermodynamic law quietly upheld.

He stopped and started. His prostate was swollen and sore. He'd forgotten his meds.

Alice drew a long breath and tried once more to doze, seeking the limpness, longing for bliss. Everything was so chaotic – the wedding, the children, getting everyone here. Couldn't he go find some golf on TV downstairs just for twenty minutes so she could rest?

He came out of the bathroom, clucking the door latch behind him. She was just as he'd left her, motionless, hands folded on her belly, feet together – only a casket was needed to complete the image.

He padded over to the dresser and snapped open his traveling bar, a tidy brown suitcase that stood upright and opened like a book, with fitted pockets for bottles, a shaker, glasses, even a strainer, all neatly packed into the velvet lining.

He poured a couple of fingers of scotch and settled into a low wing-back tucked in between the bed and the door. He sipped and listened to the patter of voices along the hallway. Once more he looked around as if he'd been mistaken about there not being a TV. But there wasn't, not here or in any of the rooms. The only TV was downstairs, where the kids fought over the remote.

A few brochures and magazines were stacked on the nightstand, with an untitled black book on top. He flipped through it. A diary, half-filled with enthusiastic entries from past guests. He skimmed it and considered writing *Couldn't find the TV!* but he just tossed it back on the table. They probably tore out the pages with bad reviews anyway.

The book's thunk ruffled Alice.

—Aren't you going to write something? she asked softly, eyes still shut.

He sipped from his glass. She was needling him. —*You* should write something.

—Maybe I will.

—What'll you write?

She sat up now.

He watched her breasts rise as she stretched and spun her hands in the air.

—Oh, I don't know. We have a couple of days. I'll wait for inspiration.

—Place needs work, Jim said. And everyone has to back their cars out if one person wants to leave.

—Why do you grumble so much? It's old… I was reading about it before… there, in that brochure under the book…

Jim slid the brochure out. A monarch butterfly spread its wings across the cover.

—It says this place goes back to before the Civil War, when it was a stagecoach stop for all the trails that went out west. You know, like the Santa Fe Trail and the others… I can't remember them all… it says in there. Some colonel or general or something made money in railroads and bought this place. Oh, and the butterflies! This farm, it was hundreds of acres, with orchards and even vineyards… who knew you'd grow vineyards here? Was once a big farm and now it's just real estate. But that's what it was, and this general, he held a butterfly festival every fall for when the butterflies came and invited everyone in town. Oh, that must have been something!

Jim tossed the brochure aside, and his eyes widened into the look he got when he was just waiting for her to finish so he could speak… and he was so predictable she already knew what he'd say.

—You want something? He drained his glass and went to the tote bar.

—No, and you shouldn't either. We still have dinner ahead and the whole evening.

He gave her a tiresomely familiar look as he poured scotch.

—We don't have time, she said. And those children could be at the door any minute.

—We just won't answer.

Alice had wanted to get out of her clothes and wash, but now she couldn't unbutton her blouse without encouraging him. She slid off the bed and took up the diary and leafed through it.

—They all say how good the food is here, she said.

—Who?

—The people who stayed here. These people. She shook the diary.

Jim laughed, —You think the owners'd leave that laying around if they didn't?

—But they did… what, you think this is fake?

He shrugged. —Guess we'll find out later. Mattie's ordered up every appetizer on the menu.

She settled in his chair and folded the book shut on her lap.

—That little girl, Alice said, I think she's adopted.

—How do you know?

—Mattie mentioned it.

—How would she know anything about her?

—She heard about this place from one of her friends. Maybe her. She told me that little girl splashed April at the pond today and soaked her.

—Not really!

—She did… said she just suddenly splashed her out of nowhere, no reason at all. Alice thought for a moment and then laughed. —Wish I'd seen it. That child is so spoiled it was probably good for her.

—Now that's just cruel, Alice. Your own grandchild…

—Is it? Do I sound cruel?

—Not in a bad way.

—Is there a good way to be cruel?

—I think so. Some people have it coming.

—April?!

—I didn't say April.

Alice huffed. After a moment, she said, —I thought you were going to ask that old fellow for an autograph.

—I was not. He was just… it was just curious, finding someone like that here. Who'd have thought you'd find an old TV star lurking around a place like this?

—I guess they have to lurk somewhere.

She could be cruel, he thought, when Alice had gone into the bathroom. He watched her shadow pass in the seam beneath the bathroom door. The seat banged down. The toilet flushed, a slow, gurgling effort, followed by a torrential roar and water splattering into the sink. He downed another, and as he strapped the bottle in place, footsteps approached their door and a lawn mower erupted outside…

FLANN HIT **PLAY** AS the mower sputtered to life. A charcoal plume swarmed up from the exhaust pipe like a cloud of bees rushing from the hive and filled the air with the rank sweetness of gas and oil as the engine found its rhythm. Inside Flann's headphones, Wu-Tang Clan chanted a cautionary hip-hop tale of drug-addled babies, gunfire in the streets, and the New World Order.

He bobbed his head and roared off through the smoke, hugging the flagstone path that curved toward the gazebo at the center of the lawn. Clippings blew up on the walk and veranda and into the pond. Rows of marigolds and petunias quivered in the mower's gusts as it passed. The ushers were sprawled on lawn chairs with beers. Flann buzzed them a couple of times until they finally quit the lawn for the porch.

He circled the gazebo and soon realized he'd have to get those chairs moved, but the fucking mower would never restart if he let go of the safety handle and the engine cut out. P-O-S the mower was and no doubt about it.

He wove through the chairs and thought about asking the ushers. Take two seconds, is all. But they had their feet on the porch rail and ignored him like he was just some wetback or whatever.

No chance. Besides, Mom'd rain down on him if she saw him ask, and she was probably watching.

Kimmy was on the veranda, doing nothing. He waved to her, but she just stared at him with that weird blank look she got, like she spoke another language or something, or maybe didn't speak any language at all. Seemed like for her living here must be how a zoo animal feels. Like she knew she didn't belong here even though everything had been fixed up just how her keepers thought she'd want it — but you could tell that she still knew she didn't belong here. Like from how she was always checking everything out, like testing the cage bars or something, looking for a way out.

How Flann saw it anyways.

He thought she could pass for a boy if she cut her hair short. Her arms hung down with her hands half open like she was always ready to grab hold of something. She was browned from staying outside all the time, and her hair swept across her brow loosely and fell to her neck like it'd been cut with gardening shears. Mom said that was because she wouldn't stay still when she got her hair cut.

He wagged a hand for her to come, but she didn't budge even

though she was looking straight at him. He waved again and got the same blank look.

Finally he pushed the mower back her way, over grass he'd already cut, and shouted over the engine's roar for her to move the chairs.

She started away from him like she was just blowing him off, and he got pissed and went back to mowing, thinking maybe he'd tie his belt on the mower handle – which Dad had told him positively, absolutely, never, under any circumstance should he tie off the mower handle to keep it running, even though it'd be fucking tomorrow before the fucking mower would start again if it fucking stopped now – but turned out she'd just taken the long way around the hedge rather than pass in front of him, and next thing, she was dragging chairs onto the walkway. Heavy wooden Adirondack chairs they were, too, and don't you know, when the dudes on the porch saw her struggling with them, first one came down, then another, and soon the whole crew was moving chairs while Flann stood by the rumbling mower with Wu-Tang throbbing inside his head.

When they'd done, one man said something to her and smiled and reached out as if to pat her on the head but she pulled back quick and startled him, and Flann saw a look of terror flash in her eyes such as he'd never seen before, and the usher pulled his hand away like he'd just tried to pet a dog and it snapped at him. But then he chilled and smiled and said something to her, and as he went back up on the porch he flicked his head at Flann like 'get to it,' and just then didn't Mom show up at the back door, thanking the men, apologizing, gathering Kimmy to her, and scowling at Flann, who swung the mower around to where the chairs had been in front of the gazebo, leaving her to glare at his back.

The house thrums with echoes, voices, footsteps in the hall, on the stairs. Doors open and shut, floorboards creak. Conversation, laughter; an eruption of thumping and moaning on the other side of the wall from the room half a flight down from hers, as if a woman is sick, and then the moaning fades and the thumping recedes into a light squeal of bedsprings, and then quiet.

Voices percolate in half-sentences, repetitions, beginnings and endings, set-ups and punchlines, answers, questions, all disassembled, unconnected. But in the accumulation of sound she finds a syntax of motion, a wholeness, a hum. The sounds go with people. Ushers and bridesmaids, the flower girl, the ring bearer, who had a tantrum and was carried screaming to his room, where the toilet that Uncle Nick repaired flushed and water flowed and a voice murmured, like his mommy reading a book. Uncle Elliot chatters somewhere downstairs. Aunt Jo's in the kitchen. Flann's music buzzes from his earphones as he passes into his room next door. The woman Alice starts to speak, and the man Jim laughs. Cars flow into the driveway. Door locks beep. Voices murmur and a woman weeps on the porch below her window.

Kim rubs the silky edge of the blanket between her fingers. Darkness is its own kind of light, surrounding the nightlight's glow. She lies awake listening, content to listen and reassemble the sounds, identify the voices, imagine the bright rooms filled with people and chatter. A puzzle, a story.

Like before she came here, a story in fragments that come out of the darkness and through the hum of sounds all over the house. If she thinks hard enough it will come back. She'll remember what came before this. In the hazy, fragile way a six-year-old may find a purpose for living, this is hers – to find out why everything changed, to fill in the images and sounds that surround the fragments. The clues are all around her, she suspects, if she can just recognize them when she sees them. If she thinks hard enough it will come back and she'll know why Daddy's gone and Mommy's dead.

An usher laughs. Glass shatters in the driveway.

She flinches and pulls her knees up.

Shards tinkled, scattering everywhere in the gravel drive. The bottle exploded when Daddy's truck rolled over it. *POP!* – like a balloon bursting.

He slammed the door.

—What the fuck?!

Loud, sharp, not funny. He looked under the truck and kicked up a spray of gravel that rattled on the garbage pails like hard rain on the tool shed. She sat on the walk, legs crossed, zooming her car through creases of dirt between the flagstones.

Gammie and Mommy's voices drifted through the screen door from inside, where the fan hummed and Poppa watched a baseball game. He liked baseball games. Kim played in the shade of the oak tree that towered over the house. It was cooler here than inside. She sometimes imagined climbing up high in the tree to where the squirrels nested, higher than the roof, where she could sit on a limb and watch the cars pass, and no one would know she was up there watching as they came and went below her.

Mommy had come outside and knelt beside her. —We'll have hamburgers when Daddy gets home, she'd said, but her face was stiff. She sat on the ground with Kim and zoomed cars. She revved and sputtered engine noises in her cheeks, then bumped Kim's car, and a smile crept into her face. Kim bumped Mommy's car, and they raced cars in the dirt and would have played some more except Gammie appeared like a shadow in the screen door, telling Mommy it was the phone. So she left Kim to play by herself.

Across the street, the Mitchell twins ran down their porch steps, the door slamming behind them. They called, —Hi Kim! —Hey Kimmy! as they trotted past and cut through her yard and disappeared into the field behind the row of houses.

Mommy looked out the door at the noise from the broken bottle.

—What was that?

Glass sparkled in the sunlight among the stones.

Daddy flicked his head at the truck. —Fucking bottle.

—You watch your mouth, she hissed.

—What's it doing in the fucking driveway!?

—You tell me? Trash spilling over, bottles laying in the driveway.

—Christ!

Mommy stepped off the porch and began picking up glass in the driveway.

Kim wanted to help, but she said, —No, no, honey. You'll get cut. And as she dropped handfuls of glass into the trash, she whispered harshly to Daddy, —Couldn't they have called?

He just shrugged.

—We were supposed to go out today.

—It wasn't like an appointment or something.

—An appointment? It was an outing, taking Kimmy to the park. We can't even have an afternoon?

Now Daddy squatted beside her and gathered glass too. —What do you want from me?

—Why should I have to tell you? They think they can just show up and we'll rearrange our day around them? And now what? He's parked in front of the TV and she's in there interrogating me about money and telling me how to make potato salad.

Just then Gammie stepped out on the porch.

—Look at you, all dirty. Let's go inside for a bath.

Mommy turned suddenly. —Oww! She grasped at her hand.

—C'mon, honey, Gammie said.

—Don't wanna bath!

—She'll have a bath later, Nancy.

—Well, she sure needs one.

Mommy winced, clutching her hand. Blood seeped through her fingers.

—And she'll need another in an hour.

Gammie shrugged, —I guess you know better.

And she went inside.

—Let me see that, Daddy said. He took Mommy's hand, which she offered slowly, almost as if it held a gift. She squinted, her cheeks rising and quivering, as he turned her hand into the light. —I don't see any glass in it.

—I'll go wash it.

She pulled her hand back, and he reached for her arm, but she turned sharply at his touch. —Oooh!

—What?

—Now there's blood on my blouse. It'll be ruined!

She trotted up the steps and let the door slam behind her, and Daddy winked at Kim, and followed Mommy inside.

The house hums in waves that rise and fall. Sounds swirl together. She watches the unmoving shadow on her wall, a familiar shape like a cat's head that reappears every night, its ears and nose, and every night at this very moment she remembers the stray calico that appeared in their yard. Mommy kept a can of food for him. She'd put a dish on the porch and they'd watch the cat. She asked Kim if they should give it a name.

Now Kim worries about Boxer getting scared with all the people downstairs, all the shoes and legs that surround him under the buffet where he sometimes hides. She can see all the feet herself from under the buffet, going this way and that, same as him.

Tennis Shoes, Balsa Planes, and a Cup of Tea

THE HALLWAY BUSTLED WITH hurried steps and laughter. The hair stylist had arrived. Freshly showered bridesmaids with bath towels swirling tipsily on their heads wandered the halls and lingered on the stairs. The women would gather in the bride's suite in their robes and drink champagne from fluted glasses etched with butterflies.

From her window Kim watched Aunt Jo and Uncle Nick sweep up grass clippings and arrange plastic garlands on the gazebo and porch railings.

The smells of bacon and pancakes drifted all the way up to her room. She padded down the narrow stairway, past the half-floor room, and finding the grand hallway empty, she ran along the carpet and would have rushed downstairs still in her PJs, but ushers and bridesmaids had settled on the landing with coffee mugs. And there was the flower girl, sitting on Kim's cushion again and cradling a cereal bowl on her lap. Her thick robe almost swallowed her up, and the turban on her head was so big she had to keep it balanced with one hand and eat gingerly so it didn't come tumbling down.

Kim froze at the top step and watched from behind the balustrade until the girl felt her presence. When she finally looked up, Kim stared until she quit looking and nestled herself beside a bridesmaid, who absently slung an arm on her shoulder as the child moved closer. The turban threatened to avalanche into her bowl. She dropped her spoon on the floor and just caught the turban in time. Kim snickered when the girl slipped another glance up at the railing and found her still there, watching. Good one.

Uncle Elliot was just coming down from his room.

—Hey, better get dressed.

—Kay.

When she returned, the landing was vacant. She rearranged her cushion and sat there herself, warming it, reclaiming it, stretching her legs on the window seat and waiting for someone to notice her sitting there, in *her* seat, but no one did, and soon she was bored. Voices echoed from the dining room. Where was Boxer? He could guard the seat. The flower girl wouldn't even think of sitting there if she saw him. Now Kim wished she'd caught the snake yesterday. She'd leave him right here. Hah! That'd be something. She stepped softly on the stairway to check out the gathering in the dining room and saw the cat curled up under the piano in a pool of yellow sunlight that somehow found its way from the tall windows and through the lace curtains and the maze of people and furniture, and all the way to the dark green rug that swirled with grapevines. He might have been no more than a throw pillow that landed there for no reason at all, white and zig-zagged with gray stripes.

Above him, the man Jim played a song. He hit a clinker and glanced around, grinning. No one seemed to notice.

In the kitchen, Kim sidled onto the stool beside Uncle Elliot, where a bowl of cereal was waiting for her.

—Milk? he said.

She nodded and he poured.

On TV a woman was making lamb skewers. She held chunks of raw meat up close to the camera. Blood and oil coated her fingers as she turned the meat chunks in her palm like dice and said how tender they were. She pierced the chunks with the skewer and as its shiny tip slid through the meat, Kim's throat tightened and she felt like she couldn't swallow.

Flann ate a sausage in one bite and twirled another in his fingers and popped it into his mouth.

Aunt Jo came in from the backyard, breathless and sweaty.

—You done yet, Flann? Dad needs help with those chairs. And you left grass clippings everywhere.

He glanced her way and his eyes found the TV again while she washed her hands. Then she stepped in between him and the TV and waited until he eased off the stool and slouched out the door.

Elliot laughed, —Kid's working your buttons!

—My buttons don't need working today, Jo said, taking up the boy's plate. The caterer will be here in an hour, and we've got to get this kitchen ready. You and Kimmy can clear the buffet as soon as they're done out there.

Elliot watched Kimmy.

—Might turn off okay after all, he said absently.

—Let's hope, Jo said.

She grabbed the broom and went out to sweep the porch.

—Not hungry? Elliot said.

Kim shook her head no.

The lamb skewers on TV sizzled on the grill.

She seemed to Elliot so fragile and small to have so much churning inside her.

He rinsed his mug, and as he peeked into the dining room, the door came pushing in from the other side. Piano music and voices suddenly filled the kitchen. Alice stood before him, clutching the door handle, startled to find herself within a breath of Elliot.

—Anything I can get you? he asked.

She looked lost, frazzled. —I didn't mean to intrude. I just wanted to step outside. I guess I used the wrong door.

—Nope, it's the right door, or one of the right doors. Still get you there. You can go through if you want, this way.

He stood aside and indicated the back door, and she took another step into the kitchen and gazed at the racks of copper pots and open pantry shelves full of spices, canned foods, preserves, rows of canisters and boxes.

—You want a cuppa coffee or tea?

She appeared to relax visibly once she was fully inside the kitchen.

Elliot's question hung, and she turned, realizing he was waiting for her to say something.

—That would be... oh, I couldn't trouble you, with all you have to do. There's tea outside... it's just... I needed to get away for a few minutes... everything's so overwhelming.

She gasped, as if stifling a sob, and then asked, —Would it be any trouble, some tea? But... may I sit in here... just for a few minutes? I didn't mean to intrude.

—Don't see why not, Elliot said, letting the door swing shut. —Just be a minute.

He put on the teapot and studied the pantry shelves. —What kind of tea you like? I don't know what all we've got. Food management's not my specialty here.

Alice searched the pantry with him, brightening now. —Oh, there, some Earl Grey. That would be delightful!

Elliot took the box back to the stove. —Why don't you just park yourself by Kimmy there? She's just finishing up her breakfast.

Alice approached the bar, where Kim kept her eyes on the TV as the woman Alice leaned into her sightline. —May I join you?

Kim shrugged and brought the juice cup to her lips, more camouflage than thirst, barely sipping from it.

—The lady's gonna have some tea with us, Elliot said.

Alice slid onto the stool beside Kim. —What a lovely kitchen! So bright, and lots of windows and daylight.

The cereal had turned soggy in Kim's bowl. The milk was khaki.

—I don't mean to be a bother, she said. It's one of those times… it just seemed like there was nowhere to… *escape*.

She laughed, as if sharing a secret.

—No bother at all, Elliot said.

She let out a long breath as she swirled her teabag, surely the first moment of relief she'd felt since she opened her eyes this morning, or no, since they got here yesterday, or no, since much longer before that. So it felt.

The rehearsal dinner last night… a disaster. No other word for it. Jim got so drunk that it suddenly seemed like a great idea to tell everyone what Alice had said about April getting soaked yesterday. Hilarious. He laughed harder than anyone and didn't even notice that Mattie wasn't laughing and April stared wide-eyed at Alice and then burst into tears. And this morning? April was hiding from her own grandmother behind Mattie's bridesmaid on the stairway landing and wouldn't talk to her, despite Alice's pleas. And all Alice got from Mattie were monosyllables. On her wedding day. Well, it was the second time around, wasn't it? Things were different this time. Or maybe not.

Alice felt like an outcast and hardly touched a thing at breakfast. One more day and it would be over. How awful to think so.

And how weird this was. She'd watched Elliot on TV for years, recognized him the moment they arrived. Now here he was fetching her tea.

And this little girl, too. Mattie said there was some story about her, some family tragedy. But to hear her tell it, you'd think whatever happened was the girl's fault. She'd said just awful things about her; that she was vulgar and rude and ragged looking; that she wasn't even sure Kimmy was a girl the first time she saw her. Piling all this on a child. Imagine! She seemed to Alice so bitter and small, her own daughter did. And cruel. Had Alice passed that on – cruelty? Was Alice truly cruel, and not in a good way? Had the cruelty gene snaked its way through the gene pool? Accepting this small kindness here in the kitchen felt like penance to Alice, an unspoken apology of sorts. She felt kinder just being here.

Kim wasn't about to eat a mouthful from that bowl. Not for nothing. No point in even poking at it. She still felt the squishy lump of raw dead animal meat from TV in her belly like some kind of pulsing blob or something, as if it were still alive and trying to escape. As if it was in pain from being killed. But now, too, the woman Alice had parked herself here.

The woman's smell reminded Kim of something, but what? Her thickness and the way her clothes rustled also seemed familiar. She was taller than her husband, with a streak of gray swirling through her dark hair over her brow. Her arms were speckled with brown spots; bracelets jangled on her wrists. Her face had a puffy softness from the powder on her cheeks. Maybe that's where the smell came from.

Now at least they were baking cakes on TV between commercials.

Soon enough, the woman Alice turned Kim's way and asked what she was watching even though you could see it right there on TV.

—Cooking show, Kim said.

—I like cooking shows too, the woman Alice said. —I was reading about the butterflies. Do they still come back every year?

Kim shrugged like how would I know.

—In fact they do, Elliot said. Not like way back when, not as many as they say used to, but they still migrate at the end of the summer.

—That must be wonderful! We'll have to come back for that. The woman Alice turned to Kim. —You must love the butterflies.

Kim took another non-sip and watched TV.

Uncle Elliot said he'd better check on the dining room, and Kim knew that meant she'd be left alone with the woman Alice, so she slid off her stool and dumped the full bowl of cereal into the sink. As Kim slipped away, the woman Alice was telling Uncle E over the food disposal racket, which he ran to hide the evidence, thank you so much and she'd been trouble enough and he said no trouble at all.

—⁓—

THE CATERERS WERE STILL inside. Pans clanked. Voices carped in wiry Asian tenors through the open kitchen windows. Jo whispered to Nick for them to hush up and get out here. She always mustered everyone along the back porch railing, including the caterers in their white smocks and caps. This image, like a promo shot for a Victorian drama on *Masterpiece Theater*, was firmly wedged into her vision of Monarch House. She imagined couples who married here turning the pages of wedding albums decades from now and sighing fondly at the gathering under the eaves of the porch who made their happiness possible.

Elliot was nearest the door. He wagged a hand inside and ignored

40

the scowl of the head chef, a Vietnamese man who muttered continually and, Jo was convinced, feigned ignorance of English whenever it suited him. Finally the cooks and servers shuffled out and stood limply on the porch, arms folded, not quite the image Jo had in mind. One lit a cigarette, but the chef told him to put it out. He went to the end of the porch, took another drag and flicked it into the driveway still lit.

Jo surveyed the gathering and courtyard and… the barn. The doors had been left open. A wave of heat surged from within her. Who? Left? Them? Open?

Nothing she could do about it now.

Elliot had been wrong about the weather, so far. Flann sighed in hollow, dramatic breaths and shifted on his feet. The chef glanced around impatiently. Kimmy fidgeted in a cotton dress that would land in a heap on the floor before the first guest ordered the first drink at the bar.

What did she remember? Jo often wondered. She was so little. And everything was so sudden. One morning she awoke and her parents were gone and the world she knew was gone. He wouldn't see the outside of a prison for decades, if Jo had a say in it. Maybe never. No maybe. Never. She had decided that she would still be alive for his parole hearing. Twenty-three years at the soonest, but she would be there. She would tell them what she'd seen at the Bueller County Coroner's Office when she had to identify her sister's battered body. She'd tell them how for years Anna would appear in the middle of the night looking as if she'd just walked the forty miles from Sunburg to Jo's door, that her cheeks would be swollen and there'd be welts and bruises on her arms and neck. *People don't change*, Jo would say. Not even twenty-five years in prison would change that… that… animal. There isn't a shred of humanity in him, she'd say. They might have files with police reports and such, but no piece of paper could tell the true story, so she'd have to tell it, and she imagined herself doing just that more than two decades from now.

And she'd want to tell them, also, about Ross's parents, mostly his mother, whom she didn't want to hate, except that… from the moment Jo went to fetch Kimmy, still dizzy from all that had happened that morning, she didn't see how it could have been different. As if the horror of Anna's death wasn't enough, Nick had quietly told Jo they should call a lawyer, too… that day, now. But why? Jo whispered. To get custody, he said ominously, adding, What if they won't let Kimmy go? Who? she asked. The grandparents. What if he gets out on bond and takes her somewhere?

That was all Jo needed.

Nick called a lawyer he knew, and they were in a judge's chambers before lunchtime. They got an order signed and then drove to Ross's parents' house with the lawyer and a social worker. Jo and Nick had only met them once, on Kimmy's second birthday at the boxy little rental house Anna and Ross shared in Sunburg. They had all squeezed into the tiny living room and balanced paper plates on their knees and talked awkwardly about the late September heat wave (the place had no air conditioning). Phil hissed randomly about taxes and illegal immigrants. Jo and Nick nodded indifferently and let his remarks fade into the rustle and clatter of gifts and wrapping paper. He seemed like someone who'd argue even when you agreed with him. Nancy didn't even acknowledge he'd said anything. Her eyes followed Kimmy, who darted among them brandishing her new toys in threatening ways. Nancy was attractive in an arch, Barbara Stanwyck sort of way. Her hairstyle and makeup betrayed vestiges of growing up in the 1950s. When she stood to her full height, which she did with great poise, she was fully half-a-foot taller than Phil. Kimmy got her height from Nancy, Jo realized. She also glimpsed hints of Nancy's high cheekbones and the spread of her eyes in Kimmy. Anna detested Nancy, but even Jo would concede that Anna could be moody. That visit predated Anna's first appearance on Jo's doorstep because Ross preferred swinging to talking, though when Jo thought back on days like this, she wondered how long he'd been brutalizing her sister. Jo didn't dislike Nancy, not then at least, but she could see why Anna did. They were both strong-willed, and Anna must have felt so… crowded in that small place.

The only conversation in the car on the way to Nancy and Phil Oden's house was a few muttered directions. The lawyer and social worker exchanged glances in the front seats, while in back Jo was near faint with grief and fear. She wept randomly; she clung to a tissue and watched the road pass. When they passed the exit for Sunburg, she felt an urge to go there, as if she needed to see Anna because they needed to talk about what happened.

K-29 ran north-south straight through the short corridor of Hill City, where the Odens lived. The downtown was lifeless and gray, with empty storefronts and deep discount signs in the windows of the few merchants who still survived here. A gaggle of cars were clustered near the lunch café and bar-and-grill. The new NASCAR speedway south of town, in Kansas City, Kansas (not to be confused with Kansas City, Missouri), had drawn most of the business away. The parking lots in the sprawl of shopping centers and discount chains surrounding the race track were always packed. The Hill City township spread outward east-west for several miles on a network of county roads that wove among farms and isolated places like the Odens', four- or five-acre properties with ranch houses, wide lawns, and maybe a

pond and outbuilding or two. They lived about twenty-five miles east of
Ross's place in Sunburg and fifty miles or so north of Monarch House
in Hawkings, which itself was part of the patchwork quilt of suburban bedroom communities that surrounded the other Kansas City, the
Missouri one, but Hawkings was just over the state line, on the Kansas
side also. Phil and Nancy and their neighbors complained often about
the crop of so-called 'ranchettes' that had sprung up on newly-parceled
farmland since the speedway came, bringing traffic and suburbanites to
their quiet country roads, but still the Odens went to the races and liked
eating at the Longhorn Steakhouse near the track.

The lawyer said they shouldn't call ahead. Jo worried no one
would be there, or maybe a lot of people. The sight of a sheriff's car
in the driveway sent a spasm of fear through her, but the lawyer said,
no, that's good.

Turned out not good exactly, but not bad either. He was a friend
of the Odens, a deputy. He answered the door. They'd without doubt
seen the car approaching on the long driveway.

Jo stood in front of the foursome crowded on the front steps.

—I'm her sister, she told him, Anna's. I'm here to pick up Kimmy,
my niece. Is she here?

The man's leather straps and heavy shoes and gun belt seemed
cumbersome in the small doorway, intrusive. He said something into
the shadows beyond the door and then Nancy appeared.

The attractiveness Jo remembered was gone, faded into a pale
emptiness. She stared bitterly at Jo and looked over the group.
Resentment and anger filled her face.

—She's fine here, where she is, Nancy said in a hoarse whisper.

—No, Jo said, she's not fine. She's coming with me.

Nancy shook her head stiffly, and the deputy stepped in beside her.

—The girl was staying here, he said. She's kind of settled in now. Seems like more excitement might upset her.

Jo heard her own voice tighten and rise. —What could upset her more than…? She paused, hesitated, restarted. —My sister told me, if something ever happened to her, I was to take care of this child.

—Her father's not dead, Nancy said flatly. She still has a family.

—My God! Jo sputtered. You can't think…

But the lawyer cut her off, addressing the deputy, pulling out the judge's order, saying there was nothing to debate and maybe he could assist in a smooth transfer of custody. That was his phrase, *transfer of custody*. Which amounted to them waiting on the steps with the sun bearing down and the temp clearing 90°F, while harried steps and voices went back and forth behind the door. Nancy argued and then pleaded with the deputy, whose voice sounded hollow and flat, as if echoing through a drainpipe. Jo didn't see Phil until the door opened again, with Nancy and Phil and Kimmy all behind the deputy.

Nancy held her in the crook of her arm. Kimmy's head rested on her shoulder, but she was stiff, alert, her eyes wide like a rabbit's at the approach of something large.

—You can't just take her like this, Nancy said.

—She belongs with us, Jo said.

—No, she doesn't.

Nancy stepped back, and the deputy put a hand behind her.

Phil scowled as if they were so many Jehovah's witnesses thrusting pamphlets through his doorway. He clutched a shopping bag with clothing in it.

—She's ours too! Nancy pleaded.

The lawyer whispered to Jo, and then said to Nancy, —We'll try to arrange something.

—Something?

—A visit.

—You can't do this! She turned to the deputy. —Don't let them take her!

—I'm sorry, Nancy. They got an order. I can't do anything right now.

Kimmy pulled at Nancy's neck when she finally leaned forward to hand the child over, and Jo swore Nancy was taunting her by allowing Kimmy to cling and forcing Jo to reach out and pull her away. It was a moment she never forgot.

Kimmy howled, squirming, flailing arms and legs, reaching back for Nancy. She thrust a knee into Jo's belly. Jo gasped and then took her firmly and tried to rub her back as she tried to squirm loose.

Nancy watched, offering no aid, her eyes liquid but her look unflinching, unforgiving. She stroked Kimmy's hair, whispered to her, but said nothing more as they left.

Once Jo and Nick had settled in the car with Kimmy between them, Jo wondered what Nancy might have told her about her mother and father – and if she even knew Anna was dead. Jo was as angry at herself for not asking as she was at Nancy for not telling her.

Kimmy sniveled and gasped. She shook Jo's arm off and looked around as if sizing the car up for an escape. She was tense and suspicious and wouldn't speak to Jo. Nick pointed out a hawk perched on a road sign. She glanced at the bird but wasn't about to be distracted from whatever had just happened. She remained sullen and fearful and weepy on the ride back to Monarch House, as if she'd just been kidnapped.

Ross was in the Bueller County jail. He'd been taken to the hospital first, Jo learned. His arms needed stitching – from knife wounds, from Anna slashing him, he said. At the trial he claimed self-defense. His attorney made Anna sound like a distempered she-beast. *She* had attacked Ross with a carving knife because he'd missed a car payment. *She* was unpredictable and volatile, the attorney claimed, and this wasn't the first time she'd done such a thing. He dragged their neighbors into court, who sullenly described Anna's shrill voice piercing the quiet street through open windows, screaming at Ross, slamming doors, throwing things. One neighbor said she'd seen Anna out in the driveway shouting at Ross over an overflowing trash pail. So it went. Anna was the bully and Ross the victim. Big, hulking, inked-up, calloused Ross, versus Anna, weighing in at maybe 120 lbs. after a big Thanksgiving dinner. Jo sat through days of this, moiling inside, enraged. One witness described Anna shouting at Ross from the front door as he drove away, spraying up gravel in his wake, while another, the old woman who lived next door, seemed to enjoy recounting whole weeks, seemed like, that Anna'd be away and Ross'd be there on his own with the little girl. For her job. So Anna said. Even then, as the trial continued, Nancy dropped a lawsuit on Jo and Nick, filing for custody of Kimmy, claiming they were financially unstable, that Monarch House was an unfit place for a child, with strangers coming and going week after week, with drinking and probably illegal drug use among the guests. The suit was suspended during the trial and finally dropped when Ross was convicted. Jo and Nick then filed for adoption. But Nancy was undeterred. She tried to block the adoption, claiming Kimmy's father was still alive and she shouldn't be deprived of the chance to know him, that it would be cruel to take her away from him.

And then the court stripped him of his parenthood too.

Whatever measure of good will Jo might have been willing to offer Nancy was fractured in the moment she forced Jo to pull the child out of her arms and then shattered in all that followed.

Jo kept her word and allowed another visit, reluctantly, on neutral ground – at the Social Services office, where they had a playroom for children and a social worker in the room. As far as Jo was concerned, that was it.

On the courtyard, applause and cheers erupted as the couple swept down the grassy aisle from the gazebo and through the archway, just beating the arrival of a BNSF freight train as it clattered through town some four blocks away. Its horn added a deafening and triumphant note to the ceremony's finale. Next door, the dogs broke into a chorus of barking.

Nick began moving chairs into the tent.

—Go help your father, Jo told Flann.

His white shirt had somehow climbed out of his pants during the ceremony. One wrinkled tail covered his backside as he loped down the steps.

—I take him to Dillard's, Jo said to Elliot, buy him good clothes, and he still manages to look like a bagger at the grocery store.

Elliot offered a sympathetic sniff and limped down to the courtyard to help with the chairs.

—Kimmy, Jo said, you can help me in the dining room.

Kim glanced at her doubtfully and once inside ran ahead, through the hallway and up to her room to get out of that itchy dress. And those shoes! Stiff leather and straps that dug into her skin like a cat clawing at her feet.

Aunt Jo was calling behind her as she disappeared up the staircase, but whatever.

She watched the party from behind her curtains. The bride and groom posed for pictures in the pine grove. Flann dragged chairs into the tent. The woman Alice talked to Uncle E, laying a hand on his arm. He nodded, and then she abruptly turned away as a brides-maid came along.

The flower girl had her picture taken. A flower herself. A cut flower. She'd soon whither. Her moment of brightness and color had almost passed. Her hair was sculpted into a delicate honey-comb of loops and curls, but the swirling pink bow at her back was already loose and her bouquet becoming cumbersome. Servers whisked about the courtyard with trays. The musicians from the ceremony packed their instruments and quietly passed through the crowd and into the driveway, as music boomed from the DJ's speakers.

The groomsmen opened gift boxes from the groom, each box a pair of tennis shoes. They changed shoes and wore tennis shoes with their suits.

The man Jim smoked a cigar.

The woman Alice scowled at the ushers wearing tennis shoes.

The ring bearer stood on a chair and flew a balsa wood plane that one of the groomsmen had given him. The groomsman flew one too, so did others, in their new tennis shoes, clutching glasses and launching wooden planes that drifted over the crowd.

The phone rang.

Uncle Nick carried the phone across the lawn and waved for Aunt Jo. He spoke into her ear with the phone covered. She shook her head no. She was angry. She took the phone, spoke, beeped off, and handed it back to Uncle Nick.

And instantly she looked up at Kim's window.

Kim hurried. Shorts, shirt, flip-flops. She scuttled down the back stairs.

Aunt Jo would be coming up the big staircase.

Cars lined both sides of West Mission Street. In the driveway, the caterer's van, with its strained English and uncertain punctuation – *"VINGS' CUISINE THE BEST"* – blocked the view from the street into the courtyard.

A brightly polished metallic-red Chevy Blazer slowed to a stop at the curb as if looking for a place to park. Nancy opened her window and surveyed the house. The front window curtains were drawn, and she saw no one on the porch or lawn.

A cook in a white smock grabbed a pan from the truck and disappeared into the house. Music throbbed from the backyard. Voices bubbled and laughed. She remained there watching the house as the stop light held back a parade of cars behind her but saw no one besides the cook. When the light changed she rolled forward at the pace of a sidewalk stroll until the first horn blared.

Phil squeezed the armrest and steadied himself as she hit the gas and they wheeled into the turn at the corner. A couple of more hard turns and a mile or so later, and they were headed north on K-29, flat, wide, smooth, where he could finally release the armrest as the car found its speed.

He settled back and read billboards.

Nancy would have been content with silence in the car, but she sensed him warming up to say something, and she knew what it was.

She snapped on the radio.

—I'll see if the ballgame's on.

—Late ssstart, he said, tapping the clock on the dashboard, which read 3:42. —Won't be till four-o-five.

She hit the button for the oldies station. Lou Christie wailed the chorus of 'Lightning Strikes Again' in a razor-thin falsetto that could crack the ice on a frozen pond.

—Lower, he said.

She drew a sharp breath and reached for the dial. Getting him settled and contented was a task without end.

He stared absently into the cars passing in adjacent lanes. A boy in the back seat of a minivan barely arm's length from his own window stared at him and then gave him the finger as he veered away on an off-ramp. Phil grunted, —Whaa… but a radio ad for easy mortgage refinancing swallowed up the sound of his voice.

Nancy hadn't noticed, or ignored him if she did.

—I sssuppose with a wedding going on… Phil finally said, but there was no more and he left the sentence dangling in the pitchman's breathless spiel about a once-in-a-lifetime opportunity to turn your home into cash.

A couple of mechanics smoking in the shade outside an auto body shop watched them pass.

—You know it had nothing to do with that, she said.

—Maybe if we'd called.

—I did call.

—From the car… we were already almost there.

—Doesn't make a difference when I call. It's just not fair. Don't you see? She won't even know who we are!

—What if they'd ssseen us?

—What if they did? So what?

She wiped at her eyes with the heel of her hand.

At home, later, she mowed the lawn while he watched the game. Row after row, criss-crossing the lot on the tractor-mower, buried in the machine's noise, the satisfying long, straight rows, the carpet-like appearance of new-mown grass, the heat, her blouse soaked in sweat. The task filled her senses and she numbed herself inside the smell of cut grass, the deep, hoarse drone of the tractor, the absence of anything but herself.

L&O, a Silver Bracelet, & Y-10k

Wasn't much doubt Flann would've been just as happy – no, happier… no, happiest – if she'd never shown up. But over time he'd settled into a sort of measured indifference toward her. Like he avoided talking directly to her and even looking at her if he could, as if she had some deformity or was one of the short-bus kids. Oddly enough, she didn't seem to resent this treatment, maybe because it was one less person for her to deal with. She sometimes got that same feeling, about being a short-bus kid or whatever, from Aunt Jo, but for the very opposite reason – because Aunt Jo was always trying so hard to make up for her being different. Either way, she knew she was different and that she'd been dropped into this place for some reason that made no sense, and she had the feeling that there was more beyond this world that she didn't know about yet, like maybe if one of the fish suddenly suspected something wasn't quite right about the koi pond and didn't even know it was a pond, only that whatever it was, it ought to be bigger, and also that something might be going on up overhead where all the quivering shadows came and went, and hands and fingers, which the fish didn't know what they were either or where they came from, would suddenly poke their way into his world and swish around and then disappear. What could that mean?

So Flann… he ranged from five to six years older than her, depending on the time of year, because his birthday was in summer and hers in the fall, and that's when she'd catch up and be only five years younger. Right now it was five. She'd just turned nine and he was fourteen.

On a school night in September, they were watching *Law & Order* with Uncle Elliot on the downstairs TV when Aunt Jo came through and began interrogating Flann like Detective Lenny Briscoe until she uncovered a math assignment that needed doing and sent him off for the book. Kim shook her head no, she didn't have homework, and watched him take the stairs in wide, unhurried steps, two at a time, like it was less effort and somehow made it slower that way. He had long legs and wore baggy black jeans that had lots of rivets and looked heavy and hung down so his boxers puffed out on his hips like icing spilling over the rim of a cupcake. Aunt Jo was always telling him pull your pants up. Kim couldn't figure why he liked wearing those pants because they looked about as comfortable as wearing a tent, but he wore the same pair almost every day. He was skinny, and his head was narrow too, like one of those new bicycle helmets, and he'd tilt his head back whenever grown-ups were talking to him like he had doubts, which he'd keep to himself, but he had doubts.

When he didn't return by the time the cops were gone and the lawyers took over, Aunt Jo told Kim, Go tell Flann I'm still waiting on him.

Kim took the main stairway, too, and then veered off on the second floor. Most of the guest rooms had televisions now. She figured he'd probably snuck off to watch one. But he wasn't there. Only one room was taken tonight, and the people had gone out to dinner. The hallway smelled of dusting spray and the thick, musty scent of vacuum cleaner exhaust. The carpet nap was fluffed up from Aunt

Jo vacuuming this afternoon. The double lamp on the sideboard glowed. It looked like two fishbowls, one stacked on top of the other, each with frosted pink glass and the whole affair sitting atop a gilt stand. Butterflies fluttered across the glass, forever still, never destined to light on nearby flowers also painted on the glass. An antique pitcher and wash basin and a few books that no one ever read stood beside the lamp. The hallway was still and quiet.

She tried the door of the occupied room. Guests often left their doors unlocked, so she wasn't surprised when it opened. Inside, the bathroom light had been left on, casting a gloomy haze of gray light across the room. They'd only arrived late this afternoon, a man and woman, but still Kim found the bed rumpled, the pillows askew and one on the floor. Bathroom towels lay in a heap on the floor beside the bed.

She went into the bathroom and peed and then splattered water on her hands and wiped them on a towel.

Guest rooms were all named for local themes and heroes — 'Overland Trail,' 'Shawnee Nation,' 'Eisenhower,' 'Wheat Fields,' 'Annie Oakley.' This room was 'Araby,' which turned out not to be about Arabs at all, or not directly anyway, but about river boats. It was named for the steamboat *Arabia*, a side-wheeler that had been dredged up from the bottom of the Missouri River after a hundred years of being buried in mud, still laden with its cargo of boots and clay pipes and bells and dishes and cast iron cookery and coins and hundreds of other items. Now the *Arabia* had its own museum, where Aunt Jo got some pictures and postcards and souvenirs to decorate this room.

'Araby' was a corner room with windows overlooking the cottonwood tree on the side of the house and the street out front.

Sitting in the corner between the windows and watching the street lights dance in the trees and looking down into the cars that passed, she felt like she was traveling in a glass bubble high up in the air where she could see everything. It reminded her of when Daddy put her up on a limb in the front yard tree and she looked down on the narrow roads she'd carved out with her trucks in the dirt so far below. She remembered the house too, some, in faint glimpses, as if clouds had rolled in, shrouding it in mist.

Daddy was in prison. Aunt Jo said he wasn't her Daddy now and he wouldn't have done what he did if he wanted to be her Daddy. At times Kim felt anger rise up from somewhere deep inside her like a wave of heat. She'd suddenly get the urge to kick one of the kids at school or drop a dinner plate on the veranda just to watch it shatter or hide out in the woods until long after dark when no one knew where she was, so that's what she did. Aunt Jo finally called the police on that one. Kim never said where she'd gone, just wandered up to the back door sometime before dawn and found the kitchen full of people and policemen and Aunt Jo in tears. But so what? She didn't belong here. She was alone in this strange world, living inside a glass bubble, and everyone else was going around like nothing had happened and they'd look at her like she just arrived from space and had no business here.

She remembered Mommy in random images – riding in the truck, wearing big sunglasses, her dark hair fluttering as the wind whipped through the cab, stubbing a cigarette in the ashtray; putting out a plate of food for the stray calico that visited their porch; toweling her hair after a shower while Kim sat on the bed and watched her breasts jiggle. But her face rarely came clearly, or her voice. Just sometimes she'd flit by and then was gone. There were many photos. Aunt Jo liked paging through albums and telling stories, but now they confused Kim because she couldn't tell what she remembered for real and what came from a photo or story.

Monarch House cluttered the past too – people came and went each week and took up room inside her that she wanted for Mommy and Daddy. Sometimes loud, tumbling, chaotic noises seemed to erupt inside her – voices, machines, TVs, footsteps. They would swell up loud and then fade to a hum, like a distant lawn mower, but still there, and she was always trying to hear and see into the noise. But during the week, the rooms were silent and empty. The doors were left open and the window shades up to keep the rooms fresh and bright. She wasn't supposed to go in vacant rooms unless she was helping clean, but she did anyway, but she didn't watch TV like Flann. Rather, she'd tuck herself into a corner behind a bed or chair, out of sight, and in the silence she could remember better and the noise would fade. The thick bedspreads and carpets and layered curtains quieted the outside sounds. She preferred emptiness…and darkness, like now. She could fold herself up inside it. There were shadows and dark places in her memory, but if she sat still, if there were emptiness and quiet, maybe she could make out what was hidden there.

Araby was her favorite room, but now, looking around at the clutter of these invisible people who'd taken over her sanctuary, she became restless and agitated. She checked out the stuff on the dresser, where she found a cell phone, lotions, coins, receipts, a pendant, and the woman's hairbrush with clumps of dark hair tangled in the bristles. Kim brushed her hair and pretended to make a call. The phone lit up and made a happy sound when she touched a button. Then she noticed a bracelet glistening in the phone's light, turquoise and silver, with intricate geometric patterns.

She slipped the bracelet on her wrist and went to the window, where it shone in the street light's glow. Wearing it quieted the noise within her, which now receded to a distant hum like the truck's engine when she'd sit by the open window with Daddy driving and Mommy beside her.

⁓

THEY LOOKED ENORMOUSLY UNHAPPY, the two of them, alone at the long dining table, with chairs for a dozen and the room heavy with knick-knacks, flowers, potted plants, and ornately framed pictures on the dark green walls. They spoke softly, as if aware of their conspicuousness. Kim watched them from the sitting room across the hall. The man was partly screened by the woman, who had her back to the doorway. Kim knelt in the wingback chair and peaked over the top.

—Be chaos is what, the man said.

His beard was dark, close-cut, trimmed as if it had been sten-ciled on his double chin. He pinned down a sausage link and sliced through it, clutching his fork like a joystick.

The woman ate quietly, nodding, vocalizing *Mm-hmm*'s when he paused.

Silverware scraped and rattled on the plates.

The woman's voice lilted upward in a question.

The man responded dryly, —But they're not fixing it. Been ignor-ing it since the fifties. Can you believe it? Some guy – whatsizname, can't think of it – anyway, this guy actually predicted all this back in 1958. They were programming with punch cards then. Think of it, punch cards! The programmers would walk around computers as big as a car that can't do a fraction of what my laptop can do today with these trays full of thousands of cards. The big programmer joke was you'd offer, like doing a guy a favor, you know, to go fetch his

58

program in the next room, where the computer'd just spit all his cards into a tray. You'd be a good guy and say you'll get it for him, but then you'd fill a tray with old discards and as you returned with the tray, you'd stumble and thousands of cards would go flying every which way, and the joke was, you had to get this, that the cards all had to be in order. One card out of order in all these thousands of cards and your program was cooked!

He chuckled. The woman nodded. She got it. The joke sounded worn, even back then, whenever.

He chewed and talked. —But so they programmed two digits for the year instead of four. Saved a lot of space with all these cards, every one of them hand punched on these typewriter-looking things, more like Telex machines or whatever, and on it went through all the pro-grams – COBOL and ACSII, then RPG, ISAM, dBASE, the whole generational alphabet soup – and it was like this genetic disease that just got passed from one computer generation to the next, and there were people who knew – like that guy… what *is* his name? – they knew even back then that one day it would fuck everything up.

—Terry!

—What?

She frowned and glanced around.

They ate silently for a few minutes. Then the man continued, quietly at first, —People think it was just neglect, you know. That no one wanted to deal with it. But you have to wonder how with all they knew about this for over what? forty years! and nobody did anything?! you have to wonder what's really going on.

She sighed and glanced at a vase on the buffet with flowers and a single bronze butterfly on a slender stem as if noticing the butterfly for the first time.

—I'm just saying, he added, it'll be chaos. Then after a pause, as if the subject's current was pulling him downstream with it, he continued, —Just look at all the timestamps out there, Microsoft, Java, UNIX. They're saying Windows is fixed, but fixing it with them probably means you got some new problem you don't even know about yet. There's one group out there… He laughed now, fully recovered from her reprimand, putting down the fork and pulling a bite from his roll and smacking the cud around in his mouth. —This one group, they're already looking out to the year ten thousand! Want us to write the dates in five digits, like zero-plus-nineteen-ninety-nine. Can you believe it? Planning eight thousand years ahead. Like what, we'll still be updating Windows in eight thousand years? Hah! But so I'm just worried about this year. Who knows if we'll even have electricity come January One. We're gonna see the dark side of humanity…

The woman set her silverware on the plate as if to say she'd heard enough about humanity's dark side for now.

After finishing off his sausage and wiping the plate with a crust of biscuit, he asked, softly, —So you want me to say something?

She shushed him, as if whispering was even too loud.

—No.

—But we can't just…

She lifted a hand, slightly, enough to cut him off.

Kim shivered and scrunched down in the chair. The rustle of the cushions suddenly seemed like the loudest sound in the house. Now there was complete stillness in the dining room, as if no one was there, as if no living thing had ever been there.

And just then Aunt Jo appeared at the door with the coffee pot.

She greeted them as if the room was full and the table crowded. —More coffee?

The woman brightened. —Oh, yes! Please… And recovering, she added, —It was delightful! Everything! Just delightful!

As Aunt Jo refilled her cup, the woman asked who was the man in the painting, and next thing it was off to the races about him being old Col. Elijah T. Fitzgibbon, who built the house over a hundred years ago, and then, Kim knew, a recitation of the whole history of the house would follow.

She slid off the chair and slipped the bracelet from her wrist. The fright of near discovery faded as she climbed the back stairs, where she put it on again. She sashayed along the empty second-floor hallway, flourishing the bracelet. She stopped at the mirror to admire how it graced her wrist. She propped her fingers lightly on her chin and slouched jauntily to one side. The bracelet suited her; it gave her color; it gleamed. She was a bridesmaid and had just had her hair done. She wore a thick, warm robe and drank champagne and gossiped with the other bridesmaids. They all admired her new bracelet; they wanted one like it; they said she'd be the next bride.

The voices from down in the dining room carried up the main staircase, louder now. The guests were up from their places.

Footsteps in the front hall, on the stairs.

She scurried to the back stairwell and listened.

Once in their room, the woman's voice shuddered like the weathervane on the garage roof on stormy nights, when the wind blew in fierce gusts from the south, chaotic, confused, but not about the bracelet. About the man, something about him made her sorrowful. You could even tell listening to her downstairs, and the way she smiled… like the wind, always whisking itself away, gone in an instant, already gone just as it arrives. Her smile never filled her face, not from the moment she arrived at Monarch House. She was always ready for her joy to abandon her; it would leave suddenly, without notice. Happiness was a packed bag and coat in hand. Now it was gone. Her voice burbled. The man's voice sounded like rocks tossed on a pile. Some rolled off; some hit with a thud; some cracked chips in the others. She whimpered. He placed a rock on the pile, but this time softly, as if abandoning the chore. Silence followed. The bedsprings creaked. The bathroom door shut. Water ran.

When they were gone for the afternoon, Kim decided to return the bracelet. It hummed with the woman's sorrow. She would hear it at night. It would drown out even the noise from inside her. It would keep Mommy away, who sometimes came into her room late at night. Kim knew she was there when the curtains fluttered or the wall creaked for no reason at all. That's how she knew Mommy had come.

The bracelet was in a make-up pouch in back of her closet where she stashed other stuff swiped from guests and their kids and from wherever. She had a matchbox car, a ZZ Top CD (which she'd never heard), a click pen with the name of a bank in Iowa, a plastic cigarette lighter (clear red and still full of lighter fluid), a phone charger, lip balm, a nail clipper, one cufflink, a poker chip, a pair of children's sunglasses, a few polished stones swiped from a souvenir shop in Branson (where the family had gone supposedly on vacation but mainly so Aunt Jo and Uncle Nick could check out a B&B down there), and an unopened pack of Skittles snatched while Aunt Jo was on line at the store.

She fetched the bracelet and went downstairs, but now they'd locked the door.

She stood in the hallway, fingering the bracelet, wondering what to do.

She knelt down and peered under the door but could only see a few inches to the edge of the rug inside the room. She slipped the bracelet on her wrist once more. It looked dull now and disappointing, like when you thought you'd spotted a coin glistening on the sidewalk and then found it was just an oily splotch of gum.

She placed the bracelet on the floor under the door, with the arc of its edge still poking out. She hesitated. It remained within reach. She could retrieve it with a fingertip. She heaved a breath and flicked her fingers, springing her forefinger off her thumb. Gone. The permanence of the act filled her. She peered under the door. There it lay at the edge of the rug, beyond reach. She rose and scampered down the back stairs and found Aunt Jo, who asked her what she'd been up to and she said nothin'.

The man and woman stayed another night. From the kitchen Kim heard them out in the hallway on their way to dinner, and just then Aunt Jo said come help fold linens in the dining room. As the woman saw Kim she looked at her the same as she did the vase with the butterfly yesterday, as if Kim suddenly caught her attention, as if noticing her for the first time even though she'd already seen her. She squinted and waved to Kim before she left, and Kim saw the bracelet glittering on her wrist.

More guests arrived for the weekend, boisterous, loud, wearing bright red hats and sweaters, all here for the Chiefs game on Sunday. They took up four rooms on the second floor, all in the same party. Monarch House livened now. Red and gold bows brightened the railings and newel posts. Aunt Jo had put a bowl filled with Christmas balls with Chiefs colors on the hearth. People came and went everywhere. They carried drink glasses and beer bottles. They asked Kim where she went to school. They recognized Uncle E from being on TV a long time ago. They asked Aunt Jo for ice and ordered her famous stuffed mushrooms.

ON SUNDAY MORNING, AS usual with guests in the house, Aunt Jo went to 6:30 Mass while Uncle Nick set up the dining room for brunch. Then she came in with several copies of the newspaper and started cooking while Uncle Nick and Kim went to church. Flann was supposed to go, too, but he'd stopped going, mostly, Aunt Jo said, because he was lazy and not because he didn't believe anymore, but it was too much trouble to get him ready and Uncle Nick said let it go, which Aunt Jo said she wouldn't if it was her going right now and maybe next week she'd roust him for the 6:30 service and see how he liked that. But today it was just Kim and Uncle Nick.

Uncle Elliot never went, but he was always up early. He'd go walking and return with a bagful of trash he collected for the recycling bin and mutter about how people just didn't throw stuff out car windows like that when he was a kid.

Aunt Jo made Kim wear the plaid wool jumper that itched her legs like walking through a thistle patch. As they parked at church, Kim saw Chelsea from her class. Chelsea saw Kim too but pretended to ignore her. Uncle Nick and Chelsea's father talked about whether it would snow early this year because it looked like it might but it wasn't cold enough today but maybe this week and they'd have to cover their flowers to save them from frost. Chelsea's father carried his own missal, a tidy black leather book that fit squarely in his hand and gave him an air of certainty about things, especially regarding church. He wore a dark suit pressed to sharp creases. His tie was tied in a triangle knot that sat perfectly under his starched white collar. His shoes clacked on the blacktop pavement. At the church steps Chelsea's family went ahead into the mingling crowd. Inside it smelled like church.

The pews were packed. The new immigrant kid Lalo and his family were squeezed into a side pew, all six of them, his mother and father and brother and two sisters. He'd just joined the class and only knew enough English to tell the lunch ladies what he wanted. Chelsea said he got free lunch, which she said with a Spanish accent. When they found seats, Kim knelt beside Uncle Nick and couldn't see much besides coats and dresses and hats. She propped her chin on the pew and wondered if Baxter, who was teaching Lalo swear words in English, was one of the altar boys. When Kim sat back, she saw Chelsea four-five rows ahead, done with her prayer, sitting in her pew and looking around. Now Chelsea spotted Brittany across the aisle and started mouthing messages to her, big, wide-faced, lip messages that Brittany was supposed to lip-read but she couldn't understand, and she kept shaking her head, eyes wide, and mouthing *What? What?* and Chelsea was getting frustrated.

Soon kneelers clattered all over the church as everyone stood and sang.

Holy God, we praise Thy Name;
Lord of all, we bow before Thee!
All on earth Thy scepter claim,
All in Heaven above adore Thee;
Infinite Thy vast domain,
Everlasting is Thy reign.

The woman beside Uncle Nick warbled in a piercing soprano. The man behind Kim growled and shifted down an octave when the melody rose on *Infinite Thy vast domain.* Kim wondered why you'd say *Holy God,* like was it necessary to call God *holy?*

Kim soon gave up on standing and kneeling. She drew pictures in the program with the stubby half-pencil from the little slot in back of the pew. Her picture showed a glimpse of the altar from behind the lady's hat in front of her, with Father Dominic leaning around it as if he was checking to see what Kim was up to way back there.

Kim thought of the bracelet woman now. For sure she knew Kim had taken it, but she didn't seem angry – that was one thing. And another was that she hadn't told Aunt Jo. That was weird. Probably had by now. Probably Kim was in for big trouble when she got home. Whatever.

She drew a new picture while everyone else sang another song.

After Mass, Uncle Nick said he needed something at Home Depot and it would only take a minute. In the nuts and bolts aisle, he opened drawers and tried to match a bolt he had in his jacket pocket. That's the sort of thing he did, going to church with a bolt in his pocket. Next thing he was looking for a Home Depot guy and said he'd be right back, and he left Kim in the aisle. Across from the bolts were cabinet handles and hinges, one of everything displayed on a board above dozens of bins filled with the items. She fingered a porcelain handle with blue flowers as if opening an imaginary vanity drawer. The bin with the item tilted open at a touch. Inside were bunches more in plastic wrappers. Uncle N was in the next aisle with a Home Depot guy in an orange apron. They were both headed down the aisle and would turn the corner any second. A forklift beeped past at the other end. She thrust her hand into the bin, grabbed one of the porcelain drawer handles, slipped it into her jumper pocket, and then shut the bin just as Uncle Nick and the HD guy came up the aisle. Uncle N got a plastic bag full of bolts and they went home for lunch.

Flann and Uncle Elliot were eating when they came in through the breezeway door. The guests had all gone wherever they were going, most of them to the game.

On TV two men in suits talked about the football game as if war had broken out, or an earthquake, or wildfires; they were serious, intense. They said, *We'll see what happens.*

Aunt Jo called from the dining room, —You back?

—We're back, Uncle Nick said.

—C'mon out here, Kimmy.

This was it.

Aunt Jo was wiping silverware and dropping it into slots in the top buffet drawer. She was always counting the silver. Silverware jangled. Kim only had one spoon stashed in her makeup case. More like she was keeping it from getting stolen.

Aunt Jo whispered in the rhythmic patter of counting, and when she'd finished one bunch, she asked, —How was church?

Kim shrugged and fingered the porcelain drawer handle in her pocket.

Aunt Jo idly separated a few dessert forks from the mound of uncounted silverware and then pulled out a chair and sat, taking Kim by the forearms and drawing her close, at eye level.

Trouble for sure.

Kim gripped the handle in her pocket. The woolen jumper itched and she wanted to change. She was hungry too and just wanted to get this over with.

—You don't like that dress, do you?

Headshake no.

—Well, it's already small on you. This rate you'll be out of it by Christmas.

Jo said this as if it would be welcome news to Kimmy, but all she got back was a shrug. She waited, hoping for more.

Kimmy was looking over her shoulder, as if something at the front window had caught her eye. Jo turned but saw nothing there. She squeezed Kimmy's arms to bring her focus back.

—Did you talk to the lady who stayed in Six?

—Unh-huh.

—You sure?

Nod.

—Well, she and her husband checked out while you were gone, but she must have liked you. Here… – Aunt Jo reached in her apron pocket – … she left this for you. She wanted you to have it.

Out came the bracelet in her fingers.

A wisp of breath swept through Kim's lips.

Which Aunt Jo caught. —What'd she say to you?

—Nothing, I swear! I saw her… I saw her eating breakfast is all.

Jo wondered what had really happened, but pressing too hard was a sure way to seal her up tight. She knew she'd get no farther for the moment.

She handed the bracelet over. Kim stuffed it into her pocket with the drawer handle.

Jo unfolded herself from the chair.

—Well, she wanted you to have it. Said you'd remember her someday, when you were older. Said people come and go in your life and you forget them. You keep that safe. Don't be wearing it around. Go on and change and I'll make you some lunch.

On the stairs, Kim slipped the bracelet on and counted her steps in the same whispered patter as Aunt Jo counting silverware.

Wild Eyes and Spark Notes Sex

The road had that Sunday feel – sparse traffic, shiny Buicks circa 1982 with old folks in church clothes peering over the dashboards, minivans packed with kids and Grandma in back on the way to brunch at Bob Evans down by the I-70 junction. A tractor stood driverless in a field bristling with dried corn stumps. A billboard promoted legal services for victims of mesothelioma. Nancy lowered the visor to block the glare of the slate sky. The sun could be anywhere. There was just glare in front of her, surrounding her, hanging over the gray road, as she drove north on K-55 alone.

She'd brought a few magazines and books, a pad of drugstore stationery paper, a box of envelopes. None of it wrapped. You couldn't wrap anything, and you couldn't bring food, and he could only wear what they gave him – so what was left? Books, magazines? He never liked reading, but still she agonized over what to buy at Borders yesterday. Everything on the magazine racks was a reminder of the life he couldn't live – travel, home repair, hunting, fishing. She wouldn't bring anything with guns in it. He liked auto racing and motorcycles, but those magazines were filled with women straddling bikes and draped over cars, wearing enough to cover nipples and pubic hair, if that much, if they even had pubic hair – she shuddered at the thought.

Walcott Correctional Facility was in Adams County, in north-central Kansas, about a four-hour drive from her home. Long stretches of highway since she got off the interstate ran past cattle feedlots, crop fields, heavy-gauge wire fencing nailed to limestone posts, center-pivot circular irrigation systems with complex networks of trusses and wheel towers. She passed few businesses or stores, but still the region had the feel of heavy industry. Grain and livestock trucks swept by frequently even though it was Sunday.

Ross had spent his first three months in Topeka Correctional, where they did psychological evaluations and counseling. Then he'd been moved to Lansing, only thirty minutes from Nancy and Phil's, and spent most of the next two years there, and that's where she thought he'd stay. But they can move you anywhere and for no reason at all, seemed like, or at least none he could give her, though she wondered what he might not be telling her about why he landed here. The question and answer just faded, as they often did with him, so she didn't press, and now he'd been here at Walcott for nearly three years. She couldn't visit every week, as she had when he was at Lansing, though she tried at first. She was still working and the drive was too much.

As she turned into the parking lot, a familiar tightness gripped her, as if her blouse was shrinking, as if the air was being sucked out of the car. Even after five years she still shuddered at the sight of the concertina wire coiled along the high double rows of chain-link fencing, pernicious and sadistic stuff. Images of mangled bodies and shredded flesh bubbled up before her.

She knew the visitor routines like a frequent flyer whisking through a familiar airport. She left her cell phone and purse in the car trunk. She wore no earrings or jewelry; she'd even left her wedding ring at home. The belt buckle on her skirt was plastic. The metal detectors were not your garden-variety airport detectors. Metal hairpins and even some bra hooks could set them off. Still, no matter what you did, there was always something.

Some women – it was mostly women who visited, she noticed – were turned away for showing up in tube tops or slit dresses or even (what were they thinking?) braless. All you had to do was read the guidelines. But still, she understood how they were all, including her, at the mercy of this insensate monolith of power. She wondered sometimes if breaking down the families was also part of the punishment – the sins of the son, as it were (or husband or brother or lover, or father too). They'd keep visitors waiting at the gates in cold and rain long past when visiting hours were supposed to start before opening them. Nancy saw a woman who'd waited over two hours turned away because the guards couldn't find her man. —Can't find him!? she'd shrieked. It's a fucking prison! Where the fuck can he go?! Well, that was it for her. She was escorted out. Nancy never saw her again, and the woman's prisoner probably lost visiting privileges for three, maybe six months. Nancy wondered what the real story was – why they 'couldn't find' that man. But it was easy to screw up. If you didn't make it through the metal detector on the third try, after you'd removed everything you could think of and they'd scanned you with the wand, you were done. No visit. Gone. Goodbye.

Once past the gates she signed in at the Control Office. The reading matter would be checked through and he'd get it later. A woman ahead of her had to re-walk the metal detector after she dropped her earrings and watch into a tray to be poked at by a corrections officer as if they were bodily waste. Alarms buzzed. Lights whirled. A female CO with a grim demeanor and hair sculpted to the shape of a football helmet wanded her. An elaborate set of keys with colorful trinkets emerged from the hip pocket of jeans so tight they might have been spray painted on. Clearly not a frequent flyer. She was advised of the three-strikes policy and opted to return to her car to readjust her personal inventory before the final attempt.

Nancy was released into the hallway on the other side. She passed through a full-length turnstile whose claw-like arms reminded her of threshing tines and then went outdoors again to cross a narrow courtyard. A CO behind thick glass watched from the other end. A metal door unlocked with an urgent buzz as she reached for it and banged shut behind her with a definitive cluck. A guard pointed her to a numbered table, where she sat without concealing her hands or holding her coat in any way that could be construed as hiding something.

The room was cool, but inside-cool, absent the moisture and life of the autumn chill beyond the walls. Fried food, fresh paint, detergent, and the faint, incongruous scent of licorice mingled in the air. She folded her coat and draped it over a chair. She was chilly but didn't want to appear as if she was ready to leave before he even sat down. She waited and watched the gray steel door in the corner where he'd appear.

The visiting room might have resembled a high school cafeteria but for the thick wire mesh covering the windows and the guards looking on from behind glass panels and others wandering the room. The room was large and noisy and barren, with nothing to muffle the din from dozens of tables, some of which included children. That was something that pained her many times over, seeing the children. Nancy hadn't seen Kimmy but once since she'd been taken from her front porch over five years ago – the visit promised by the lawyer that day, a brief and unsatisfying reunion only weeks later. Even prisoners had more time with their families.

Nearby a black man was helping his son with homework. The boy might be close to Kimmy's age. His father was a fearsome-looking man with a heavy mustache and otherwise unshaven. Tattoos crawled out of his collar and up his neck in ominous, viney ways, and his face bore the blank, drained, you-cannot-tell-me-something-that-will-shock-me look of having done terrible things even before the terrible thing that finally landed him here. He held the pencil awkwardly and puzzled through whatever it was, maybe arithmetic, with his kid. Nancy imagined Kimmy sitting here with her now, a school book on the table, eyes wandering everywhere, but soon settling into her homework as Ross struggled along with her.

Yet Nancy also doubted he'd have the patience that man had, or even care as much as he seemed to. She was always the first to mention Kimmy when she visited. More than once, driving home after seeing him, she wondered if he'd even have asked about Kimmy if she hadn't mentioned her. He'd just given up, so it seemed to Nancy, and maybe wouldn't even think about his own child but for her.

He'd been sentenced to life. He would not be in prison for less than twenty-five years – a 'hard twenty-five.' He'd be fifty-seven when his first chance for parole came up. Kimmy would be twenty-nine. And Nancy would be… well, she lived with the arithmetic. As bizarre as it would have sounded if she'd ever said so – so she never did – time was shorter for her than for him, and she believed she'd lost more than he did.

It seemed unbearably unfair that this is what her life had come to.

She had a secret nickname for Ross's natural father. The Animal.

She'd never told anyone, not even Phil. It's possible that those words in that form – *The + Animal* – had never passed her lips. His real name had so faded from her consciousness that there were moments when it didn't even come to her and all there was was The Animal. About the time when Ross was old enough to start school, Nancy left The Animal and moved in with her mother. She checked groceries at the Food-for-Less on Parallel Parkway down in KCK and was determined to have Ross's childhood bear some semblance to what she thought of as 'normal.' She wanted him to believe he was just as good as kids who came from families with two parents, at least one of whom had a job a link or two higher up on the food chain than Nancy's. The appearance of normalcy, she decided, was as good as the reality of it. Nancy made sure that Ross participated in everything, even when he didn't want to, which was often, as if he felt the burden of being embarrassed for both of them because he was the only kid at, say, the Pinewood Derby, whose mother helped him build his car, which did turn out pretty bad, she had to admit.

Another single mom who worked at the grocery store told Nancy, —You fake it till you make it, don't you?

Which carried her a long way.

She lived in fear of the day The Animal would suddenly crawl back into their lives. She felt as if she were living in a house with a big snake under the porch that could be anywhere when she stepped out the door.

Ross played baseball. He was good at it, too. Since he was big, he played first base. He could hit and always tried to stretch a double into a triple or a triple into a homer.

She hadn't seen or heard from The Animal in two-three years, when finally one night it happened. He showed up at a little league game. Over time she'd almost been lulled into believing it wouldn't happen, or at least there'd be a warning, a phone call, an intuition, something. But on this hot summer evening, as the treetops whooshed in a breeze that could not seem to find its way down to the stifling field, she missed seeing his Ford Torino rumble into the parking lot and glide slowly among the rows of cars like a boat docking in a marina; missed him leaning under the concessions truck awning to ask if he'd found the right game where his kid was playing; missed him hanging over the chain link fence and lighting a smoke while he checked the place out until he spotted her in the stands; and missed him sidling along the fence, closer to where Ross was at first base.

She missed him until he gave a familiar two-note whistle that he could do by curling his tongue into a little chute under his lip. Ross turned instantly at the sound, and the moment she saw the boy's head turn toward the fence, she knew who it was even before The Animal's gaunt, ashen face, shaded by an oversized, sweat-stained John Deere cap, looked up at her as if she were the only person in the stands.

She felt like prey. She shuddered. The night's late summer heat bore down on her. The game might have been on mute.

He clomped up the bleachers, weaving among the other parents and offering his saccharine *'Scuse-me's* and *Thank-you-muches* as he passed – the over-politeness just another clue to his volatility, the courtesy of someone who doesn't really know how to be courteous and doesn't believe in it anyway, who thinks courtesy is a sign of weakness, so when it's necessary or useful to be courteous he play-acts it, like bad melodrama.

He was thinner than she recalled, just a runt, in fact, with gaunt, sun-dried arms that had the texture of old orange peels and a pair of sticks for legs that he always concealed under dirty jeans no matter the temperature. Yet the threat of sudden violence was as much a fixture in his appearance as that dirty, oversized cap.

And now all that baggage had rumbled into her evening and clomped up the galvanized aluminum seat planks and plopped itself down beside her.

—How's he doin'? was all he said.

Nancy mumbled the score.

—What about him? Get a hit?

Not even using Ross's name, she noticed–

—Yeah, got a hit in the first.

—Good.

He nodded, his lips pushed up in approval, a proprietary nod, as in, *I'm pleased. You all can carry on.*

She smelled the booze and noticed how Ross kept glancing up to the stands. He was excited, eager to please his father.

The Animal lit a cigarette, cupping his hands around the Bic lighter, more gesture than shielding the flame from the nonexistent wind. His movements were studied; his intonations dramatized.

The side was out and Ross flicked his head at his father as he trotted to the dugout and fetched a helmet and bat. He'd be up second, waiting on deck.

The first batter knifed a ground ball into centerfield and rounded first. When the ball came back to the infield, he began a taunting, wing-flopping dance, daring the second baseman to throw. The second baseman glared as he walked the ball to the mound and put it in the pitcher's glove.

Now Ross came up, looking toward the stands again as he stepped into the batter's box. The Animal was aroused. He stood. The cigarette hung from his lips as he clapped and grunted, —C'mon now! Right now, boy!

Ross kicked dirt from the box and banged the bat on the plate, a series of brisk thumps. He fouled off the first pitch and took another as the ball went high and glanced off the catcher's mitt, clanking into the chain-link backstop. The runner scooted to second and now taunted the catcher, who ran the ball halfway to the mound and tossed a lazy arc to the pitcher.

The Animal stayed on his feet, pulling a final draw on his smoke and flicking the butt under the bleachers. Cheers welled up.

Nancy clapped. —Get one, Ross!

The Animal glanced at her as if she didn't know how to cheer.

The pitch came in. Ross swung hard and met the ball with a sharp wooden *clop!* An unmistakable sound. And no foul ball or grounder either. The sound of the bat's sweet thickness finding dead center of the ball's radius, as it was stopped instantly and its course reversed and it took flight on a glorious rocketing delivery from gravity, from filthy hands and oily gloves and grass stains and dirt, when it changed sides and now belonged briefly to the offense and had the attention of every set of eyes in the park, an immeasurable moment, as the ball found its way deep into left center, where two fielders converged, and the runner rounded third and Ross pedaled hard for second.

They'd played him deep, and the team was well-coached. The cut-off man darted onto the outfield grass behind short and the centerfielder launched the ball in a hard throw that left him tumbling to his knees as Ross ran for second. He never showed a hint of slowing down or sliding, even as the third-base coach waved him to hold-up. Ross was a heavy runner. Elbows chugged, steps thudded. He wheeled for third from deep in the hole. The throw came true from the cut-off man, and the third baseman, a kid easily a head shorter than Ross, snagged it and leaned forward to tag him as he slid. But he didn't slide. He plowed into the kid chest first and sent him tumbling into the coach's box. The ball got loose and rolled away.

Ross saw the kid lift a hatless head from the dust and look in the wrong direction for the ball. He thumped home and stomped on the plate, and instantly, with a sharp, fisted jab into the dusty air, the umpire called him out.

The wild cheers from the crowd behind Ross's team bench faded and morphed into a universal groan.

The Animal glared, his face blossoming into wild-eyed rage. Nancy knew what had happened. A few other parents did too. So did Ross's coaches, who shook their heads and muttered.

The bleachers behind the other team erupted in cheers and welled up again as the third baseman stood and his coach dusted him off.

Confusion and rage mingled and churned as The Animal sought for something to do with his hands, maybe wishing he hadn't tossed the cigarette so he could toss it now, flick it sharply in some dramatic, signifying gesture to punctuate his anger.

—What the fuck was that?! he exclaimed. His coach, he ain't even out there protesting!

Nancy shrugged. —Ross's out. He was out at third before he ever went home.

—Why?

—Supposed to slide is why.

—Ain't no rule about you gotta slide.

—There is in little league. To keep them from getting hurt. Just like what happened.

—Bullshit! Kid's fine. Looka him.

She wanted to tell him to stifle the language, wanted to tell him too that if he'd ever come to a game he'd already know this. But now she suddenly wondered why he was here, why tonight, this game, right now. Why had he suddenly appeared?

Ross was back on the bench, sullen and pissed. Hoots of approval continued from the bleachers across the field. The Animal was still standing, staring across, trying to pick out who was hooting.

Nancy sat down and most others had too, and finally, to her relief, so did The Animal.

After the game, while minivans with sweaty parents and dirty kids angled into the single-lane exit from the lot, The Animal told Ross he'd made a fucking good play and the bullshit sliding rule was a bullshit rule and he'd make it a point to call whoever the fuck you had to call in little league to get it changed, which Nancy knew (and hoped) he'd forget by morning. He told Ross, too, as if passing along sage baseball wisdom, that Ross'd sent a message loud and fucking clear that shouldn't nobody try to fucking tag him out. Ross nodded. The Animal tussled the boy's hat and told him to wait in the car. He'd done with parenting for now.

Then he turned to Nancy for the predictable come-on, which in his dim way he figured might have some chance of success if he first demonstrated his fatherliness, which had been thus shown. Couldn't even get laid with some of the rung-out white-trash bitches who hung around the white-trash places he hung around, she thought, so here he is, hitting on the lay of last resort. It was all so transparent it was almost funny. But she did finally wrangle free, and he roared off in the Torino, definitively, theatrically, with the predictable, message-laden spraying of gravel and burning of rubber; thankfully, she noted, the opposite way she was headed, and without so much as a *See-ya-soon, sport,* for Ross.

He didn't show up for another game that summer, though now she found herself casting jittery glances toward the parking lot between pitches. The next time she heard anything more about him was from a Leavenworth County Sheriff's deputy, who came to the house to say there'd been an accident and he was sorry to tell her that her husband was deceased. That was his word. *Deceased* – officious, definitive, a word you needn't doubt. When Nancy shut the door behind the deputy, a numbing sense of cold relief filled her, as if everything around her had settled into a sort of distant hum, like highway traffic you hear at night though it's miles away. She was finally free. She never shed a tear for him. His blood alcohol was so high he'd probably gone through half a case of beer and a few chasers besides before getting behind the wheel, which for his lanky hundred fifty-sixty pounds, give-or-take, mostly take, would have made even the front porch steps a hazard. He and one of his buds were in the Torino with a Rush cassette blaring when they went off Muncie Road and into a ditch just a few miles from Lansing Correctional, where Ross later did some of his time. The music was somehow still playing when the fire department arrived to unwedge him from the windshield and dashboard. Nancy knew the place. She drove past it every week on her way to see Ross while he was in Lansing.

He had poisoned her every day just by living and being a possibility.

She was glad he died and at peace with that gladness.

His death had fertilized their lives.

At a table near the gray steel door, a couple engaged in a woozy, moist, undulating kiss. Their hands remained on the table as they leaned over it and rolled their heads and worked their lips as if compressing a Spark Notes version of elaborate and unrestrained intercourse into this one-minute kiss. She watched with the detached compulsion of a rubber-necker passing a car wreck. The woman gave a post-orgasmic shudder when they separated, and in a half-formed thought, Nancy wondered if the woman had acted the shudder for her man's sake or if she had now, after however long he'd been incarcerated and she'd been visiting him, so compartmentalized and focused her needs, and his, that she actually experienced one in that brief exchange.

When Ross finally arrived, he looked thin, sallow-faced, with pockets of shadow in his cheeks — too much like his father. He was about the same age as his father when he died, and she'd never seen the resemblance more clearly. He was much bigger, which he got from her, but his head and shoulders had slumped into the same droopy posture as his father, tilting forward, as if he was about to reach for something. His denim work shirt hung loosely from his shoulders and bloused out in the back, and he'd begun to acquire a similar wiriness to The Animal that was enlivened by a tensile edge of suspicion, even aggression, that found its way into his arms and the curl of his hands as he walked.

He kissed her on the cheek and glanced around before he sat, a quick look, as if to make sure it was safe to sit, to leave himself vulnerable. She'd heard enough chatter among visitors outside to know that he lived this way, they all did, always tense, always suspicious.

His look was expectant, as if she needed to explain why she'd come.

—Phil wanted to come, too, she said, but he's just not up to it.

Her first words to him… they sounded like babble.

—S'all right. You don't have to come neither.

—Of course, I do… I mean, I want to.

He nodded and glanced around.

—So how is he… Phil?

—Not great. Has to take it easy, you know.

—What happened? He sick?

—No, not sick, least nothing the doctor can find. I don't know what it is really, just he's slower, tires out more. The long car ride… he says… – she lowered her voice – … says he has to use the bathroom so much, you know.

Ross nodded but said nothing.

She drew a breath of detergent-licorice air. He seemed impenetrable, like this place. She just wanted to open him up some, like the people at other tables who were talking back and forth, conversing. That's all she wanted.

—I brought a few things, she said, some books and magazines.

—Thanks.

—Couldn't wrap them, not that it's an occasion. Just, you know…

—I know. It's okay.

—You look thin, she said. You getting enough to eat?

—I can get enough. Just don't seem that hungry sometimes. Besides, some a that crap, who wants to eat it?

—I'll put some money in your account. They have anything decent you can buy?

—Snacks 'n such.

—Well, don't use it all on cigarettes.

—I won't.

—You been here long enough that… well, they say when you can apply for a job?

He shrugged. —Won't be till I'm in medium. Don't know when that'll be.

—You haven't… you haven't had trouble, have you?

—Nothing really.

She paused, hoping he'd fill in whatever that meant, but he just looked off toward another table where a CO approached a couple whose hands had been joined too long. They opened their hands, palms up. The guard nodded and stepped back.

—Brought some writing paper, she said, and envelopes, so you can write.

He sniffed, the closest he'd come to a grin yet. —Not much to write about, like you can see. Guess I just told you what there is.

—I wasn't thinking of me, Ross.

The glimmer of humor faded. —There's no point, Mom. Wrote once and it just came back.

—That was years ago. You should try again. She just turned nine… was last month.

He squinted as if maybe doing the math or recalling Kimmy's birthdate.

—How's she doing?

Nancy caught her breath, an almost undetectable gasp. She stopped herself short of asking how he could ask such a thing.

—I don't know, Ross, she said slowly. I don't get to see her either.

He thought for a second and then said, —I did know… that it was her birthday. I knew that.

—I know you did. Of course, you wouldn't forget. I just thought maybe if you wrote… well, there's no harm in it. At least Anna's sister might read it. Maybe she's softened up some. Must be having to tell Kimmy something. You know, she's old enough to visit. I was looking around here… all these kids who come see their dads…

—I ain't her dad.

Nancy grabbed his hand now, sharply, instinctively. —Don't you say that! Don't you ever say that. You'll always be her father, no matter what the court says, or anyone! She'll want to know who you are, Ross. She'll need to one day. Nothing can change that. It's something you have to live for. You have to be ready for it. That day will come… a letter'll come back from her, her name'll show up on the visitors list, or maybe it won't be till you get out, but that day is going to come. You have to be the person she'd want to know.

Her sudden move had caught a guard's attention, who cast a look their way and approached the table. Nancy lifted her hand to show him it was empty. Ross turned his over too, languidly, without looking up at the CO, who wandered past.

The hand check drained the urgency she'd felt just a moment ago.

Ross seemed impatient. She talked about whatever came to mind, football, people he'd known, anything to fill the time, to keep him from feeling like being back wherever he spent the rest of his days was better than sitting here with her right now.

In this part of Kansas the unencumbered wind blows almost ceaselessly from the south, and as she walked to her car later, she left her coat open to let the cold wind blow through her and cleanse the stink of that rank, stifling place, though the wind could not reach the places inside her that most needed cleansing.

Nearby in the parking lot a woman sobbed and shouted at the people with her. Nancy heard enough to know what happened. Wasn't the first time she'd heard a story like this one. The woman's husband had just transferred to Walcott and she'd been told his visitor card would transfer with him – but it didn't, so she couldn't visit until he filed a new one, which took weeks to process. She'd driven all the way from Winfield, nearly five hours, only to find out she couldn't visit her husband on their anniversary.

Nancy wondered if Ross might get transferred again sometime. Who knew why anything happened here?

—~~~—

MANDEL LAY ON THE top bunk reading a Western novel. He favored Westerns that took the Indians' point of view. He was always saying how much you could learn from Indians.

Ross didn't have much interest in Mandel's literary insights.

If Indians were so fucking smart, he'd say, how come whites ended up winning?

Mandel was doing a thirteen jolt for a combination parole violation and crank-trafficking conviction, and for the unregistered Beretta .22 and Taurus 9mm the Kansas Highway Patrol found under his seat. They'd stopped him on I-70 (speed limit 70, min. 40) for going 38 m.p.h. on his way from Topeka to KCK, where he planned to deliver the 150 grams of 'strawberry quick' in his trunk to a couple of business associates down on Quindaro. This version of crystal meth masked the bitter taste of lye and battery acid with strawberry flavoring to make it more kid-friendly. The cops also found a digital scale and a box of baggies with the corners clipped to make 'twists' for easy distribution of the product in small quantities, and also, in the cupholders, an open 40-ouncer of King Cobra and an unopened can of Red Bull.

—Shoulda had the Bull steada the doobie, Mandel often said.

And there was the doobie.

Ross tossed the items from his mother on his own bunk down below.

Mandel glanced up from his book, gauged Ross's movements, then refocused on the page.

The barred door rolled shut, clanking as it crossed the transom

85

and then clicking electrically as it locked. In an hour or so it would open for dinner-call.

Next thing, Mandel knew, Ross would say something.

Ross pissed, huffing as he stood at the lidless stainless-steel bowl and then spitting as it flushed. Then he swiveled the stool out from the table fixed to the wall and sat, empty-handed, looking around. The only thing different in the cell was the reading and writing matter.

—Might be something you'd wanna read, he said, flicking his head at his bunk.

Mandel stared into his book. —From your moms?

—Yeah, coupla books, whatever. One a them looks like the ones you read.

—I'll check it out.

Ross took up one of the paperbacks. On the cover a seriously yoked Indian with glistening bronze skin, thick black hair, and Caucasian features brandished a spear as he rode headlong into a throng of cra-zy-eyed, stampeding buffalo. Hovering over the scene, as if in the sky, was a hot Indian woman, also with lustrous bronze skin and flowing black hair and a Caucasian face. Her deerskin garment hung in place on the tenuous, frictional grip of her nipples. Hormonal steam drifted up from the cover like dust from the stampede.

Ross smacked the book on palm of his hand. Mandel raised an eyebrow.

—You ever think, Ross asked, that maybe it'd just be better if they didn't visit at all?

—Huh, hasn't been much of an issue for me. Kay-doc'd never let the few peeps who'd even bother coming to see me get on the vis-itors list. And one dude just got sent to Lansing. Who knows, might run into him sometime.

—S'just like, I don't know who she's visiting *for* sometimes, if it's for me or for her.

—People don't know what it's like till they been in here, Mandel said.

—Like as if you still got obligations. They expect shit from you, but what can you do?

Mandel let the question hang, read another sentence or two, and then asked, —So what, you still got some bills or something? Nothing you can do about it now. All you can do is the time.

Ross let that truth hover and fade and then said, —She wants me to write to my daughter.

—So why not just call?

—They'd never take my calls. Sent back the last letter I wrote.

Ross pulled a sharp breath through his nostrils and curled his lips into a sneer as he leaned back against the wall. —What good would it do? She probably don't even remember me, and if she does, who knows what that bitch sister's told her.

Mandel turned a page. The Indian princess in his story had run away from her tribe for a nighttime tryst in the forest with a cavalry officer. They'd just met up by a babbling brook with antelope hanging out nearby, even though it was nighttime. The leather thong holding up her deerskin garment had slipped off her shoulder, which glistened in the moonlight. Mist hung over the babbling brook. The cavalry officer took her in his arms and her heaving bosom pressed against his broad chest. Mandel wanted to save the good part.

He shut the book and ventured, —So maybe your moms is right and you ought to send another letter.

—You serious? Ross snarled.

—Depends if you want to, I guess.

Ross shrugged. —Don't know if I want to. I mean, what'd happen then? Like what if she did write back or whatever. Not gonna do her no good to hear from me, or worse yet, come up here. My mom, she was talking about how these other kids come visit, you know. But kids, they shouldn't be here. You see them out in visitors just sitting there and looking around like what the fuck is this place, and then too, what do they think of their daddies when they come here and have to get searched and they see the walls and bars and razor wire and shit? Don't see it. Ain't gonna happen anyways.

—I guess. Up to you, man.

—Besides, what would I even say? Tell her about what it's like here and shit?

He drummed his fingers on the table.

Mandel started to lift his book, but Ross said, —I ain't hardly thought about her. I mean, I have, but not like I'd ever see her again or she'd visit here or something. That's another thing too, is Mom, she stirs all this shit up, and then it takes half a week to put everything back to where it don't bother me one minute to the next, and by then she's here again, talking about Kimmy and when her birthday is…

—That's her name, your kid's? Kimmy?

Ross paused and nodded.

Mandel watched him drift off. Down the hall a con started bellowing random chunks of rap, as if singing along with his earphones.

—Sorry, man, Mandel said.

Ross shrugged. —Don't matter. I guess I just ain't said her name in a while. Her mother wanted to name her that, not even Kimberly, just Kim. That's her actual Christian name on her birth certificate, but it didn't even sound Christian to me. Plus, I thought, why do you want to give her a nickname for a name? Plus too, it sounds like a chink name, you ask me. But Anna said she'd read some book in school about a boy with that same name and that's the one she wanted. And I said, a boy? Why give her a boy's name? And she said, it's a girl's name too, and besides, he was smart and clever, she said, this kid in the book, and a survivor, and the name would be easy for people to remember. So I said okay, but we started calling her Kimmy anyway.

—So how come your moms wants you to write now?

—Oh, not just now. She always talks about her. I think she's tried to see her too. Well, I know she has, but like there's shit she ain't telling me.

—What sorta shit?

—I don't know. She don't tell me, but I'm guessing she's gone to their house, maybe calls them. She just sounds so desperate, you know. Probably is. Plus too, Phil's sick, she said.

— …?

—My step-dad.

—What's he got?

—She didn't say, just he wasn't up to the drive, would have to take a piss every fifteen minutes. But that too… I mean, I don't know if he just don't want to come up here or if he's really sick cause maybe she probably wouldn't tell me that neither.

Ross's story had begun to interest Mandel almost as much as his book. He'd shared the cell with Ross for almost six months and this was the most he'd heard about Ross's family in all that time.

—Seems like, Mandel said, you wouldn't want to tell her what it's like in here but instead you should be asking her what it's like out there.

Ross squinted doubtfully. —Tell who what now?

—Your daughter, Kimmy… Kim. If you write, you'd want to ask her stuff about her life, you know? So that way she'd have to write back.

Ross huffed and puckered his lips. —She ain't never gonna see the letter. Her aunt won't let her.

—She might. You don't know unless you try.

—Thing is, that's something pisses me off, is how I gotta go through that bitch and it's up to her.

—Ain't right, Mandel said softly.

Ross's head shake was almost indetectable. Mandel took up his book but soon flopped it face down on his chest and shut his eyes. One thing that helped with the time was sleep. You'd wake up an hour later and another hour'd be gone, which made you one hour closer to your date.

Hot Laps, Shoes for Everything, and the Foreboding Lightness of a Gift

ON A COOL FRIDAY in late October, Flann thought he was going to Cottonwood Speedway. Supposed to be him and a couple of others, and Shawn was driving, who'd just mounted woofers in his Dodge Colt and hung a cherry-bomb glass pack on the exhaust. Flann imagined them all buzzing up K-29, woofers thumping, car humming – a satisfying image. But… one thing… Flann wanted shotgun.

Told Shawn, pick him up first. But then like what if he had to get out to let the others climb in back, then what? Colin might pull some shit like standing there and waiting till Flann got in back, which Flann decided no fucking way. Pulled that shit once before but not this time. He'd fight him too.

But so Flann was generally amped. Never been to Cottonwood, and this was the final race of the season. A half-mile track in rural Bueller County, just outside Hill City. Was supposed to be the fastest dirt track in the Midwest, so Flann heard. Heard too that bikers swarmed the place and sometimes there were fights in the parking lot. Going to Cottonwood was all he thought about all day at school.

But then around 4:32 p.m. Shawn called and it wasn't good. He'd had a fender-bender. Said he caught the corner of some white bitch's minivan in the parking lot down at Prairie Mall. (Flann thought it was cool how he called her a white bitch even though he was white too, and so was Flann.) The sun's glare did it, Shawn said, and there was like no damage to the kiddie wagon neither, leastways you couldn't hardly tell unless you looked close, but the white bitch went batshit crazy because she was like strapping one kiddie in the back seat while another was standing beside the car when Shawn clipped it. Shouldn't've been there, Shawn said, the kid shouldn't've, but the w.b. blasted Shawn an earful and then called a cop, and finally later her husband called Shawn's father and said he was like going too fast, which was totally bogus and plus the kiddie wagon was hanging over the line from the parking space and plus what kind of mother lets her kid play in a parking lot and whatever, but bottom line, he couldn't go, with or without whether he drove, so sorry, man, gotta be another time, which Flann knew would be at soonest next April. Fuck, man!

Jo asked what happened when she saw the watery disappointment in his eyes. He gave her the bare bones story, minus the fender-bender, the cop, and the white bitch parts, which now distilled left, —Can't go tonight, and —Goin' upstairs.

Nick was easily found by following the banging noise to its source, which was a basement window he was replacing after a soccer ball scored a goal through it last weekend. Jo wanted to charge the guests for the window, but Nick said a pane of glass only cost a couple of bucks and he could put it in himself and it wasn't worth losing their future business, which Jo wasn't sure she wanted.

—Window casing's so old, I had to replace that too, he said, as she made her way through the basement maze.

He was on a ladder, fitting a length of wood into the empty

window, which now opened onto the patio. His glasses were skewed and sweat glistened on his brow.

—Found some rotted wood that needed replacing, he added. Couple others I should do too. Maybe we should invite them back.

Jo scowled and glanced around, wondering what else they might find if they looked too closely at the heaving walls and ancient pipes and wiring criss-crossing the joists overhead.

—Why I came, she said, is Flann.

Nick knew about the outing and how pumped Flann was to go. Now they commiserated.

—Maybe you could take him, she finally said.

Nick pondered that. —Don't think going with me was what he had in mind.

—I'd worry less, for sure.

—Suppose I could, if he'd want to, but what about Kimmy?

—What about her?

—Maybe she'd want to go too.

—No, she wouldn't. And besides, what'd Flann say then?

—Maybe she would. Wouldn't be fair to leave her out if I take him.

Jo looked around vacantly and thought for a minute. Why was everything so complicated?

A hard-shell suitcase from 1950-something caught her gaze in the shadows. It belonged to Elliot, and she knew from moving it to make room for Christmas decorations that it was still packed full, and not with clothes. Too heavy, and it rattled. Books, scripts, records? Who knew? She'd always been curious about it. She'd even suggestively asked Elliot a couple of times if he wanted to unpack it, or if there was anything he might want to donate to Goodwill, but he always waved a hand and said, —Naah, just leave it. And never offered more than that. She tried the latches one time and found it locked, which only thickened her curiosity.

The question of who was going to the racetrack still hung.

—I just don't think she'd like it.

—She wouldn't, or you?

Jo looked off toward the suitcase again. —What do you think's in there?

—Dunno, Nick shrugged. Memories, I guess.

—Just that… seemed like he didn't want to talk about it.

—Maybe he doesn't. Bad memories, maybe. So, what about Kimmy?

—It's just… this… it's so *them*, you know? *Him.* Car racing. And the noise. I've heard it's loud.

—Leaving her out might make her feel… left out.

—I would if she was my own, keep her home. Little sisters expect to get left out. It's a rite of passage. That's the thing. It's like you can't even make the decision you would make because you end up compensating for something that you don't even know if it's real or not. Oh… I'm not making sense.

He shook his head. —You're not, but there's no sense to any of it.

—Maybe she should go. She does better with you. I wonder how Anna would have done with her. Anna was difficult, too, but different. Quick-tempered, but Kimmy… I don't know. She just resists me in all these little ways… helps with the dishes, but then puts things where I don't want them and keeps on doing it after I tell her not to, or maybe just *because* I told her not to. Won't stay out of the guest rooms either. And she looks at me sometimes – oh, God help me for saying it – like I'm a zookeeper and she's staring out from behind the cage bars. I just don't know what I'm doing. How do I know what part of anything she does is because of what happened and what part is just because of how she is, how she'd be if Anna was alive and raising her? Maybe it's this place, all these people. I wonder how she sees them, all these strangers coming and going. Jo drew a long breath and settled on a nearby trunk. —Maybe we should give up this place, Nick. I've thought about it. Maybe we should just find some little place in a suburb outside of Seattle or Santa Fe or somewhere far from here. Maybe God's telling me that this is what I'm supposed to do – just take her far away from here, and from *him* and *his mother.* Maybe this is just too much for all of us.

Her voice faded, quaking.

Nick came down the ladder and took a step toward her, but she raised a hand.

—It's not just that.

—What… what is it?

She rustled in her apron pocket and pulled out a wrinkled envelope.

—This… this came.

Nick instantly recognized the scrawled handwriting. The return address was a single-digit post office box in Walcott. Above it were Ross's last name, first initial, and prisoner number. The letter was addressed to *Kimmy Oden, c/o Monark House,* etc.

—When did this come?

Jo looked away, squinting, as if noticing something unusual in the detritus all about them.

—Coupla days ago.

—Days? And you… you've been…

—Had it in my pocket since then. She snatched the envelope from him and snapped her fingers on it. —You see this! You see this? Doesn't even use her right name!

Nick nodded.

—Why now? she asked. All of a sudden now, out of nowhere! We haven't even heard from his mother in what… close to a year, isn't it?

—Why did you keep it? Why not just send it back?

—I don't know. It's just maybe… I was so angry seeing her name written like that, I couldn't even bring myself to deal with it. And I didn't want it sitting somewhere she might find it.

—You gonna open it?

Her head flickered no.

—We have to send it back just like this, she said. There's no one here by that name.

⌇

—Not here, Jo said from the back seat.

—Why not?

—We'll get blocked in.

Nick dropped into gear and rocked forward on the uneven, hard-packed ground. He parked the minivan facing the exit lane. Jo hoped they could make an easy escape later, if not sooner.

Clouds of dust swirled up from the limestone gravel drive as a parade of trucks, SUVs, and Harleys rumbled past.

—Maybe I should follow them, he said.

—This is fine. Just keep the windows up with all that dust.

She hit the door lock for the dozenth time since they'd pulled up behind the line of traffic out on Beecham Drive waiting to turn into the speedway. When they finally did turn, they found themselves sitting bumper-to-bumper on the railroad tracks. Jo watched nervously in both directions until Nick could pull into the field. An impotent click announced that the locks were still locked. Flann sat up front with Nick, and Kimmy rode in back with her.

Bikers revved their engines. A jacked-up truck with huge tires

96

and an enormous Confederate flag fluttering on a pole went by. Smoke billowed up from tailgate parties all over the parking lot. Men in baseball caps and sleeveless T-shirts, with tattooed arms, necks, and who knew what else, strutted past beside women with big hair and defiant looks. Beer cans and cigarettes were fixtures in every hand.

An undefinable and unfocused anger drifted through the noise and fumes. It felt larger and more seething than the mere fact of this many people congregating in one place with this much alcohol. Jo couldn't understand what fed it, but it was all-too familiar. She considered telling Nick to take them home right now. She steeled herself for whatever lay ahead.

They got out and followed the crowd.

In the distance they heard the buzz and whirr of heavy horse-power, high-compression, fuel-injected engines echoing through a khaki haze of dust.

Nick lined up for tickets. Flann and Kimmy watched what they could see of the track from the ticket booth. A file of pick-up trucks whisked around the turn.

—Has it started? Jo asked.

—Naah, Flann said. They're just smoothing the track. Look, they're not even racing.

She wondered how he knew this.

Kim wandered across the walkway and perched herself on the railing. Down the slope in the parking lot, hundreds of gleaming bikes were lined up, row upon row, all leaning to one side, front wheels tilted at the same angle. There was a decidedly martial quality in the sight. Bikers rumbled and chugged into the lot, swelling the constellation of sparkling chrome and glinting fenders. Rivets twinkled on their black leather jackets and vests. Engines growled in low, understated ways. A few bikes sported oversized American flags.

A new pack had just rolled in and now cruised through the ranks, not so much looking to park as parading, checking the place out, letting themselves be checked out, rolling past the grandstand, as it were. They all wore red bandanas and black leather vests with red lettering that she couldn't read from up the hill. They finally dropped their feet to the ground and backed into slots alongside the others.

The bikes felt familiar, and happy, and watching the men straddle their machines, feet on the ground, resting on their seats, she remembered straddling a leather seat and grasping the handlebars as she went airborne on the rolling hills of a field of bluestem grass. The bike's rear wheel sprayed up dirt and grass each time it caught the ground. She laughed and shrieked with joy. She recalled, too, the pleasant sensation that came after the engine was cut and the sounds of everything that wasn't the bike returned and the chill of evening felt fresh and new once more. How the bikers felt now – she knew this.

The railing suddenly shook, and she grabbed hold to keep from tumbling off. Flann climbed up beside her.

—'M gonna get one a those, he said.

The new riders now strode down the row, bandanas off, wiping their brows, greeting other bikers, beers in hand.

—Check that one out! Flann exclaimed. He pointed to a sleek maroon bike with cream fenders that swooped low to the ground. Its fringed leather saddle-bags looked like they belonged on a horse.

—'S an Indian, he said. Hog's big competitor. You gotta wait a year to order one.

—You got time, Kim said.

—Kuh, he snarled, you'd be scared shitless on one a them. And he bolted off the railing as Jo called.

The Hot Laps had already started by the time they settled on bench-seats behind a blackened chain-link fence that ran fifteen-twenty feet high. A sign warned spectators not to climb on it. Jo could hear Elliot remarking that for sure some moron had climbed up there if they thought they needed a sign. He'd stayed behind to mind the house for a few hours. As they were leaving he told them that the race cars got four miles to the gallon. —Thought you should know that, he added. —Whatever, Flann muttered.

A half-dozen cars roared around the dirt track, packed so close together you could barely have swiped a credit card between them. They ran like this for a couple of laps and then spread out. On the steep banks of the turns they spun at near right angles to the infield, spraying geysers of mud in wide arcs behind them. After a few more laps they exited the track on the far straightaway and another group roared on.

Jo sat between Kimmy and Flann.

—Who won? Jo asked.

Flann laughed, —Nobody *won*! It's Hot Laps! They're just warming up, showing their stuff.

Kimmy'd said nothing since they settled. She rested her feet on the vacant seat in front of her and propped her chin on the arch of her entwined fingers.

—You like it? Jo asked.

She nodded without looking away from the track. The place had consumed her since they stepped past the ticket booth and walked the crowded promenade behind the bleachers. Everything about it. The eddying currents of people on the walkway. The concessionaires selling pennants and clothing and food. The souvenir kiosks. The permeating mix of cigarette smoke and carbon fumes. And below them, the track – a half-mile oval of glistening, tamped mud the color of chocolate pudding. She was so distracted by all of it she'd have bumped into people or been knocked over if Jo hadn't finally taken her by the hand and led her through the crowd until they settled in their seats.

The cars mesmerized her. The stock cars had finished their warm-ups, and now the angular Grand Nationals roared thunderously onto the track in a close pack like a single organism. She felt the noise as much as heard it – a chorus of half-a-dozen cars all howling at such a pitch that it shivered through her chest and tingled her feet. The GNs looked like metal wedges painted in bright colors, vibrating and shaking as they passed, slithering through rapid turns on the straightaways to test their steering. She'd noticed how much sweeter the fumes smelled when these cars came on the track. Flann said it was because they were burning nitro fuel, and some of them alcohol too. He said they'd do one-forty, one-fifty m-p-h easy once the races started.

When the Hot Laps ended, the pick-up trucks returned to smooth the track's surface. A couple of men worked a synchronized dance between laps to lay down the white chalk starting line.

Off to the right, on a hill overlooking turns two and three, fans had backed their trucks and vans up to the fence so they could watch from their tailgates. The Confederate flag truck was up there. So was another truck that had raised its own flag pole on the rear bed some twenty feet high or more with an American flag as big as the truck itself fluttering from it. When the announcer greeted the tailgaters up on the hill, they all waved and blasted their horns.

Soon everyone stood for a prayer. A long one, too. The minister prayed for the weather, the drivers, the pit crews, the fans, somebody's wife who'd just had a baby, somebody else's grandma who was in the hospital, elected officials, the president, everyone in America, and soldiers wherever they were. Kim wondered why you'd leave anyone out. Why not just pray for the whole world?

She mostly looked around while they prayed and sang the national anthem. On the infield, the firemen and EMT guys stood at attention, helmets and hats on their chests. Then everyone cheered as a squadron of tow trucks raced down the straightaway and gathered in the infield. Perched on one tow rack was a burly man in a sleeveless cammie shirt with his hat backward. A couple of others in backwards baseball caps stood on each side like his honor guard or something. He waved to the crowd and a cheer welled up like everyone knew him.

Aunt Jo sat on the edge of her seat as if she didn't plan to stay, which Kim knew she did – this was just how she sat at baseball games or wherever with strangers around. She clutched her purse against her belly with the strap still around her shoulder.

A couple of rows down, a man with a braided pony-tail and hunting cap lit a cigarette and leaned back, stretching his arm around the woman beside him who had dark hair with blonde streaks that looked like they'd been done with a yellow highlighter. The smoke wafted back. Aunt Jo scrunched her nose and fanned herself.

The first race started. A pack of stock cars entered the track and circled the oval, building speed, roaring even louder than during the Hot Laps. The cigarette smoke faded into the fumes.

After three warm-up laps, the flagman unfurled a green flag and twirled it in tight figure-eights as the cars roared over the starting line. They hurtled forward and spun mud as they fishtailed through the turns, aligning themselves for the straightaways ahead.

Flann whooped and shouted. Even Aunt Jo seemed taken with the spectacle as the sideshows now gave way to the drama of the race itself. One heat followed another.

Suddenly a popping noise erupted, out of sync with the roaring engines. A car slowed and veered toward the infield as two others turned onto the straightaway racing head-to-head. The inside car clipped the disabled car and sent it spinning in the mud. The flagman waved yellow, and the tow trucks came to life.

—What happened? Aunt Jo asked.

—Dunno, Flann said.

The pony-tail man leaned around and said into the air, —Ignition… blew his ignition. Shoulda got his ass off the track sooner. Took the leader out with him.

—Oh, thank you, Aunt Jo said brightly, as if he'd just held a chair for her.

Pony-tail man flagged a little wave with his fingers and turned back to the race.

Flann dropped his head in shame, wagging it from side to side.

Aunt Jo scrunched her shoulders like *What?* but Flann just rolled his eyes. Then Uncle Nick shrugged *Who knows?* like whatever. Then they both turned back to watch the tow trucks.

Everyone cheered when the wreck was cleared. The tow guy bowed from the back of his truck as it passed the grandstand.

At intermission, Aunt Jo and Uncle Nick had a big debate about whether to buy Flann a T-shirt. Aunt Jo thought they were too expensive, but she finally agreed and said if he was going to have one, Kimmy should too. So both kids got racing T-shirts and then Aunt Jo took Kimmy to the restroom, where she put hers on and promptly went outside while Aunt Jo was still in a stall, even though she'd been told to wait.

The races had started. Across from the rest room the railing was crowded and she couldn't see, so she wandered down the promenade. Evening had fallen. The trees and woods beyond the glow of the stadium lights looked like charcoal silhouettes. Farther along the walkway she could see the field of RVs and trailers outside the track where the drivers and their teams stayed, like a huge campground for race cars.

The heat on the track had finished, and she could see cars lined up behind the gate for the next heat. She stepped into the open space in the handicapped area where there was lots of room. Only a few old people were there. A man and two woman sat on the bench nearby. Beside them was a man in a wheelchair wearing a veteran's cap full of pins. The woman nearest cast a look Kim's way, and she wondered if the lady was going to tell her she couldn't stand there, but whatever. The cars were on the track now. As they came around the near turn, Kim noticed the woman still watching her, and she looked back, like what? The woman grinned strangely and said something to the man beside her, who looked at Kim and shrugged. Kim watched the race. The winner took his victory lap and spun fishtails along the straightaway in front of the grandstand.

—Oh!

A syllable was enough. Kim didn't need to turn around to know Aunt Jo'd found her.

—I looked everywhere for you! You were supposed to…

Her voice suddenly broke off in a breathless, sharp way that Kim had never heard before. She turned now and saw Aunt Jo and the woman on the bench staring at one another. Aunt Jo's hand found Kim's shoulder, and she felt herself being pushed behind her aunt, who never took her eyes off the woman.

The woman rose from the bench and approached slowly. Her eyes were fixed on Kim as she stepped toward them.

—It is you, Nancy said.

Kim felt Aunt Jo's hand trembling. Her whole body seemed to quake.

—I knew it when I saw you, the woman said to Kim. I was sure. I just couldn't believe it.

Aunt Jo was unmistakably frightened. She stiffened and her hand tightened on Kim.

—We're…we were just leaving, Aunt Jo said. We have to go.

But she didn't move, as if frozen with fear, like in a dream when you can't run away, hard as you try to move your legs. Kim had never seen her like this. She wondered if the woman was about to attack them. She approached slowly, as if finding her way through a dark room. She tilted her head to look around behind Aunt Jo at Kim with curiosity, even wonder.

—I've waited so long for this…to see you again, she said.

The weirdness of it, the puzzling things the woman said, and most of all the strange mixture of joy and sadness on her face now frightened Kim, who hadn't been afraid of a thing in the world just moments ago. The joyful roar of the cars began to melt away as the rushing hum that usually only came at night returned. She trembled and pushed herself behind Aunt Jo as the woman approached.

Aunt Jo now seemed to recover. She pulled Kim close and kept her shielded, but neither did she rush them away.

—Please, Jo, the woman said. You're already here. She's already seen me. Please.

She called Aunt Jo by name. Everything was so confusing.

Kim felt her aunt's body relenting, but to what she couldn't tell, only that a quiet feeling of resolve had coursed through her as she turned slightly and looked down at Kim and then at the woman.

—You've frightened her, Jo said.

—It's true, Nancy responded. I don't mean to. It's the last thing I want.

—I suppose this was bound to happen sooner or later, Jo said stiffly.

—I suppose.

The woman squatted, making herself even smaller than Kim, who watched her fearfully.

—You don't remember me, do you, Kimmy?

Kim stared at her but didn't move or say a word. She knew Kim's name, too.

Her face was flushed, her eyes glassy. Her lips trembled. Kim clung tighter to Aunt Jo.

—I'm…. She glanced up at Aunt Jo and started again. —I was your Gammie. Do you remember me?

Her words were muffled in the cacophony of cars roaring past on the track, but the word *gammie* shot through Kim and she shuddered as if from a sudden chill, which Aunt Jo felt too. —This is too much, Nancy! She's terrified.

The woman ignored her.

—I'm your Gammie. You used to come to my house when you were little. I've missed you so much… for so long…

Tears streamed down her cheeks. She was close now. Her eyes were shadowy and her skin worn in a fine web of lines and wrinkles. She looked weary and sad.

—Over there, she said, that's your Poppa. You remember him?

The man on the bench stared glumly at them. The woman beside him and the man in the wheelchair were watching too.

—She doesn't remember you, Aunt Jo said. This isn't fair. You have no idea…

The woman reached out, slowly, as if letting a dog or cat sniff her hand before petting it. She touched Kim's arm lightly. Then she stood slowly, with effort. She was taller than Aunt Jo and stood erectly. She pushed tears away with the back of her hand as if brushing away a fly. She seemed stiffer now.

—You have no idea either, Jo. It didn't have to be like this.

—How it is was your doing.

With that she took Kim and turned to go, but the woman grabbed Aunt Jo by the arm. —Wait! Please, just a moment more. It's been so long.

—I knew that coming here was a mistake, Jo said, shaking off Nancy's hand, her voice cracking. —My son likes all this… this noise. She flicked a hand toward the track. We came for him. That's all. We don't belong here. We're leaving now.

—Jo, Nancy said, please wait. I can't even think of all I have to say. This is so… unexpected. Oh my, to see Kimmy, how tall she is, what a young lady… and you got a brand new racing shirt tonight, too, didn't you?

Her voice faded and she drew a hand to her lips at the sight of Kim in the baggy white shirt with a race car blazing across her chest and the memory of a tiny racing shirt from long ago.

—I can't do this, Jo said. Not here. What a nightmare this place is, and now this…

—Jo, please let me visit. Wherever you say… at your house maybe. Things are different. So many years have passed.

—This isn't fair, Aunt Jo said, for me, for us… to get blindsided like this.

Her voice quaked. A new heat had just started and the engines roared up so the two women had to lean in close to hear each other, and Kim couldn't make out all they said. But then, the woman squatted again and put her hands on Kim's shoulders as if to pull her close. Kim stiffened and the woman settled for taking her hands, but she ominously said she'd see Kim soon and then they could get to know each other again. Back at their seats Jo stared off vacantly as if the track wasn't there. Nick asked what happened, but she only shook her head. At times her jaw just seemed to fall away, as if she forgot to close her mouth. She looked gray and tired.

The joy of the races was gone. Kim didn't care who won. Why would you just keep driving around in circles like that? Who cared who got there first? After all the noise and fumes and praying and crashing and tow trucks, you just ended up right back where you started.

—⁓—

It was a busy time. Weekends brought squadrons of SUVs to Monarch House with adventurous names like Mountaineer, Yukon, Expedition, Land Cruiser, Explorer, Pathfinder. Their tinted windows and gleaming grills made them seem invincible. Kim imagined guests traveling through forests and over mountainous roads to get here. When the car doors flew open, she noticed how much stuff was inside: water bottles and rumpled clothes and food; dollar bills crumpled like candy wrappers in the consoles; cell phones in the cupholders, if the new arrivals weren't still talking on them as they climbed out. Uncle Elliot said cell phones could blow up a gas station if you talked on one while you filled your tank. That'd be something, she thought.

Kids piled out of back seats cluttered with video games and headphones and CD players; with greasy Styrofoam fast-food cartons, half-full bags of Cheese Doodles, empty pop cans, and scatterings of Fruit Loops. And shoes. Shoes all over the car. Shoes for everything.

Shoes for walking and different ones for running, shoes for riding in the car or coming in the house, shoes for watching TV or eating breakfast. Seemed like she never saw anyone in the same shoes twice.

They all had so much stuff.

The uncles lugged bags into the house. She helped too and sometimes got tips. Once upstairs, they'd seal themselves up in their rooms, the guests did, just like in their cars. Up and down the hall, TVs went on and stayed on all the time. People talked on cell phones. Kids wore earphones and played video games. The games didn't much interest Kim. Flann showed her how to do his, but she found it boring and preferred checking the compost heap for toads and snakes or going on the swings next door at the church, where the new sexton said why shouldn't she play here, when Aunt Jo asked if she could go on the swings. Swings are for children, aren't they? he said.

Daddy'd hung a swing from the tree out front. He made it from a car tire and tied it off on a tree limb. Gammie said Kimmy'd get her clothes dirty on it, so she bought a new one, a regular swing set from Walmart, Poppa called it. The box was heavy and clanked when Daddy brought it in from the car. She told Daddy put that one up instead. The only place for it was out back by the garage, but there were no shade trees and the ground wasn't level, so it rocked off one leg when you swung. It squealed too, like as if swinging hurt it. And it was hot and lonely out there. The front yard was shady and cool. So the swings out back sat idle, and soon Mommy told Daddy, —Now it's just gonna turn into a rusty eyesore. You think she could've asked first if we wanted one? You gonna take it apart when we move? We're not staying in this dump forever.

And Daddy got mad and shouted at Mommy, and next thing his

arm just flew up from nowhere with his fist clenched like a bulbous knot on a stick of tree wood, and Mommy careened back across the kitchen and shrieked.

—Took half a day putting it up, he said, so don't be tellin' me she ain't gonna use it!

Mommy was rumpled, crying, shaking, her blouse half-pulled out of her skirt. She covered her head as if expecting another blow or maybe waiting to see if he unbuckled his belt and slipped it through the loops like a snake sliding through the weeds.

He drained his longneck, dropped it in the trash, and slammed the fridge door when he got another. —You wanna go swing? he asked Kim, who was sitting on the big book they put on her chair to raise her up at the table. She shook her head no and scuttled down and ran into the front room, and next thing, the screen door slammed and his steps faded on the back stairs. After his truck roared out, Mommy packed up a bag and they went to Aunt Jo's where Kim slept in the big bed in Araby while Mommy sat by the front window and smoked.

<hr>

WHEN GAMMIE AND POPPA arrived, Aunt Jo took them out on the veranda because guests were sitting in the parlor and dining room. Poppa wore a bolo tie with an arrowhead medallion. Gammie carried a gift box wrapped in pink paper and took in everything as they passed through the house. Aunt Jo brought coffee mugs outside. Kim sat between her and Uncle Nick.

Gammie and Poppa were like characters who suddenly appeared for real out of a story book or movie, now free to wander about in unpredictable ways and say and do unpredictable things. Until now, they had been vague, shadowy images flitting through dreams whose stories she only remembered in fractured ways. But at least that's where they stayed, so you'd know where they were, and they didn't show up in person. And she sensed that that's how they felt, too, disoriented from finding themselves in the not-story realm, suddenly real, sitting right here, as if the strangeness of being here overwhelmed them too.

Gammie said how wonderful it was to be here and how much she liked the house. Poppa nodded with a fish-eyed look over his glasses. Kim said yes-no-and-I-don't-know and shrugged when they asked questions.

It worried Kim how Aunt Jo seemed to warm up to them. Gammie kept asking about the weddings and where the guests came from and such, and Kim could see Aunt Jo visibly starting to relax. She brightened whenever she chattered about Monarch House, and today was no different.

Soon Gammie said she'd brought a gift for Kim. The box had a foreboding lightness when it landed on her lap, and sure enough, out from the crinkly tissue paper came a dress, a woolen jumper in lavender. Gammie said Advent was coming soon and maybe Kim could wear it to church. It had the same prickly steel-wool texture as her plaid jumper and Kim found no comfort in hearing Aunt Jo say she thought it was lovely, and then Gammie said she had to guess at the size but she'd exchange it or get it fitted or whatever was needed.

Next thing, wouldn't you know, they made her try it on, and it was just as scratchy as she thought it would be, plus it was too big.

Kim stood before them with the dress hanging from her like a rain poncho.

Gammie fussed with the shoulder straps and ruffled the pleats and said with a laugh how she'd thought Kim had grown so much when she saw her at the races that... oh, well, she'd just grown so much!

No, this won't do, Gammie said. It's too big even to have fitted. She thought for a moment and said to Aunt Jo, looking straight at her and nowhere else, and with a sincerity in her eyes that was unmistakably sincere, —We could, she said, if it would be okay with you… I mean, only if you thought so… we could take Kimmy back to the store to get the right size… just, maybe… just for lunch and to the store, if that would be okay. They still had other dresses like this, but you never knew what might be left a few days from now with the holidays coming and all. Or maybe she'd like something different. Would that be okay?

And she never looked away, not to Poppa or Uncle Nick or even Kim, but just seemed to place her fate in Aunt Jo's hands, as if something decisive was taking place, as if the future was about to change in ways you couldn't describe, but for sure, everything was about to change.

Aunt Jo's face went flat. All the furrows in her brow just faded. Gammie must have found a way into some feeling deep inside of Aunt Jo that she'd tried to push down so far that it would never, ever come out again, but now it did, because it was obvious she'd been touched by Gammie's sincerity, so that whatever pain Gammie had known, Aunt Jo now glimpsed it, and next thing her eyes flitted toward Uncle Nick and then Kim, and she pursed up her lips and nodded lightly, and said, —If Kimmy wants to go, I think, maybe, just for lunch and to the store, like you say, I think that would be okay. What do you think, dear?

And now they all looked at Kim. All of them at once.

AN HOUR LATER, KIM found herself squeezed into a booth beside Gammie at the Denny's on Metcalf Avenue in Overland Park. Just her and Gammie and Poppa.

Poppa told her twice on the way over and once after they got seated that you could have breakfast all day here, didn't matter what time it was. Gammie said Kim could order whatever she wanted, and Poppa said it would be the Grand Slam for him. That's what he always got, he said.

The menu was so big and had so much stuff and so many pages that Kim didn't know what to get, and she wasn't hungry anyway. The waitress came and looked at them like she was collecting homework papers. Kim said she'd have the Grand Slam too, just to order something, just because she didn't know what else to say. Gammie said was she sure she could eat the whole thing, and Kim shrugged and nodded.

The people at the next booth smoked cigarettes. Aunt Jo and Uncle Nick would've been out the door soon as they caught a whiff, but Gammie and Poppa didn't even seem to notice while they all ate and watched cars go by on Metcalf.

The eggs on the plate were runny and gross. Kim pushed the sausages away and ate the pancakes, which had whipped cream on them, but all she could taste was the cigarette smoke from next door.

Gammie chattered about dresses. Seemed like all she could talk about.

—Have you seen my daddy? Kim asked.

Gammie froze. Poppa looked up from his Grand Slam breakfast with his fish eyes and a glob of gross eggs dripping from his fork.

—Yes, Gammie said. Yes, I have… I saw him last week.

—He's in prison, isn't he?

—Yes, he is.

—He's gotta stay there a long time, right?

—That's right, he does. Gammie put down her fork and turned toward Kim before asking, —Do you remember him?

Kim smeared whipped cream around her plate with her fork and nodded.

—What do you remember?

—Nothin'… stuff.

The waitress came by and asked how everything was tasting and if Poppa was still working on his plate, and he said yes, he was still working on it, and when she'd gone, he added that he was still eating too.

—Never mind about that, Gammie said, and turning back to Kim, asked quietly, almost as if afraid of being overheard, —So do you remember coming to my house… when you were little?

Kim shrugged. —What's it like in prison?

Gammie let her breath go as if blowing seeds off a dandelion puff.

—It's very big. Lots of other men live there. I visit him every couple of weeks or so. We talk about you. I'll be seeing him again soon, and now I'll get to tell him I visited you and that you were asking for him.

—Don't tell him nothin' about me, Kim said sharply. Don't talk about me! I don't want people talkin' about me!

—Of course not, honey, Gammie said quickly. Not if you don't want. Well, maybe we shouldn't talk about all this just now.

Poppa looked at her like maybe we weren't supposed to in the first place, which Kim didn't miss. She'd heard enough whisperings at home over the past few days. You didn't have to be grown-up to know stuff was going on.

It was back to dresses and such for now.

Hers had come from the mall just up the road from Denny's. There was a big sale on and the store was mobbed. Women spun furiously through clothing racks, clanking and rattling hangers, wedging themselves around one another, carting armloads of clothes into dressing rooms. The place was a maze of pastel chaos. Poppa shuffled behind, and Gammie told him to come along.

They passed a crowd of women at the perfume counter, where the smell was as thick as lawnmower fumes and stank even worse. Poppa spotted an open bench beside the escalator and plopped himself there. Gammie said you all right and he said yes, he'd wait here and she said fine we'll just be over in Misses.

Kim and Gammie plunged back into the chaos on the other side of the escalator, which Kim hoped they'd get to ride. Gliding up and down looked a lot better than bumping around in the swarms of people down here, but they weren't going up.

Gammie guided Kim through canyons of clothing racks until they stood before one filled with woolen jumpers identical to Kim's. The sight was overwhelming. She imagined a thousand girls all lined up in the same dress – all alike, all the same, all named either Chelsea or Brittany.

—Now, Gammie said, let's find a smaller one.

She walked her fingers expertly through the rack as if it were a filing drawer.

Kim waited stiffly beside her.

Gammie finally unhooked one from the rack and checked the size.

—Thank goodness we came today. It's the only one left in this size.

She held it up to Kim and said cheerily, —This might be just right! But then she noticed that Kim's color had faded to a jaundiced pallor in an alarming way. —Are you all right, honey?

Kim shook her head no. —Gotta go to the bathroom.

—Oh… do you think you can you hold it a little while?

Kim tightened her lips and gave one firm head shake, leaving no doubt.

—Well… okay… I'll just hold onto this dress and then we'll decide…

Nancy didn't see a restroom sign. She finally found a clerk, who wagged a hand vaguely toward the back of the store.

Phil was still seated by the escalator.

Nancy waved as they passed, but he was scowling at a boisterous group of black women gliding down the escalator and didn't notice.

She fretted over whether to send Kimmy into the restroom alone or go in with her, leaving the last-one-in-its-size dress outside, which a sign said she must do. The sending-Kimmy-alone-in-to-a-public-restroom fear won out, and the dress remained outside, draped on a chair.

Kimmy had rushed ahead of her all the way, stepping quickly in the direction the clerk-lady pointed. Now she went straight into a stall.

Nancy arrived as the door shut and latch clacked and Kimmy's pants dropped to her ankles as she backed up to the seat with her feet dangling over the floor.

—You okay, honey?

Another stall door opened, and a roar of industrial flushing swallowed up whatever the child said, if she responded at all. The woman from the stall strutted past the sinks on her way out, and Nancy waited until the door shut behind her to ask again, but this time the abrupt gurgle and sputter of diarrhea was all the response she got. Nancy mentally tallied what Kimmy had eaten and got angry at Phil for pushing that big breakfast on her. Then she remembered the dress outside on the chair and said to the stall door, —I'm just stepping out for a minute, honey. I'll be right back. To which there was no response. The feet were motionless, the jeans now crumpled on the tile floor against the base of the stool. She'd need more than a new dress before they were done here today.

Outside, the dress was gone. No clerks in sight. The iridescent red sale tag must have been a glowing invitation to some other shopper, though Nancy didn't care what price she paid today. She'd have happily paid full price and then some just for the pleasure of pulling a dozen dresses off the rack and spending an hour watching Kimmy model them. Phil would be stewing by now, she thought, as she returned and found Kimmy at the sink, trying to get water from the touchless auto faucet.

—You feel better now, honey? Nancy asked.

—I guess.

Kimmy washed and then dripped water over to the drying machine, which roared to life when she banged the chrome switch with a fist.

Nancy had noticed how heavy and quick her movements were. She pushed through the door sharply when they left, banging it against the wall, and walked ahead as if it didn't matter if Nancy followed or not.

Nancy caught up to her in the aisle. —We should check on Poppa.

His mood had turned foul. His lips had tightened into a walnut and he leaned forward at the edge of the bench, gripping it tightly, just as he did at the doctor's office when the nurse came through the door and he expected to be called next and then wasn't.

—Where've you been? he demanded.

Nancy whispered, —She needed the bathroom.

—What?

Nancy told him again, louder.

—Well, I need the bathroom too! And I waited ssso you'd know where I wasss.

—Fine, she said stiffly. Go ahead. We'll wait here.

—Where? he said, struggling to rise. Where is it?

—For God's sake, Phil, settle down. Just follow that aisle. We'll be here.

She'd waited so long for this, and now the day seemed to be collapsing like faulty scaffolding, and Kimmy hadn't even tried on one dress yet. Maybe they could make a fresh start somewhere less crowded. She'd have to call Jo, she knew, and now she worried about what to say, and what Jo would say.

Kimmy was peering into a jewelry display case across the aisle.

Mostly cheap costume jewelry, Nancy saw – necklaces, rings, bracelets in gaudy designs – but there was something dazzling about its cumulative effect, how the color and glitter and sheer quantity of items blended into an enticing, even compelling sight that drew you in despite its obvious cheapness. An immense sadness overcame her watching Kimmy – she was still in the grip of such sights. Maybe Nancy would buy one for her.

She asked for a couple to be put on the counter. The clerk pulled out several trays and then wandered off to another customer. Earring racks enclosed them on each side like shrubbery, which Kimmy began to spin. Nancy wondered if she might be old enough for piercing. Nancy held up a necklace, a thin gold-plated chain with a cross, but Kimmy only shrugged and seemed to lose interest.

—Let's try it on and see how you like it then.

She latched it on Kimmy and tilted the mirror her way.

—What do you think? Here, pull your hair back.

Kimmy flinched when Nancy touched her hair from behind. She stared into the mirror, but she seemed more interested in her face than the necklace.

Nancy glanced toward the restrooms. There he was, looking

around as if he'd just emerged on the other side of the looking glass, and sure enough, he started down the wrong aisle. She'd have to fetch him. She fumbled with the necklace latch, but it didn't come easily so she left it on. He'd already disappeared.

—Stay right here, Kimmy, she said firmly, at this counter. I'm just going to get Poppa.

Kim nodded and spun one of the earring trees.

The gold chain scratched her neck. No way she'd wear it. But maybe if Gammie bought something they could leave. Poppa was grouchy, and the store was crowded and chaotic, and the people, they just seemed to claw at everything, like the dogs next door when they smelled something and pawed at the dirt. The place was hot and noisy, and her stomach was gurgling again. And all the stuff, there was so much stuff! She'd never been in a place like this. Aunt Jo had never brought her here.

The trays under the counter gleamed in gold and silver and stones in all the colors of a sixty-four box of crayons, seemed like. She wondered what the names of the stones were and where they got dug up and who dug them and did they find them in some big mountain of Electric Lime or Razzle Dazzle Rose or Mango Tango? The whole place was like that, so much stuff, so much of it, and how eager and desperate and even angry some of the people were as they rustled through clothing racks and the way they talked to clerks, like show me this and gimme that, and they'd just point and talk to clerks like they were slaves or whatever.

The earrings hung on little white cards that dangled and rustled when the rack spun. She wiggled it, sending a ripple through the rack. One pair shook loose and landed face down on the counter. She turned it over, holding the card in the palm of her hand. The label said Emerald, but she thought Screamin' Green. The color reminded her of oak leaves in summer time, layered on top of one another, thick and rich, how they fluttered when a breeze lifted them. The noise and chaos all around seemed to melt away in the color; she now realized how noisy it was here. A constant hum and rumble had surrounded her ever since they arrived, but now, as she studied the rich color of the earrings, the noise became faint and distant. It was the color: it sucked the racket in and concentrated it in a lambent glow. She cupped the card with the earrings into her palm and slid it into her jeans pocket, and just then Gammie emerged from between the clothing racks across the aisle with Poppa.

—Oh, do you like it, honey? she said. It's just right for you. Let's get it. It'll be for church.

Nancy paid cash, and the clerk handed Kimmy a crinkled plastic bag with the boxed cross and chain inside and said it would look lovely on her.

—Let's go out that door, she said. I'll bring the car around and we'll call Aunt Jo, she told Kimmy, who dawdled behind as they left, sweeping her hand along the racks of skirts and blouses she passed.

As they neared the door, Nancy said, —Come along, Kimmy. You stay here at the curb with Poppa for just a minute while I get the car. It'll just be a few minutes… what? What is it?

A stout man in a brown suit with a clip-on tie had emerged from the clothing racks and now stepped in front of them, blocking the way.

Nancy said, —Excuse me…

But he cut her off. —Ma'am, I need to ask you and the little girl to come with me.

Sammiches

ABOUT THE LAVENDER DRESS… Nancy seemed so… what?… distant, when they dropped Kimmy off. Barely mentioned it. She was less talkative than earlier, and for sure less cheerful. Not less… not cheerful at all. The dress seemed like an afterthought. That was it. And she'd been so pleased earlier… about seeing Kimmy, about bringing this gift. You could tell she'd put a lot of thought into it. Don't overdo, but still, make it something special, something that will leave an impression, a trace of herself: Kimmy wearing a dress for church that Nancy had chosen. And now…

Something happened. Must've… but what?

Jo wondered.

Things were hurried. The house was full. Jo was cooking when they came through the breezeway door in a flurry with Kimmy leading the way. She went straight to her room without a parting word. All Nancy said was they couldn't find a dress in her size and here's the receipt and maybe Jo could exchange it for something she'd like. Jo was busy. Nancy didn't want to be a bother. She didn't want to be in the way. They'd be off. She'd call.

Of course she would. Jo knew this wasn't the last visit. Oh, no.

But all she got from Kimmy was couldn't find a dress, nothin' happened, and could she go outside now, which she did. Jo even mused darkly that maybe Nancy'd bought the wrong size in the first place just so she could suggest taking Kim off to the store.

—That's pushing it, Nick said.

—I suppose. But something wasn't right. I shouldn't have let Kimmy go off alone with them. I wonder what Nancy told her.

—She was probably bored, and Nancy was probably disappointed to find out that she really does hate dresses.

—God knows what she thinks. And now what? They're like living symbols of everything I want Kimmy to forget. I have no idea how to fit them in. But something happened. I just hate to think what. If they started telling her about Ross or… oh, this was wrong. I should never have allowed this. And I'm not about to spend their money either. If Kimmy needs a new dress we'll buy it. Here, do something with this.

—But it's brand new!

—I don't care… just do something with it.

She thrust the box with the dress into his hands, and he quietly stuck it in back of the minivan.

The next day, while he was running an errand up on Market Street, he dropped the box into a Salvation Army bin in the parking lot of the old mission church building, a landmark of sorts in Hawkings, its earliest Christian church and school, where children from the Kaw, Lenape, Potawatomi, Kickapoo, and other nations and tribes, some emigrated by force from elsewhere on the continent, were brought to be disabused of their native superstitions and forbidden to speak in their native languages. The building was later occupied by Methodists for a couple of generations, and when they outgrew it, it stood empty and boarded up until a wealthy patron of the Hawkings Community Players died and left the theater company money to take over and renovate the building. Elliot had lately joined the group, becoming its new Scrooge that Christmas season and for several yet to come. But casting him as Scrooge had consequences. The old Scrooge, who'd played the role for years, was demoted to Marley, and Marley was demoted to Mr. Fezziwig, who in turn became Portly Gentleman #2, and so on. Nothing happens without consequences. Another thermodynamic law upheld, more or less. Marley's ghost seemed especially bitter clanking around in his chains that year.

Elliot was a curiosity. His new role drew attention to him and his family, and soon stories about his decline into obscurity and, from what some heard, poverty, were shared, embellished, and steeped in schadenfreude. But for a few, his was also a story of redemption. His Scrooge was resonant. When Christmas morning finally rolled around and he awoke to find it was still early and the big goose was still hanging in the market and Tiny Tim could yet be saved, schadenfreuders all over the dark theater wiped their cheeks in artful ways, as if scratching an itch or brushing back a loose spray of hair. And the moistest eyes were those of Elliot's Wednesday night Alcoholics Anonymous crew, who filled a row near the front of the house and didn't care a whit if anyone saw them wiping away tears. They passed out tissues and shook hands and slapped each another's knees triumphantly. Stories of redemption were their favorite kind.

The lavender dress did not go far. It may not have been mentioned in Monarch House again, but it was seen – glimpsed in church at the early service, at first doubtfully, and then curiously, by Jo, who decided it was probably one of a hundred identical dresses that came from the same rack at the Jones Store. Or was it? The girl wearing it looked to be a little older and bigger than Kimmy, about the right size for that too-big dress. Her mother, an undocumented Mexican immigrant, had paid $2.50 for it at the Salvation Army store. The girl wore it every Sunday to church and then carefully hung it in her closet when she got home – her only dress – so she could watch her brothers and sisters and cousins while her mother and aunt cleaned offices at the corporate park on the west side of Hawkings. One of the cousins in her charge on those evenings was two years younger than her, the same age as Kim. His name was Lalo and he sat next to Kim in class.

THE NEW MILLENNIUM CAME. Water still flowed from spigots where it flowed before. Electric lights burned through midnight on the year's final day. The Internet hummed. Planes did not fall from the sky. Stock markets did not crash, for a while yet, anyway. Millennial fanatics receded to wherever they came from until the next Armageddon was at hand.

Winter settled in. A bleak winter. Little snow fell that year, so the cold was a dry see-your-breath kind of cold, the kind that found its way indoors no matter the thermostat setting and wore away at you.

Nick drove Kim to school on a sub-zero February morning and Elliot came along for the ride.

—They pay God-knows-how-much to paint words on signs and no one even knows how to spell them, Elliot snorted.

Kim clutched her backpack and watched the sign pass.

Tiffaney Downs. Its sky-blue letters swirled across a panel of stained wood braced on each side by sturdy limestone pillars. The sign had the look of a lonely outpost with a single parapet up top from which to defend the subdivision against invading hordes from rival subdivisions.

—What's wrong with it? Nick asked.

—If it's supposed to be Louis Tiffany, like *Tiffany* lamps, that's not how you spell it. Imagine living someplace with the name spelled wrong!

Frozen leaves collected in an empty fountain below the sign and on the faded green tarp that stretched across the neighborhood pool like a trampoline. Hoarfrost coated the brown grass.

Tiffaney Downs was a valley of drab shake rooftops, row upon row of them, interconnected by a maze of roads and cul-de-sacs. On this cold morning, countless plumes of gray smoke streamed up from chimney pipes on every roof.

The turn into school was just past the next subdivision, *Pointe Grande*, which on a previous trip had set Elliot off about what the French had to do with suburban Kansas, where only two hundred years ago, he would have them know, there was nothing but tallgrass as far anyone could see, and the only ones to see it were Indians, who had to stand on the backs of their horses to look around, so tall was the tallgrass. And now look what's here! he'd said, *Pointe Grande!* … when there's no *pointe* (he laughed at his own pun) and no one even cares whether the point's *grand* or *grand-ay*, or how big it is, for that matter.

At the left-turn signal into the school's driveway, only a few vehicles at a time could whip under the light before it changed. Cars then paraded around a loop in front of the school, where children piled out and teachers bundled in parkas as shapeless as Michelin men (though nearly all were women) directed traffic with little wooden stop signs like ping-pong paddles and herded packs of children through the doors.

—They're not supposed to do that, Nick said.

—Do what?

—Stop like that, in front of the school. Look, see that teacher out there in the red coat? She's trying to get them to drive up to the end of the lane so she can move the traffic up.

Kim realized it was her teacher, Mrs. Blanchard, but said nothing.

A white Suburban had stopped at the overhang in front of the school. A line of cars behind it waited. Nick sat motionless through a green light. Mrs. Blanchard came around to the driver's side and waved at the SUV to pull forward, but there it stood. The driver appeared to be arguing with her. Meanwhile, on the other side of the car, doors opened, shadows disembarked, doors shut. Then the vehicle lurched forward as a group of kids stopped in the crossing lane to let it pass.

Elliot let out another signifying snort and let that stand for a comment.

When the uncles had finally sluiced away in the slushy wet lane behind her, Kim headed up the walk to join the herd. Chelsea and Brittany hovered by one of the overhang's pylons, both shivering in matching denim jackets with fleece collars and short skirts, their pale thin legs, like dried corn stalks, pressed together against the cold.

They ignored Kim as she passed, or pretended to. Mr. Wilkinson, the principal, waded among the children. He called them *chaldran*. Last fall he spent all day on the roof to raise money for the school library, which wasn't called a library but the *Resource Center* (Uncle Elliot really got launched on that one), and as school let out that day he hollered down from the roof,—Bye, chaldran! Bye, chaldran! Now he made his way to the front doors, and as the herd pressed forward, Kim felt herself nudged as Chelsea and Brittany pushed past her. Brittany offered a hoity 'Scuse me, as she quick-stepped to catch up with Chelsea.

<hr>

SNOW BEGAN TO FALL during the morning. Its mesmerizing motion and whiteness filled the wide classroom windows, and the chaldran watched in amazement. Chelsea and Brittany whispered and stared at Kim through slit eyes. Baxter put his head on the desk. Lalo sat at the same table as Kim. He stared at the worksheet, but Kim saw the blankness in his eyes. The words were alien. Wouldn't have mattered if they were in Spanish; couldn't read much of that either. He grinned and shrugged helplessly. Next period he'd go to ESL class, same time as Elisa went to Special Ed, so everyone figured not speaking English was the same as being retarded. Jeremy and Baxter got him to teach them swear words in Spanish. They went around saying *¡Mierda!* until one of the lunch ladies heard them; then they got sent to the office.

Lalo pushed the math worksheet around on the table and finally slid it toward Kim with a puzzled look. A few random numbers were scrawled into the answer spaces just to put something on the sheet. Writing numbers was what everyone was supposed to do, so that's what he did. He clamped the pencil in his fist like a knitting needle stuck through a ball of yarn.

She glanced at the paper and shook her head like *Not even close.*

When Mrs. Blanchard sat down at her computer, Kim pushed her paper his way and he copied her answers in large awkward figures.

Kim looked up to find Chelsea watching grimly.

Chelsea had a long neck. Her head bobbled. She nudged Brittany and whispered. Both girls watched Kim and Lalo for a moment and then Chelsea burst out, —She's cheating!

Baxter and Jeremy came out of their stupor. Everyone brightened as if an electric current had zapped the room.

Chelsea's arm stuck out like a rod.

—What's all this? Mrs. Blanchard said, rising.

—Them! Cheating! Chelsea said, shaking her finger.

Baxter laughed and Jeremy echoed the same laugh, like laughing in the round. Lalo laughed too.

—They *were-ere*! Chelsea exclaimed.

The boys' laughter threatened to drain her news of its gravity.

—I saw them too! Brittany added, as if trying to plug the gravity leak.

Mrs. Blanchard told everyone to go back to their work.

What disappointment there was as the drama melted away and Mrs. Blanchard sat down with Lalo to go over the math problems. How unfair!

The snow continued, and for the rest of the morning every time Chelsea looked up she found Kim watching her in a way that seemed even more threatening for its blankness than if Kim had frowned or squinted. She stared back, or tried to, but what she saw now in Kim's eyes came from depths beyond her reckoning. She was faced down by some unnamable thing embedded in the deep structure of Kim's life, absorbed in the same way a tree absorbs a foreign object stuck in the crevice of its limbs over time – a chunk of metal, a bottle, a shoe – until it's immoveable, yet still recognizable for the thing it once was, though impossible to dislodge, forever part of the tree.

The morning's work was done and the kids were getting antsy because it was almost time for lunch, when Kim suddenly asked, —What's a chelsea?

Mrs. Blanchard was rooting around in the supply closet.

Chelsea sneered at Kim.

—What is it? Kim taunted. A saint? Is there Saint Chelsea?!

— …!!

—Never heard of Saint Chelsea, Kim said, grinning at Baxter and Jeremy, who brightened at the prospects of this new game.

Brittany looked expectantly at Chelsea, waiting for a snappy comeback, but Chelsea only bobbled her head and snarled. There was on her lips the faintest hint of a fearful tremble. The quiet, placid dog that always suffered her abuse had just snapped back.

—What's a Kim? was all she could muster.

The boys laughed. Brittany huffed.

Kim snickered.

Lalo leaned on his elbow, grinning. You didn't need much English to figure this out.

—Hah! Don't even know what your name means! Kim said. Just something your mom made up probably. Couldn't figure out what you were and said oh, it must be a chelsea, and your dad said whatever.

Kim threw up her hands, like whatever, and the boys howled.

Mrs. Blanchard emerged from the closet like a spelunker from a cave and brushed herself off.

—That's enough! she said.

But at the next lull, Kim said, —I know! They saw it on a sign, like Chelsea Downs. You're a subdivision! You got named for a subdivision! Hah! Chelsea Downs!

Jeremy and Baxter squealed with delight while Chelsea huffed short, dramatic breaths.

—Chelsea Downs! Baxter sputtered through his giggles. —Yo, Chelsea Downs!

Jeremy giggled too and echoed Baxter. —Yo… Chelsea Downs!

Brittany glared at Kim, but before she could come up with her own insult, Kim said, —Probly right down the road from Brittany Pointay! What is a point-ay? Or a chel-say?

The two girls were still huffing with rage after Mrs. Blanchard told Kim to hush up and marshalled the class to line up for lunch.

Out in the hallway the boys howled and chanted Brittany and

Chelsea's new monikers as the classes mingled and others joined in with no clue of what the chanting meant. It was just fun to say.

Lalo found Kim in the cafeteria and sat beside her.

He laughed as he opened a wrinkled paper bag. —Chelsay point-ay!

She smirked triumphantly. —What do you got for lunch?

He squinched his shoulders. She wasn't sure if he didn't understand her or didn't know what was in the bag.

Out came a loose sandwich, partly wrapped. She squinted at it, like watching tadpoles in a pond, and then pealed back the bread. A reddish paste smudged the bottom slice. She sniffed.

—What is that?

—Sammich.

—No, I mean what's that? She pointed at the smudge.

—Sammich.

—Your mom make that?

—I make.

He tore it into two ragged halves and offered her one.

—No way, she said. She unwrapped a slice of Aunt Jo's carrot cake and held it out. —Here, eat this.

He nudged the half sandwich at her.

—Okay, I'll take that if you take this.

He sniffed the carrot cake, miming her, and then bit and watched her as he chewed, waiting for her to eat his sandwich.

She smelled it again. Meat-like, maybe ham spread. She bit off a corner, away from the whatever-it-was. —Good, she nodded.

Now he wolfed the rest of the cake.

He found her each day after that – at lunch, on the playground. He would jump the line going into assemblies to sit beside her and wave to her at church. His English was limited to a handful of words and short phrases. She learned some Spanish from him, but mostly they pointed at things to communicate. He couldn't tell her where he lived before he moved here. His mother picked him up after school in a beat-up red Mercury.

⁓

Late one cold afternoon after basketball, she found Lalo sitting in a corner of the front hall vestibule.

—Hey, Lalo, what're you doing here?

Shrug.

Nick was waiting in the car and saw her talking to a kid on the floor who got up and followed her down the walkway.

—Can we give Lalo a ride home?

A glance at the boy shivering in a too-big sweatshirt was enough for Nick. When they'd climbed in back, he said, —Hi, Lalo.

Lalo nodded fearfully.

—Your mom or dad late picking you up?

He shook his head. Not no, just no response.

—So where do you live?

The boy's eyes widened doubtfully.

Kimmy said, —Maybe if you just drive, he can tell us where to turn.

—Don't think that's a great idea. Nick took a breath and asked haltingly, —¿Dónde … (?)… vive … usted?

The boy brightened and whitewater rushed through his lips. Nick clung to a familiar word here and there from his desultory high school tour of Spanish, and with a lot of pointing and nodding, they found their way to a green duplex in a row of tract houses that Nick didn't know had sprouted up on the west side of town, where there'd been only farmland the last time he got out this way. The

130

yards had little shrubbery. The thin barren saplings on a few lawns looked like you could uproot them with a good yank. Snow patches had shaped themselves to the shadows between houses.

The shades were drawn at Lalo's house, and the red Mercury was parked in the driveway.

—Here? Nick asked before he let the boy out.

Lalo nodded, a jittery shudder.

—I'll walk up with you, Nick said.

—Me too, Kim said, and she hopped out before Nick could stop her.

He had to step quickly to catch up with the children.

His knock fell hollow on the door. Children's voices and TV noise echoed from inside, then the patter of steps, then the door was opened to a crease by a girl who couldn't have been older than five or six.

Lalo started past Nick, who dropped a hand on the boy's chest and asked the girl, —Is your mom here?

She looked at him, open-mouthed, with wide, dark eyes. Her thumb hung limply from her lips.

—Your mom?

She stared for a moment and then retreated.

—Mama! Lalo shouted into the room.

A short woman in jeans and a loose T-shirt now appeared and looked groggily at Nick.

—Ah! She waved Lalo inside and smiled weakly at Nick. —*Gracias*, she said, and began to ease the door shut.

Before it closed, Nick asked, —Everything okay here? you okay?

—O-kay, she nodded and repeated, o-kay, now smiling at Kim, and this time she did shut the door, leaving Nick to wonder what to do next, if anything.

He considered knocking again but didn't know what he'd say. The boy was home with his mother. What else was there to know — or ask? Maybe she was sick, maybe she needed help.

Jo said don't worry about it, but she did pack an extra sandwich in Kimmy's lunch the next day.

Nick couldn't stop thinking about them while he grouted the shower stall in number six.

THIS TIME THE HOLLOW knock on the door echoed through the neighborhood. The street was quiet and empty. No one was outdoors. Their footsteps on the front walk had seemed loud and intrusive.

The red Mercury sat in the driveway and the shades were drawn, same as last time. Voices echoed from inside, in Spanish — a woman's, scolding, impatient; a child's, resistant. Then hurried footsteps, and the door opened.

Nick stood there with a box of groceries in his arms and shopping bags stuffed with clothing at his feet, and Kim at his side, also clutching bags, who spoke up before he could say a word.

—Remember us? We brought some stuff!

Lalo's mother peered dimly through her suspicion. Plainly, unexpected knocks at the door seldom brought welcome news.

The prospect of insulting these people with charity hadn't occurred to Nick in a concrete way until this moment.

—We thought, he said, ... we thought a few things might be helpful... for the children.

She peered stiffly at the bags and snapped, —¿Cuánto?

Nick puzzled over the question, looking down at the bags. —No, no. No money, no dinero. It's a... how do I say it?... it's a... I don't know the word.

Lalo appeared at the door and smiled when he saw Kim.

—Hi, Lalo! she said.

He grinned widely.

—Tell your mom it's a gift, it's free. How do you say that?

— …?

—Free?

—*¿Gratis?*

—Ah, that's it, Nick said. *¡Gratis!* He pointed at the bags.
—*¡Gratis! ¡Para sus…hijos!* he added, more proud of his Spanish
than the offering.

She remained wary and shook her head until Lalo pointed at Kim
and issued a torrential explanation of which Nick understood zero.

Finally she opened the door wide. —*Gracias,* she said.

—*De nada,* Nick responded, imagining briefly that they were
now conversing in Spanish.

—*/\/\/*—

KIM SAT IN A stall studying the handwriting scribbled below an erect
cock that looked more like a thumbs-up sign. The image had been
there for some time, etched into the paint. It appeared following a
weekend basketball tournament when boys from the visiting school
had used the girls room to change.

But the caption was new.

Kim sucks spic dick!

The final stroke of the *k*'s swooped upward. The *i*'s were dotted
with tiny circles. Wasn't hard to figure who wrote it.

Kim thought about kicking their asses but decided to write
something instead, in Spanish. Trouble was she didn't want Lalo get-

133

ting blamed, so she left him out of it and looked up the words herself in the library.

The next day she wrote on the back of the stall door,

> *¡Mierda Chelsea gustos tan bueno,*
> *que podía comer todo el día!*
> *— Bretaña* ☺

She dotted the *i*'s with circles. Happy faces were a Brittany thing.

Trouble soon followed. The drama of imminent crisis permeated the clique and all of its satellites.

The girls traipsed indignantly into the Resource Center to look up the words in the same Spanish-English dictionary Kim had used.

The crisis erupted.

The clique rallied to Chelsea, while poor Brittany, the imputed author of the lines, didn't get to be a victim too. The girls surrounded Chelsea and left Brittany on the margins. In fact, her name *was* at the bottom of the lines, wasn't it? Hmm.

They eyeballed Kim and Lalo. They whispered and spread rumors, and even, through some bizarre logic known only to them, assigned joint blame for the graffiti to both Kim and Brittany, with obvious assistance from Lalo — who probably could not have written that much Spanish himself.

Naturally, such doings didn't go unnoticed for long before adult authorities got involved. Mr. Wilkinson himself went into the girls room to inspect the stall, with a couple of female teachers clearing the way and guarding the door. The scrawling about Kim had miraculously been scratched over in the meanwhile.

She took the blame — without shame, without remorse. She said nothing about the earlier graffiti, but she did tell Mr. Wilkinson, insisted even, that Lalo had nothing to do with it (though she left him to figure out for himself whether Brittany was complicit – which he decided she was not). In her usual way, she left the adults to do all the talking, fill in her blanks, assume what they would.

It was ISS for Kim.

In-School Suspension.

⁓

ELLIOT LAUGHED OUT LOUD when Jo got off the phone with the principal.

—For talking Spanish?! Hah!

—Writing it, and it's not funny. Where's Nick? We have to go down there.

—Last I saw he was putting new towel racks in number three.

Upstairs, as she passed Araby, she noticed the rumpled bed. Kimmy'd been in there again. The strangest thing was how it was only a couple of times they stayed in this room, Anna and Kimmy, and you'd think she was too young to recall it. What else did she remember, Jo wondered?

She was prickly, Anna was. Could be more difficult than a regular paying guest, and clueless about whether the room might be needed. Jo smelled cigarette smoke one night after she'd gone up to bed but couldn't bring herself to tell Anna not to smoke. So she laundered everything after they left – blankets, bedspread, everything. Even had the drapes dry-cleaned. Plus, she'd had to change a reservation. A guest said something about the smoke, too, and Jo decided that next time she'd tell Anna not to smoke – but oh, that was the thing, wasn't it? There always seemed to be a next time.

As Jo straightened the bed, she noticed drawing paper poking out from under it,. Kimmy's pictures were not exceptional for their

135

drawing, but they had unique angles and poses you'd never think of. These showed Elliot looking down the stairwell from his room and Boxer behind the chair legs under the dining table and a view of the backyard from Kimmy's window, with some figures down below looking up, maybe Jo and Nick. There was one of a motorcycle airborne in a field of grass with two riders, their hair flying back in the wind. A few crayons and pencils were loose under the bed. Jo knelt to see what else was there. She scooped everything out of the shadows and discovered a fountain pen. Its finish was marbled in midnight blue and the top unscrewed to open it. This was an expensive pen, not something Kimmy'd been given. Jo recalled a guest last fall asking about a lost pen. This was it.

—Probably found it in the cushions, Nick said, when she showed him.

He reacted to the ISS about the same as if he'd just discovered that a corroded washer was causing a faucet to leak. A head nod, an understated *hunh*.

⌁

ANIMALS CAVORTED. BOATS SAILED through constellations of green speckles on the yellow walls. If you looked long enough, the speckles took on figures and shapes. Longer still and the figures moved, like clouds on a still day or the surface of the koi pond or the sun setting through the trees.

The room wasn't much bigger than the pantry at home. Under the desktop her fingertips blindly found lumps of gum so dry and hard they felt like rivets.

She was supposed to sit here all day doing homework or whatever. No one could talk to her. Seemed like every time she moved an inch, Mizz Pritchett (she'd buzz the word *Mizz* like a bumble bee

136

if you said it wrong), who was Mr. Wilkinson's assistant and sat outside his office in front of the big glass window where his office was, would look over her computer monitor and glare. Her frizzy purple hair bounced around like a balloon on a string behind the computer monitor. She kept an eye on Mr. Wilkinson too, like she was afraid he'd sneak up on her with an axe or something. Sometimes Kim would squirm around and scrape the chair on the floor just to get Mizz Pritchett to look and keep her from whatever she was doing. Then Mizz P would squint at her, and Kim would stare back until she sniffed and went back to her computer.

Mrs. Blanchard brought some worksheets for Kim during the morning. She smelled like the perfume counter at the store where Gammie took her.

The office they had to go in that day was no bigger than the ISS room, but it was all white, walls and ceiling, and the bright overhead fluorescent lights made it seem like light was being squeezed into the room, like the room would explode if you tried to cram one more ounce of light in. Gammie sat on a hard plastic chair with her knees bent sideways up against the tiny metal desk where the man in the brown suit sat with his papers. Every so often he'd look at Kim like she was a spider he'd just noticed crawling along the base board and he was about come around and stomp on her. She stood against the wall and Poppa sat in the only other chair, and a policeman soon came, filling the doorway with dark blue, sucking some of the light out of the room. He winked at Kim and talked to the brown-suit man in a sharper voice than he did Gammie, who said she would gladly pay for the item — that's what they called the earrings now, 'the item' — and said she wanted to make it right. But the policeman didn't seem too bothered about it. His shoulder radio burped and hissed, and Kim realized there was another policeman in the hallway when she heard the same sound out there.

Gammie pleaded, the officer nodded, the brown-suit man folded his massive hands on the paperwork on his tiny desk and scowled. When the policeman left, the brown-suit man, who smelled like the inside of a car trunk, came around his desk, huffing as he did so, and bent over in front of Kim and told her, next time he caught her stealing he'd send her to jail. Now Gammie got pissed and said he needn't talk that way to a child, and the man frowned at Gammie and told her to keep a better eye on her next time, and Gammie said there wouldn't be a next time here or anywhere, but especially not here because she'd never set foot in this store again, and the man said that was just fine.

Outside, Gammie squeezed Kim and said never mind what that man said, that she would never, ever let anyone take her to jail. And she said, too, if you don't want to tell Aunt Jo about what happened it's okay because nobody got in trouble and she'd keep it a secret too. And Kim didn't care so she said okay, and Gammie said okay and next time they'd go somewhere different. Kim noticed her wiping her face while she drove home to Aunt Jo's.

And so far, nobody'd said a word about it. She only saw Gammie and Poppa a couple of times at home since then, and Gammie'd given her a look, a little eyebrow flicker was all, but it was like, now they had something between them, something they'd done together that no one else knew about, and she seemed to like that after all, as if maybe she wasn't so sorry about Kim swiping the earrings or whatever, so Kim didn't worry about whether she'd get told on about it or not.

Mr. Wilkinson came out and handed Mizz Pritchett some papers and he smiled through his bushy mustache like Teddy Roosevelt.

Mrs. Blanchard brought Kim's lunch bag to the ISS room. She brought her own too and sat in the other desk and said she'd eat with Kim if it was okay with her, and Kim said shrug.

—My, you must have a big appetite! she said when Kim unpacked her lunch.

—Not all for me.

—Oh?

—Unh-uh.

Pause…

—Who's it for?

Shrug…

—I see.

Mrs. B. opened a plastic container and poked at cottage cheese with a spork.

—He's not here today, at school, she said.

Kim unwrapped a sandwich. The bread was Aunt Jo's, which was soft and brown, and Kim pressed a stiff finger into it, studying the hole she made. The hum returned, filling the room now so it drowned out Mrs. B. and the keyboarding out in the office; it surrounded her, like the static rustle of dried leaves when she buried herself in a pile Uncle Nick had raked up. Every move she made rustled the leaves and drowned everything in static.

Mrs. Blanchard touched her arm. —I thought you knew, she said. It has nothing to do with you, or this business.

Kim pressed another finger into the bread.

—It was… well, his family, they moved away, is all.

Kim's fingers were moist with egg salad. Mrs. B.'s voice was somewhere outside the leaf pile, beyond the static. Kim could hear her but not hear her at the same time. She wondered where Lalo had gone but already knew that Mrs. B. wouldn't know.

Mrs. B. put her food down and slid closer. —I just found out this morning. It's not your fault. It was because… I guess they had to move. Sometimes it happens.

Kim was the fish. How people stood over them and watched and wouldn't leave them alone just to be what they were but instead they were just there to be watched. They didn't exist for themselves but only so people could watch and taunt them.

She said nothing. She stared at the bread. Finally Mrs. B. left her own lunch on the other desk and went outside.

First she talked to Mizz P., who warbled back in her Mizz P. voice about there was nothing she could do, and next Mrs. Blanchard said where's Mr. Wilkinson, and Mizz P. said he was outside with the custodian, and Mrs. B. went off to find him.

Kim rejoined the class after lunch. Was supposed to be in ISS all day, but Mrs. B. got her out.

Lalo's place was vacant and his stuff gone.

Brittany huffed and Chelsea bobbled her head, but Kim didn't care. The static drowned them out too.

'Hell is un-cool'

YOU COULD SEE, IN the distance, on the east side of the yard, through two rows of chain link fencing trimmed on top with corkscrews of concertina-wire like the edging on a fancy cake, a street… no, call it a road… lined with boxy ranch houses. American flags hung over a couple of garages. Christmas lights brightened the gutters when it was the season to be jolly. Big-wheel trikes and kickballs were strewn in front yards. Distant and small, but there. Familiar shapes, easily recognized even when the objects were barely visible. The houses were incongruent to the landscape, as if a subdivision had been started and never finished. Seven houses, three on one side and four on the other. Ross had counted them the first time he came out in the yard on his first day here and the number hadn't changed in over three years. All just plopped there amid the vast patchwork of cropland that surrounded them. A few snouts lived there. Helluvathing, bringing your kids up with the WCF looming over you every day and lit up all night too. Without a doubt, the lights would glow on the curtains and shades of every window that faced this way. Ross wondered which ones lived there, which snouts. Couldn't see far enough to tell, but for sure he'd seen snout uniforms getting in and out of a couple of pick-ups over there.

Ross often lingered at the end of the yard, beyond the basketball courts, and watched the houses for whatever was going on, cars coming and going, kids playing, whatever. There was farm activity too — tractors and combines trundling across fields, leaving wakes of dust as vast as the horizon to drift off and settle wherever it went. You didn't see people so much with the farming, just machines milling this way and that, tines spinning, chutes blowing grain into hoppers that rolled alongside them. But the houses — kids'd be playing outside, mom and dad fucking inside. You could imagine what you couldn't see. That made it more interesting. Food cooking, TVs on, phone calls, beer in the fridge. And always, women in the shower, in the bedroom, maybe not in the bedroom. You could just make it up, whatever you couldn't see. But the distant glimpses gave you something to work with, a frame, a stage, actors, people.

Watching was sort of a compulsion of circumstances, of this weird geography of the prison and this clump of houses stuck in the middle of nowhere, like watching a soap opera on a waiting room TV while new tires got put on your car. What else was there? Behind him were limestone walls, barred windows, metal doors, hundreds of bored and very tense men in denim work shirts and jackets and baggy pants wandering from here to there on the yard with no purpose other than not being wherever they just were. Behind him, too, was the utter sameness of each day, drab, colorless; filled with noise, always metallic noise, always echoing, never just a sound by itself, but sounds always filling the vacuums between other sounds, all layered over one another — random howlings; sharp, indistinguishable utterances that fell short of language but were full of meaning nonetheless, full of pain, frustration, anger, despair.

Ross mostly stayed away from others. He didn't trust anyone and didn't like most — and he didn't believe he belonged here. Even now, after years in prison, he remained convinced that at some point whatever bureaucratic or legal snafu brought him here would get sorted out and the day would come when a snout would tap him on the shoulder while he was eating – he had a dozen scenarios along this line that he played in continuous loops – and say you need to come with me, and he'd be led away through hallways he'd never walked to an office he'd never set foot in and there he'd find his lawyer and prison officials, and probably his mother too, all waiting, all smiling, his mom smiling anyway, and there'd be papers to sign, and then he'd get a change of clothes and next thing they'd be off to a steak dinner somewhere beyond the boxy ranch house horizon, and so the nightmare would end – with beer and steak, and maybe with him returning to the restaurant later to retrieve the waitress he'd flirted with all through dinner. That was how he imagined his prison term ending.

He didn't socialize and never attended group counseling sessions, except the required ones, and he kept his mouth shut in those. No classes, no basketball or handball, no job training, and especially no church. You could see all around you, far as he was concerned, what all that amounted to once the training and group sessions were done and it was back to reality on the yard and in the cell blocks. The niggers still clung to their own, even now, yelping and hooting like a buncha chimps over by the free weights while one of them tried to break his push-up or chin-up record or whatever, and shit, couldn't those bastards do anything without making a racket? Always talking out loud to no one and to everyone at the same time – and you couldn't understand half of what they said anyways.

Same everywhere you looked. Spics over by the handball courts where they always hung. Clumps of cons here and there – faggots, druggies, bikers, Nazis, and just plain zombies. Keeping clear, keeping your mouth shut – it wasn't just because he wasn't one of them; it was how you survived too.

But none of them matched the Jesus-people for irritating. Most of the rest didn't even pretend you could trust them, but the Jesus-people, that was their stock-in-trade, breaking that down, that wall or shield of distrust or whatever that kept you alive. They were downright creepy, is what, cultish. They smiled this cult smile, this robo-glow, and they were always ready to drop into fifth gear with the Jesus talk.

They'd crowded into his view now, the Jesus-peeps had, four-five of them, hanging with their preacher, a con named Wade, the so-called *Reverend* Wade. He was doing a twenty jolt for killing a vestry member in his congregation who'd been diddling his wife. Church down near Fort Hays or somewheres.

A snout sauntered past and nodded at Wade and his crew like nothing, like the Lord had sent some of their sunshine his way too, even though if it had been the niggers or spics clumped together like that he'd have broken it up. As the CO passed he looked at Ross like he was considering whether to spit in his direction and then decided it wasn't a good enough place to spit and strolled on.

Mandel now came by, shoulders hunched, collar turned up, looking like he was hanging on some KCK street corner waiting for his cell phone to ring. There's a look you get once you get fucked up with that shit, in particular the meth, that you never lose, no matter that you've been straight inside this place for the past six years. He still had that gray, skeletal, missing-and-crooked-teeth, druggie look, and he was stuck with it. Ross'd seen him coming across the yard but never looked his way. You always knew who was where and who was approaching your own personal perimeter.

Outside the wire, at one of the houses, a car pulled in and a woman carried grocery bags inside with a toddler at her hip. A snout house. Hard to believe you'd live where cons could actually see your wife and kids. Maybe just rentals, Ross pondered for the first time. That'd be something, he thought – when he got out? to build more houses over there and rent them to snouts. You could plop four houses on one acre of that farmland – or eight duplexes, maybe more. He'd be their landlord. It was a satisfying thought.

—'Sup, man, Mandel said.

Ross snorted and lit a smoke. He didn't offer Mandel one and Mandel didn't ask, even though he was out and wanted one too.

Mandel started chattering about it being an election year or some shit and he was trying to decide which candidate he liked. Ross didn't bother reminding him that they weren't allowed to vote.

The Rev looked Ross's way just then. He flicked a smile and head nod as if returning a greeting, as if Ross had nodded first, which he decidedly had not.

—Shit, Ross hissed, not even a word, more like part of his breath.

On the basketball court, the niggers played in their beaters even though it was about 42°F, give or take, and grunted and bellowed in fine, crisp timbres that always made Ross think the lines of their jungle ancestors were running clear and straight through their genes and chromosomes and blood. Along the south wall, two snouts passed each other with a nod, while up on the tower, shadows with caps moved around behind tinted glass, looking out over the yard. On the west side of the yard the laundry fans threw off a plume of exhaust and rumbled as they always did, part of the incessant white noise and tidal motion of the place.

Mandel ventured, —So you gonna try again?

—Try what again? Ross knew what he meant, and it irritated him being asked.

—Writing your little girl, like you did.

Ross let a drag of smoke curl through his lips, took a breath of cold air, and made Mandel wait a beat or two before he responded, long enough to let him know the question wasn't welcome.

—Kuh… letter came back. What's the point?

Mandel tried to think of the point, and then said, —Point is, man, you don't even get to find out what your kid'd think. That ain't right.

Ross frowned. The furrows between his eyebrows curled like new-plowed soil. —What's it to you?

—Ain't nothin'… ain't nothin' to me. Just I seen you writing that first one. Writing ain't easy. Don't seem right, is all, I guess. Your moms, she keeps comin' here, you know, and like I told you, I gotta meet her someday so I can and thank her for the books 'n shit, and but here's what you should do… you should send *her* the letter…

— …?!

Mandel noticed how Ross now glanced his way. He'd hit on something. —No, you should, man, he said, more confidently. She could like give it to your little girl, pass it along. Didn't you tell me she gets to see your kid from time to time?

—Yeah, but…

—But what?… ain't no but… send it to her, man. She'll give it to your daughter.

The Rev had wandered their way and was now within earshot.

—Not easy, is it? the Rev asked vaguely, invitingly, with a knowing sort of glow.

Ross glanced off into the distance and let the conversation drop.

—What's that, Rev? Mandel said.

—Holding family together in these… circumstances.

—Don't believe we were talking to you, Ross said.

—That is so, the Rev said softly. Didn't mean to intrude.

But his posse had sniffed the challenge, the tone, and drifted toward them in a ghostly sort of way. If they'd been bikers or spics or whatever, they'd all have been staring Ross down now, but these dudes were just… *present*, looking off in different directions, but still here, listening, alert.

Ross would've been just as happy to wander off and leave Mandel and the Rev behind to talk about the election or the weather or whatever, but for one, he didn't want them talking about him, and for two, walking off would have set an unacceptable precedent. Conceding the personal space, that is. Getting run off – and by this bunch, at that. If it'd been the niggers or whatever, he'd've faced them down, got in the fight, maybe got his ass kicked, but still, message sent, message received: Ain't backin' down. But these creeps, they just talked until they wore you out. And Ross knew that tomorrow or the day after, he'd come out here to enjoy his little glimpse of life beyond the wire, imagine the snouts' wives all soaped up in the shower, ponder a real estate empire where there was nothing but soy beans and corn and dust right now, and here they'd be, these fuckers, taking up the space, his space, and probably inviting him to join them as if they were gracious hosts offering him a vacant rocker on his own front porch.

Nope. No indeed. Wouldn't do. Just would not do.

Ross ground the butt under his toe, spread his feet defiantly, and looked off into the distance to where a host of sparrows crossed the sky in a dark, undulating cloud.

The Rev broke into Ross's concentrated effort at indifference.

—Davey Wade, he said gently, sincerely, as he stuck out his hand.

Ross squinted suspiciously. Putting your hand in someone else's, leaving yourself one-handed even for a moment out here wasn't something you did lightly. But the downside of offending him for no reason came with risks, too, that you might not find out about for days or weeks or whenever you least expected it. Also, he did not, under any circumstance, want to let himself in for an impromptu sermon – and with this dude it was inevitable.

Ross had tried church once.

At some point, and prompted by what Ross couldn't say for sure, Anna had decided that they should bring Kimmy up in a Christian home, as she put it. She'd picked a church too. Didn't look much like a church, but that's where they went – this big, modular building, like a tractor warehouse, on a few barren acres surrounded by corn-fields just off K-54. Out front, a 7-Eleven-like marquee posted witty gems that changed weekly.

> *Always remember that Hell is un-cool*
> *Free Trip To Heaven… Details Inside*
> *God grades on the Cross, not on the curve*

Inside, the place was about what you'd expect in a warehouse – ribbed paneling, slatted windows, birds flitting around in the steel roof joists overhead. The altar, which looked to Ross more like a stage than an altar, was a carpeted platform with draperies hung behind it and not much else – a couple of gilded high-back chairs, a podium, a cross. The most prominent feature was a projection screen that showed glorious sunrises and eagles in flight, which they watched until the service began. Then it showed the prayers and hymns. But its main use was to show the bullet points from the preacher's sermons, which were the central feature of going to this church – him talking about the Bible. When you arrived ushers handed out pamphlets with the same identical PowerPoint images that appeared on the screen. The preacher called his sermons 'lessons,' and he'd announce more than once during the sermon that they were also available in books and DVDs you could get for a 'small donation' at the end of the service on the way out.

Kimmy liked going to church, pretty much, Ross thought. He'd hoist her up and bounce along with the hymns. She bobbed her head and made up her own words. Anna brought crayons, and she'd draw on the pamphlets during the sermons. He didn't know what she got out of it, but Anna said the whole point was just going, *her* going, getting in the habit, so he took them, even though getting up on Sunday mornings was getting old.

The preacher was smart, Ross thought, and told good stories. Ross favored the ones in which God was disposed to improve your worldly circumstances in exchange for token donations to charity or maybe helping someone whose car had broken down. Next thing, wouldn't the good Samaritan discover that the person whose car broke down was rich and the Samaritan's delinquent mortgage had suddenly, miraculously been paid off – in full! The preacher had a huge inventory of stories like these.

But it was no tit-for-tat deal with God, he always reminded his flock. No, no. Rather, they would *prosper* in God's love. So what this meant, exactly how this worked, confused Ross, though it seemed dazzlingly clear when he sat in the pew with Anna and Kimmy and heard that wealth and happiness were maybe just one spare tire and a handful of lug nuts away. The key word was *prosper*. The preacher, Ross noticed, never said outright that you'd get rich for coming to church – but rather that you'd *prosper*. But soon Ross began to have doubts. He began to have this dim feeling that there was something circular about the whole pattern of the preacher's 'lessons,' which usually left the congregation hanging except for a strong hint that the full meaning of the lesson would be revealed in the DVDs and books 'available for a small donation' in back of the church. Or that next week's 'lesson' would clarify some of the questions about how *prosperity* would come to 'the people of God.' Like it was all designed just to keep you coming back for more – and buying DVDs and books to tide you over. Meanwhile, all over the church people were taking notes like a sonvabitch, and if a car happened to break down out on K-54 after church, you'd see a half a dozen cars from the church all pulled over, heads poking under the hood, three-four men to help to change a tire, and cell phones stuck in everyone's ears to be the first to call the service station.

They'd been going there a month or two when Ross's mother asked where they went to church one night when they'd gone over for dinner. Anna said the name of the church, but Nancy just squinted a look of nonrecognition, a skeptical look, as if some judgment, you could see, was forming and it wasn't a good judgment, and Anna picked up on it the way you'd pick up on the slightest change in temperature when a draft brushed over the hairs on your arms and you sensed the change instantly even before you could think about it, and there it was. What followed was first a lengthy set of directions on how you got there, which you couldn't miss, Anna said, maybe a little tartly, just off 54 about two miles east of Sunburg. Nancy didn't recall seeing it, she said, and Anna said it'd been there a year or two, to which Nancy responded, —Oh, it's not a regular church.

This was headed nowhere good.

—*Regular?* Anna asked. Her hairline had this way of pulling itself back, like the skin just got tugged from behind and the thin lines on her brow would go flat and her eyes would dim. The look was unmistakable.

So now they were talking without looking at each other, Anna and Nancy, as Nancy named some *regular* churches, like Methodists and Presbyterians and Baptists (which she and Phil were, she said, even though she knew that Anna knew this), and Anna said she didn't think God took particular notice of *regular* or *nonregular* as long as they were all Christian churches, and Ross made a joke about leaded versus unleaded and Phil chimed in with regular or decaf, but no, these comments did not help.

Then his mom said, as if trying to wrap things up and have the final word, she just hoped Kimmy would be brought up in the right spirit, to which Anna, having the final word, said —You don't need to worry about Kimmy's spirit.

But no, there would still be another final word, as Nancy paused and drew a long significant breath and said she was just trying to understand was all, and so made it look like Anna was the one who'd made something out of nothing, which did not escape Anna, how Nancy did that, because that's all Anna talked about later as they drove home. But none of it amounted to anything because they only went to that church a few more times because now the preacher's 'lessons' had begun to veer off more and more to how much it cost to keep the lease on the building and he was looking for people to make *commitments*, as he put it. The preacher's wife even called them at home one night and asked for a donation (demanded was how it sounded to Anna), so they quit going, and they were glad to have Sunday mornings back to stay in bed while Kimmy watched *Davey and Goliath* on TV, which made them feel like they were still taking good care of her spirit.

Mandel had picked up chattering with the Rev as Ross's gaze drifted off. He was just then telling the Rev how he still couldn't believe the President had gotten an actual blow job in the Oval Office. He said so with more admiration and wonder than disillusionment. But, he added somberly, it nearly made him lose faith in the institution, in government itself.

By now snouts were coming into the yard. The cons would line up and be counted. A few would be randomly searched. As if knowing what mattered most to Ross at that moment, as if he somehow had figured out what the game really was, the Rev wandered off with his flock, Mandel now among them, and left Ross to his space, not so much, Ross suspected, conceding it but more as if he was making a gift of it.

'Things I cannot change'

ELLIOT HADN'T GONE OUTSIDE to do yard work. A squirrel had knocked the feeder down from the oak tree out front – again. Squirrels ate better than the birds, Elliot often said. He refilled and rehung the feeder, then yanked a couple of weeds near the porch, and next thing it was another and another, until he was walking around with a fistful of weeds, which he didn't want to leave somewhere because he might forget them, and there they'd be, wherever. So he trekked out to the compost bin and then got the broom to sweep up the birdseed he'd spilled – hands were shaky some days lately, he'd noticed – and after he swept the porch, he got out the hand clippers to trim the yews.

Never used the electric. The cord was a hassle, and the racket probably passed for music in hell. Plus, mostly, that is, these clippers reminded him of the ones he trimmed shrubs with at the old house in St. Louis when he was a kid. Maybe were the same ones. It was possible. Nick had ended up with a load of old tools after his father (Elliot's brother) died – a hand drill, two or three planes and levels, braces of all sizes, assorted chisels, a couple each of bow saws and marking gauges. Nick had no clue how to use one of the wrenches until a church member from next door picked it up and said he'd only ever seen a photo of one of these. A Morange Patent Wrench, he called it, with a surprising (and to Jo suspicious) acquaintance with this curiosity. He showed them how you popped open the bottom of the handle and cranked the wrench to whatever size you needed. He offered Nick five dollars for it, but Jo said, no, they'd keep it for now, and he said let him know if she changed her mind. Which convinced her there was some value in the tools – a lot more than five-dollars-a-piece worth. She said they should decorate the house with these antiques – they'd suddenly been promoted to antiques – and put price stickers on them too. But how much to ask? That'd take some research. Meanwhile, most of the tools had ended up in a pile in the corner of the barn. Elliot figured some might have even come down from his own father. These might be the very same clippers he'd held in his ten-year-old hands. Imagine. He did, as he wrapped his fingers around the darkened ash handles. He'd have to ask Nick later.

Everyone was out and the house was empty. No guests. Middle of the week on a sunny and warm April afternoon. The quiet inside had turned oppressive and Elliot was looking for something to do outdoors, where it was pleasant and languid. He decided he was glad the squirrel'd knocked the feeder down and the yews needed trimming. He'd had a fifty-year hiatus from chores like this. Everywhere he'd lived or traveled, the shrubs were already clipped – by others, and usually not when he'd see them doing it either. He felt on days like this that he was the person he was supposed to be, finally, after all these years, all these decades, and there wasn't much more to him than this either.

He had a nagging feeling he was supposed to do something inside, only he couldn't remember what. Didn't matter. It'd keep. He found the sound of the clippers soothing. He snipped and clipped.

Clip-clip-clip, clip-clip, clip-clip-clip.

Above him, the flag hung limply from a post beside the front porch steps. Others hung on porches along West Mission Street too, had ever since last fall. Just went up and never got taken down, and now they were getting faded. He'd said one time, just off-the-cuff, just off-handed like, that without any particular occasion for having the flags up after so long, what would be special about putting them up? Seemed like it would drain the color off July Fourth. And, too, who'd be the first to take theirs down? Soon people'd start noticing who *didn't* have a flag up. Now that was something to think about. But Jo did not think it was something to think about and said that was the flag she put up after the attacks and that was the one that would stay up.

Which it did, day and night, light or dark, rain or shine, through the snow and sleet of winter and the first T-storms of spring. And now its red had a pinkish tinge and its blue looked purplish and its white had turned gray. Funny, he thought, how particular she was about the house's appearance, yet this fraying flag still hung here. Pointing this out didn't seem prudent, and Elliot didn't much care.

But he'd begun to find the somber and reverential way people talked about not only the attacks but even just the flag, well, it was unsettling, disturbing even – all the little flags you'd see on cars whipping in the wind and the bumper stickers and T-shirts that appeared out of nowhere with slogans that also seemed to come out of nowhere and all of a sudden were everywhere. *These colors don't run! United we stand! Freedom isn't free!* All that sorrow had turned angry and needed somewhere to go. Elliot had begun to feel uncomfortable with it, even fearful at times, but he wasn't sure what it was he feared.

Still, he had the day's warmth and serenity. The bird feeder was full, he had yews to clip.

Next door, Dawit, the sexton, came down from his apartment over the old estate carriage house. He and his wife Ayana were from Ethiopia. Ayana was pregnant when they arrived. Jo brought clothing and whatever other baby stuff she could find among Flann's things. The baby turned out to be a girl, and more than once Jo said vacantly that nothing of Kimmy's would fit until little Rose was about four.

Dawit smiled broadly at Elliot and waved, but Elliot didn't notice, so the sexton opened the garage doors, rolled out the lawnmower, and went about gassing it up.

When it rumbled to life and the afternoon's quiet got sucked into the engine's roar, Elliot did notice. He snarled at Dawit's back as he roared off to the far side of the church, leaving behind a cloud of oily blue fumes.

Elliot hacked several times and then went back to his task. The sticky dampness of his shirt hadn't bothered him until now, nor did he feel any urgency about finishing the shrubs, which bordered the house all the way around the corner and along the driveway like an emerald choke collar. But the untrimmed bushes now appeared spikey and just seemed to taunt him. Soon the mower rounded the corner to work this side of the church. The engine thundered in the canyon between the two buildings, where fumes lingered in the shimmering ripples of heat rising up from the concrete.

Dawit waved to Elliot, fellow toilers in the sun, the good cheer of camaraderie, except, Elliot noted, he was toiling in the shade of the oaks on the church side of the driveway while Elliot got nothing but the hot sun beating down on him, with the siding and pavement convecting the heat and fumes into a stifling, invisible cloud.

Elliot wagged a half-wave and went back to his task.

The heat was inescapable, and he found it hard to breath. Plus the bending over was getting to his back, which pained him each time he stood up and bent over again. He felt clumsy and fat and sweaty, and could think of nothing but the noise as it swept over him in waves with each pass of the mower. Sweat dripped from his brow and rolled down his arms. The clipper handles became slippery and the shrubs more awkward to reach. His hands shook as he clipped. He wanted only to sit and rest but suddenly didn't think he could make it to the breezeway steps. He lost focus with the clipper and snipped into the air near the shrubs.

Seemed like the engine finally went off, but the fumes lingered, enveloping him.

He heard footsteps.

—Elliot! You all right?

Hands grabbed and pulled at him.

—Elliot? Can you stand?

The voice was light; it danced over the consonants; it fluttered through the vowels. It was a bird come from the feeder: it twittered, it chirped.

But the hands were strong, powerful; they elevated him. He felt lighter than he had in years.

⁓⁓⁓

KIM FLICKED A FINGER on the crystal punch bowl as she passed through the dining room, leaving a single note ringing behind her.

In the kitchen, Aunt Jo was putting away groceries.

—Don't do that, she said. Elliot's resting.

Kim looked into the parlor. His hair sprouted over the back of the club chair like a clump of gray weeds.

The sexton Dawit said he'd brought Elliot inside after he got faint in the heat. Said he'd been trimming the shrubs, which amazed

157

Jo and Nick. Elliot refused to go to the hospital, had even taken a sharp tone, which surprised them even more, but Nick finally got him to compromise on a doctor appointment in the morning.

Kim squinched her shoulders oops and let the door close behind her.

Aunt Jo told Uncle Nick, —The light's blinking on the message machine. Check who called. And then she whispered, —He was supposed to be inside minding the phone. What was he doing out there in that heat?

Nick shrugged dunno and opened the calendar book and played the messages.

—Well, we'll have a couple of rooms taken this weekend, he said.

—That's something. I remember those people, that last couple, from years ago… a wedding party.

—I'll call them after lunch.

Kim went around the counter and started poking through the grocery bags.

Aunt Jo said, —I'll make you something in a minute. Here, put these vegetables in the refrigerator.

As Kim took the bag and rattled open the veggie bin, Aunt J leaned over the uncle's shoulder and whispered, —He shouldn't go anywhere tonight.

—Doubt if we can stop him. It's his meeting night and then rehearsal. Hasn't missed his meeting in years.

Kim was supposed to go to rehearsal tonight with Uncle Elliot, too, and didn't want to miss it.

Nick said, —They want 'Overland' again.

—Maybe they liked it better than I thought.

—I was going to paint that bathroom this week. Some peeling in the corners. Don't know if it'll be ready. Lemme go take a look and

I'll figure out what to do before I call.

When he left, Aunt Jo frowned at Kim.

They'd already covered dinging the punch bowl, so now what?

—You need to wear more than that, she said.

—More than what?

—You know what I'm talking about. That top's not enough.

Kim groaned. —It's a pain, and I hate wearing it! And besides it's hot today and I don't need it yet.

—And that's too loose by itself.

Kim looked down at her blouse. Nothing showed. She barely poked dents in front, which got lost in the folds anyway. The thing was hot and stupid, wrapping yourself up with straps and clips and whatever. She was so happy to get home and take it off, couldn't get upstairs fast enough.

—Why do we have to wear clothes at all when it's hot? Why couldn't I just go around naked, if I want? What's wrong with that?

—In a perfect world, not a thing, but that's not the world we live in.

—Maybe we should act like it's a perfect world and that's what it would be.

—Some days you make my head spin, Kimmy. It just makes people uncomfortable is why.

—Well, that's on them.

For the jillionth time Jo stifled the temptation to mutter how like her mother she was – smart and willful, and more given to her instincts than her brains, or no, maybe it was just that she reasoned her way through things so quickly that it just seemed that way sometimes. She'd work out the whole argument and all you were left with was what she wanted minus the part where you discussed it. Jo continually found herself in these circular arguments with Kimmy. She worried about whether this stubbornness would morph into other behaviors, and whether Kimmy had inherited any of the traits that led Anna to end up with *him*. Maybe in some unconscious, bizarrely psychological inverse way she was leading Kimmy down the same deadly path.

Jo blamed herself for everything – the fights at school, the fire last summer in the dry brush down near the storm tunnel in the park. The fire department had to be called, sheriff's deputies appeared at the front door, and Jo knew – *knew!* – that Kimmy'd been put up to it by those boys daring her, which was another thing, always playing with boys. She never seemed to get along with girls. She'd never had a girl as a friend, at least never more than a day or two. And then there was the time she ran away and the police (it was an off-duty Hawkings city cop this time) found her all the way out on K-29 in the middle of the night riding her bike to Anna's house in Sunburg, even though she'd never been there and had no idea where it was or how far, only that she thought it was somewhere in the direction she'd been headed, which was north.

But Jo's lowest moment came on the day the mystery of the room thefts was solved. Of course, she didn't know they were thefts then. Just every so often guests would say they'd mislaid something. Would Jo please call if she happened to find a pendant, a cell phone, a set of rosary beads? She and Nick searched drawers, seat cushions, cabinets. They argued with one couple, who claimed things had been moved around in their room and someone had been in there. (That one got so nasty that Nick actually raised his voice.) The first time or two, Jo thought other guests might be the thieves. After several more incidents, she suspected Flann.

But then, while she was cleaning Kimmy's room one afternoon, sorting clothes and pulling things out of the closet for Goodwill, she found the make-up case, and inside the complete inventory of every item any guest had ever asked about, and some they hadn't — some still in store packaging, too. Odd things: one of those 'page-up' paper holders that they sell at the check-out counter in the office supply store, a potato peeler, a drawer handle in a plastic bag from the hardware store. What could she have wanted with these things? Why would she take them?

Jo sat on her bedroom carpet, cross-legged, flushed with warmth and shame and fear — but fear of what she didn't know, only that the sensation was familiar, the same one she often felt in the weeks and months after Anna died, as if she was whirling through some blinding and deafening storm and had no idea where she was or if a tree limb or brick might suddenly fly out of nowhere and knock her dead. This *thing*, this finding, it seemed to go to the center of every-thing — their home, their life. Every search they'd made for a 'mislaid' item, every conversation or phone call they'd had about one — they all ran through her imagination like so many slow-motion replays. She felt empty, drained; she wondered what else she had to give. She sat on the floor for most of an hour poking through the stuff, examining each item, wondering which stores things came from, recalling which guests belonged to what, wondering if she should call them now, what she would say, and mostly what lay behind all this, what troubling, disturbing motive Kimmy had for doing this, and what comfort she found in it. None of these items had ever appeared anywhere. So far as Jo knew, Kimmy'd never used them, wore them, played with them. That bracelet, the one the lady gave her — that was here; it was part of this story too. She'd stolen it; it wasn't a gift; it was a… what? a reprimand? Or no, it *was* a gift, an offering, a remembrance of some sort. That's what the woman said

– that Kimmy'd remember her. The woman knew something then
that Jo still didn't understand, for if she did maybe this wouldn't have
happened. She wanted to call that woman, invite her back, give her
a free weekend, talk to her for hours, send Kimmy off with her for
a picnic, an outing; they'd all go. In just that brief encounter the
woman had understood Kimmy in ways Jo still did not.

She was shaken for days afterwards. She mistrusted Kimmy –
and vilified herself for that too. Nick said, predictably, that she was
making too much of it, but she knew she wasn't because it went to
the heart of something very troubling, but she didn't know what.
It was like an immense mathematical problem that Jo hadn't a clue
how to solve because she didn't even know what the symbols meant,
so she couldn't decipher the question. Jo feared a blow-up when she
and Nick confronted Kimmy with the stolen items, but the opposite
happened. She shut down, froze, as blank-faced as a statue. Jo found
herself doing all the talking, even though all she wanted was to get
Kimmy to open up and tell her why she'd done this. But she just
sat and stared at the make-up case and items on the table and said
almost nothing.

—I dunno.

—Just cause.

Shrug.

Jo sent her to her room until dinner, less as punishment than so
she herself could recover from all that raged within her.

—It might have cost us the business, she told Nick. What if someone had put it on the internet?

And then she wondered if maybe someone had. So that's what
she did for the rest of the day instead of chores and fixing dinner –
search the internet to see if guests had put the word out to lock up

your valuables if you visit Monarch House. But none had, and they all gloomily ate packaged mac & cheese for dinner that night, with Kimmy stirring patterns in her bowl until it was time to clear the dishes.

The thefts stopped after that, Jo thought. She couldn't be sure, but she wasn't bashful about searching Kimmy's room while she was at school. Guests hadn't mislaid anything lately. Jo kept a close eye on her at the store, and told Nick to also, but she also didn't believe that was why she'd stopped stealing things, if indeed she had. It seemed more like she'd outgrown it or just passed through it, and what worried Jo now was whether that impulse would mutate into some other behavior that hadn't shown itself yet – like going around naked.

—At least put on something more than that, Jo said. Your Chiefs shirt's clean. Go put that on.

—I will in a minute, Kim said.

The concession didn't escape Kim. She could skip the bra if she put on the red T-shirt. Sometimes that's how you win – you take what you want first, then make others try to win back pieces of it, like checkers, at the end of the game, when each player starts trying to win kings with the few pieces they have left. It's a new game then.

—You'll do it now, Aunt Jo said firmly, as she washed her hands.

Kim watched her without moving.

Aunt Jo took cold cuts out of the refrigerator. —What do you want for lunch?

Elliot appeared in the kitchen door. —Did I hear lunch?

—Just cheese, Kim said.

—I got chicken and roast beef.

—Just cheese, Kim repeated.

Elliot laughed. —You keep forgetting, Jo. She's a vegan now.

Kim pursed her lips and said flatly, —Those are dead animals in those bags. Maybe you should be there when they die if you're gonna eat them.

Jo shrugged. —Fine, cheese. And now, stopping in mid-stride between the refrigerator and counter, she added, —I'll make that while you change.

Kim stared back, but before she could draw the aunt into a staring showdown, Elliot said, —Well, maybe Kimmy's right, so I'll have a cheese sandwich too. Are there any of those bread 'n butter pickles left? They're great on a cheese sandwich. Don't you think so? he asked Kimmy.

Who scrunched her nose and went upstairs satisfied. She'd made Aunt Jo's head spin. She looked down at her breasts before she dressed and prodded them. They seemed such paltry things to have such power, like walking into a room shirtless was such a big deal. Why should it be? What'd it matter? They were just skin, flesh, little nipples to feed a baby with someday. Which made her shiver to think of. People got so weird about them, as if there weren't better things to think about, as if eating dead animals was less important.

⁓

Coffee grounds dusted the countertop with each pass of the scoop from the can to the filter. Tremors were worse when his arms were still. They often felt like someone else's. Motion helped. Doing things. Making coffee.

Elliot thought about what he'd say tonight as others shuffled about and got settled at the scarred folding tables they'd pushed together to form one big table with barely enough room to squeeze around it.

Down here, down the concrete stairwell on the side of the building and then across a cavernous hallway to the meeting room, it was always the same time of day: night. Didn't matter how bright and sunny it might be outdoors. The room was windowless and barren. The fluorescent overhead lights gave the place an antiseptic feel, like a treatment room at the doctor's office. The faux-mahogany wallboard had warped, negating even the illusion of real wood. A few outdated posters gave the room some color. One was for a storyteller's services at birthday parties. Elliot had briefly considered taking up something like that for a few extra dollars, but he didn't mostly because it would mean that much more driving for Jo and Nick getting him around – hardly cover the gas. The room's décor fell well short of cheery.

Elliot still had rehearsal after the meeting. The director knew he came late on Wednesdays, and that's just how it was. Next week were run-throughs, tech rehearsal, dress rehearsal, and then the new play opened. But right now he was here and not much else mattered.

Metal folding chairs scraped and clanked as more people appeared. Big group tonight, looked like. The inside seats at the table were for newbies. Couldn't escape once they got seated, the joke was. Lame, sometimes just not funny, but it persisted. The ranking wasn't so much a formal thing as an unspoken tradition. The uninitiated would plop themselves at the end of the table in front of the percolator – nearest the back of the room, that is – until someone said in a genial but clear way, devoid of any lilt that might sound like a suggestion, let's slide down so everyone can get in, and he or she would (maybe a little intimidated that someone had noticed them after all, that they'd indeed managed to attract attention though they wanted at all costs to avoid just that). Elliot and Leo and a couple of others took up the end seats – long-time members, long-time drunks with years of sobriety accumulated among them but the tales of their personal tragedies encrusted on drooping jowls and sagging eye bags and dried skin and patches of whiskers missed shaving, and for Lydia, the only woman end-seater, the dyed hair and smoker's-pallor beneath a coating of beige pancake makeup. Leo bypassed the genial part when he delivered the let's-slide-in message. Genial was not a word that came to mind when you thought of Leo.

They shared a look, did these end-seaters, a proprietary look – Elliot was in charge of the coffee, Lydia brought the collection box for coffee supplies, and Leo and a couple of others fetched chairs and arranged tables — so yes, proprietary – they got things done, made the meeting happen, as it were – but that was only on the surface of why they looked as they did – sincere, grim, lacking any sense of irony, though not immune to humor. What they wanted, what they expected, what they hoped for was to hear a story that was authentic, sincere, true – truthful; that's what gave them that expectant and proprietary look. They passed no judgment on misdeeds, never held speakers in censure for what they might've done while they were drunk. They'd heard it all, and they'd done a lot of it themselves. No, what they would judge was the tale's authenticity – and not whether *they* believed it, but whether the teller did, the drunk who now sat sober at the big table, squeezed in with the others, taking his or her turn, telling his or her tale of a night (night*s*? weeks, months, years?) in jail; a car wreck (couldn't call them *accidents* here, could you?); a house fire; of violence done to spouses and children; of conniving to borrow or steal money from loved ones (or anyone); of ruined holidays, wasted savings, lost jobs and homes, and so the litany went, a catalogue of regret and sorrow and death, of loss and despair. But here they were, newcomers and not-so-new alike, and all that mattered to the Elliot & co. was truth, and they were greedy for it. The truth was always a story you wanted to hear. You gained redemption from hearing it, from living the story with the teller, from giving him or her an audience for the tale. What story was complete without a listener? That storyteller whose poster hung on the wall could probably learn something about telling stories if he sat through few sessions here. Who knows? Maybe he was here.

Elliot hadn't spoken in some time. The regulars knew him, knew his story, knew they could find him on late-night TV, had long gotten over the novelty of having a celebrity among them. To the younger people he was just another old guy who sat by the coffee pot. He might have spoken more often but the sameness of his stories, and even his own voice, had begun to bore him. Too, he found he got more from hearing others than from talking himself. Listening, he'd decided, was a lost art in America, where everyone seemed to be starring in the movie of their own lives. No, he mostly preferred listening these days. It was a trait that made him a lot of friends among the regulars. Funny how that is, he'd noticed, the less you say, the more people like you.

He wondered, too, if whatever he did have to say might not be sufficiently on topic. Whole bunch of things on his mind lately that weren't about drinking at all. In fact, some days, for reasons he could not explain, he didn't feel any more urge to have a drink than he did to eat a poison ivy salad. Weird, but three-four days after a meeting, he'd realize an entire day had passed in which he hadn't given booze a thought. Then when something did prompt it, like a TV commercial or seeing a guest with a glass of wine, he'd think, oh yeah, just remembered, slipped my mind. *I am an alcoholic.* He'd whisper those words to himself and add, *Must not forget.*

He found it difficult to express the pleasure he'd discovered in being sober and then forgetting that he was *sober* without sounding, well, maudlin, or worse, preachy. He took nothing for granted. He was here. He wanted to be here. He believed it was, in fact, vital to be here – and he'd keep coming back, as they said (a lot). Plus he had friends here, real friends, people he valued – the people he sat beside in front of the percolator. And plus too, he made new friends all the time. But it wasn't like he woke up every morning celebrating his new life of sobriety either. His life was anything but new – he was old, and now had Parkinson's (he'd known it long before his spell this morning), and doing things was an effort, like going to the bathroom, which was a chore, a pain, an event. Rather he felt something more subtle, more passive, less easy to express. A calmness, an understanding. He didn't know anything about Zen, but he thought maybe this was what it was all about, this sense of being in touch with so much that surrounded him, with the immediacy and presence of all the varying life forms, animal, plant, and human bound together in some organic way that he couldn't define or describe or fully understand, but that had motivated him, without even knowing how or when the urge first came upon him, to pick up trash when he was out walking and to lament whatever damage anyone did to the whole, whether by war or pollution or throwing a sandwich wrapper out a car window or by just plain being generally unpleasant. Maybe he'd been numb or stoned for so long that this was what you were supposed to feel when you weren't. How could you be sober and think that invading another country or dumping poison into a river were good things to do? Such thoughts didn't easily lend themselves to the kind of stories most people told or expected to hear at these meetings.

Also, much of what was on his mind was not, he believed, his to share – even in the confidence of a place like this. Jo and Nick didn't talk finances with him, but it was plain that things were getting tight. Didn't take an accountant to notice how slow business was most weekends. Jo was often glum, quiet, worried. Nick was the same as always, but he did more with less, took on jobs he might've had people do in the past, like replacing a furnace motor – some job that was, but he did it, you had to give him that. He'd even mentioned working part-time, see if maybe his old company might want him back for some consulting work. They still drove the same car, too, though it was ten years old and had over a hundred thousand miles on it. So Elliot worried too, silently, privately, along with them, so to speak, the way others might pray.

And there was Flann, who was always in one kind of trouble or another, nothing but grief for Jo, but now, this time, he'd gotten into something that might stick, might indeed change his life, and it was for sure what worried Jo above all else these days. He'd been picked up with one of his friends for dealing small quantities of meth and reefer to twelve-thirteen-year-old kids. Bad enough, very bad indeed, but – and this was one of those things that made you thunk yourself on the head when you heard it – they were just around the corner from an elementary school. Couldn't see the school from where they'd parked on a quiet neighborhood street in a new subdivision out at the western edge of town. The school was on the next block, but still inside the one-thousand-foot zone where dealing drugs got elevated to a felony charge. Flann claimed he didn't even know the school was there and they weren't even selling to the kiddies from *that* school – just (as if this explained everything!) *this* (where they'd parked) was where the *middle-school* school bus dropped off the *middle schoolers* from the *middle school!* Yes, of course, that explained everything. Flann and his buddy were the only car on the street, a car that none of the old folks peeking out from behind their curtains or mothers standing on front porches waiting for their kids recognized, though they had noticed how it appeared with some regularity in the afternoon, and how kids would stop by this shady looking vehicle and not so discreetly stuff into their pockets and backpacks the recycled Marlboro cigarette boxes (which were *red* and *white*, and easily seen at the distance of a front porch or parted curtain) that Flann & friend had repackaged with a handful each of doobies or a few teenas of crank. Until one afternoon when the neighborhood came alive with a chorus of unearthly, high-decibel whirrings and bleepings, and four cars converged on the stunned twelve-year-old standing at the driver's window of Flann's white Ford Escort with two very agitated seventeen-year-olds inside. They were in deep, deep shit, Flann & friend were. Jo and Nick couldn't come up with the cash to bail him out for two days. The kids could get a couple of years in juvey – or possibly adult. Or maybe, just maybe, if they were really, really lucky on which judge caught their docket number, they might end up on some kind of probation along with a menu of restrictions that included household confinement and drug education classes. But not guilty was not an option. That's what Jo said the lawyer said. Poor Jo and Nick! The court dates and lawyer appointments went on for months, prolonging their agonies of doubt and worry, while he – in the kind of sublime oblivion you could only account to a shortage of brain cells or just being seventeen – blamed everyone else for his troubles because no one seemed to get that he wasn't selling dope to the little kiddies, *only the older ones*.

Monarch House was swirling in a vortex of troubles that in some way, Elliot believed, began elsewhere, maybe in the fear that spread outward from the attacks last fall and now manifested itself in the chip-on-the-shoulder way people displayed their patriotism these days, if patriotism was even the right word for it, or the imminent war, or the roiling stock market, or the idea (which Elliot believed even affected doubters despite their protests to the contrary) that the warming of the planet and its dire implications for civilization had led to a subconscious form of collective despair that was playing itself out in unsavory ways. Calamity seemed to be everywhere, and Elliot thought it was having its effect on them, direct or otherwise, while the family waded through its private troubles as if they had little to do with the outside world – the slowdown in business yes, maybe, some, but all the rest of it too, for sure, he thought.

Of course, the fog of sorrow that brought Kimmy to them had never fully lifted, and as Jo feared, it only thickened when the girl's paternal grandparents came back into the picture several years ago – living reminders of who she was and who her father was, and still was, and how her mother had died. Now, lately, she was asking more questions about him, at once both curious and angry – and it was the anger that worried Jo the most, that Kimmy would grow up, was growing up, with a festering hatred for him that would only serve to fuel her curiosity in a vicious feedback loop that would in turn nourish more hatred and leave her to grow up bitter. So Jo limited her contact with the grandparents to short, infrequent visits to bring a Christmas or birthday gift, but that was never enough for Nancy, and you could see, never would be. Her solicitude betrayed itself in the measured way she spoke, as if her sentences had been rehearsed, as if she were transforming herself into some caricature of the kind of people she thought Jo and Nick were – trendy suburbanites who played golf on weekends and drank sparkling water and exotic coffees. Of course, they were nothing like that, and Nancy's charade came off heavily, badly, only serving to underscore her resentment. She could barely conceal her curiosity about small evidences of their slowing business – that the house seemed quiet today or whether Jo had a big wedding party coming up. And then the grandfather, Phil, had let slip to Elliot how Nancy hoped she'd be able to take Kimmy to visit *her father* (Phil's words), sometime, *when the time was right*, he added with a confidential nod, the right time being whenever Jo could be sold on it. So there it was, in front of Elliot, an agenda, *the* agenda. Phil was about the same age as Elliot. They always seemed to wind up sitting together in the way old men did, left to chatter in desultory ways about the weather, the downturn in the economy, the decline of civilization. Elliot tried to limit their talk to the little they might agree on, but there were almost nothing. Phil's off-handed slurs about Muslims, blacks, immigrants, anyone different from him, made Elliot bristle, but he let them pass – for Jo and Nick's sake, for Kimmy's.

Elliot had come to his own conclusion – unspoken, unshared, and based on little more than instinct – that Kimmy had seen more the day Anna died than she remembered, or shared, at least. He'd heard a news report recently about a woman who could remember everything in her life. Everything, every detail. Name a random date and she could take you through what she did, said, ate for breakfast-lunch-and-dinner, wore to school (or to work or the movies), what songs played on the radio that day, and what the newspaper said, if she was old enough to read because she could even recall in the same detail everything before then, back to crawling on the carpet as a baby. So he wondered about all that might be going on inside a being so slight, so young.

He snapped the top on the coffee maker. He liked that they used an old two-gallon percolator, a clanky beast, one of those tall, aluminum cylinders that every church basement seemed to have. The red light glowed reassuringly when he hit the button, and just as the first burps of coffee spurted into the glass cap, he slid into his chair at the end of the table. The coffee smelled warm and pure; its burbling offered a comforting ambience; without it, without the ritual of making it and enjoying its smell and the percolator's rhythmic burps, how much harder would all this be? It was the incense and Gregorian chant of this little room.

A couple of new faces had appeared tonight. A man about Nick's age, but unlike most of this group, dressed in a fitted suit that couldn't have run less than a grand. Elliot thought he recognized him: the father of one of those brats Kimmy'd had run-ins with years ago. He looked like he'd unravel at a touch.

The chair beside Elliot squealed as Leo settled in. He was Elliot's sponsor, a retired soldier whose drooping lips and squinting eyes were fixed in a permanent look of suspicion. His white hair was buzz-cut on the sides and flat on top, and you could not converse with him for five minutes without learning that he'd been a 'full-bird' colonel in the Army with ten thousand men ready jump at the snap of his fingers. He and Elliot were as different as two people could be, yet in the years since Elliot moved to Hawkings and joined this AA group, they'd become so close they could communicate in eyebrow flickers and gestures that bordered on telepathy. Leo thought Elliot was a fool to believe in global warming and never failed to point out the error of his ways when temps dropped below freezing, while Elliot liked to ask Leo if the nation had acquired enough nuclear weapons yet to blow up the solar system. But they both admired Leo's hero, Gen. George S. Patton, though in their own ways. Leo believed no general in modern history compared to Patton for courage and vision, while Elliot's admiration was directed to George C. Scott's movie portrayal of the general and his regret that he'd never played such a role.

Leo worked an unlit Cohiba Corona Especiale around his cheek like a ruminating cow and winked at Elliot as he sat down. Whenever someone asked him how he managed to buy Cuban cigars, he'd take the thirty-dollar log from his mouth and study it and grin and say he'd gotten his addictions down to this little vegetable product and Elliot's coffee and he figured that was good enough to ride out the last of his days, and that was all the answer they got.

After Lydia passed one of Leo's old cigar boxes around for the coffee fund and the meeting times were announced (mostly for the benefit of newbies), Leo whispered, —We ain't heard from you in a while, Elliot.

To which Elliot shrugged, —Maybe next time. Couple others may have something to say tonight.

Leo snarled and nodded, a quick, approving jerk of his head, as if Elliot had just told him the troops were ready for inspection.

—⁓—

UNCLE E WAS ALREADY here, at the theater. Despite Jo and Nick's protests, he'd walked himself to his AA meeting, and then it was two blocks over to the theater. Said he was fine and he'd walk just like he did every night when it wasn't raining or snowing. He was always saying that he liked how he could walk himself most places since he moved here. He walked everywhere. The library, the bank, his meeting, now the theater. Where else did you need to go? he'd ask Kim, as if she was the only one who might know.

He'd stayed with the theater group ever since his first role as Scrooge, and Aunt Jo was glad of it, and glad too, she said, that all the walking kept him healthy, and he even looked a little thinner than he used to, she said, though Uncle E said he worried that if he got too thin they'd only cast him in crowd scenes or something because

174

being paunchy was part of his character. Said he'd've been out of work years ago if he trimmed down and got all svelte and such. That was his word, *svelte*, which was a cool word. Aunt Jo laughed and said she wouldn't go that far. —*Svelte!* she snickered.

The rehearsal was already going on when Kim arrived, so she stepped lightly as she climbed the narrow wooden staircase to the balcony, which was empty, but the floorboards creaked as she shuffled alongside the balustrade, and so did the seat when she settled on its thin, cracked leather. The place was old and hollow, and every sound carried and echoed. The balcony seemed to groan with fatigue. She imagined all the people who'd sat up here for who knows how many years from back in the day. She wondered if it'd just come crashing down sometime when it was full of people all clomping around up here. That'd be something.

On stage, Uncle E read his lines from the script and sometimes ignored it when he knew them. His hand shook holding the book.

The director kept interrupting and telling them go this way and that, pick up an umbrella or a cup here and leave it over there. The interruptions bothered one of the actresses. She huffed when the director stopped them

Kim helped Uncle E with his lines at home. She'd learned all of the huffy actress's lines and whispered along as the actress read from her script.

Finally the director said the techs needed the stage, and the rehearsal broke.

She looked for Uncle E to wave, but he just went off into the wings without looking up, like he'd forgotten she was coming.

Voices burbled backstage. Work lights in the wings and rafters threw weird shadows on the unfinished set and gave it a skeletal look.

Soon a girl in the play came upstairs and said hey and sat right beside her even though the whole balcony was empty except for Kim.

—How come you're up here all by yourself? she said.

Kim shrugged I dunno and watched the empty stage.

She was a couple of years older than Kim and went to Flann's school. She played the youngest daughter. Her character ballet danced everywhere, even to answer the doorbell or set the dinner table. Right now, for rehearsal, the girl wore bright yellow tights, a paisley mini skirt, and a parti-colored sweatshirt with rhinestones. She told Kim the mini skirt was her Mom's from back in the day. —Helps me get into character, she added. My real costume is a tutu, but I was thinking I'd wear something with it, you know, to brighten it up, like a scarf or a beret or something, maybe both. The whole family's supposed to be a little weird, so that's what I'd do, or her, you know, my character. I get myself mixed up with her sometimes.

Kim didn't think she really got herself mixed up. She sounded more like she wanted to sound as if she did, but whatever. The girl's flighty conversation and bizarre clothes did not conceal a familiar curiosity. The girl knew about her, or thought she did, or had picked up fragments of gossip. Some kids'd just come out and ask if her daddy was in jail, and why, and others, probably like this girl, would nose around until they could bring it up. Even Kim just saying Aunt Jo or Uncle Nick instead of Mom or Dad in front of others made them wonder what the deal was.

The girl chattered – gossip about the cast, how bitchy the huffy actress was, the director was gay, so forth. She said her name was Doreen, but call her Dory, and she knew Kim's brother in school, which Kim thought might be a phony cue for her to say he's not my brother and then next thing it'd be a dozen more questions, so Kim just nodded and let Dory figure that one out on her own.

As one of the tech guys passed across the stage, Dory leaned close to Kim and whispered, —You see him, that guy with the hat and mustache?

Kim nodded.

The man was gathering up a length of lighting cable like a lasso. His jeans looked about two sizes too large, and he wore a hat with a colorful band and feather in it. Kim liked the hat.

—He's crazy, Dory said. Totally.

Kim knew she was supposed to ask why he was crazy, but she just waited.

—You can ask Elliot, Dory said. One night? we were coming in for rehearsal and you shoulda seen it. I was like coming around front from the parking lot? and a couple of the others had stopped and were looking up and I was like whatever, and first I thought it was the sunset? which was all orange and streaky, but they were all looking the other way from the sunset, and then Ginny nudged me and pointed up at... you know the tower out front, the bell tower? he was like up there, and I couldn't believe it cause he was *standing* on the ledge outside the tower, and I was like how'd he even get out there or something, cause you gotta climb up through the rafters and there's no bell up there any more and omigod there's bird shit everywhere cause I was up on the platform where you pull the bell rope? and it was gross, but he was like *way* up, on the outside, not even holding on to anything but just standing like you would for the national anthem or whatever and looking off at the sunset, and I was like omigod, and nobody said a word or called him or whatever. Maybe they were afraid they'd frighten him, and somebody whispered, 'Is he gonna jump?' but I was like don't even say that and nobody answered and then he turned around without even looking down like he didn't even notice all of us down below watching him? and then he went inside the tower and disappeared and next thing I saw him backstage and I said, 'What were you doing out there, Lufkin?' That's what everyone calls him is Lufkin, but it's not his name but just he always wears this tape measure that says Lufkin so they call him Lufkin, and he was like whatever. Just shrugs and says, 'Watching the sun go down. Dja see it?' And I was like nooo, cause I was watching you, but I just said yeah and he said, 'Yeah, beautiful night,' and goes back to whatever. Can you believe that?

Kim could… believe that, and she thought it was cool, too. She pictured herself standing out on the steeple ledge and watching the sun set and seeing all the rooftops and treetops and buildings and all, and she wanted to go up there too. Maybe Lufkin would take her. Aunt J would have a shit fit, but she wouldn't have to know.

⁓

KIM LUGGED THE TWO big, heavy bags up the stairs and down the hall and through the doorway and parked them on the carpet in the middle of the room.

The woman said call her Alice and said she remembered Kim from a long time ago when she was little and did Kim remember her. Which Kim said no, even though she did, and even remembered soaking the little girl at the pond too, but the woman Alice went on like she'd said yes.

She said her granddaughter was the same age as Kim and did she remember her? surely she must recall them… playing (she seemed to search for the word)… at the pond? did Kim remember that?

Unh-huh.

Well, anyway, her granddaughter was learning baton twirling and now she had a little sister the same age as Kim and her granddaughter were back then, last time she was here, the woman Alice. Was Kimmy sure she didn't remember?

Headshake.

Kim waited, wondering if she'd get a tip, but the woman wandered about the room, checking out pictures and knick-knacks and such, and saying, oh, it's still here, and I remember this, and we'll have to write something in the diary this time, do you still leave diaries in the room? (nod) you do!? how delightful! On this went until Kim finally made it out the door, tipless.

She passed the man on the stairs who said did you lug those bags up here all by yourself and she said yup and thought maybe he'd tip her, but he didn't, but when she got to the bottom of the stairs he leaned over the bannister and said thanks and she said no problem without looking back.

Aunt Jo was looking at her computer in the kitchen. She asked if Kim got a tip and when Kim said no, she shook her head and snorted like she did when somebody did something foolish.

THE ONLY OTHER GUESTS for this weekend cancelled, so it was just these two. They ordered appetizers and made their own drinks in the parlor and were disappointed to learn they were the only guests, so they watched the news on TV.

Alice told Jo – confidentially, just between them – that it was her idea to stay here. They were here for a conference in Kansas City, but she didn't want to be stuck in a downtown hotel where she'd run into her husband's colleagues (they were all doctors) or, even worse, their wives, every time she stepped into the elevator.

—You can't imagine, she said, even more confidentially, how obnoxious some of them are.

Jo inferred that her husband did not want to stay at Monarch House, but she cared less about their motives than having a room occupied. Maybe they'd refer another wedding. Jo treated the woman's confidences as if they were old friends from her last visit six years ago. Her husband seemed pleased that the rooms had TVs now, which they had for quite a while, but he said it as if discovering that the place had finally gotten electricity and running water.

Jo could imagine…

※

WITH JUST THE TWO of them here, the sole guests in this big house, and for the *whole weekend*, Alice now felt conspicuous, embarrassed even. Certainly so for trying to make Jo her confidante after a couple of drinks. *Obnoxious*? Really? How awful she must sound! Obviously things weren't well here. Few guests. Well, just them – and on just the kind of autumn weekend when you'd expect people to go off to a place like this for a couple of days. How quiet this big house was. And you could see that things were… not run-down, but worn. The carpets and furniture showed wear; the bathroom fixtures were aging; the walkway had cracks. Oh, everything was neat, clean, tidy – but that was just it: how much more work it must be to keep up the old, keep it fresh, make it new, even if it was obvious that things were anything but new – and not in a quaint, charming, B&B kind of way either. No, the effort showed through, which made the appearance of things all the more… sad, even pathetic.

This was all wrong. They shouldn't have come here. Alice should have just gone along and played the role she was supposed to play. She belonged at the hotel with the other wives, drinking their way through long lunches on the Plaza after they'd exhausted themselves shopping while their husbands dozed through their conference sessions until it was time to rouse themselves to go to the bar and then dress for the banquet. What caricatures they'd all become. How little had really changed.

And now… she felt like a curiosity. And transparent. She rambled and said ridiculous things as if to fill in the vacant space that surrounded her, them. As if to explain why they'd come here – maybe to conceal it. No, not maybe. Even Jim didn't really know.

Whatever she expected when she saw Kimmy, the encounter was less than that by far. Alice was just another guest to the girl, another set of bags to traipse up the stairs. The girl was a rail. What was it like to be that thin? Alice couldn't remember. Sticks for arms, long slender legs. She'd grown tall, too, much taller than April. She was nearly eye-to-eye with Alice. But the girl was cheerless. She didn't seem reticent so much as non-engaged. Observant – and probably smart – but disinterested. Alice had tried to open her up, make small talk, but she stood by, waiting to escape. Probably waiting for a tip – how could Jim be so thoughtless? No, how could *she*, Alice? She didn't even think of it. Jim always took care of those things.

But what had she expected from this child? Some greeting? recognition?

What a thing it was to be so forgotten, to fade into the haze of someone's past. Alice knew she was expecting too much. The girl was just a child then. What could they have possibly meant to her? How many people had come and gone over the years for a child living in the midst of a business like this, but too, what a unique way to live. That's what fascinated Alice – that you could have a life like this, that people lived lives that weren't predictable, expected. That they came into the world in ways that were so uncertain – and sometimes so tragic.

You could say the same for anyone, Alice supposed, but her own grandchild April was already so insulated that the girl couldn't imagine people living differently than her – nor could she empathize with anyone who did. Baton twirling!? Oh, could Alice ever open her mouth and say something that wasn't absurd or pretentious or just plain stupid – something that wouldn't leave her cringing a few hours later, even if she hadn't been drinking? April would become what she would become because Alice was what she was – and Jim, and Mattie, and all of them.

No, Alice belonged downtown at some expensive restaurant, paying exorbitant prices for daiquiris and crème brulez, treating the wait staff shabbily, surrounded by all her packages and shopping bags, the detritus of her life, ever floating in her wake, in the backwash of her days. Trying to be different, to be herself, always seemed to backfire, maybe because she wasn't really trying at all, she thought. Maybe she was just filling in the colors as she thought they'd be filled in for someone who really was different; maybe she was just acting as someone would act who was simply being herself.

She couldn't say for sure what had prompted her curiosity about this family. Maybe paging through one of Mattie's wedding albums. There was a photo of the Monarch House family and staff all lined up on the porch as the wedding began. Alice didn't even recall noticing them at the time. The photographer had caught them – and not even a set shot. Rather, from off to the side, as if they were posing for another camera – but there was no other camera. They weren't posing at all. They'd lined up at the porch railing in a way that struck Alice, after all these years, as stunningly sincere, making themselves participants rather than observers at a wedding in which they had no relation to the families. Giving themselves a stake in it – and even in the marriage, you could say, since they were now witnesses, since they too had joined the moment of heavy silence when the minister asked if anyone objected to this marriage (Alice wondered if she should have spoken up, if only to say, we have to stop living this way, perpetuating this emptiness, this vacuousness, for generation after generation, but of course, she never would have done such a thing, nor did it occur to her at the time) – and there they were, on the porch. The photo reminded Alice of some domestic drama she'd seen on PBS or somewhere.

Mattie, she recalled, had said, had told her there was something unusual about this family, something about the little girl, who wasn't the proprietors' natural child, but what? Years ago, of course, she'd never have found out. It would never have occurred to her to go to the library and look up such things, probe reels of newspaper microfilm for hours to find out whatever there was to learn. Snooping like that was simply too overt, too shameful, too much trouble. Just making such an effort meant admitting she was indeed a busybody with nothing better to do than spend her days poking into others' lives. And too, it would have been so public, so obvious, so blatant. Well, those were reasons enough to stay out of anyone's business. No, she never would have acted in such a way. But now?… type a few words into the search box… names… phrases… click through the pages of links that appear. Click open this one or that one. Oops, watch out for the weight loss ad, the find-your-lost-classmate ad, the male enhancement ad… back to the results page… and there were so, so many results, so many links.

Arriving here now, finding herself alone in Overland Trail with Kimmy, sharing gossip with Jo, Alice brimmed with information about the Pughs, the Odens, Elliot, even Ross's prison. She'd read news accounts of the murder, the trial, the appeal, even the custody battle, which had only included Kimmy's initials, not her name, but still, it had all become public. She'd read about Elliot's career and its disastrous end. She'd even found a shocking Web page posted by the girl's imprisoned father seeking women to come visit him – and the more she looked, the more she realized that there really were lonely women out there who were indeed stupid enough to do just that. Her first discoveries had left her so dazed that Jim asked that evening was something wrong, and she'd said no, just her Prempro prescription had expired – she was feeling a little flushed, she'd be fine, but wasn't it a bit warm in here?

Now, being here, in this place, confronted with the reality of the lives in which she'd submersed herself, she realized how tainted she was by what she knew. She could not betray it. A stray comment, an idle remark, and what would she look like? A stalker?

She meant no harm, even felt affection for these people. The old man had been kind to her when they last visited. He'd once been so successful and now he was bell-hopping bags up to guest rooms. And the child – what tragedy pervaded her life? What memories might she still carry even if she didn't remember sitting beside Alice at the breakfast bar or splashing April at the pond? Alice felt the weight of all she knew, the magnitude. Nothing like that had befallen her or anyone close to her, and in some perverse way she felt a gap in her life because of the absence of such tragedy.

She and Jim had been left to themselves by the fireplace. She felt ridiculous sitting here with enough appetizers for a dozen. Just them, Jim's tote bar, and all that food.

Finally, thankfully, it was time to leave for dinner.

He'd already had too much to be driving, but she didn't care. Let them die tonight. She would quietly neglect to fasten her seatbelt.

He wouldn't notice. He wouldn't care either.

Or if not that – more amusing, at least – maybe he'd catch a DUI. Oh, wouldn't that be fun? Yes, it was time to go. One more stuffed mushroom. Drain the glasses and leave them to be picked up and washed. Pack up the traveling bar. Time to go.

'A great storm of wind'

DORY SAID COOL YOU came we gotta paint some flats.

Kim didn't know what a flat was but Dory led her through the theater and out back to where they were all laid out on the grass while Uncle E went off to rehearse in a meeting room and Lufkin and the others hammered and clomped around on the stage, where the light pipes hung down to where they could work on them. The rafters were all lit up and someone was climbing around up there and they shouted back and forth.

The flats were like big blank picture canvases on wood frames, all of them white and in different sizes and some with openings for doors and windows. Dory said the dutchmen are finally dried, which… what? She showed Kim where strips of muslin coated in a glue mixture were laid over the seams between some of the flats and feathered at the edges so when they dried it looked like there was no seam at all.

They each got a paint bucket – sienna for Dory and ochre for Kim – and were told which flats to paint. Actors wandered about reciting lines; hammers pounded and the electric saw buzzed from inside. Traffic whooshed by distantly on Market Street. It was warm and bright, a perfect day for painting flats.

But the sky soon began to darken, and they had to work fast to move everything into the garage out behind the church where scenery was stored. Above them an ink blue ocean moiled and churned as if the sky had come alive. The clouds seemed close, and fast, like dark gray icebergs sweeping past on a strong current. Everyone hustled to get the flats moved, and none too soon.

The rain came all at once, not gradually. More like it was unleashed. The theater roof leaked, and they ran about with buckets and spread tarps over the seats. It was pretty fun, Kim thought, but the rehearsal was done and so was working on the set. Dory said Kim should come and help again and Kim said okay. The director said he hoped it didn't rain on opening night.

No question about walking home. Nick pulled up close to the side door in the minivan.

—Where's Elliot? he asked as Kimmy climbed in.

—On the phone, she said.

—Hunh, must be talking to Leo or one of his group buddies.

Elliot finally appeared and dashed for the car. The back door was easier, so he and Kim sat in back, soggy and grinning.

—Aunt Jo's gonna think I let you walk, after all, Uncle Nick said.

—I would! Kim said. Can I?

Uncle E laughed.

Rain continued through the evening. The pond flooded and the gutter drain pipes ran like fire hoses. Tree limbs cracked. The shutters on the barn windows flapped and blew off in the heavy winds. The table on the veranda went over with a metallic thunk. Kim wondered if the fish in the pond would swim off in the rapids running down the driveway and into the street. The rain pounded and thrummed the porch roof so loud you had to shout across the kitchen.

When the woman Alice and the man Jim arrived from their dinner, Uncle Nick and Aunt Jo waited in the breezeway with umbrellas and said leave the car where it was what was the difference no one was going anywhere tonight.

The woman Alice's dress was soaked, and her hair limp and wilted. Strands stuck to her face like vines, but she laughed as if it was the most fun she'd had all night.

Aunt J said would they like some cocoa or tea after they got dried off and changed.

—Oh tea! the woman Alice said. That would be lovely!

—What a drive! the man said to no one in particular, and then to his wife, —I'm having something stronger and then going to bed.

But she seemed thrilled about the storm and having tea and all. She came down alone and sat in the kitchen where everyone had gathered because the usual rules about who could go where didn't seem to apply. Besides, they were still the only guests in the house.

The hail spattered lightly at first, like a handful of pebbles tossed on the flagstones and porch steps, and then for a minute it seemed like it was done, but no, it wasn't, and here it came, like a truck-load of golf balls got dumped from way up high. Hailstones ripped through the trees, tearing away at the young leaves and branches and pounding the back porch roof, but no, that wasn't all either for now a huge one, big as an apple, came crashing through one of the veranda windows and startled everyone.

Outside, the barn windows shattered. The cars were getting pounded and dented and their windows broken. It felt like maybe the whole house would cave in, but the hail still didn't quit. Aunt Jo said what's that when some large black chunks of something tumbled down on the grass and veranda and Uncle Nick said it's the roof, those're shingles, and Flann said holy shit! right in front of the guest, and the Aunt swatted his arm and told him hush.

Uncle Nick looked pale – the same kind of pale he looked the day they took Boxer to the vet for the last time; it was the pale of too late to do anything, of running around trying to mop up here and pick up there won't matter and all you can do is watch until it's done, and now the woman Alice wasn't so delighted when she saw what was happening to the house. She sat solemnly at the breakfast bar and gripped the mug in both hands and smiled sorrowfully at Kim.

Hailstones bounced on the grass and driveway, knocking each other around like croquet balls. Across the way at the sexton's apartment the outside lights went on, and Aunt Jo said I hope they're okay.

When the hail finally let up, which it did almost as abruptly as it began, even though rain still fell in sheets, she told Uncle Nick go over and check on them, we'll get that glass inside.

He soon returned with Dawit and Ayana, who clutched her baby as if the hail might start up again and come right through the kitchen ceiling.

—They can't stay there tonight, Uncle Nick said. It's coming in through the roof.

Aunt Jo told Ayana, —Well, you'll stay here with us.

She led Ayana off through the dining room, and now Flann burst in through the back door with hailstones as big grapefruit in each hand and said, —Looka these! We gotta save 'em!

Everyone admired the glistening hailstones. He put them in the freezer, and Kim wanted to see Aunt Jo's face next time she opened it.

The hours that followed were a chaos of brooms, dustpans, rain jackets, doors opening and shutting, and trips to the sexton's apartment and the barn.

The chaos lasted days. Dawit's family moved into the room Kim once shared with her mother long ago, and the man and woman stayed on because their car had to be towed and repaired. They kept their room and the man Jim rented a car and returned to his practice in Wichita, but the woman Alice said she'd just as soon stay, and maybe she could help. Kim later heard the aunt grumbling to the uncle that she'd get more done without guests in the house, but she couldn't turn her out if she wanted to stay, could she?

Outside, the house and outbuilding were a patchwork of tarps – on the roof, on the siding, covering broken windows out on the barn, and over at the sexton's apartment.

Uncle Nick and Dawit went this way and that with ladders and tools.

Aunt Jo was always on the phone about repairs and insurance and such, but the storm was so big that everyone was trying to get the same stuff done at the same time and she was tired of punching through menus and listening to music loops while she waited to talked to someone, to a human, she always said.

Alice would ask what can I do to help while she sat alone at the dining room having breakfast.

—We're just fine, Jo would say, apologizing for the mess and whisking dirty dishes off the table.

Then Alice would go off for a walk while Jo made up her bed. She mostly stayed in her room during the day, watching television and talking on the phone. When she came out, she'd wander awkwardly around Nick up on the ladder or wedge past Jo on the stairs with a hamper of laundry, who greeted her cheerfully and asked did she need anything, and Alice said no, but did Jo need some help? and Jo said how nice she was to ask but everything was under control. She brightened at dinnertime, Alice did. She ate at Monarch House with the family because she had no car. Jo said to Nick, —Well, we can't just leave her to walk all the way into town and then home in the dark, can we?

Coming down to dinner in the kitchen, with Ayana chopping vegetables and Jo going this way and that with steaming pots and Kimmy setting the table and Flann and Elliot poking around for something to munch on and Nick washing his hands in the sink while Jo said don't wash here when I'm cooking and Dawit saying that he'd already washed his hands upstairs and how good they smelled because of the fine soap in that room – with all that activity humming about, that is, coming down to dinner in the kitchen was the highlight of her day.

But then at the table she felt that she had imposed, that she wasn't a guest in the true sense of the word at all, but only in the business sense – and 'guests' at bed and breakfast inns didn't eat dinner with the owners. So her discomfort led her to talk too much, as if it were up to her to fill the gaps in conversation, as if they were leaks in the fragile dingy in which she bobbed about, all by herself, the only 'guest' in the house this week. She chattered aimlessly; she completed others' sentences. She went on about the lake house Mattie and Glenn were building; about the trip she and Jim took to Montana because they had planned to go to Spain but what with the war and so forth, well, they went to Montana instead but the mountains looked so dry and she hoped it would snow next year so the glaciers would come back (Elliot pointed out that glaciers didn't come back in a year, but she didn't see why not); and of course, she couldn't leave out April's baton twirling… again? Oh, how could she have mentioned it yet again? Afterwards, later, drinking wine alone her in room with Jay Leno on TV, she sank into remorse as if it was a deep and familiar mattress. She wanted to ask Ayana about the hardships of her life, to ask Elliot about what had really become of him at the end of his career, to ask Jo about raising the orphaned child of her sister who had died so horribly, and most of all to visit with Kimmy about growing up in this marvelous house. But she couldn't. She wasn't part of this family and would never be. That's how families were – what it really meant – you had to share the experiences, suffer because of others to whom you belonged. You couldn't join; you couldn't hear about it. It was experience that mattered, not gossip. You had to have a stake in it.

On Friday Jim arrived near dinnertime. Alice wanted to go out to eat. That's what they'd planned, and she was already dressed. But Jo saw him coming in the main door before Alice and invited him to dinner too. *Just meatloaf, easy enough to put out another plate, already thought the lady was eating here.* Well, Jim had been driving for hours. He was beat. Sounded like just the thing. Upstairs, Alice fumed, but it was done.

—Maybe the old guy'll share a couple of tales from his glory days, Jim said brightly. He wasn't so beat after all.

Then down to the kitchen, tote bar in hand. Alice still wore her going-out-to-dinner dress, while everyone else wore whatever they had on all day to clean and repair the house.

Jim needed *something* before dinner, he announced to the kitchen. Who'd like to join him? He ceremoniously unsnapped the tote bar on the breakfast counter and began setting out its contents as if laying out the altar for Mass. Jo moved aside a colander of broccoli and the bowl of mashed potatoes and shook her head, no thanks, nothing for her. No? Nick? No? Elliot? Nothing for you? How about you folks? he asked, but Dawit and Ayana declined too. He tried explaining the custom to them, a little louder, in simple sentences, so they'd understand. Cocktails were a custom, he said, a tradition. Alice was melting in shame. Ayana responded simply, too, in her normal voice, that she didn't want to drink alcohol because she was nursing and didn't want the baby drinking it too. Dawit brushed Jim off cheerfully. No thanks, too much to do after dinner. So Alice and Jim drank their cocktails at the breakfast bar while everyone buzzed this way and that until dinner was served. Alice was quieter than usual. Was she feeling well? he whispered. Yes, fine, she said timidly, casting the slightest of smiles Kim's way, who was setting out water glasses and returned the slightest of frowns, the kind she reserved for intruders.

The car was finally ready, Jim said. The shop was open until noon tomorrow. He had to drop off the rental in the morning and they'd be on their way.

Over dinner he asked Nick about the house repairs and prodded Elliot to talk about his show business days.

—So who're some stars you knew… people I'd have heard of?

Alice winced.

Elliot studied Jim for a moment with an easy but penetrating look, as if suddenly they were alone at the table. Drunks do make it hard to care about them. Certainly this one did. Maybe somewhere inside this man was a person who might be worth offering a hand to help him out of the abyss into which he'd tumbled, but despite all the lofty thoughts and inspiring aphorisms Elliot and his friends shared on Wednesday nights, he was damned if he could find that person down there right now. And he knew too, that that person, if he was down there, would have to reach up before Elliot or anyone else could extend a hand, for he wouldn't take it, Elliot also knew, unless he went first. But there was this woman. She was stuck down there with him – too afraid to reach out, lacking even a shadow of her own to fear in this dark place. You could see her just fold herself up beside him. Sure, she'd been chatty all week, but Elliot knew that none of them really knew her, that she hadn't shared herself, that she was holding back, hiding behind all the chatter and boasting. In the few syllables Jim uttered, in the glance Elliot cast his way, he saw the whole history of these two people. The details were incidental. He'd lived it himself twice over in the course of two marriages, and compared to this little nothing moment, in ways that were worse by magnitudes.

What he could do for the woman right now, for everyone at the table, for that matter, was to humor this drunk, play the role in which he'd been cast by this arrogant and obnoxious director. Elliot had dealt with worse. Jim might be a doctor and think he walked on water, but Elliot had been pushed around by professional assholes who thought they could fly, who thought God spoke directly to them, if indeed they weren't confused about who was Who, as a few seemed to be. This was amateur hour, and Elliot was the only professional in the room.

So he stepped onstage. He told a tale of summer stock theater that went back some fifty-odd years. He took them on tour of the Straw-Hat Circuit up and down the East coast in the dreary and humid heat of July and August, through barn theaters and old churches and town halls. He told them how belligerently gnats treated sweaty actors in stage lights in a time when air conditioning was unheard of in these shaky old barns; how more than once the actors in his company had come upon snakes and rodents in the wings and dressing rooms. He shared a story of an old-time silent film actor in his company who couldn't remember his lines because he'd never had to learn lines until now, and about the actor's famous actress-wife, who befriended Elliot, who was then just a twenty-year-old kid trying to make his way among these seasoned professionals. She called Elliot continually, he said. The wall phone would light up in the green room and she'd ask for him. She was chummy, patronizing, even flirtatious, and Elliot was flattered. But she was also jealous. She wanted Elliot to give her reports on her memory-challenged, über-handsome, lecherous husband, who fucked every walk-on or apprentice or usherette in every town they played if a girl so much as smiled at him. Course, Elliot didn't say fucked at the dinner table, and he left out the time the actor was charged with statutory rape because some apprentices and usherettes and even walk-ons were not always old enough to be described as consenting adults – and not all of them were girls, so Elliot left that part out too. Oh, he colored his tale in the flavor of summer stock theater as Gene Kelly and Judy Garland portrayed it. It was the good-old summertime, with strawberry patches behind the barn theaters and stage managers smoking corncob pipes. It was the summer stock theater they wanted to believe in, not the one he lived, but it served the purpose. And it even had a hometown clincher he could throw in for the family's amusement, because, it turned out, this handsome silent-film statutory rapist actor had spent his boyhood right here in this very town of Hawkings before he'd gone on to moderate fame, immoderate fortune, forgotten lines (probably never learned in the first place), a wealthy and famous wife, and a trail of girls and a few boys who without doubt had lived their lives – and perhaps a few still did – with a bitter memory tucked away of their long-ago past in summer stock theater and their much-too-close brush with moderate fame.

Elliot finally took a bite of luke-warm meatloaf.

—Never heard of that guy, Jim said. You make any money doing that summer stock thing?

—If you look up summer stock in a thesaurus, Elliot said, you'll find the word poverty beside it.

Jim nodded a thought-as-much nod, drained his wine glass, and fetched the bottle from the counter.

—Anyone else?

Alice pushed her glass his way, and as he poured, she ventured, —I thought it was interesting, Elliot. Sometimes when I'm watching Leno or Katie, I just think that these people that come on… some of them… not you, Elliot… well, I just liked them better before they opened their mouths and I found out what they're really like…

—You think that's what they're really like… on Leno? Jim said.

—No, she said. It's just… oh, I don't know… they're just not the same.

Elliot had a mouthful. Someone else was going to have to ride in to save her this time. Jo began to speak up, but Alice wasn't finished.

—I see them in a movie and love their acting, and I think how deep it was, how moving, but then I hear them on a talk show and they talk about all these stupid things, and some of them, they just sound so shallow.

—Turns out they're human after all, Jim said.

—So that's what it is to be human, being shallow?

—Not what I said. His voice scraped across the table like a wood rasp.

That hung for a moment before Alice hissed, —Well, you should say what you mean.

A dense, foggy silence drifted in, which Jim broke with all the subtlety of a fog horn by pointing at Kim with his fork. —So what is that, that meatless patty thing?

—Oh, Jo said stiffly, it's a veggie mix I made up, beans mostly, some seasoning. Mix it up in the processor.

Kim, who had only poked at her food since the last round of attention came her way, now puffed up her cheeks and stared at the pepper mill.

—So is it good? Jim asked her.

She'd gone numb. Nick spoke up, —I like it…

But Alice cut him off, turning to Jim. —Let her be! You don't need to know what she's eating. Are you taking up vegetarian cooking now?

—It was just a question, he said. What's got your fur up?

—My fur's not up at all. You never care what's on your plate as long as it's meat and potatoes, so what's the difference? What is it you really want to know? You just don't want anyone being different from you. If Kimmy doesn't like meat, what's it to you?

Flann, it was plain, hadn't found dinner so entertaining in quite a long time, while Ayana and Dawit looked on as if watching a nature program about some exotic mating ritual in the animal kingdom.

Jo was ready to clear plates, even if everyone wasn't done.

Jim was flushed with booze and anger. Clearly Alice had poked at an exposed nerve only she knew how to locate. As Jo got up from her place, gathering dishes, Jim turned to Alice and said, —Well, just tell me again, please, why it was that you insisted on staying here all week? To *help* these folks? What possible help could you be? You wouldn't know which end of a paintbrush was the business end. So what was it really? Why are we even here tonight?

As much as Jo detested this man, with his traveling bar and patronizing tone and drunkenness and how he treated this woman, she was curious too. Alice's presence here all week had been if not a mystery, certainly odd. But Jo wondered, too, if she'd misjudged the woman and her intentions. The storm last week had thrown everything into chaos. Now, in the serpentine workings of her own guilt mechanism, Jo wondered if she was to blame for this… this *scene*, or whatever you'd call it. Maybe she should have found something for the woman to do. Maybe Jo was really the snob for thinking this woman one. Oh, it was all so muddled. But that's what men like this one do, isn't it – muddle your thinking, make you believe their rage is your fault. Bullies. Jo knew something about his kind.

—Alice was good company all week, Jo declared, snatching for Jim's plate from the opposite side of his wife and so making him turn away from her. The plate was still a work-in-progress, but as far as Jo was concerned, dinner was done – and the bar was closed.

—We were glad to have her, she added. We heard all about your granddaughter. Why your daughter's wedding was nearly one of our first. It helped launch our business. (A fabrication, but useful if it shut down this man's steam vents. Flann glanced at her like what are you talking about, and his mother glared back like stifle it.)

For her part, Alice would have welcomed death at that moment, not so much because of the humiliation had Jim heaped on her – on both of them really, though he would never admit or even realize it – but because of how narrowly she'd skirted exposure. Her face was flushed and warm. Her skin felt transparent. She thought she was no more than a breath away from hearing him announce – just as he had announced at the rehearsal dinner years ago what she'd said about April – that while he was at home this week he'd discovered the record of her computer searches, of all she'd learned about these people. Or perhaps he'd just seen through her, as he could do, as if she had Saran Wrap for skin, and now he was about to expose her folly, her curiosity, her snooping, and worse still, was about to belittle her for the waves of empathy she'd felt for this girl and her family.

Not only wasn't it her right to feel such things, but she was a fool for feeling them. He would expose her for all of that. And maybe he was right, after all. Maybe it was as much as she deserved.

They left before breakfast. Alice went quietly out the front door and waited in the car. Jo didn't even offer them coffee when the man came down with his bag.

He frowned when he saw the bill – full price for the entire week. Jo was itching for an argument, but he paid it without giving her one, and she left him to carry his own bags down the front steps.

Maybe She Won't Be Either

NANCY COULDN'T DECIDE WHETHER to remain in the car or go in now, and if she did, should she find a seat right away or wait in the lobby?

All she could think about driving down here was how they'd react when they saw her and what she'd say. But why shouldn't she come? The play was a public event. Anyone could go. What was so wrong with her going too? Still, she knew Jo wouldn't want her here and would resent her not calling first. But Nancy resented having every minute she spent with Kimmy overseen, managed, controlled. Their visits had become a ritual, right down to the plate of cookies that was always sitting on the buffet when she and Phil were ushered in. Then they'd sit like Victorians in the so-called *parlor* sipping coffee while Kimmy opened a gift and dangled her legs impatiently until the torture ended. That's what her Gammie and Poppa had become – a trial, a ceremony, something to endure. It wasn't right, so Nancy decided to come see the play on her own. She'd buy a ticket, pay her own way. It's a free country.

But wasn't it just like her to land here almost an hour early? The sun was still high over the granary silos on the west wide of town. How much more obvious could she be sitting here, nearly the only car in the lot? A door on the loading dock was propped open with a sandbag she first mistook for a sleeping dog. People came and went. A man with a wide-brimmed hat with a feather stood at the edge of the dock and smoked. She was as hopeful of catching a glimpse of Kimmy or Elliot as she was fearful they'd see her. Elliot wasn't encouraging when she spoke to him, though she'd always felt there was some affinity between them. He was close in age to her and Phil, and Phil seemed to like him, said he thought Elliot saw things the way he did, mostly. She'd called Elliot at the theater a couple of weeks ago to ask what he thought about her coming to the play. He said it was up to her. Couldn't speak for Jo, he said, and couldn't talk long either. A huge storm had moved in. Everything was in chaos. Were they getting the same weather up her way? Nick was waiting outside in the downpour. He had to go. Nancy recalled that night: fierce winds, sheets of rain falling sideways, tornado sirens. They should have gone down to the basement themselves, but Phil wouldn't budge so what could she do? They might have been killed. A dozen or more homes down by the airport were leveled in a microburst. Phil would've let them both die rather than leave the TV and go downstairs for an hour or two.

A girl in a ballet costume appeared in the doorway and said something to the man in the hat. He shook his head with the dismay of someone who'd just been reminded yet again of how helpless the rest of humanity was without him. He crushed the cigarette under his boot and strutted inside. More cars filed into the lot. A cream-colored Town Car with a landau roof swung bruskly into a nearby space. Three men and a woman got out. The woman didn't seem attached to any of the men, just with them. The driver's hair was white and buzz-cut to a flat plane on top; it sloped downward toward his brow and gave the impression that you could put a ping-pong ball up there and watch it roll down and bounce off his nose. He chomped on a huge, unlit cigar and walked ahead of the others. The woman's face had a worn look. Her hair was dyed a rusty shade of red and was rippled and limp, yet when she laughed Nancy was struck by the notion of how happiness improved a person's looks. She had friends, something to laugh at, people to laugh with.

No question about bringing Phil. He might have come. He wasn't as sick as he claimed. Mostly he just didn't want to go anywhere these days, just wanted to stay home. But Nancy was better off without him here, she decided. He'd fidget through the play. He'd for sure need to use the bathroom.

Patrons were arriving now, drifting toward the main door around front. The Town Car crew had gone in also, but they soon reappeared, all four of them, and trooped around the building and up to the loading dock, where the buzz-cut man, still leading the way, marching more than walking, stepped into the shadows inside the doorway and reemerged with Elliot, who was partially costumed in suit pants, suspenders, and a V-neck undershirt. He looked different in the sharp glare of the low-hanging sun – sickly and garish, with dark eyebrows and his hair combed up. Of course! He wore makeup. His friends gathered around him and shared jokes. Then Kimmy appeared and lingered at the door. They hadn't noticed her yet.

Slouched against the doorpost, arms folded as if she didn't know what to do with them and her weight on one foot, she could have been her mother. Nancy hadn't known Anna at that age, but surely that's what she would have looked like and how she'd have stood. Nancy recognized a familiar trace of cockiness in Kimmy's posture. How strange this was. The child had hardly known her mother and yet she could project an attitude, a state of mind, so familiar that it seemed for a moment as if Anna had been reborn.

She has chip, Nancy sometimes said of Anna.

Just how she isss, Phil would hiss.

But the smallest things set her off.

Kimmy had only just started to walk.

They'd come to the house for a cookout, Ross and Anna and Kimmy, and you could see, anyone could – it was obvious to Nancy, at least, and Phil too, she thought – that something was going on between them even before they arrived. Whatever it was, you couldn't be sure, but it wasn't hard to guess. Ross couldn't find work, and Anna'd just lately gotten a job at the grain co-op answering phones. So it was money – it was always money. This might be the biggest meal they had all week, not that Anna was much of a cook anyway. Nancy had asked Ross to bring some ice, but doesn't he show up empty-handed, and she knew the reason, too. Didn't have two dollars for a bag of ice. He quietly hit Phil up for a ten and then drove back to the store, halfway back to Sunburg, that is, a gallon of gas and most of an hour gone because he didn't have eight quarters somewhere in the house. Meanwhile Anna had sent Kimmy down to play in the yard and settled herself on the deck like the place was her own.

Nancy spotted Kimmy from the kitchen window wandering out beyond the mowed grass and into the weeds. It was hot – July-in-Kansas hot, when the south wind blows into your face like a furnace draft. Might be snakes out there, and they were quick this time of year. And there was Anna, taking up the Sunday paper, soon growing bored with it and stretching out in the sun, eyes shut, as if… as if, Nancy thought, even now, she and Phil and Kimmy weren't even there.

The image was still fresh – Anna lounging, showing herself off was how it struck Nancy – her legs lean and smooth, silvery streaks glowing along her shins in the sunlight, toenails polished in a ghastly shade of dark purple (money enough for the nail salon but couldn't afford a bag of ice!), her head back as if nesting in her hair, this picture forcing itself on Nancy, even now. Yes, she was attractive, in a gritty sort of way. Not beautiful, not a knockout – she could have done something more with her hair, Nancy always thought – but neither could you easily turn away when she smiled at you. And it wasn't only her features, Nancy realized, that men, that Ross, would see in her. She was poised; she lifted her chin when she listened; her eyes brightened so you'd believe whatever you were saying to her mattered. It was all a convincing act to Nancy, who found her self-absorbed and noticed how quickly she turned a conversation back to herself, her own experiences, what she liked and didn't like, and wasn't she so easily crossed too.

Kimmy was waist high in the weeds now.

Nancy slid the door open and stepped out on the deck. Anna must have heard her, couldn't have been so deeply asleep already. The only sounds were the light rustle of the wind in the trees, the door hissing shut, Nancy's footfalls hollow on the wood. But Anna lay still, unresponsive. Her dark eyebrows sloped into a frown. They naturally fell that way – and Nancy wondered if her personality hadn't shaped itself around them, an instinctive sense of resentment, a voice that sharpened into easy defensiveness when she was questioned about the smallest thing, why she bought this brand instead of that, went to one hairdresser rather than another. She lay motionless. Her hair was walnut brown, layered and feathered, and she had small drooping breasts beneath her blouse, flattened now as she lay on her back, but barely curving from her chest even when she was standing. Nancy imagined Ross's lips on those breasts, felt a momentary sensation of his tongue on them as she'd felt it on her own when he was an infant.

Nancy stepped to the edge of the deck and didn't see Kimmy now.

—Where is she?

Anna tilted her head forward and squinted in the sun, her eyes barely slits.

Then Nancy spotted Kimmy, well beyond the rim of cut grass, where the lawn ended and weeds began, sloping down toward the hedge trees and pond.

—Playing on the lawn, Anna said.

The words faded behind Nancy as she took the steps down to the grass.

Kimmy stretched her arms wide, like a bird's wings, and swept her hands along the milkweed blossoms. The bluestem grass folded easily under her naked feet, already toughened from playing barefoot outdoors. She wore only shorts and a diaper, and her soft pink skin dissolved in the field's palette of colors and the texture of its motion as if she were part of the flora.

Nancy swooped her up from behind, surprising her, abruptly pulling her away from a milkweed pod as she grasped for it and closed her fingers on emptiness.

—Come along, honey. You shouldn't be out here.

The rank diaper's odor rushed upwards in a stiff backdraft just as Nancy recognized the soft, clayey moisture spreading along her arm and belly.

With the baby straddling her hip, she thumped past Anna, who'd lain back and now struck Nancy as almost purposive in her stillness, her head on the cushion, her eyes shut as if she'd shut them knowing Nancy would pass, carrying the child, that Nancy's problem was not her problem. So it felt as Nancy pushed the slider shut behind her. She found the baby bag where Anna'd dropped it by the front door, threw a bath towel on her bed, and lay Kimmy down to change her. The diaper had to be pealed away. Her legs and crotch were coated in moist, greenish clay. As Nancy bent over to remove the diaper, her elbow brushed the damp stain on her own blouse, and with an oath, she unbuttoned it and crumpled it on the floor. So there she was, wiping futilely with towelettes no bigger than the palm of her hand and finally realizing, just as she would have twenty-five years earlier, when Ross was no older than Kimmy, that the simplest thing to do was to run the shower and both of them get in.

The truck pulled into the driveway and the front door opened, and just then also, the slider opened and shut in back. Then she heard footsteps and whispering in the front hall.

Ross's voice preceded him as he leaned in the bedroom door.

—Everything okay?… oh.

He backed out as his mother, bent over the baby, looked over her shoulder in her bra.

—You go in, he whispered.

Then Anna's voice, flat, vacant. —I can do that.

Without looking up, Nancy said in barely a whisper, —No point now. We're both covered in it. I'll take her in the shower.

—Go ahead and shower, Nancy. I'll clean her up.

—She needs a bath too.

—I'll give her a bath.

—Oh, it's just as easy if I take her in with me.

Nancy stood upright now, facing Anna in only her bra but arching her shoulders back, as if fully dressed, shielding Kimmy from Anna as she folded the soiled diaper into a thick wad, like a garage mechanic unbending himself from under the hood, hands covered in grease, immune to it, unfazed, oily rag in hand. The filth now quarantined her with Kimmy. Anna'd have to plunge in if she wanted some of the action.

Nancy still held the diaper. To reach the waste basket she'd have to step away from the bed, so with the muddy wad still in hand, she scooped Kimmy up in the towel and brought her into the bathroom, tossing the diaper into the trash, and now turning on the shower.

Anna followed her across the room. —I'll take her in the other bathroom.

—Why waste the water? Nancy said, and then turning to Kimmy, added, —Isn't that right, honey? Wanna take a shower with Gammie? She bounced Kimmy on her hip.

—Yah!

—Well, okay then. And to Anna she said cheerfully, —We'll just be a few minutes.

She set Kimmy down on the bath rug, loosened the clip on her bra, and dropped it in the laundry basket. She smiled at Anna, who stiffened but looked at her unblinking, refusing to drop her gaze from Nancy's eyes, until she turned and left the bedroom.

Nancy opened the car window and drew a breath of thick, humid evening air, and now chided herself for sitting here and thinking ill of Anna. What right had she? But memory plagued her, wouldn't release her. She wondered what all these years of tension and stress and fear were doing to her that she should sit here thinking such things, that her life had come to this, to sitting in a parking lot like a stalker so she could watch her only grandchild among these strangers. Up on the dock Elliot noticed Kimmy now and drew her into the fold with an arm around her thin shoulders. The others fawned; she nodded and mumbled, reticent, uncomfortable with the attention, aloof. She doesn't belong among these people, Nancy thought. This was a terrible mistake, her growing up with Anna's sister. Who knew how different her life might have been if…? Well, there were many ifs.

Elliot soon disappeared inside with Kimmy, and the foursome trooped back around to the main entrance, with Buzz-Cut marching on point for the squad.

After she pulled the key from the ignition, Nancy shuffled the items in her purse so the letter would be handy, easy to grab and deliver. She wouldn't have long, but she'd only need a moment alone with Kimmy, who she was certain would conceal it, would keep it secret, if only from curiosity, if not from some deeper need that Nancy was sure she felt.

Nancy went inside and bought a ticket. The theater felt small and close. The house lights were up and the seats still only half-filled. People chatted in the aisles. She couldn't easily slip in and watch the play anonymously, as she'd hoped. She felt conspicuous, but glancing around, she realized Jo and Nick hadn't arrived yet.

Elliot's friends sat up close to the stage. They'd left one seat at the end of the row. If she couldn't be inconspicuous tonight, she might as well make herself known. She went down the aisle and asked Leo if the seat beside him was taken and he smiled and said it was now, by her, and he pushed the cushion down for her and turned back to his group. They were debating whether a mission should be launched to colonize Mars now that ice had been found beneath its surface.

—If we don't, Leo said, shaking a stiff forefinger at the man farthest down the row, it's gonna be the Chinese. You watch what I'm telling you. You'll wake up and find out they've already set up camp there.

—You been reading too many Tom Clancy books, the man said. Just look at what they gotta do before they could even think of colonizing it. And the cost!? Phew!

—And how long it'll take, the other man added.

—Them Chinese got time, Leo asserted. They got time and they got people, and at the rate we're going, they're gonna have all our money too, but that's a whole other story.

—So, but just think about it, the farthest man said, leaning in front of the woman, who followed the conversation as if watching a tennis match. It's not like they can just put up their red flag somewheres up there and say the whole thing's theirs. I mean it's huge, and plus they'll just be parked at some little outpost, and what? they gonna start the first Martian world war if we happen to land on the other side of the planet, whatever, ten thousand miles away? so that'll the first thing we gotta do on Mars? is set up intercontinental missiles to take them out? And mind you, we'll be living inside some kinda bubble dome, and it'll take a year or two just to get there, and we won't have enough food or water, and that's what we're gonna do is start a war? Hah!

Leo scowled.

The woman spoke up. —Be just like us, wouldn't it? First thing we do on a new planet is start a war. Off to a great start, first thing.

Leo shook his head and turned toward Nancy. Catching her eye, he grinned in a scowling sort of way, like you see what I have to deal with, this warped logic, these half-wits, but he conveyed it warmly, without malice. She was glad she'd sat here.

The theater had mostly filled now.

Nick wondered if he'd find three seats together. He spotted a few people he knew, all seated and the rows filled. He recognized Leo's gray head and one or two people with him. He was talking to a woman whom Nick couldn't see as the lights dimmed halfway. An usher found seats for him and Flann and Dawit on a side aisle, toward the back. The lights went to dark almost as soon as they were seated, and the play began.

—⁓—

THEIR FACES WERE BRIGHT: they shone, they greeted him, they welcomed him. Applause went up as he entered. You couldn't get that in a TV studio. He held his first line until it faded and then settled to work. He was where he belonged; he would be good for them. He'd give them his best, better than he ever got paid for.

A few steps downstage, in the spillage of light, he spotted Nancy beside Leo.

Even as he went about his business, his dialogue, his cues, his blocking, he mulled this over, this odd sight, the two of them sitting together. What would come of that? Leo'd been a widower for close to twenty years and hadn't remarried. Maybe it was just the stage lights, the glow they cast on things, but Leo seemed especially buoyant, sitting there, watching the play.

He was just saying, Elliot was, telling his stage family why he liked graduation speeches so much. He'd just come from a graduation, just heard a graduation speech, indeed. He was taking off his coat and limping about the stage with his cane and saying that he attended graduations whenever he could. Nope, didn't know any of the graduates there, not a one, just liked the speeches. Inspirational, uplifting. People needed more of that.

So this business out there, out in the audience, well, he'd use it. Fit nicely into the mood on stage. Yes, fit nicely. Could the people in this bizarre family up here be any stranger than the real ones out there?

—⁓—

KIM WATCHED FROM A loft in the stage-right wing where the lighting pipes were tied off. She leaned on a heavy rope coil and dangled her legs. So much more to see from up here. She was eye-level with the network of cables and lights over the stage. Below, actors moved about in the wings like ghosts, waiting their cues. Behind her, Lufkin worked the light panels and whispered into a headset.

Down on stage, Uncle Elliot's character was discussing taxes with a tax collector. He kept telling the man to explain exactly how his money would get spent if he paid all the back taxes the man said he owed. The tax collector got fuddled trying to explain it, and the audience laughed. Uncle E raised his eyebrows and wrinkled up his face and kept pointing at the man with the stem of an unlit pipe that Kim was in charge of making sure was on the prop table before the play began.

Lufkin whispered into the headset as he lowered one of the cranks on the light panel. —One-one thousand, two-one thousand…

It would take a full minute to edge the lights down only a few degrees. You could barely see the light dim outside the window as dusk fell.

Dory stood directly below her now, awaiting her cue. She was supposed to stay over at Monarch House and sleep in Kim's room. Had pretty much invited herself, Kim thought, letting it be known in front of Aunt Jo that her mother had to pick her father up at the airport tonight and it was so much extra driving with dropping her at the theater and such, until Aunt Jo said, —Well, you can just as easy stay with us. And that was that. Dory was gleeful. Plus she was supposed to get Kim's bed and Kim would get the floor. —Why can't she just use a vacant room? Plenty of 'em, Kim'd snorted earlier to Aunt Jo, who responded stiffly, —It'll make too much work. So Kim was in a bad mood when Dory got there a few hours ago, and then the girl comes out of the shower and down the hall in a towel, parading it past Flann on the way, and once back in Kim's room whips

the towel off and starts trying to get Kim to take off her clothes too
so they can 'do stuff,' she said. Well, so Kim didn't want to do stuff, and
then Dory worried she'd spread rumors about her being gay and Kim
decided well maybe she would and maybe she wouldn't and Dory'd
just have to wait and see… which sent Dory into spasms of terror,
whisper-shouting breathlessly at Kim that she wasn't gay and doing
stuff was nothing and she'd better not tell anyone, and Kim said shrug.

Dory hadn't spoken to her since they left the house, since before
that even. She'd called her mother to come pick her up after the play
no matter how many miles she ended up driving tonight. Aunt Jo'd
been after Kim about what happened, but Kim just said nothin'…
which was true… nobody did any stuff. Kim thought maybe she'd
try being gay for a while. She figured she could try either way or not
at all. Mainly she didn't think she'd ever be either.

She fingered a clump of sawdust on the floor and sprinkled some
on Dory, who brushed at her hair as if at a mosquito or gnat and
unsprang a curl. Then she looked up and sneered at Kim, but Kim
just stared back like a face in a picture.

⁓

It'd easily been three hours since Nancy used a bathroom. Staying
in her seat through intermission wasn't an option, but she wondered
where Jo was, and if she'd already seen her.

Leo's group got up as if on command. She'd already learned that
he was in the Army. She always wondered what a 'full bird colonel'
was but now she as too embarrassed to ask. But it sounded impres-
sive. More than just your average colonel.

Leo slipped hastily into the aisle to walk beside her. The sensation
was familiar, though it'd been a long time since a man paid attention
to her. He complimented her glistening American flag brooch and

212

said she wore it so well, so proudly. For Nine-Eleven, she said, and he said amen to that with a sharp, somber nod.

People milled at the back of the theater. There was Nick, on the side aisle, still seated, talking to a black man who sat beside him. He hadn't noticed her yet, but his son had. The boy stared at her all the way up the aisle. She hadn't recognized him at first. Maybe his hair color had changed. That was it. Obsidian. A sickly black, like coal, blacker than human hair should ever be. He wore it close cropped on one side and hanging long over the other cheek. It looked at once ridiculous and disturbing. He eyed her as she went up the aisle but said nothing to his father.

Leo had moved on to golf. Did she like to golf? No, she said, she'd never be good at it, and he said, well that's the first mistake most people make, thinking they'll get good at it, and he laughed, and she did too.

When she returned from the ladies room, Leo was chatting with Nick.

But where was Jo?

As she joined them, Leo began to introduce her.

—We know each other, Nick said, nodding uneasily to Nancy.

—I'm Kimmy's grandmother, she told Leo.

—Her grandmother…? So you know Elliot too?

She offered a tepid nod, as if owning up, though she wasn't sure to what. Should she have told Leo? But what reason would she have had for just announcing it? She didn't know him or how he knew Elliot, and wasn't even supposed to know that they were even acquainted. Explanations were… complicated.

Leo still looked puzzled. —You're…?

—Her grandmother, Nancy asserted, and quickly added, on her father's side.

Leo thought for a second, as if measuring out the lineage, assembling the parts of this complex machine, and then scowled approval and looked around toward the stage, where the curtains were drawn.

—Well, she's doing a fine job, is Kimmy, he said. All those props. She's helping with the props, right? he asked Nick.

—That's right, the props, Nick said.

—Lots of them, too, Leo said. Why every time one a them actors picks something up, it's a prop, right? Like that pipe Elliot's been waving around, right? And his cane?

—I think so, said Nick.

—That's a lot to do, you think about it, he said, now turning to Nancy. —Big job, it is, props.

—It must be, she said, and hesitating, she turned to Nick. —I haven't seen Jo yet.

—Stayed home tonight. Guests at the house. She'll come tomorrow.

Nancy hoped her relief wasn't visible. She asked about Elliot's health. Leo folded his arms and squinted, refocusing so he could listen hard as Nick described the last doctor visit and trying to get him to move to a downstairs room and his stubbornness, at which they all nodded. A lovable stubbornness it was, they all agreed.

The house lights flickered just as Dawit returned from the lobby.

When Leo and Nancy settled back into their seats and the theater went to darkness, he said, —You're full of surprises, aren't you?

—I suppose I am.

⸎

The lobby was crowded and lively. Everyone had a plastic cup with wine except Kim, who got ginger ale, and Elliot's friends, who also got ginger ale. People told the director what a great play it was, what a great choice, and he said I thought so too. He said the part was made for Elliot, don't you think? And they said yes, he was even better than Lionel Barrymore in the movie, and the director agreed. Yes, thank you so very much.

Dory waited at the door, clutching her backpack, her hair still pinned up in an intricate weave that reminded Kim of strawberry vines.

Gammie seemed nervous. She asked Kim what she did backstage. Just props, Kim told her. Like you had tables where the actors picked up books and toys and other stuff, and you rearranged things on stage between acts, and that was it.

Her every word prompted admiration. Colonel Leo stood close by Gammie and kept saying, Well that's really something, imagine that.

When Uncle E finally came in, everyone cheered.

Dory's mother leaned in the front door of the lobby, hesitantly, with a puzzled look on her face. Dory tried to hurry her back out the door, but she stepped inside and looked around. Uncle Nick saw her and wove through the crowd. His hands fluttered, his head tilted. He slouched a little lower, maybe to hear better, maybe apologetic. Kim easily imagined him saying how sorry he was that Dory couldn't stay overnight and maybe she'd come again soon and they had lots of room, and whatever. Then they were gone.

Uncle Elliot was surrounded by patrons and the Colonel and his other meeting friends, as he called them. Gammie and Kim remained on the far side of the packed the lobby, alone now. Gammie suddenly clutched Kim's arm, her eyes large and moist and dark.

—I have something for you, Kimmy, she said, … just for you.

She slid out an envelope from her purse and thrust into Kim's hands.

—It's from your father, she said. He wanted to write to you. He's tried before, but his letters… oh, I shouldn't even say that much, but this is for you, from him. Put it away and read it when you're alone. I haven't read it, so it's just between you and him. She looked around nervously and added, —You're a young woman. You'll want to know things. You'll want to understand. I know you have many questions. I'm certain of it. So put this away for now. Save it for later, and if you want to write back to him there's an address on the envelope, or you can just give me a letter and I'll bring it to him. I just hope… all I want… is for you to maybe someday get to know him. Things were complicated back then, when you were little. Not everything was how it seems now, all these years later.

Uncle Nick was making his way through the crowd, and the Colonel too, who'd remained by Nancy's side all evening. Gammie patted Kim's hands in a nervous attempt both to conceal the envelope and get her to hide it. But Kim made no effort to put it away. The handwriting was heavy and thick, but the most startling thing was seeing her name written as *Kimmy Oden* in the broad scrawl that she knew for certain was her own father's hand, even though she'd never before seen it. A sudden and sharp chill shot through her. She'd never seen her name written that way, nor heard it, nor even thought it herself. She'd been Kim Pugh for as long as she could remember. These two names had never been attached. The very appearance of it was jarring, as if it was someone else's name, not hers… as if she was someone else… or there was someone else that was her, so she suddenly didn't know who she was.

She squinted doubtfully at Gammie, who leaned over and wrapped her hands around Kim's, still grasping the envelope, and said firmly, —That'll be something for later, just for you.

Kim doubled it over and shoved it into her jeans pocket as Colonel Leo came up beside Gammie and told her how proud she should be of Kimmy. Then Uncle Nick came along and Gammie asked him if they were busy at Monarch House these days.

Just then Kim noticed Flann lingering behind the open theater door, watching her and Gammie. He hung back, out of the traffic, a faint look of disgust curled into the half of his face that wasn't shrouded in hair. His look wasn't only for her, she knew. He was afraid… of all these people, of saying something that sounded ordinary, of being seen in the clothes Aunt Jo made him wear, of talking about the play, about props, about school, about the weather… the things people were talking about all over the lobby. Sometimes he was friendly to her when no one was around. They were both different, he told her, and nothing would ever change that because you can't change who you are. It's fate, he said, and you can't control it, and she knew he wasn't talking about her but about himself, and that his anger was at *his* fate, whatever that was. He couldn't control it; it was trying to make him into something he didn't want to be; he'd have to talk about the weather and look ordinary and be like other people, and that's what made him angry, and fearful. When he said these things, she could see that such thoughts tumbled around inside him and gave him no peace. Now he flicked his head and she flicked hers back. They did that sometimes, flicked their heads, like code for being different. But she wasn't afraid, like him. The weather and other stuff like that were never things she thought of wasting her breath on, so she didn't worry about whether she might, was all. And too, she knew he wouldn't say anything about what he'd just seen.

Cowboys and Hamlet

—KNOW WHAT, MAN?

—… hunh…?

—Like, some days? I think this is the best place for me.

Down the row a con howled, coyote-like, a piercing, woofing sort of howl. Another con growled shut the fuck up. Snout footfalls started that way. Ross recognized the last voice. The checkers player. Never got beat. Moved fast too. Soon's you made your move, before your hand even cleared the board, he'd smack his piece down on a square, smack it hard two-three times as he jumped you. If you could slam-dunk at checkers, that's how he moved. Cheating somehow with all that razzle-dazzle shit, Ross figured. Heard he worked at a cattle feed-lot out near Garden City before he harassed and tailgated a guy thir-ty-forty miles down I-70 who'd cut him off up the road. Then beat him into a coma at a rest stop as the poor bastard's wife screamed into a cell phone and his kids looked on from their beamer. Dude's girl-friend watched too, eyeballing them while she smoked a cigarette in the idling pickup. She ended up a witness at the trial. Weren't married, so she had to testify. Fucking with this dude wasn't something you'd do lightly. Ross played him checkers once and lost a pack of cigarettes, which you could only smoke outside anyway so what the fuck.

The howler let loose another, and the checkers player yelled, —'M tryin' to sleep, so shut the fuck up!

A snout voice snapped something to the effect of both of you either shut the fuck up or I write up your asses and then you land in de-seg, where I won't have to listen to your shit up here for a month. And won't be no fucking checkers down there neither.

Ross held the pen over the pad, still suspended. Twice now he'd started to write and then stopped – once for Mandel, a second time for the howler and checkers dude.

—Know what'm sayin? Mandel asked.

Ross dropped the pen on his lap. —Tryin' to write a letter.

—Yeah, so much fucking noise in here, Mandel blithely observed. Never stops. That's the one thing I'd have if I could get my wish is some quiet, just, like, to sit by a lake and listen to birds 'n shit, that's what I'd wish for.

Clueless. Didn't surprise Ross that he didn't catch the barb. But now Ross thought about what he missed too, which after the obvious ones was driving. He missed driving. Get laid, get drunk, eat steak, get laid again. And drive. Alone. By himself. Going anywhere, or nowhere. Out on some county road, where he could open it up and let the wind whip through the cab, with the engine humming in a deep, steady, tight rumble that gave notice that there were plenty more horses in this stable. Swallowing up pavement, leaning with the turns, gliding over hills, where the speed and trajectory gave you a brief and joyful taste of weightlessness. No radio, no music. Just the heavy decibels of the engine fluttering through the seat cushion. All the rest – fucking, eating, drinking – that was shit you had to have. Hard to think about anything else without fucking first. But this – driving with nowhere to go except what was in front of you – that was pure pleasure. Fucking might be a pleasure too – but it was also a need, like breathing. But redlining, pushing one-ten, one-twenty, leaning back as the truck propelled you forward and all that mattered were motion and speed – that was living.

—Who you writing to, your Moms?

Ross knew that Mandel knew that he never wrote to his mother, so what Mandel really wanted to know was if he was writing to Kimmy again, but Mandel also knew how touchy Ross was on that topic.

Ross hadn't written to her in months. Maybe it was already a year. Time moved on a different scale in here. Glacial. Months might pass between parts of a conversation you'd have with someone on the yard who'd maybe got moved to de-seg or another facility and then showed up again. No reason given or asked. Just pick up where you left off.

Mandel was – transparently to Ross and slyly to Mandel – ever curious about Ross's family. Had none of his own, never got visitors or mail or packages.

Ross wasn't about to get into it, mostly because the whole business enraged him in ways he had no words for but which would morph into physical tightness so intense that his body felt like it might implode. He clenched his jaw and drew a sharp breath as he imagined yet again the day Anna's bitch sister snatched the girl from his mother's arms years ago, as she'd described the scene to him many times, more than he wanted to hear. Once was enough. Didn't need to hear it more than that, but it was like a mantra with Nancy. Then the bitch sister cut them all off. Four years old, the last time he saw Kimmy, the night he left her at his mother's house. Hadn't seen or talked to her since then.

She got him to write, Nancy did. But the letters came back, unopened, unread, with the word REFUSED written in bold, dark caps on the still-sealed envelopes. A personal insult. His hands trembled when he saw the envelopes in his mail. It was as if the walls of his cell had just been redoubled, the grated window and bars sealed with poured concrete. He wasn't imprisoned but entombed. Not only was his body confined here, but so were his thoughts, his words. Jo's handwriting was meant for his eyes, her message to him, and even now, as Mandel's layered question triggered a mental circuit that fired up Ross's rage once more, his hand twitched, a visceral token of the fury and hatred that rushed through him.

Worse still to Ross – and Mandel knew nothing of this – was that when he finally gave a letter to his mother to deliver, the bitch cut her off too after she found out. His mother hadn't even told him, or wouldn't have, if he hadn't dragged it out of her during a visit. She was moody, depressed. He asked what happened, what did Kimmy say, but she couldn't tell him, of course, because she didn't know. She hadn't seen the girl after that and probably wouldn't see her again for a long time. She gave the letter to Kimmy at some play or something, and a few days later she got a call from Jo, who said don't call here or show up here again. Ever, she added. Not ever again. Short and bitter, that call was. Nancy could barely get it out when she told him. But don't blame yourself, she said, because what she wanted most, even more than for herself, was for him to get to know her, his daughter. She was glad she tried, she said. The risk was worth it. And Kimmy did get the letter.

But Ross didn't blame himself. Nancy had pushed him to write. It was her idea, not his. He'd done it to please her, but the idea that someone could put something this big, this vast, over not only him but his mother too… his hands trembled and he sucked air in stuttered breaths through his teeth.

—So like it's true, ain't it?

— …

—About me belonging here. Like when they picked me up? I was like – you ain't gonna believe this – but I was like… *relieved*. I remember that, feelin' that way, relieved. The fucking nightmare was over. It was outta my hands now.

Mandel rustled on his bunk overhead. Ross knew every creak, squeak, crackle, and groan that mattress made when Mandel's lanky, drug-addled body turned this way and that.

—All I ever wanted to do was dope… all I thought about from the time I opened my eyes till I shut 'em… dope, that's all… moving it, selling it, doing it. All I thought about. But then, when they collared me, I knew it was done, that I wouldn't be getting high for a long time. Could get something in here… but man, the price is too high, grabbing your ankles for some ugly shithead or getting mixed up with one a them nigger or spic gangs or something. So it was like I don't have to worry about that now, do I? It's gone. Off my back. Don't have to keep wanting it. I was fucked up, man.

—You're fucked up now if you think you're better off in here, Ross muttered.

—But I'm afraid it's all I'll want, you know? when I'm out? Just a couple of years till I get a hearing. I'm afraid this is like, being here, I mean, it's like… whatever, suspended animation or something, and so when I get out I'll just go back to being what I was… what I am, I mean. That's who I am and being here don't change it. It just keeps me from fucking myself up, and probably a lot of other people too. Like, this is the way things should be, keeping me away from being what I am, keeping me away from others. It's better for everyone, ain't it? The preacher, he gets me thinking about shit, you know?

Like, he don't tell me what to think, but when I hear him say shit, I realize that that's what I was already thinking but I didn't have the words for it. One thing he says that I like is 'Either you do the time or the time'll do you.' That's one I like. Wrote that one down and kept it.

The snout from down the hall passed by now. Even with his back to the front of the house, Ross felt him looking in.

—I get really tired of hearing about what the preacher says, Ross snorted.

—It's true. Just falls outta my mouth sometimes, like I don't even think about what I'm saying.

—That's a fact.

—He says I shouldn't focus on myself, you know, but on what I can do for someone else… just, like, one person, what I could do for them, but the thing is, I thought of something I want to do, but I can't decide if it'd qualify, but so what the thing is I'm gonna do is…

On the hall you could hear leakage from a half-dozen CD headsets buzzing and droning, a perverse sort of ambient forest noise, metallic, insistent.

— … so like you know how I'm always reading books, like Westerns 'n shit? I decided I'm gonna write one a those, but different, you see, it's gonna have its own twist which is that like it'll be about… but first I gotta tell you… you know how I been takin' them GED classes? So the teacher was telling us about this story where this guy, he's like a prince or whatever back in the day? only his father the king gets murdered and he knows who done it, the prince does, because some ghost tells him, and but he dicks around forever about killing him, but when he finally does kill him, he dies too. Part of the rules of the story, teach says. He's gotta die too. But so I figured I'd take that story and make it into a Western in which the prince is an Indian prince and his father the chief gets knocked off, and all he can think about, the Indian prince, is getting revenge on the brave who done it who's now a chief, but so he wants to kill this chief who murdered his father, but instead the Indian prince learns about Jesus from a missionary and gets saved, but only... I still haven't worked out the ending yet cause I still think even though he gets saved he oughta get to kill the phony chief what killed his daddy and get to be chief steada getting killed hisself like the prince back in the day, but I ain't figured the whole thing through yet, but that's the basic story of it, the Western I'm gonna write, but I ain't figured the end yet, and what I'm trying to imagine is if I can just have an imaginary reader, like one person, who I'd be writing it for, who'd like the book and get the story and maybe get saved too, so I'm trying to imagine them reading it steada me writing it, so they'd just think about the story and then get saved too, so what do you think?

Ross wondered why the prince – whichever, the old-school one or the Indian one – would dick around about killing whoever killed his father, and too, this rule about you gotta die just cause you get revenge, that was fucked up, and then there was the bigger curiosity, which knowing Mandel maybe wasn't so curious after all, which was how come, if he was going to write a book, Ross'd never seen him write anything.

But if he asked, if Ross did, there'd be no end of this in sight.

—Don't think nothing, he growled.

He tried to refocus on the letter, which until Mandel reminded him of the aforementioned, was all he'd been thinking about. It wasn't really a letter, rather the draft of an email, but he wanted to write it out first, get the wording just right. His time at the computer was limited, so he didn't want to sit there thinking of what to say or have other shitheads peering over his shoulder. No, just write it out and have it ready to go, that was the plan. He still had the pad on his lap but couldn't decide on the right word. Already crossed out *longing* and *desire*. Didn't want to sound desperate. He'd just gotten two e-mails from his web page at *MeetaCon.com*, and he figured to answer and see what happened next. But what he couldn't decide, too, was if it'd be some kind of two-timing to write back to both women at once? A brief fantasy buzzed through his head in which both women discovered they were here to see him on the same day and a catfight broke out in the visitors room. He'd be fucked then — lose visiting privileges for months. More likely, they'd both probably turn out to be dogs. Hadn't sent photos with the e-mails. He'd keep his options open. Like blind dates, that's what they were. The unfinished sentence absorbed him once more.

Hope?

Hopeful, hopefully, hoping.

Hoping to hear from you soon.

Didn't want to sound horny either. Besides, he was thinking long-term to the prospect of finding a woman who'd marry him, and then when he finally got to Medium and got a job, he could qualify for conjugals and get laid for real. This was gonna take time, but time was his capital. He was just laying the groundwork now so he wouldn't have to jack off forever to the tune of Mandel's snoring and the chorus from hell that filled the nighttime when the lights dimmed on the hall.

He took up the wrinkled printout of his homepage and admired the layout and photo of himself. He looked good, he thought, in a jacket, in front of the fireplace in a fancy hotel lobby. It was from the Granary Co-op Association banquet, the last time he'd gotten dressed up like that. Anna's dress had a thin strip of lace that curved elegantly under her boobs and gave the effect of lifting and highlighting them. She looked hot. She did. You just couldn't say otherwise unless you were a fag or something – and even they'd probably concede how good she looked, probably good enough to turn a fag back to normal. Anna fluttered from one table to another, dragging him along to shake hands with all these farmers and their wives from all over the state, who sat stiffly in their suits and dresses as if they were afraid the clothing would crack if they moved. Networking, she called it. One of her favorite words. But the shop talk… well, it left him out – corn futures, winter wheat, no-till farming, forward contracts. He finally shook loose and found his way to the cash bar and talked shotguns and NASCAR with a couple of farmers from Salina. Brothers they were, who worked a farm started by a grandfather several greats back who'd come from Germany before the Civil War and settled here in Kansas. Ross soon began to feel a bit of resentment, thinking about how these two hicks were running twelve hundred acres they were just born into. Translated into dollars, he knew, the value of their place made them each a multi-millionaire, and plus, Ross learned, they got an annual subsidy from the government. When he heard that, resentment began to turn into outright don't like these motherfuckers. Here he was scrambling and hustling and working his ass off for everything he got – and little enough it was, too – and here was the government paying these hicks to turn their crops under! Everything was rigged, he figured, so he'd get screwed while people like this, who just had it handed to them, only got more. By now, he'd downed his fourth or fifth, fingering his way through the twenty-two dollars he had in his pocket and dropping a buck into the tip jar with each beer so it wouldn't look like he was cheap or broke, and churning inside, trying to reason this thing out: Don't grow the crops you can grow and pick up a check for stuff you didn't grow or bring to market or sell, and in turn that kept the prices high, so you'd get more for what you did sell (and so get paid twice over, he reasoned), and plus (and this was the real zinger) now a loaf of bread costs four bucks at the grocery store, which *I'm* paying because the price of wheat is artificially high, and plus too, all this propping up is being done with *my* tax dollars. What the fuck? This is one major-league rip-off!

So far, he'd absorbed it, measured it out, to see if maybe there was something he'd missed, some gap in his reasoning. This whole event, after all, this whole big banquet with the railroad people and grain brokers and farmers – all here, all dressed up in suits and ties and the ladies in taffeta dresses, and his woman looking hotter than all of them – they were all here because this giant system *worked*. Everyone was making money – and that's what it was all about, right? But Anna, she wasn't making that much. She was just clawing at the edges of it, trying to scrape whatever shavings she could off the granite monolith of this system. Just to be here tonight, she'd run up five hundred bucks on their charge card for the dress and hair stylist and getting her nails and toes done, the latter of which were hidden in her shoes anyway. And another hundred for a new jacket and tie for him. The dress and the hair and whatever, they were an *investment*, she said. The farmer brothers from Salina were by now going on about how you wouldn't think you'd even have to worry about the farm bill getting passed this term, but with a Democrat in the White House and another running the Department of Ag, well, you just didn't know, did you? Should've been a slam dunk.

—So lemme get this straight…

The place was warm. The starched collar scratched and dug at his neck, and it was tight, which just seemed to push the heat up into his head, forcing it there, so the only way he could keep the two men before him balanced and aligned properly was to stare straightaway in between them, and so he ended up fixing his gaze on the bartender as he smiled and poured a glass of wine for a fat woman at the bar and as Ross from the side of his mouth raised the question with these two wealthy Salina farmers of why they would possibly need a *handout* from the government. Well, that was the trigger. They both stiffened, and one of them, who up until now had been talking in what seemed to Ross your regular good clean grammatical English, which Ross would be the first to say he was no expert at but he knew the difference, said flatly, —Ain't no fucking *handout.* And he fixed his dark liquid eyes on Ross and tucked up his chin so his thick wormy lips seemed to droop off to the side. Looked like parking lot time, not that Ross would have waited to get to the parking lot. He was perhaps one second, maybe two, from letting his beer bottle slide through his fingers and taking a swing right there before the bottle thunked on the floor, not just because of what the man said or even might say, but from being stared at like that. Oh yes, he'd have joyfully taken a swing. He'd straighten that motherfucker out most definitely on the definition of *handout*, but just then the other brother spoke up. —We oughta get back to the table, he said, and nudged his brother, who continued looking over his shoulder at Ross as he was walked away.

She drove home, showering him with waves of industrial-strength silence in between torrential speeches about didn't he know this was *business!* and they weren't there to *party!* and what the fuck was that with telling that *raunchy* joke that wasn't even funny to a table with *ladies* at it! her prospects' *wives*, is who! And on it went, the funny thing to him being that she didn't even know about the two brothers and the almost-fight in the parking lot or maybe right there at the bar.

As they neared the toll booth on I-70, she waved the ticket at him and said she needed the toll, which he knew would be two dollars and change. He fished in his pocket and came up with four crumpled singles, which he stared at, trying to calibrate from these remaining dollars how many beers he'd had, with a buck in the tip jar for every beer and a buck-and-a-half each, and with trying to multiply with the half dollar and then add in the buck tip, the answer kept slipping away into the dark void of higher mathematics each time he thought he had it, which he was even worse at math than English, he'd be the first to tell you. So then he realized that you could add the buck tip and the buck-and-a-half-a-beer together, so that made two-fifty-a-beer, and subtract two-fifty from the twenty-two dollars he originally had *one unit of two-fifty at a time!* Which he did: *19.50… 17.50…* (No, *17!* – that's right, *17!*) Then *14.50.* But he soon lost count of how many units of two-fifty he'd subtracted and had to start over again, which was the point – how many was it?

The car hit the slow-down strips before the toll booth and it felt like they were all of a sudden touching down on a runway. The brightness of the toll plaza, which was clear and bleached white and surreal, now accompanied by its own sound track of hissing tires and whining brakes as Anna's window slid down, made it feel like you'd just entered the Twilight Zone. She didn't even ask for the money again, just rattled the ticket at him, and he handed over the four bills. She counted them out like an irritable cashier and dropped one back in his lap.

The noise and fresh air and sweet aroma of diesel exhaust fumes at the toll booth brought him around. As her window hissed shut and the car sped into the darkness on the other side, he crumpled the dollar in his fist and said what the fuck. He lowered his own window, sucking more cool air through his nostrils, lit a cigarette, and then flicked the bill out the window.

They fought the rest of the way down I-70 and then on through the exit north for Sunburg. He kept telling her, just shut the fuck up and drop it — about the banquet, about *business*, about her *prospects*, about her fucking *networking*, about his jokes, and now about the dollar bill, which that last one she just couldn't let go of. She should've just been smart and shut up. Wasn't his fault. If she'd've just shut up… but no, she wouldn't, so just as they were coming up on a four-way stop on Fairlane Road, still about four-five miles from home, he let her have it, a good, quick shot, with the back of his left fist, that caught her cheek-bone straight on and sent her head thumping into the window. Her hand jerked the wheel and pulled on it, sending them careening toward a ditch, and he grabbed the wheel, fighting her grasp and pulling it back, now overcompensating, which sent them wheeling and fishtailing toward the other side of the road, where they plowed a couple of deep furrows into a front lawn at the corner before they came to a stop.

The intersection was empty and the house dark, but now a light went on in one window and then the porch light.

—Stupid bitch!

He climbed out and loped around to the other side and yanked her out onto the wet grass, where she landed on all fours.

—What the fuck is wrong with you?! she screamed.

Her dress was ripped where he'd grabbed her, and her hair dangled over her face as she looked up at him and then dabbed her fingers at the bruise on her cheek. —You sonovabitch!

He landed a foot in her torso, as if punting a football, and sent her rolling across the grass. She gasped and coughed as she tried to right herself, dizzily tumbling over again before she got to her feet, wobbly, filthy, tearful.

They were in the shadow of the truck, away from the front porch light, which was dim and barely lit even the passenger side, nearest the house. A shadow filled the front doorway, maybe an old woman. Ross stood over Anna as she stumbled around in the darkness, looking for a missing shoe. He thought with satisfaction of the expensive toe nail job that no one got to see now sliding around in the mud and grass.

—I'm done with you, you bastard!

She found the shoe and put it on and then started away, trudging into the darkness toward the road. Not a single car had passed since they landed here.

The shadow in the doorway was gone and the front door shut.

Calling the cops, Ross figured.

—Get in the truck, he said.

—Fuck you!

—Just saying it once more… get in the fucking truck!

Nada. She trudged toward the road.

He caught up with her in a few strides, grabbed her by the hair, pulling her head down so she was helpless to do anything but follow, and marched her around to the passenger side, shoved her into the seat, and slammed the door.

A heavy woman's figure now appeared in the front window.

He fishtailed the truck again and farmed up the lawn – a parting gift for the nosy bitch in the window – before cutting diagonally back toward the road and bouncing over the shoulder and through the intersection. Too dark for her to get his tag number anyway.

Anna didn't even weep as he drove, just sat there, dour and filled with hate, looking away, out the passenger window.

He hated her less when she was like this – when she was hating him, that is – than when she was running around with her business cards, sucking up to those old farmers, *networking* her way through that herd of bloodsuckers who take government handouts while they run the price of bread up on everyone else. In fact, he really didn't hate her at all at such moments. He even found a kind of sweetness in her silence, her near stillness, how her movements had suddenly become small, limited, purposive. She was like a child who needed disciplining, and now that that was done, you didn't have to nurture your anger toward her any longer. She got it. She wasn't going anywhere. She knew he'd never let her take Kimmy – and she'd never leave her behind.

He left her to herself when they got home. She iced the bruise and slept with Kimmy fully clothed. In the morning, he ate cereal and watched cartoons with Kimmy while Anna stumbled around the house, ignoring him, showering. She might have locked herself away for the day except he said he was taking Kimmy to his mother's for dinner. Anna didn't want to go, but she didn't want him taking Kimmy anywhere without her, so she went too. He knew that what she needed most to shake her out of this mood was a good fucking, so that's what he did, on Sunday night after they got home, when Kimmy'd gone to bed and the football game was still on in the living room. He fucked her right there, on the sofa, and by Monday, when she had to go back to work, she was fine – couldn't hardly notice the bruise on her cheek at all, which she pancaked pretty well – and he didn't hear no more shit about *networking* either, or about farming up that lawn.

—Them e-mails you get from those women? Mandel suddenly said, from that website? how do you even know they're legit? Like some punk out there might just be pranking you.

Ross had been doodling on the paper – a picture of a dog's head, with a long snout and pointy ears, one of the only figures he could draw. He tried shading in some fur but now the doodle was a mess, didn't even resemble an animal.

He blew an exasperated breath, as if Mandel had interrupted his writing again.

—Thought a that, he said, but what the fuck. Worth a chance, right? Figure it's a numbers game. Like I got two so maybe one's legit. Probably get more, too. Sooner or later someone's gonna show up at the gate if I keep writing them.

—True that, Mandel said.

Ross wiggled the pen in his fingers and thought for a moment. He crumpled the page with the doodles and unfinished sentence, thinking he ought to get these women to send photos. Maybe that's what he'd say.

Opening Night and June Allyson Drops a Line

Winter passed and war came. Like Superbowl Sunday. Like opening night for a blockbuster movie. Like Christmas. It even had a trademark slogan: *Shock and Awe!* And graphics and stirring, urgent music, and news anchors who read from teleprompters in grave and heavy voices. It had dark-skinned villains in black beards and ragged clothes. And it had heroes. Legions of heroes. Soldiers were soldiers no more: they were heroes. America embraced war. America's Superbowl. America's blockbuster! And Americans embraced the season, the movie, the game, the war in the way Americans embraced such events... by shopping. For that was, the leaders said, how this war would be won, not with Victory Gardens and rationing coupons, not by driving less or lowering thermostats on cold days – no, the war would be won in the trenches of shopping centers throughout The Homeland, as the country was now known. The true American heroes would be those citizens who stiffened their resolve, held their heads high, slapped yellow-ribbon magnets on their SUVs, and undertook missions to the nation's malls. They would pretend the terrorists didn't scare them by pretending there was no war. And soon pretense became reality. And for many, for most, soon, there was no war. It simply did not exist.

And then, less than three months after the invasion, on May 1, 2003, the movie ended, the game was over, the war was won, the mission accomplished! Somewhere off the coast of California, a Navy S-3B Viking fighter jet made two flybys over the aircraft carrier *USS Abraham Lincoln* before sweeping onto the deck for a thrilling tail-hook landing, snatching the last of four cables before it ran out of runway. Then the cockpit dome opened and out popped… the Commander-in-Chief! In full flight gear! The first American president ever to make such a landing, or such an entrance. Helmet cradled in his arm, he'd come to deliver the good news. *Mission Accomplished!* It was over. America had triumphed – again! Another victory for the history books. On to Memorial Day. Time to dust off the barbecue grill. *War is over!*

———⁘———

DEATH MAKES YOU DO things you haven't thought about doing in a long while, like going down to the basement and opening an old suitcase with your past stashed away in it like Dorian Gray's portrait, only Elliot didn't have a magic spell to keep him young and handsome too.

Not his own death, of course.

No, it was Phil.

Nancy called, couldn't have been five minutes after Nick and Jo left for Kimmy's school carnival, and said he'd died that afternoon. Elliot couldn't quite ingest the news for the shock of hearing her voice on the phone – or her fortunate timing. He wasn't sure she'd have gotten a word in if Jo answered, or that Jo would even have answered if she'd seen Nancy's name on the caller ID. As if reading Elliot's thoughts, Nancy said she hoped he'd be the one to pick up the phone. He was easier to talk to. They should all know – Kimmy should know – her grandfather died today.

Watching TV, she added musingly, and then hmphed an empty laugh, as if there was something ironic, or maybe just fitting, about

235

him dying in front of the TV. She told Elliot she knew he was gone the moment she saw him. Not a chance he'd just dozed off. His head was slumped back and his mouth open in a breathless yawn that couldn't mean anything else. She even wondered if he hadn't somehow held off until she was out of the room and then departed, so to speak, like he wanted to be by himself to do it – a notion that Elliot faintly understood, though he didn't say so, for he'd heard of people going that way, mostly older folks, it seemed, and he even understood it in a way that he didn't want to share because it had a closer proximity to him now and felt more like a secret you kept, like a kind of inside knowledge among the club of those within sight, than something you talked about, and besides, this was Nancy's moment and he didn't want to be talking over it. She narrated all this in a flat voice, almost numb, which wasn't the thing that most struck Elliot about the call, that being the unmistakable note of relief he also picked up in her voice, as if some great burden had finally been lifted from her shoulders.

He'd been sitting in the parlor reading a script for a new play by one of the theater group members which not only had a part for him but was transparently based on his life, though maybe exaggerated a magnitude or two. The Elliot-character in the play (lamely named Ernest) was homeless, bouncing through shelters and homeless camps and sometimes sleeping in cardboard boxes in back alleys or in the woods along the railroad tracks, but always within the orbit of a generic, mid-sized, all-too-recognizable Midwestern town. As he traveled his customary routes, Ernest would collect trash to be recycled in a satiric parody of Elliot's environmental ways. Sometimes, when he was lucky, he'd find a short length of copper piping to sell, but his main customer, the junkyard owner – a vicious take on the same funeral home director who had buried Anna some nine years ago – would accuse him of stealing it from a construction site, which Ernest had not, though he couldn't convince the junkyard owner otherwise, who still wasn't above buying the metal at a fraction of its value. A clerk at the grocery store (this time a particularly cheap shot at Kim's friend, Karl, who still packed their groceries every week) would remind Ernest, who always seemed to forget, that they didn't pay refunds on bottles or cans here like they did back East, where old, homeless, sadly comic, and not-too-bright Ernest came from, leaving Ernest confused about where on the planet he was and how he got here.

So when Nancy called, Elliot, the real Elliot, was plodding his way through this thin script, steeped at once in the chaotic meta-experience of the playwright's caricature of him while trying to imagine himself playing a character based on himself. The whole thing was a kaleidoscopic mess – and Elliot thought that's just what an audience would think too. In fact, he didn't see what could possibly interest an audience in this play, not only because he wasn't that interesting a character after all, once you put him down on paper and lifted a few quasi-colorful lines from his conversations (diluted now by the playwright's mealy paraphrasing), but because the play didn't have much of a plot, which, Elliot thought, was what people wanted most, wasn't it, a good story. Just tell a good story is the thing. Rather the play's only point seemed to be to caricature, rather cruelly, a number of townspeople, and Elliot thought (generously, it's worth saying), well, maybe it could have some interest in a *Spoon River* sort of way – and there would be no shortage of drama or potential entertainment, he conceded, in seeing how the caricatured responded to seeing themselves on stage – but really, the play just wasn't any good, mostly because it was simply mean-spirited; it lacked compassion; it had no heart and wasn't worth anyone's time or money, and certainly none of his effort. Oddly enough, he wasn't even offended – maybe because it was so bad that it was laughable – though he was sure others would be, and perhaps even a few on his behalf, he liked to think. But he'd already decided that he wouldn't do it, though if they went ahead with this nonsense, he was curious to see who would end up playing him (which, when the play finally was produced, turned out to be the long-displaced Scrooge).

After Nancy's call he aimlessly scanned a few more pages. A couple of guests passed through and stopped to chat about the war. They didn't think it would last much longer. Clear out a few dead-enders, they said. Mop up some isolated spots. Sounded more like housework than war, but Elliot just nodded passively, and the guests went off to wherever they were going, leaving him to page through the cartoon version of himself on his lap and think about how war just didn't seem that big a deal to people – they even seemed to like it, he couldn't help thinking. News of Phil's death left him feeling hollow, not so much from a sense of personal loss as a sense of waste. The relief in Nancy's voice was all that echoed from the quiet pass-ing of an entire life which had been lived for every breath of some eighty years or more, and now it was gone and Phil had joined all the dead of the ages in anonymity, leaving behind just a sigh of relief on the lips of one of the few who would still briefly, for the remain-ing length of her own time, remember him.

It's not difficult imagining how such a cloudy personal atmo-sphere would lead you down the stairway and across the basement to the honey-colored suitcase with thin brown stripes that looked like it would have been at home on a steamy train platform sometime in the way-back between W-Ws One and Two.

Damn thing was heavy, too. He hoisted it onto a chair beneath a naked lightbulb and unlocked it and imagined Nick and Jo discovering what was here once he'd gone off to wherever Phil was, and for the most part it would be curious but not surprising, the sort of things you'd expect to find: old LPs, scripts, photos, a few master tapes from his TV show, a fifth of Johnny that he'd stashed just-in-case for the day he'd want it (good to know it was here); some worthless stock certificates; a half-finished scrapbook of clippings that he didn't half-finish himself but rather his second wife did (or didn't), and for a moment he missed her and wondered if she was still married to that French violinist. He had handwritten notes from a few old-time stars which might be worth something (maybe Jo could sell them on the computer like she was some of the antiques in the house – hmm, those old records might be worth something too). He found a Mason jar full of coins and realized it was so old the quarters and dimes might be silver, so he put that aside too.

He didn't have some particular something he was looking for, but rather felt an instinct to submerse himself in his life's detritus, to touch things that had last been touched when the bag was packed, which predated his rehab and went back to the life before that, from which he had passed away as definitively as Phil. Elliot now lived, he thought, in a kind of afterlife. Maybe eons ago that's where these notions about afterlives and such began, he considered; that your life itself contained the full spectrum of all that some of the more literal-minded religious types (and there seemed to be a lot of them these days) thought happened after you died, and before too. That maybe hell and heaven and reincarnation and all those other notions that governed entire civilizations, past and present and probably still to come, were really all wrapped up inside the life you were living, but in ways that were unrecognizable because you were inside it and no more aware of it than a fish was of water.

His circle was small these days, so the news of Phil's passing had depressed him, and mucking through this old stuff was just feeding the gloom. He brought the letters, the LPs, and the jar of coins upstairs and was sitting in the kitchen studying the liner notes on Miles Davis's *Sketches of Spain* when Jo and Nick and Kimmy arrived.

Jo had the glazed, traumatized look of surviving deep submersion in adolescent chaos. Nick was typically unfazed.

Kim wore a twisted balloon hat shaped like a giraffe.

Didn't seem like the right moment to mention Nancy's call.

—What's all this? Jo said.

Kim slid onto a stool beside Elliot and peered at the money jar as if it contained a toad or small snake. The balloon hat wobbled as she moved. The giraffe's neck and head sprouted a foot or so over her head.

—Some stuff you can maybe trade on your computer, Elliot said. My token offering to the commonweal. Might be some silver in that jar, he added.

—Really? Kim said.

He opened it and poured a scattering of coins on the counter and picked through them as if sorting pieces for a puzzle.

—Here, here's one! He held a quarter up to the light. —Look, from 1958. They stopped using all silver sometime in the sixties, thereabouts.

Her eyes followed the coin as he waved it around as if watching a June bug.

He found one with copper to show her the difference. Soon Nick joined the search.

—Well, those are yours, Elliot, Jo declared, and we'll be just fine without them.

Elliot shrugged. —I'll just get ripped off by some dealer, and besides, I didn't miss 'em before and won't miss 'em now. Do more good if you just put it toward the house. And these too.

The letters shook like dried leaves in a light breeze as he handed them to her.

She paged through and suddenly exclaimed, —Oh, Elliot! Here's one from James Cagney and another from Kitty Carlisle, and these are from Van Johnson and Barry Nelson and Eleanor Parker!

She shuffled the pages, eyes wide, and then looked up. —It's a who's-who of movie stars! I had no idea you knew all these people. She chuckled and added, —And there you were telling that doctor who was so full of himself about that old summer stock actor who nobody remembers, when you knew all these people! No, no, Elliot, you have to keep these. They're a treasure. She glanced down again and read the next letter, and sighed formidably at the sight of June Allyson's signature. A weepy memory of watching *Little Women* on TV with Anna when they were children tumbled out.

The giraffe's head looked up as if a thicket of Serengeti grass had rustled threateningly.

Jo patted her shoulder and said softly to Elliot, —These are yours. I wouldn't think of selling them. But you'll have to tell us about all these stars. You've been keeping all this to yourself, Elliot. How did you know June Allyson?

—Not much of a story about June, he said. I was on her show whenever it was, back in the fifties or something. Just a thank you note, is all. They're not worth a thing to me. Not sure why people put such stock in old papers like that. You can do that computer auction thingy of yours and see what some fool'll pay.

He tapped his fingers into the air.

The giraffe had returned to grazing in the coins.

—Maybe we'll frame them, Jo said. Probably have frames that'd fit downstairs.

Nick was idly pushing coins around on the counter. —I'll have to screw them to the walls like they do lamps and pictures in motels, he said.

Elliot laughed. —That's about the most cynical thing I've ever heard you utter.

The silver coins were starting to take on an order, as silver dimes and quarters joined their own kind in wallpaper-like clusters.

The giraffe was staring at him now.

—Guess what, Uncle E, Kim said.

—What?

—We saw Lalo.

Elliot frowned puzzlement.

—Lalo! she repeated.

—Oh, you remember him, Jo said, that Mexican family a few years back.

—Ah! Elliot turned to Kim. So what happened to him?

—Dunno. We hardly saw him.

—He was with some other kids, Jo said. I'm not even sure he saw us.

—He did, Kim said. I waved, but he looked like he didn't recognize me. Maybe I look different. Do I look different?

—You're older, Jo said. And you had on that headgear. (Jo flicked a finger at the balloon hat.) —Was years ago last time you saw him, she added. And besides, he probably couldn't break away from his friends.

—I ain't seen him in school.

—*Ain't?*! Elliot said.

—Yeah.

⸺⁓⸺

ELLIOT HAD ALREADY DECIDED to attend Phil's funeral by the time he shared the news with Jo and Nick later that evening.

No question about them not going, but Jo did concede to sending a card (Nick's idea) and having Kimmy sign it too. No note. Just their names beneath a generic message of condolence from the ranks of Hallmark's lyric poets.

Elliot got Leo to take him, who seemed oddly moved by the death of the spouse of someone he'd met only once. Elliot had known Leo for years, but he'd never seen him dressed so well. His cologne filled the car. As they drove, he asked Elliot why the rest of the family wasn't going.

—Even for the brief time that they'd reached a détente of sorts, Elliot said, things were never good between Jo and Nancy.

—But they're the girl's grandparents.

—Just Nancy… Phil was Kimmy's step-grandfather, but she'd never known the real grandfather on that side when she was little, and from what I hear, it's just as well.

—She remember them from back then?

—Better than she lets on, I think, but she never got comfortable with having them around either, which just encouraged Jo to keep them at arm's length. But even so, for a stretch they had some regular contact. Poor Nancy. I do feel for her sometimes. She was so desperate to have some relation with the girl.

—Well, that's not right, Elliot. I mean, I know we're friends and I respect your family, and I like them all a lot, but that just don't seem right. Seems downright unfair, you ask me.

Elliot nodded. —I can see how it'd look that way, but for one thing you never saw how bad things got way back years ago, when Kim's father went on trial. Nancy's always believed she was cheated twice-over, first by the law, because she clings to the idea that her son is innocent, and a second time by Jo, who was meanwhile worried that Nancy'd try to convince Kimmy he was innocent too. One thing Jo wanted at all costs, and still does, is to keep him away from her.

Leo's Town Car was over ten years old, but he kept it looking new. Not just clean, but new. He cleaned in the crevices around the dashboard dials and in the cupholders, and around the door posts and hinges where grime accumulates and most people never bother cleaning, but where you felt newness without realizing why. Leo's doorposts and hinges gleamed. The carpet pile was fluffed up from a recent vacuuming. Leo never smoked in his car, though he chomped on a Corona as he drove. The car shone inside and out. Drops of water still clung to the windows from the carwash. Said he ran it through at oh-six-hundred hours, when there was no line.

—What's the other? he asked.

—Other what?

—You said 'for one thing' like there was more than one thing. What else besides that?

—Oh, it was the letter.

—Letter?

Elliot sniffed a laugh.

—What? Leo asked. What's funny about that?

—Well, in a way you were part of it.

—Me?!

—Yes, you remember the night that play opened last year?

Leo nodded. Neither of them had mentioned that this was his only thread-like connection to today's doings, apart from chauffeuring Elliot.

Elliot continued, —I didn't witness it myself, but apparently when you left Nancy alone with Kimmy to go fetch her a drink or something, she passed along a letter from the girl's father.

Leo thought for a moment, and then said, —I recall that, the two of them talking when I came along. But that don't seem so bad. Seems like she'd be the very one to pass along a note. Probably did all the time.

—Well, if she did, that's the only one we ever heard of, but the point is, that was *verboten*, the one thing Jo wouldn't have. She'd sent back a bunch of letters unopened that came from the prison, and Nancy wasn't even supposed to talk about him with her. That was a condition of her visits.

—That's downright cruel, Elliot.

—Not for me to judge, but Kimmy's seen things for sure that none of us should ever have to see, so Jo's been very protective of her, and well, let's face it, her father's a convicted murderer, and he'd abused the child's mother for years before he killed her.

—But you just said it ain't certain that he did kill her.

—Oh, he did. There's no doubt.

—But Nancy doubts it, Leo said, his voice gathering a tinge of defensiveness.

Which Elliot noticed but let pass. —Thing is, he said, she wasn't supposed to pass along this letter, and she broke a trust when she did, and then she and Jo had a hell of a fight when Jo found out, and so Nancy hasn't seen Kim since that night.

Leo pondered this, and then asked, —So what'd the letter say?

—We don't know, Elliot shrugged. No one does, only Kimmy. But she got very moody after that night, after the play. Even moreso than usual. She was always quiet. Seems to like her own company best, but you could tell there was more going on inside her than she let on. Jo's never felt easy with her either. God knows she tries, but some people just don't mix easy, and that's always how it's been with them, but so, Kim got worse than usual, quick-tempered, brooding, holing up in her room, and finally, after a week or more of this, Jo walked in on her and found her reading the letter… probably rereading it for the umpteenth time. Jo knew instantly what it was when she saw the envelope on the bed. She wanted to read the letter too, but Kimmy wouldn't let her, though she did find out how she got it.

—So Jo still ain't read it?

—No, not her, not even Nancy. No one but Kimmy and her father knows what's in it. Nancy delivered it sealed.

—And the girl ain't said what was in it?

—Not a word. Jo's not above searching her room… though there's a good reason for that, which I'll tell you another time… but I don't think she would, not for the letter, and besides, if I know Kimmy, no one would find it even if they took that room apart board by board, if that's even where she stashed it.

—That's a hell of thing, Elliot, Leo said thoughtfully. Wonder what's in it.

—Me too.

Elliot and Leo finally arrived at a small cemetery in a remote corner of Bueller County, where Phil's people from three generations back were buried. They passed into the place beneath a white wrought iron archway suspended from two plain white poles at the end of a gravelly lane off the main road. A white utility shack stood off to one side. There couldn't have been more than a few hundred grave markers, most of which were discreetly set into the grass. There was little to suggest this even was a cemetery until you were upon it. Farmland surrounded the place on all sides. It was, Elliot reflected, the kind of place you could settle in for a long time and not worry about a thing. Quiet *was* the sound of the place, not merely a by-product of having the little road noise there was absorbed by trees and hills; it was the sound the place made, and there was nothing to disturb it, even visually – no utility lines or highways or buildings or signs. Just the hills billowing off in the distance as if they'd been tossed across the landscape like a flung blanket. Eternity took on a new character here for Elliot, and it was much larger and more inviting than anything he'd ever imagined.

He and Leo soon joined a handful of Phil's cousins and a few former co-workers who'd gathered around Nancy at the gravesite. Considering Leo's remote connection to these folks – he'd never met Phil as a living person, after all, and only had the one encounter with Nancy – his mood was decidedly lugubrious, especially when the time came to take Nancy's hand and express his very sincere sympathies for her loss. He was very sincere. And very sympathetic. He looked squarely into her eyes and told her if there was anything, anything at all, that she needed, she should call on him, and he said it with the conviction of a man who'd once had ten thousand men at his beck and call and wasn't in the habit of saying things he didn't mean. She was moved, too, as she was by Elliot's presence, which felt to him as if they were taking up once more that odd conversation from last week when she called to tell him Phil was gone, just picking up where they left off, and as if he, in some strange and inexplicable way, embodied all that she was missing family-wise at the moment, all the people who might have been at this funeral but for the turn things had taken so long ago, which didn't seem so long ago at all when an event like this came along, when the absent were as present as the few cousins and former co-workers who were now clumped here and there just beyond the immediate perimeter of Phil's final resting place, wandering about the cemetery, studying the older stones, even bubbling into laughter here and there – well, they hadn't seen in each in so long, had they, and when would they see each other again?

So her grief, Elliot could see, was for that larger loss, which Phil's death had the unintended consequence of accentuating. However difficult Phil been for her to manage – and you couldn't be around them long without seeing how difficult that was – he was all that was left to her.

There would be sandwiches and salads, one of the cousins told Elliot and Leo as they were leaving, and fruit bowls and cakes, and beers and coffee, at Nancy's house, just a little something was all, so the house wouldn't be empty when Nancy got home, the cousin added, and on a personal note, she whispered, could they come? There were so few here, after all, and it would be so nice if they did. Leo appeared to have room on his calendar. The upturned parabola of his lips and arched eyebrows conveyed to Elliot that they had to eat lunch anyways, but Elliot said no, but thank you so much, he had a doctor appointment still ahead, to which the cousin said nothing serious I hope and Elliot said nothing at all, just the doctor's wife had ordered some new furniture and he needed Elliot to come in and pay for it, and they all laughed, and Leo said, as they wound along a narrow county road that Elliot could no way ever again tell anyone how to find, you ain't got no doctor appointment, and then, after a pause, do you? And Elliot said no, just seemed like a family thing is all, those folks getting together, though the real reason, which he didn't tell Leo, was that he knew, could foresee, that is, how explaining who he was and how he knew Nancy, and even how he knew Leo, and maybe having to explain it five-six times over, for all you knew, was just the kind of conversation she didn't need in her kitchen on that warm afternoon while the cousins and former co-workers enjoyed their reunion and sandwiches and fruit bowls and so forth, and avoided saying anything unpleasant about Phil – or about anyone else who might not have been able to attend the funeral.

A Language of Lies

Like he'd seen her too. Maybe just didn't want his friends to see him talking to a girl in a balloon hat, or maybe a white girl in a balloon hat, or maybe a white girl.

On Monday a.m. she scoped the commons before first hour and there he was with the other Latins, where they always hung out by the railing that overlooked the back doors. He was still shorter than her and most of the kids around him too, but he was the liveliest in the group, at the center of it, as if he'd been among them forever, even though he'd just shown up here whenever, a week ago or something. His black hair was long and parted in the middle and hung over his ears and neck, and swayed like curtains in a breeze when he turned his head.

Other kids never hung out with the Latins because all they talked was machine-gun fast Spanish. Sometimes a white kid taking like Spanish II would try talking with them and then they'd say a whole bunch of shit back which you had no idea of whatever and that'd do it for that kid for talking to them ever again.

But none of that would've bothered her a lick. She didn't go talk to him because she knew he'd seen her too and remembered her and there was no mistaking that, when you see someone and they see you too, but so if he just wanted to hang with the other Latins, whatever, but she wondered how long he'd been around because the first she'd seen him was Friday at the carnival, and like maybe he'd already seen her first. She just wondered is all, and plus mainly, where had he gone for all these years? She was curious about that too.

Tulsa first, she soon learned, where his family lived with an uncle's family and his papa worked on a lawn crew with Lalo's uncle, but the house was crowded and his mama didn't get along with Lalo's aunt, and so they went to Wichita and spent a winter there, and then a couple of other places that Lalo said he couldn't keep straight. For a while, he said – could've been weeks or months, seemed like forever – they just stayed in the car and it was hot and you could hardly sleep and sometimes they'd get waked up and told they couldn't park there so they'd drive off to somewheres else and try to sleep there, but Lalo couldn't sleep so he'd watch cars passing on the highway and wonder where people were going and who they were and what their houses looked like, but here, this had been the best place, where both his papa and mama got work before they left and another uncle was here now too, but this was a different uncle, his mama's brother, and she missed him and they stayed with him for a while and then got an apartment. They'd got evicted from the house way back because some neighbors complained about them being Mexican and all. The landlord didn't care long as he got his money but then people kept calling and complaining and whatever, and finally he made them leave.

Lalo told her all this while they sat on the brick wall in front of school where she waited for Uncle Nick to pick her up every afternoon. She had a math paper to finish so when Aunt Jo asked if it was done she could say yeah and that'd be that, but she was just drawing on the paper and knew he was coming her way down the walk but she waited till he said hey Kimmy before she looked up and there he was. His English was good now, not so much English-teacher good, but he could say what he wanted to say, but she noticed how he spoke English like it had a bad taste in his mouth, or like clothes that didn't fit but he'd just got used to wearing them, or no, like it was a work-job that the only reason you'd ever do it was for money like when Flann got that job at McDonald's but he hated being there every minute and he smelled like stale French fries at the end of his shift, and his clothes were smelly and stained and Aunt Jo made him take his shoes off in the breezeway: that's how English sounded on Lalo – a language of bitterness and hostility and survival, maybe how it sounded to him too.

If he was glad to see her, he didn't show it. He acted more like she was the newcomer and he already knew his way around, had friends, was too cool for homework (he was empty-handed, no books or papers or backpack). He made no mention of seeing her and didn't ask about her life in all the time since they shared sandwiches and she sat beside him in class. She thought maybe if she could speak Spanish he'd treat her differently. She wondered if English was just a language of lies to him. She still remembered some Spanish she'd learned from him, and she took it in school too, but now she feared looking like other kids who tried talking Spanish to the Latins. She was sure he'd laugh at her if she tried.

He'd only started up school again the day before the carnival, he said. Been in lots of schools, he added, sometimes only a week or two. Was nothing. Didn't even remember their names, most of them. Somewheres to go while his mama and papa worked. His family lived in an apartment building down near the mall.

—So how come you just sittin' here all by yourself? he asked.

—Homework, she shrugged.

—But I seen you in school too, and you don't hang out with no one.

—No one I want to hang out with, I guess. Doesn't bother me.

—You still the same. You got bigger and stuff but you don't try to look like them other white girls. I could remember that, how you was different from them. See, like you just wearing the jeans and the shirttails out, 'n they all gotta be in the skirts and fancy sweaters and all the bangles 'n the hair in all colors. Hah! You wouldn't never wear that shit. I could tell.

He said this with only a glance her way, a flick of his hand. He was looking out toward the parking lot, where a teacher had piled his bag and books on top of his car to unlock it. Lalo's feet swung free and he kept jittering his right foot and banging the heel against the wall. She sat cross-legged on top of the wall.

—He don't got no key fob, Lalo said.

—Who?

—That teach.

He jerked his head that way.

—See, he's gotta unlock the door with a key. Just drives a old piece a shit.

Kim knew him, Mr. Hanley, the science teacher. Everyone knew about his room because it smelled from all the rabbits and snakes and all the other creatures he had in there. The ceiling was hung with planets and moons for the solar system. Kim couldn't wait to get him next year. She thought his class would be cool.

Mr. Hanley's car sputtered and left a plume of gray smoke as he drove out.

Lalo shook his head, like what a fool.

She remembered kids making fun of the car his mama drove to pick him up at school.

—You still live in that big house? Lalo asked.

—Yeah, the same house.

—'N you still live with your aunt?

—My aunt and uncle.

—I remember her. She made good cookies.

Nod.

—So I heard about how come you live there, which I didn't know about before. Whew, man, I had no idea about that! But I was just a kid 'n all that time when I knew you, you never said nothing, so who knew? But so you ever go see your papa in prison? That's where he's at, ain't he?

His voice had a flat, bland familiarity with prisons and prison talk, as if asking another kid about their papa in prison was no different from asking where you got your Nikes (which she didn't have but Lalo did).

All the while she had the notebook open on her lap and continued drawing an intricate vine along the edge of the paper that now entwined the whole margin and snaked around the binder rings. Flowers blossomed into faces. A faint tremor somewhere inside her found its way into her hand and then into the shading around a girl's face among the petals.

—Huh? You ever go see him?

—Unh-uh.

—I would, Lalo declared. The two words came out like one and he nodded sharply, like part of the sentence. His foot stopped jittering as he waited for some response and when she said nothing, he added, —I'd go there and spit in his face, that's what. I'd sneak a shank inside and kill him. That's what I'd do. You ever think a doing that?

The words, in English, sounded like dogs barking, like those dogs that used to live next door but finally the people moved away and

Aunt Jo was so glad the day they moved, but like just the least little nothing would get them started, like just looking their way. Then the lady next door would shout at them to stop, and that became part of the noise too and drowned everything out worse than the lawnmower because at least the lawnmower wasn't full of rage like the dogs and the lady.

Maybe if she could've answered in Spanish, she'd have said something. Maybe they'd be talking about something else, he would, they both would.

Daddy's letter said he swore he didn't do it, that it wasn't his fault.

Anna had attacked him, he said. (He called her *Anna* and not *Mommy*.) She'd got crazy, he said, and attacked him with a knife and cut him bad too. He still had the scars, he said, and they reminded him every day that he didn't belong where he was.

At first, when she first read the letter, Kim didn't believe him – and for many readings after that. It was five pages long. His writing was a sloppy and chaotic mix of printed and cursive. He'd write a small *o* followed by a large comma, so you'd think the number *9* had just appeared on the page for no reason. One line of writing trailed upwards and the next downwards. Spelling and such was bad too – *geting, hopefuly, ascared, can not, had drank, gig was up, would of, its', bussiness*, so forth. You couldn't trust writing like that, rambling, sloppy, stupid. That was it… he sounded stupid. That was how she first read the letter.

She already knew about the knife wounds. She knew that the prosecutor said he cut himself to make it look like Mommy'd attacked him. She'd known that for a long time.

But still, through the rambling, illiterate mess of his writing, she could hear his desperation, his plea for someone to listen and believe him… and that she was his last hope of anyone who might. Maybe it was because the writing was so bad that it *was* convincing, after all. Well, not convincing, but you couldn't ignore it either. What if it was true? What if the judge and jury were wrong? Gammie believed him. Was a lie a lie just because enough people said so? Was that how the truth worked, just keep saying something enough times and then it's true?

She didn't know what to think, but she wondered about it a lot.

The other night, when Lalo saw her, she had decided, before she ever saw him, that as long as she had on the balloon hat she wouldn't have to wonder. She'd be someone else, someone who didn't think about such things, or not even someone but some*thing* – a giraffe, who lived on the plains, who could see farther, breathe different air, and remember nothing. There were music and lights and games. For a little while she was a giraffe.

The school parking lot was mostly empty now. A few neighborhood kids played basketball on one of the courts. You could hear the baseball team practicing on the field around the side of the school building. A comforting and familiar hum came to her from somewhere inside – a welcome sound that softened the harsh noises prickling all around her like skin prickles in summertime. But then, it wasn't inside her but outside too. The noise came from an engine rumbling up the hill, still out of sight beyond the trees, on the access road. A gray Mustang turned into the parking lot, cruising slowly, rumbling, glistening – proud, quick-tempered, a predator. Its deep engine rumble echoed through the near-vacant parking lot, almost detached from the car's motion, like how an animal's growl isn't what makes it run fast.

thuh-thuh-thuh-thuh-thuh-thuh-thuh-thuh-thuh-thuh-thuh-thuh-thuh...

As the car approached, its resonance absorbed everything around it – noise, light, movement. There was nothing but the car. When it stopped before them it roared, a territorial roar that sucked in the remnants of the untranslatable words inside her – words for which she had neither English nor Spanish. Yet the engine's roar wasn't fearful but welcome. Its noise had found her inner rhythm, expressed it, comforted her.

A Latino kid leaned out of the passenger window and drummed the side of the car like bongo drums as he called in Spanish to Lalo, who laughed as he answered. The first time he'd laughed since he sat with her.

—We goin' to Dairy Cream, he said. So you wanna come?

The mistake jarred her. *No, no… it's Dairy… Queen.*

And the correction jarred her too, though she hadn't even spoken it, hadn't corrected him, as if those words had something to do with the letter too, or should have, as if some connection was made, something about ice cream, strawberry ice cream, and sitting on the curb, almost like they were now, and people getting ice cream at Dairy Queen. It was all shadowy, like fragments of a dream you can't remember later. The story-line is lost; the people in the dream have no faces or names. She was there that day. She'd always known that, but never for herself, from her own memory, only from the fact of it, from what others told her, and now from what the letter said, and from Lalo calling *Dairy Queen* by the wrong name. What could that mean? All that she knew about that day came from outside of her, but it was trying to sync itself with whatever she'd forgotten, like the engine's roar finding the rhythm of her own protective hum, which sheltered her, keeping others out and herself in.

She just shook her head no.

—C'mon, Lalo said. We bring you home after.

—Can't, she said. My uncle's gonna be here.

Lalo hopped off the wall with a shrug. —Maybe you come another time.

—Maybe.

He climbed into the car, and it roared and squealed down the hill to Dairy Cream.

⁓

WHERE FLANN DID HIS UA when his color came up was a storefront on Shawnee Trail Road she'd passed a hundred times and never noticed till now, while she sat in the car and waited for him. No markings on the building but the street number. Must've been something once. Something tropical. The cinderblock siding was painted turquoise with pink decorative brick partitions on each corner screening the trash and such from the street. The paint was faded and pealing and chipped.

Flann loped up the broken concrete steps and disappeared inside. All she could see through the door was his back at the counter before he disappeared. The windows were blocked out with brown paper. A couple of kids hung out on the side of the building smoking cigarettes, and she recognized Dory.

U-A. As in urine analysis. Part of the deal. He was assigned a color and had to call a number every day and a recording told him the color of the day, and if it was his color, he had to come and piss into a cup by four p.m. or he'd be back in court and up Shit Creek. That's why Aunt Jo and Uncle Nick let him drive, because they didn't have time for it and said it was on him to get himself here or face the consequences. No way they'd have let her come but they weren't home, so she said I want to come too, and here she was.

She wasn't allowed inside, but he told her this old dude stood there and watched you piss. Imagine getting that job, he said, laughing, watching kids piss all day, wondering which one's gonna snap and turn around and wet you all over. They had mirrors over the urinals so you couldn't switch out the cup with a clean sample. One kid, he told her, was always going around at school trying to collect other kids' piss for his UAs. Imagine that, he said, begging kids for their piss. That's when you know you're fucked up. Besides, you get caught and then you're really fucked. She figured she'd never be able to piss with someone watching her, like piss on command or else. But he didn't care, just went in and ten minutes later he was out, like nothing. And now, as he got in the car, Dory noticed her and blew cigarette smoke upwards and turned away.

The woman from behind the desk leaned out the door and told the kids git. Dory made a face at her and went off down the sidewalk with her friends.

—What's she here for? Kim asked.

—Who?

—Her.

Kim nodded toward Dory.

He squinted. —Hah! I know her. Coupla nails is all.

He said it like she was an amateur. A year in state prison, maybe two, was hanging over him if he didn't get here on time. Just as Flann hit the ignition the old dude inside turned the window sign to **CLOSED** and pulled the shade down on the door.

—So where you wanna go? Flann asked.

—Go?

—Yeah, let's go somewheres.

They got tacos at Taco-Bell and licked their fingers as they cruised up and down Shawnee Trail. They buzzed through the Sonic lot, where Flann's friends hung out, but only saw some Latins, but not the gray Mustang and not Lalo.

He made sharp turns and quick stops and starts, Flann did. She leaned this way and that, same as him. He slumped down low with his seat tilted back like a Barcalounger and steered with the heel of his hand or sometimes just a finger.

His woofers throbbed as if the car had its own heartbeat. The bass notes quaked in her chest.

She pondered where to go.

—How far is Sunburg? she asked, but the music swallowed up the last word.

—Where? he shouted.

She squeezed it into a space in the music.

—Sunburg.

—Dunno. Gotta go up K-29, I think. Never been there, but I seen signs for it. Twenty-thirty minutes, I guess. I dunno…. He lowered the volume and asked suspiciously, —Wait… why you wanna go there?

She shrugged. —Just do.

He was used to her vague answers. You couldn't get nothing out of her sometimes. Who knew what she was thinking?

—You know how fucked I'll be if the peeps find out?

—I won't tell.

—Don't guess you will either.

Another shrug.

—C'mon, Kimmy. You gotta tell me something.

—Just want to is all. So forget it. So never mind.

He thought for a moment and said, —I don't know, Kimmy. Maybe you shouldn't go there. Might not be good. How come now all of a sudden?

His sudden protectiveness sounded strange to both of them.

She frowned a like-whatever frown. —No reason *now*. Just cause we can, is all. If you're too scared…

That last even sounded weird to her. Just something that came out.

—I ain't scared. Just… you've never been there, have you?

Headshake no.

He pondered that as they came up on the railroad crossing at Market Street. A train was almost done passing. The gates would lift in a moment. A few blocks beyond was the turn for Monarch House.

—Guess I'd wanna see it, if it was me, he said. Your house, right? You wanna go see where you lived, don't you?

It wasn't just the house. She hadn't even thought about it as just *the house*. It was the *place* – and all that made it *that place*: the roads and streets, the stores, the trees, whatever surrounded them when they lived there. It was the idea that they had all been there that drew her.

And too, it had been pulling at her for a long time, maybe without her even realizing the source of this constant tugging sensation, but now she recognized it. The older she got, the more time passed, the closer that time and whatever happened back then felt, as if it was all circling back on her and now had her trapped. For one, the letter had come. That was months ago, but every day seemed like it had just arrived that day. She didn't reread it often, but it was there, with her (and taped securely to the bottom of her desk drawer, where Aunt Jo would never find it, she was sure – and sure too that Aunt Jo had looked). He'd stepped back into her life out of nowhere.

And Gammie, too. It was just an accident that she'd ever shown up again, that Kim had wandered into her line of sight at the racetrack, but it was a clue of some sort. It meant something, as if Kim was in a stage play, like Uncle Elliot, only the characters in this play were real but they didn't suspect that anyone else might not think they were real, or that there was an audience out beyond where the lights blocked everything out, only now the lights had faded and the audience members were stumbling into their world; the characters were still characters but they were wandering about the stage without the familiar light that insulated them, and without scripts, too, without knowing what to say next, having to figure it out for themselves, and now they were even wandering away, off the stage, outside the theater. You had to wonder what was out there – you had to find out.

—You'll get in trouble, she said. Forget it. Turn here.

—No, no. It's cool. We got time. We can go. Besides, I wanna see it too. Never been there neither. It's like where your life started. Sunburg's up past the outdoor theater cause I saw a sign for it when we went to see Cannibal Corpse and Deicide. I heard sometimes they sacrificed a chicken or a cat or something on stage but they didn't. Probly got told not to or whatever. You gotta hear some.

He flipped down the visor-wallet with his CDs and put on Cannibal Corpse, which came on like a chain saw revving its way through an oak tree. The singer shrieked as if he'd fallen to the bottom of some deep cave, or as if he'd been buried alive: *Fucked with a knife!! Fucked with a knife!!*

Flann's head bounced like he was pounding a stake into the ground with his forehead.

After a couple of songs, he lowered the volume and said, —Know what?

—Unh-uh.

—I'm joining up.

—Joining up?

—Like the Army.

—You are?

He nodded and grinned a thin, cocky snarl and pushed the hair off his brow. He had scrawny arms and hadn't done any sports since Little League. Nothing about him jibed with the images of soldiers on TV.

—When?

—Soon's I graduate… May… then I'm gone.

—Do they…?

—No! And you can't tell 'em neither. Swear you won't!

—But how?

—Recruiter at school, is all. Said soon as I'm outta school I can join.

—You can do that?

—Be eighteen. They don't need to sign nothing then. But you gotta swear!

—Why?

—Cause they'll call him or something and cancel it or whatever. Mom will, you know she will. Kimmy, you gotta swear!

She did. She swore. Why not? He told her about the recruiters. They set up a chin-up bar at in the commons at school and every-one was doing chin-ups, but Flann could barely do one, but the recruiter told Flann, he said he'd guarantee – *gâr-ōwn-fucking-tee!*, he'd whispered to Flann, and right there in school, too, the fuck-ing recruiter did! – that Flann'd be doing twenty-five by the end of Basic. The recruiter jumped on the bar right then and pumped twenty without even breaking a sweat, just like that. Did a couple one-handed, too.

Flann said *BDUs* and *high-speed, low-drag* and *Big Sandbox*, which was Army-talk for Iraq, like she'd know what he meant, like he'd always talked that way.

—But the main thing? Flann said, about joining? was because they attacked us.

—Who?

—Fuckin' ragheads is who! Sometimes, Kimster, it's like you… like you're on another planet or whatever or something.

Flann shut the music off when they passed the sign for Bueller County. Soon they turned off the highway and followed a sign for the Business District, which sounded like there'd be skyscrapers or something.

Main Street was wide and flat and empty, and only about four blocks long. They found themselves on a two-lane county road with the speed limit back up to sixty-five and the town behind them before they realized they'd passed through it.

—Go back, Kim urged.

Flann did a huey and drove through at a crawl this time.

They passed a couple of churches, a post office with a flagpole taller than any of the buildings, then a steakhouse in a red-brick building that had the look of an old warehouse. The appliance store didn't have a single car parked near it. A few people passed on the sidewalks and a handful of cars and pick-ups lined the street.

They felt conspicuous, as if any moment someone might step in front of the car and ask what they were doing here.

None of it looked familiar to Kim.

A couple of hundred yards past the other end of town, the road turned to highway, and once more Flann looked for a place to turn around. He pulled into the parking lot of a grain storage facility, where a boxy, white modular office building with green awnings was dwarfed by a half-dozen or so gray, poured concrete silos, which once you were right beneath them and looking up were an imposing, even terrifying sight. There was something alto-gether unhuman about them – windowless, doorless, uninhabitable, and meant to be so, for people anyway. The Cannibal Corpse singer might have been shrieking his ungodly lyrics from the bottom of one of these towers, with not a human soul to hear him.

Flann and Kim gaped at the structures for a moment before he made the turn in the parking lot. As he started to pull away, Kim said, —Wait!

He jerked to a stop. She was staring at a sign on the side of the building: *Sunburg Grain Dist., Inc.*

—What is it? he asked.

His eyes followed one of the towers up to its corrugated roof. An intricate network of pipes and trusses were joined to a steel conveyor belt than ran from a crane-like elevator at the back of the whole arrangement and fed all of the towers. He stared at the silo as if wondering if it was about to topple over on them.

—This was where she worked, Kim said.

—Hunh?

—Here… she worked here.

—How do you know?

—The name. Aunt Jo said so. At home there's a picture in one of the albums of her at a desk in there.

Flann waited as Kim studied the sign, and then asked, —So you wanna go inside? You think they might remember her?

She blew a long, wispy breath. —Never thought of that.

—What?

—That anybody'd know her.

—Probly do, Flann said. Place like this, everybody knows every-body. Bet somebody does.

She shuddered. —No, no. Just drive!

His wheels spit gravel as he pulled away.

They soon approached the town's center again.

—So what now?

—Turn there, she said abruptly, pointing to a side street on the left. —Down that way.

—You remember this?

—Unh-uh… just… she walked sometimes… we did… into town. Couldn't be that far.

The neighborhood felt small and close. The trees were thick and towered over the cottage-like houses that lined the street. The homes were a mix of tidy, well-kept places with neat lawns and manicured shrubbery alongside run-down houses with patchy yards peppered with plastic gnomes and wooden ducks with spinning wings and porches crowded with broken toys and rusting barbecue grills.

The few people they saw were white, as were the people in town.

Kim whispered, —There!

She nodded toward a house with a For Rent sign. Across the street was a small brick church that looked like it'd been reborn from a former life as an ordinary ranch house. Its vestibule was an awkward addition to the side of the building, and the steeple didn't reach the treetop of a nearby cottonwood tree.

—Where?

—Across from the church. I remember the church… and the driveway. We had a driveway… went around back to the garage. See! There was a field out there. Looks like more houses now.

Flann pulled up in front of the church and they studied the house. It was like the others – hobbit-like, a sash window on each side of the front door, a tiny porch that two lawn chairs would crowd.

The shades were down. The place looked vacant.

—That's where you lived, Kimmy, Flann said, in a near whisper. It's like… I never thought about it being real, more like you just had this ancient past, like that wasn't hardly real, like a myth or something. But there it is.

He shut off the engine and asked, —So what do you think of it, of seeing it? You remember anything?

—The tree, she said. The oak tree by the driveway. It looks different now, changed its shape. But it's an oak, it's old, has to be the same one. Lawn's grown in now, too. Was mostly dirt. Living room's the window on the left and their bedroom was on the right. Kitchen and my room were in back.

—Fuck! he muttered. You say it like it's imprinted, like you could just walk in there and you'd know right where everything was, like if it was the same furniture and shit inside you could walk through it in the dark. You've been holding back. You remember a lot more than Mom thinks you do.

—I don't know what I remember. It's just there. The house is there. Not hard to figure out what's in it.

—This is all weird 'n shit, coming here, is all. I'm just sayin'. He paused and glanced toward the house again, and then said, —Well, we came all this way, so let's check it out. Looks empty.

He was out of the car and halfway across the street before he realized she hadn't budged. He returned and went around to her side.

She sat stiffly, her face blank, staring off as if whatever she was looking at was far away.

He rapped a knuckle on the window and she looked up without opening it.

—You all right, Kimmy? You wanna leave?

She shrugged and climbed out.

He said, nervously, —Maybe we shouldna come here. You wanna go?

—No, like you said, we came all this way.

She could reach up and touch the tree limb where Daddy'd sat her without even standing on tiptoes. The bare dirt and flagstones where she'd pushed her trucks around were now a thick lawn and poured concrete walkway, and the driveway had been paved too.

They peered through a sieve in the front door blinds. The house was empty. Sunlight streaked the wood floor from the kitchen window in back. She shuddered, imagining a familiar boot suddenly stepping into the light. She could see the kitchen doorpost. Mommy had died in there. Kim was outside, playing in the dirt by the tree, the oak. The twins across the street, next door to the church, came running outside to play just then. She looked around now. There was the house, still there. They ran by, heading for the field out back. They called, —Hey, Kimmy! as they passed. She waved. She wanted to go with them, but they streaked past, between her house and the one next door, where the old lady lived, and were gone. Then shouting erupted from inside. You couldn't even make out words in it. The noise surrounded her – terrifying sounds, like animals howling in some dark forest – all she could do to drown it out was zoom her trucks through the dirt and make motor noises. *Vrrroooom! Vrrroooom!* Chairs banged and crashed, and cabinet doors, and utensils clanked, then an abrupt, isolated shriek and then quiet, which was more terrifying than the noise.

There was another day like that, too. She awoke from the weight of Mommy leaning on her… still in her dress, her new dress that she'd fussed over and sashayed in front of Kim before she went out… now torn. Frayed ragged strips of fabric fell across her arm and shoulder; her face was red and splotchy, her mouth thick on one side, swollen and sickly red, putrid red, like rust, and her cheek thick too, and dark blue and purple. Kim studied her face before she awoke, the lines and streaked makeup and her thick breathing through lightly parted lips that couldn't fully close for the swelling. Finally her eyes opened only to thin creases, as if she couldn't open them more than that, and she groaned as she recognized Kim and awoke almost as if realizing she was alive.

That was a different day – but the day Mommy died… that was the last day Kim had ever seen this place.

Daddy'd come outside and pulled the front door shut and locked it, which was different because they always left the door open when it was hot. It was always hot in summertime then. That was the only way she knew summer. Having AC or not wasn't something she knew of then, only heat. Same up and down the street. Doors and windows always open, everyone's, you could hear everything, up and down the street – TV shows, dishes clattering, kids fussing. You'd know everything about everyone because it was hot. But now he shut the door and locked it. Never did that. Mommy was still inside and he locked the door. He snatched Kim up from the ground without a word, so quickly that her hand was still in motion pushing a toy truck through the dirt, and now it flew like a plane. He grabbed it from her and tossed it on the gravel and put her in the pick-up truck and they drove away. The truck roared down the street. He slammed the gearshift up and down, then up again and down again. He said nothing, didn't even look her way as she slid back and forth on the seat, gripping the armrest for the turns, pushing herself back from the dashboard when he braked. Seemed like they drove forever.

She knew better than to say anything, even then, at four. She wasn't so much afraid as more like she already knew there was no point. He'd just grunt or tell her to hush up. They always landed somewhere when they went in the truck – at the store, at Gammie's. Nothing to be said. The ride was long – and hot and tiresome and boring. She leaned on the door and felt the truck's engine rumbling through her body, a noise, no, more a sensation that blotted everything out – fatigue, hunger, missing Mommy, wondering where they'd be whenever they got where they were going. The truck's rhythmic growl and its motion compressed themselves into a vibration that coursed through her, absorbing her discomfort and, soon, her growing fear, because this was different somehow than other truck rides. Something was different. She felt lonely even though she was beside him. The noise was familiar, and stayed with her, though she never knew where she first heard it. After they'd driven for a while, a long while, he said, —You hungry? want some ice cream?

She nodded and said, faintly, —Kay.

They were around back now, she and Flann. He was peering in the garage windows, his hands cupped around his eyes like a diving mask. Kim was up on the back porch, trying to see into the kitchen through the back door, whose blinds were also drawn. All she could see were glimpses of floor tiling. It was in there, on that floor that Mommy lay dying while Kim ate ice cream. Mommy didn't know she was dying, didn't know she was gone, gone then, gone now. Her body was still trying to live even after her mind went dark, and then she was gone.

Kim sank onto the porch steps and imagined her slumped on the floor, bruised as she'd been in bed that morning, now bleeding her life away while Kim knew nothing of what had happened – but he did… he knew she was here, knew she was dying, and he left her here and sloshed ice around the bottom of cup and ignored the people who wanted his table.

—We should go, Flann said. He was standing before her, had come up the steps and she never heard him.

She nodded and let him lead her away. He even opened the door when she climbed into the car. He'd never done that.

She never looked back as they pulled away. He followed the road ahead to avoid going through town again. She said nothing, and he didn't ask. Several miles west of town, he found his way back to K-32 and turned east toward home, and soon they passed a Dairy Queen on the left.

He broke the silence in the car and said, —We're already wicked late, 'nother fifteen minutes don't matter. You wanna take a break, maybe stop for an ice cream?

He began slowing for the turn when she burst out, —No! Don't! Don't stop here!

Her voice quaked.

—What?! What is it?

She gasped, —Not here! Don't stop here!

—Okay, okay.

He hit the gas and glanced her way, wondering what just happened.

She watched the place as they passed it – the patio was still there, the curb where she sat, the window on the side of the building where they got ice cream. New sign, new blacktop in the parking lot, probably new everything inside, but it was the same place, the very place he'd taken her and she'd sat licking strawberry ice cream while Mommy died – and that bastard chewed ice from the bottom of a watery Coke.

She leaned back in the seat, shaking, tearful, gasping in short breaths.

Flann sputtered, was she okay, it was his fault, he never should have brought her here – but what? what happened just now? Maybe it all just caught up with her at once, was that it? But she said it was nothing, just let's go home.

They hit rush-hour. 'Wicked late' wasn't even close when they finally arrived. The look of the house broadcast lateness. The porch lights and dining room lights glowed with lateness. A shit storm was coming. They knew it as they turned into the drive.

Flann said quietly, —Won't tell 'em nothing, if you don't want.

And he didn't, and neither did she.

A Night at the Movies

Tacos at Taco-Bell was all Jo ever got out of them.

Plus 'nowheres' and 'just hangin' out is all.'

But they seemed to get on better after that day, even if there was a distinctly conspiratorial flavor in their eyebrow flickers and whisperings.

The missing afternoon faded into spring.

Flann graduated… barely… didn't miss a UA, didn't test positive, passed his exams, just… he seemed oddly motivated.

After the ceremony, Kimmy asked Jo could Lalo come to the party.

Jo was delighted. Of course he could.

Nick prodded burgers and sausages out on the veranda (a veggie burger for Kimmy), while Leo supervised grilling operations and some church friends told Elliot how dreadful the community play-ers' latest offering was, how vicious, how shocked they were, how awful it was! Why people, they said, some people, just got up and walked out right in the middle — and none too quietly either. Elliot sensed they were hoping he'd add to the general melodrama that surrounded the play but just said he'd hadn't really given it a thought. They seemed disappointed.

Dawit threw horseshoes with Elliot's meeting friends out by the barn, and Ayana snatched her toddler from the edge of the koi pond before she tumbled in. Flann slouched in a lawn chair and seemed vaguely surprised whenever someone congratulated him.

Kimmy hadn't appeared since they returned from school.

Jo was about to fetch her when Lalo appeared from around the corner by the driveway. A deep rumble of heavy horsepower erupted out front and then faded, and Jo realized that was his ride pulling away.

He wore blousy gray pants, white basketball shoes and a black mock T-shirt. He studied the gathering as if uncertain he'd found the right place.

—Lalo! she called, waving.

He waited for her to come to him. His eyes had none of the humor she recalled. He looked expectant, as if a stranger on the street had just tapped him on the shoulder.

—Kim said I could come.

—Of course! We're so glad you did!

She leaned forward to clutch him, but he sensed what was coming and slid back as if shifting his weight, avoiding her grasp.

She was disappointed. After all these years – and all she'd done for him and his family…

She walked him over to Nick, where Leo shook his hand like a greeter at a chamber of commerce breakfast while the boy scanned the yard. Just then the back door swung open and Kimmy swept past Jo and across the courtyard… wearing…

… a pink tank top with spaghetti straps, faded blue jeans with floral vines embroidered along the legs (and tighter than anything Jo'd ever seen on her), a single thin braid sprouting from her hair, and no shoes.

Retro-hippie with an attitude.

And she'd never bothered this much with her hair.

Even Flann noticed. Jo watched him follow her across the lawn with his eyes. Nick couldn't conceal a double take as she sidled up beside Lalo just as he was about to hear from the Colonel about the ten-thousand-men-jumping-at-the-snap-of-his-fingers and such, and Jo saw – no, you could not miss it (even Nick, in his unmindful way, noticed) – how the boy scoped her up and down and didn't so much grin as purse his lips and offer just the slightest nod of approval before they wandered off to watch the horseshoe players.

And then, yes, Lalo pulled out a cell phone and tapped it with his thumb and talked, while Kimmy stood by, and then he snapped it shut, and they watched the horseshoes fly and clank in the pits.

Jo went inside to stir the beans on the stove. There was much to think about.

—⁓—

The Mustang's backseat swallowed you up in smoky gray leather, and you sank down low behind the front seats and peered through the tiny window, a wedge of glass no bigger than a heating vent, as if you were going underwater in a submarine.

Lalo's cousin Angel leaned around from the passenger seat and laughed and said something in Spanish, as Macario clicked through the gears.

—He says, you should see the look on your face, Lalo said.

Kim snickered. —You should've seen the look on my aunt's face.

Lalo laughed too, and she recognized the sound of it and the look in his eyes from long ago.

Angel spoke no English and Macario only some, but she couldn't hear much from up front over the engine's rumble anyway. Macario tapped the console and a song resumed with a nifty Flamenco guitar riff in fuzzy electric tones.

Aunt Jo said the movies was all and then straight home, and she made Kim wear a sweater and take Uncle Nick's cell phone too,

275

which was cool and she flipped it open like she was checking
messages and then stashed it in her hip pocket and tried to think
of someone to call.

Macario held the seat as she climbed out at the mall. Then he and
Angel walked ahead across the parking lot.

—He got a uncle, Lalo said, nodding at Macario, that did a jolt too.
Jolt.

She'd never heard the word used like that but she got it instantly.
Lalo'd told the boys about her.

It was late dusk at the mall. The sky was charcoal gray but not
fully night. The pavement was warm from the day's heat. Sodium
lights hummed and glowed overhead, and the colorful marquees
welcomed them.

They studied the movie board and bought tickets to a kiddie
movie, which when she looked at Lalo like not really, he grinned
and shook his head, and after they'd passed the ticket-taker, he said,
—We gonna bounce, is all. Don't matter what movie, so we buy the
kiddie movie like a joke.

They bounced through *Lord of the Rings: The Return of the King, The
Matrix Reloaded, Terminator 3, Bad Boys II, Pirates of the Caribbean,* and *X2.*

The boys chattered in the hallway between theaters. She asked
Lalo why Macario and Angel liked the movies so much when they
couldn't understand them.

—What's to understand? he said. It's just fights and car chases and
whatever. We just watch the fights 'n stuff.

He hung his arm around her in *X2* and showed her how to play
Tetris on the uncle's cell phone.

His fingers dangled over her breast as she played the game and
the X-Jet barely escaped a flood, though Jean drowned, sacrificing

herself to save the X-Men by spinning a telekinetic wall around the jet to hold back the waters so they could take off.

Lalo eased a hand up under her breast and moved closer, watching her play, his head on her shoulder now. The game pulled her in and she didn't want to stop. The little yellow blocks fell like heavy rain as she tapped left and right, up and down to fill the spaces. She quickly got good at it, so now, without moving his hand from her left breast, he showed her how to move up another level, but when she began to play again, he squeezed her tightly, painfully, pushing on her breast, and she squirmed, shaking him off.

He laughed. —You ticklish.

—Didn't tickle, she said. It hurt.

A few rows back someone shushed them. All three boys turned at once and peered threateningly into the rows of flickering gray faces behind them, every one now stiffly focused on the movie screen. Lalo sent a middle finger into the air like a flagpole, and the boys all howled with laughter.

Later in the hallway, Lalo leaned into Macario's ear and whispered in Spanish, though she wouldn't have understood him even if he'd spoken aloud. Macario nodded.

—We goin' to a party, Lalo told Kim.

—Can't, she said. I gotta go home.

—Oh, you can, just for a little while.

She shook her head no. —Aunt Jo said I gotta come home after the movie.

They climbed into the car, and Macario spun rubber and fishtailed as they turned onto the highway. She and Lalo laughed as they swung this way and that in the back seat. Macario revved the engine at the next light, jerking the car forward as if it was growling and pulling on a leash. As they waited for green, the people in the car beside them stared straight ahead with the same blank, fearful, rabbit-like, we're-ignoring-you-but-we-know-you're-there look as the people in the movie.

Lalo had his arm around her as the car swerved on the turns and heaved forward at green lights.

—Just for a few minutes is all, he said. It's on the way. Just be for a minute.

—I can't, she said. If I'm late, she won't let me go out again for a month or who knows when.

Angel said something to Lalo, who nodded and agreed to whatever it was, which Angel then relayed to Macario, who flicked his head yes as he downshifted. Then a block or two farther on, he turned on to a side street and took several more turns through a neighborhood.

—Where's this? Kim asked.

—It's just for a minute, Lalo said. It's on the way and then we take you straight home.

The car slowed as they cruised a block lined with cars. The party house was obvious – windows glowing, people spilling onto the porch and lingering by cars with cigarettes and bottles, Latin music throbbing into the night air.

Kim folded her arms. —I said I gotta go home.

Macario parked a block or so from the house.

—Listen, Lalo said, it ain't up to me. They just gotta stop here for a minute to see someone, that's all. Not even going to the party. Not to stay. Be no different than if we sat through part of another movie.

—I'll wait here, she said sharply.

Lalo and Macario jabbered back and forth, and then both boys in front got out and shut the doors, leaving Kim and Lalo in the car.

—I'll wait too, he said.

Lalo's phone beeped a few minutes later. He laughed when he saw the text message.

—They want us to come in, he said.

—I thought they weren't staying.

—Just take a minute. He swayed and jittered his shoulders like a dance move, and said, —Can't hardly hear the music from out there. He reached between the seats and hit the CD player on the dash, and music surrounded them – a driving four-four beat, with Spanish lyrics coated in a metal singer's throaty voice.

Lalo settled in beside her, pushing his shoulder into hers, smiling. He swayed with the music and slowly drew her into its rhythm. Her anger drained as the music found its way into her limbs. They giggled. He took up her hand and rocked it to the beat of the song. Soon he nuzzled into her hair and she let him kiss her. She'd never been kissed before, not like this. His lips were warm and strange – they seemed to greet hers. He kissed her easily, gently, as if awakening her. But the next was harsh, like pushing through a door. His lips flattened hers on her teeth and didn't release her, and then, abruptly, his mouth widened and his tongue pushed through her lips and rubbed against her teeth. She pulled back, but his mouth kept pressing on hers, and now his hand was up inside her sweater.

She curled stiffly into the corner of the seat, and he moved with her, surrounding her. His breaths were shallow and quick and urgent. He went for her neck when she turned away, first licking it and then biting her as he pulled at her blouse. She felt the strap break on one side. His fingers swarmed her breast like a rodent scratching all over it, and then his grip tightened and he squeezed until she shrieked, —No! That hurt! Get your hands off me! But still he pressed her,

squeezing her breast as if wringing out a sponge, and she screamed
again, but the guitar and drums and heavy leather and thick glass
swallowed up her voice. She squirmed and struggled, but he coun-
tered every move, trapping her in the corner, yanking her sweater off
her shoulders and pulling her blouse down and now the bra, until
her breasts were exposed and he began to lick and gnaw on one as
he groped the other, and then his hand slid down to her pants and
began working the belt open.

She screamed and fought back, shouting in a voice that sounded
like it belonged to someone else. She batted at him and kicked anything her feet could find, upholstery, legs, feet, anything. Now he'd
pulled her pant waist open but couldn't get the pants down without
unzipping her, and he couldn't grasp the tab as she squirmed and
struggled, so he suddenly drew back, as if regrouping, and pinned
her into the corner with one hand planted stiffly on her chest, giving
himself room to swing, and then smacked her hard across the cheek.
The blow stunned her into stillness.

—What's wrong with you, bitch?! he shouted. Just be still. You
gonna like it. You white bitches all the same – all uptight and then
once you get it, you can't get enough.

His face was shadowy in the dim street light. She shook and
panted like a chipmunk she'd once seen trapped in a drain pipe
until Uncle Nick released it, but she was suddenly no longer
afraid because this shadowy face belonged to a stranger, so she had
nothing to fear from hurting it, and now she screamed and swung
wildly at him, holding her fingers claw-like so her nails would
catch his cheek.

—Ahhh! he cried, as she swiped her nails across his face.

She pounded him with her fists, scratching, writhing, fighting viciously. She kicked hard and reached for the wheel to pull herself up front.

As she wedged herself between the seats, he tried to pull her back, yanking at her pants, but once she got hold of the wheel he'd have had to cut her hand off to get her to release her grip. She finally pulled herself through and tumbled out the passenger door, landing face down on the grass. He stepped on her back, as he climbed out, holding her down. Her screams echoed up and down the dark street, —Let me up, you fucker! Let me the fuck up! Get off me, you fucker!

And he did, looking around, dazed, realizing that everywhere heads had now turned their way.

He fell back against the car, spent, head down, sniveling, dabbing at the scratches on his face and neck with his fingertips. —What the fuck's wrong with you? he whimpered. You think you're too good for me. Your old man's a fucking con. You think cause you're white you're too good for me?!

She turned away. Others watched as she got up and pulled up her blouse and buckled her belt and brushed the dirt off.

And then, as she turned to ask what the fuck was wrong with *him*, she saw the scratches on his cheek and neck – and it was *those*, on his neck, the scratches on his neck, that she recognized. She'd seen those scratches before, up close, just once, in the same light. Raw, fresh painful-looking, cuts – still red and moist, before the blood had clotted and dried, the skin sweaty from heat that had carried over from the afternoon and into the evening so it seemed like the sun hadn't set at all, only it got dark. A million invisible cicadas hummed everywhere forming immense walls of sound on either side of Gammie's driveway. They'd driven forever, seemed like, and then got ice cream, and then Daddy took her to Gammie's house, and sleepy now, she felt him pull her from the truck. She rode his hip up to the front porch, and as she bounced against his shoulder, right there before her eyes were the scratches, at the end of her nose, that close. For a few moments that's all she saw, staring numbly, compulsively, fixedly, without wondering how they got there or what she was even seeing, just staring at what was before her eyes until they reached the steps. And she forgot what she'd seen as soon as he put her down on the walk. She climbed the steps herself, one step at a time, until Gammie scooped her up and said what a mess you are, what with ice cream all over your favorite shirt.

And she understood now: *the letter was a lie.* For certain. Without doubt. It was a lie. Even Gammie didn't know. She'd just accepted what he told her and lived with the injustice it implied. Only Kim knew the truth now… and him. Mommy had fought and struggled with him before he took Kim for ice cream. He'd already killed her… or worse (it seemed worse… no, it was worse), maybe she wasn't dead yet; she was slowly dying while Kim ate strawberry ice cream. Anna had scratched him as she fought for her life, and then he killed her and went back and slashed himself to make it look like she'd come at him. He wasn't cut when he took Kim to Gammie's. His arms weren't hurt. But his neck was already scratched. And he'd made Gammie live with this lie, too, convinced her he was defending himself, even though he couldn't convince a judge and jury. They could only speculate about what happened, the judge, the jury, all the newspapers, even Aunt Jo and Uncle Nick. No one else knew for certain, until now.

If Lalo didn't look so pathetic right now, she might have kicked him the balls just to give him something to remember.

Macario came running up just then, with Angel trotting behind him.

—What the fuck? Macario said, looking inside the car and reaching for Lalo, who shrugged him off. —*¡Que poco mierda!* What the fuck did you do to my car?!

Angel grinned dumbly at Kim.

The music was still blasting inside the car. Macario shut it off and came over to her and said, —He told me go to the party. He said you'd wanna come in, but then when you didn't he said leave you alone out here, said you wanted to be here alone with him.

Turned out he did speak English.

—Fuck him! she said. And fuck you too!

And as she turned and started down the block, she added, —*¡Vete a la mierda!*

Macario caught up behind her and she readied herself for another fight, but he was subdued, maybe, she realized, worried she'd bring the cops.

—I'll take you home, he pleaded. I'll leave him here. He don't have to come. I won't hurt you. Just take you straight home. How you gonna get home?

—I'll get home, she said, without you.

She wandered the dark neighborhood until she heard traffic noise from the main road and found her way there. Lalo had put Uncle Nick's phone on silent in the movie, so she hadn't noticed the calls from home until now.

She followed the light and noise until she came to a car dealership on the highway. It was closed but flooded in light. Out front two gleaming Hummers were parked on massive limestone boulders with no obvious way to drive them up there or back down again. An American flag as big as a house flapped heavily from a pole alongside the display.

Calling Flann was a possibility, but she feared he'd go after Lalo – and probably get his ass kicked by a posse of Latinos or else get himself arrested, or both, which would fuck up his life for good, with probation still hanging over him.

She'd never prayed much, but now she prayed that Uncle Nick would be the one to answer when she called home.

Sunday in the Park

ON A WARM SUNDAY afternoon in late September, as dried leaves rustled in the wind and the dismal end of yet another dismal season of Royals baseball mercifully approached, Nancy and Leo sat on a balcony overlooking Mill Creek Park. A southerly breeze blew sprays of mist from the fountain on sweaty joggers and mothers with strollers and young couples with hands sunk in each other's back pockets. Sudden gusts of wind carried frisbees away and flapped the banners and signs of a small group that had gathered at the street corner to protest the war in Iraq.

—Can't even describe how it irritates me seeing that, Leo said, his voice measured, the space between each word as pronounced as the words themselves. He settled back in his chair and sipped iced tea, adding, —Just as well I've got my back to them.

—There aren't many, Nancy said.

—Shouldn't be none, he sniffed. Back in the first world war they had a law, and those yayhoos out there? they'd have been arrested.

He nodded approvingly.

The small band pumped signs at passing traffic. One man dressed as Uncle Sam strode through the crowd. Another occupied a camp chair near the curb waving an American flag with a peace symbol in place of the field of stars.

—I didn't know that, she said.

—Criticizing your government during wartime was against the

law, is what it was. Don't understand why we let these people get away with that now.

—It makes sense, Nancy said.

He rested an elbow on the railing while a server topped their water glasses.

When he'd gone, Leo said, —But let's talk about something cheerful. So did you like those pictures?

—They were… different. She hesitated before settling on the word.

He huffed a laugh. —True diplomat is what you are.

She laughed too. —No, no, it's just… I'd just never seen anything like it.

—Me neither. I coulda picked someplace better to go, but just, I'd passed that museum up there dozens a times and never been inside so I thought, why not? Might be interesting, and then I thought, maybe Mrs. Oden'd like to see it too.

—I did, she said, and searching for something good to say about the weird paintings that had puzzled them both for the past hour, added, and so close to the Plaza.

And too, she told him, please call her Nancy.

Which he promptly folded into his observation that the paintings might have been done by children with finger paint and he just liked to see a picture of *something*… a sunset or mountain or something. What's wrong with painting pictures like that? he wondered.

She agreed. That's what art should be, she told him, but she also wondered, why would anyone spend so much money to build a building just for those paintings and strange statues? Maybe there *was* more to it. Maybe you shouldn't dismiss it so easily. She wondered… but for now, it seemed easier to let it go.

When they'd ordered dinner and watched the frisbee throwers

for a few minutes, he said, — I hope you don't think I was being forward calling on you.

—It was thoughtful, she said. I haven't been over this way in a while, and such a nice afternoon, too.

She sensed him fishing, dragging his line lightly beneath the surface waters. This was maybe the third or fourth time they'd observed what a nice afternoon it was. They'd left the car at the Kemper Museum of Modern Art, across the park and up Main Street a block or so, and strolled down the hill to Figlio's, about which Leo said several times you couldn't find better lasagna anywhere. She worried he'd be offended if she didn't order it. She hardly had any appetite, and now they'd arrived at that moment, after the museum outing, after the stroll, after they'd ordered dinner but before it arrived, when non-conversation is supposed to give way to something more, but she didn't want more than this, the lingering warmth of the day, the puzzlement of modern art, even the distant drama of the antiwar protest down in the park, which had postponed a little longer the arrival of this moment, when she was supposed to open up, share of herself, talk about things that matter. This all felt so new… and yet so familiar. And he seemed so intent.

—So tell me, he said, predictably, how are you these days?

She glanced at the protesters and watched Uncle Sam bob through the crowd.

—I'm fine, she said. Still working…

She trailed off, hearing the evasiveness in her voice, knowing he'd hear it too. He'd been nothing but kind to her. He deserved more than that, but some instinctive fear held her back, as if knowing that once she opened up there was no turning back, as if it was herself that she feared more than him.

All that in a moment, a breath, a glance away from the table and back again. She'd had no one to talk to for months. He waited on her to finish the sentence; he knew the other side of things too, she was aware; he didn't need the background, the footnotes. He would understand.

— … oh, but this'll probably sound awful, she said, it's terrible, I mean… but I almost feel relieved at times.

She felt like a bystander overhearing her own conversation now.

He nodded thoughtfully. You could not doubt his sincerity. He was a man who listened well. She knew how Elliot knew him – the iced tea on the table seemed almost emblematic. She might've ordered wine, but not today. She had tea also.

—Ah… that's perfectly natural, he said slowly. I lost someone too. You shouldn't have a lick of guilt after all you did, all you been through.

She offered a light shrug and looked off again. Cars had lined up in front of the protesters, waiting for a red light. Voices carried from the open windows of a white SUV as the occupants shouted obscenities at the group.

Leo turned at the noise and scowled. —Be all right with me if they got out and beat them to a pulp.

The sudden harshness in his voice felt like sandpaper scraping an open cut, but she said nothing. The light changed, and the white car squirted through, middle fingers fluttering from its windows and a chorus of *fuck you's* fading as it drove off.

—You just wonder, he said, what happened to all that feeling we had after Nine-Eleven, you know. Now they're out there like a band of hippies or whatever.

When dinner had been served, Leo said, —Maybe you heard about Elliot's nephew's son joining up.

—Why no.

He laughed. —Guess the boy really sprung it on them too. Was early in the summer. He'd had a little run-in with the law a ways back, but the Army'll straighten him out. You can believe that. Seen it over and over again.

—What sort of trouble?

—Some dope or something. They'll make a man out of him. The kid looked like a twig, always mopey-looking, know what I mean? Shook hands with him one time and thought I had hold of a dish rag.

She offered a knowing grin and asked, —So… is he gone?

—Went to Basic sometime in June. Sent him to Jackson, I think. Oughta be near done by now. Most of 'em coming out now are going straight to Iraq. Get a week or so at home after their training and they ship 'em right out.

—Just like that?

He nodded through a bite, and then abruptly said, —Here, that fish looks awful lonely on your plate. You should try this.

He took up his soup spoon and passed a hefty portion onto her plate before she could protest.

She took a spare bite.

—You see! You can't find better. So the boy… I ain't heard for certain where he's at now. Have to ask Elliot when I see him, but I'd be surprised if he ain't on the way, or at least got orders. They're pouring everything into it now. Everything we got. Doubt if it'll last another two months, maybe three.

He took another bite and then said, —So, speaking of them… and don't be shy about telling me it's none of my business neither… but do you get to visit your granddaughter from time to time?

It was inevitable, this question. She'd known it from the moment she agreed to the outing. Wouldn't have mattered how evasive she was. What else did they have in common? They'd sat together at a play a year ago. Well, when you looked at it that way, she'd chosen him, hadn't she?

She rested her fork on the plate.

Knowing this was coming and being ready for it… two different things entirely.

—Now, now, he said, waving a hand, it's none of my business, and I'll say it for you.

—No, that's not it. I suppose you know them better than I do. She snickered, ironically, bitterly. —Maybe even know my granddaughter better. Well, that's it, isn't it? She's not my granddaughter, after all.

—What's that?

—Well, I'm sure you must know, it's all legal. Settled years ago. They took away my son's fatherhood. The sins of the son, I guess. I've lived with it for over ten years. I never meant ill toward them. I used to see her for a holiday or birthday. They allowed me that much. Always just for short visits, formal, you know, never part of anything, never the kind of family visit when there's clamor in the kitchen and you put on an apron and help set the table or stir the gravy, so what's there to talk about? We sit in the living room and talk about nothing and I give her a gift and she opens it and pretends she likes it and says thank you after being prompted, but you know, I'm right about this one thing, and they just don't understand, that sooner or later, no matter what my son did, no matter how guilty or evil or whatever anyone thinks he is, sooner or later she'll want to see him. You just can't blot that out of a person's life. You can't blot that out. She's known where he was since she was little. I guess

I understand them not letting her go up to… to see him. I never agreed, but I can understand how that might affect a child, but she's a teenager now. She's got to have questions. I know she does.

Her hand shook as she took up the fork, not even to eat but merely to move herself along, to navigate this dark passage and get to the other side, because eating, the act of it, the movement it required, was the next thing she could do to speed her way through, though she had no appetite at all… and really wished she'd ordered a glass of wine.

Leo reached across the table and squeezed the hand with the fork, which she allowed, for a moment, before she set it down and folded her hands on her lap.

—I didn't mean to upset you, he said.

—No, no, it's nothing you did. I shouldn't dump all this on you. It's just so close to the surface, you know. It's always there.

—You can dump on me all you like, Leo said. There's not much I ain't seen, but I still can't imagine what you've been through.

For the first time this afternoon she felt vulnerable. He was indeed sincere, but there was hopefulness in his sincerity, desperation even. He was lonely, but she did not have the strength to be the object of yet another man's needs.

It felt like such an effort just to keep up her end of the conversation. But she saw no reason to spill it all now – the letter, the whole history of her exchanges with Jo. She hardly knew this man. And he may not be altogether forthright either, for he must have heard a good deal more about her over the years than he let on.

The dishonesty that most bothered her, however, had nothing to do with him or here and now. It was simply this – that she'd kept the secret of Kim's shoplifting for all these years, never told a soul, but the end result was that from the moment she'd dropped Kimmy off that day, it only seemed to make her more distant. Perhaps from shame, Nancy conjectured, wanted to believe. But despite her own humiliation, Nancy had hoped it would have been something, some history, an experience they had shared that in some strange way would eventually have brought them closer together… a dark secret, a story that might even have become laughable as it aged. But nothing of the kind happened.

—It's just, she said, you never know how a thing's going to change your life. She, my granddaughter, was at *my* house that day, not theirs. I'd given her a bath the night before. I was going to make her breakfast and take her out for some new clothes… and then everything changed, and it's felt like, I don't know, like I've been living in that day ever since, like that day never ended with all the nightmares that came with it…oh, how I babble…I never stop thinking about it, but…this is terrible, to sit here on a nice evening like this and you've been so nice and here I am going on….

She gazed off at the band of protesters in the park and let the sentence hang, mindless of him, the restaurant, the food on her plate, and he, graciously, she recognized, did not feel the urge to fill the silence with talk. But now, watching the group moil about with their banners and weird costumes, she squinted into the evening's fading light and studied the crowd, looking intently now, as if she'd just spotted a rare bird in the dense foliage of a tree.

—What? Leo asked. Something happen?

—It can't be… I don't believe it!

He turned sharply to look.

—I think that's… I'm certain of it… that man in the overalls and fedora… that's Elliot!

Leo stared hard now. —By God, that is him!

—Oh, no!

—What?

—With those women, holding the signs?! That's Kimmy!

—No!

—It is! The girl in the white shirt and watch cap.

She was pumping a sign at the passing traffic. Uncle Sam came by and patted her on the head.

Nancy was too agitated to eat another bite.

Leo's head spun. Just minutes ago he thought they'd linger on the balcony over coffee and stroll the Plaza after dinner. He'd even planned to spring for a horse carriage ride, imagining the two of them in one particular carriage he'd seen shaped like a pumpkin and trimmed with white Christmas lights. But there'd be no recovering from this. He thought he might just punch the lights out of one or two of those hippies down there. One in particular had especially got under his skin, that man parked in the lawn chair with the mock American flag. The flag hung partly on the ground, which, even if it wasn't the real thing, burned Leo every time he looked down at the park.

He paid the check and she apologized a dozen times while he took one final, longing glance at the slab of lasagna still on his plate, and they left.

The scene had changed by the time they reached the park. The protesters were gathered in a circle under an oak tree with yellowing leaves and were singing. They held candles with paper cups for windscreens. Nancy's anger rushing down here now withered as they neared the somber group.

Elliot's hand trembled with his candle, but he sang vigorously. Kimmy was farther along in the circle from him and held a candle too.

She didn't sing but watched the flame and cast glances at others in the group. They hadn't noticed Nancy and Leo yet.

The protest signs lay on the grass and propped against trees. Angry horns sometimes blared from the street. Nancy startled at the noise, while Leo now found himself glaring at belligerent cars. They stood by as poetry and prayers followed the song, and when the group finally broke up and Elliot saw them, he glowed with delight. Kimmy had gone around to collect the extinguished candles into a box.

—Of all the people! Elliot exclaimed.

Leo frowned and said nothing as Elliot greeted Nancy, who could only sputter his name through her rejuvenated anger.

Kim now appeared, hair hanging rumpled and loose from under the watch cap. She hadn't seen Gammie in almost a year, since the play, since she'd passed along the letter full of lies.

Kim had never told anyone what happened with Lalo and what she'd realized that night. Probably nobody'd believe her anyway, she thought. It was so long ago and she was so little, they'd say. She even doubted it herself sometimes. Gammie'd never believe her. She even began to resent her for disbelieving something she'd never been told. Kim could hear her saying, *How could you remember something like that? You were only four! That's impossible. Your imagination's playing tricks on you. We already know what really happened.* And probably, too, she'd blame whatever Kim said on Aunt Jo, which meant, too, that Gammie still thought it was Mommy's own fault that she got killed. All this and more Kim had pondered. And now she found herself resenting Gammie, too, for showing up and spoiling the day. It had been a great day, with all these cool people and the signs and banners and the wind blowing and all the cars and people shouting at them and them shouting back.

Nancy did not help her own cause, though she couldn't have imagined all the ways it had already been damaged, when she greeted Kim with, —What are you doing here?

Kim thrust her hands into her jeans pocket and said, with a note of cheery defiance, —Protesting the war, what else? Did you see Uncle Sam? He's over there! Isn't he cool?

—We saw him, Nancy replied stiffly.

Before Nancy could reboot, Kim turned to Leo and said, —Hey Colonel Leo, know what one of the cars called Uncle Elliot?

—I can imagine what they called him, Leo said, eyes wide, glazed. And looking harshly at Elliot now, he asked, —What are you doing bringing this child down here?

—She wanted to come, he said.

—I did, Kim asserted. I wanted to. It's cause of Flann.

—What about him? Leo asked, and turning to Elliot said, —This is how you act with a soldier in your family? This is how you support our troops?

—I can't think of a better way to support them than by ending this war, Elliot said.

Nancy asked Kim, —Does your aunt know you're here?

She grinned at Elliot, who smiled. —Matter of fact, Nancy, they don't. They think she's at the theater with me, so I guess we're in a world of trouble now, mostly me. We came down with Paul over there. You see him? Elliot wagged a hand at a cluster of people still gathered near the tree.

Leo now recognized the man in the Uncle Sam outfit as one of their AA group and replied in a tone that you couldn't have distinguished from a parent talking to a kid, —Well, we'll take you home!

—Good, Elliot said, because I'm starving.

—Me too, Kim added.

They started down the sidewalk, but Elliot stopped to talk with a woman holding a sign proclaiming, *'THE RIGHT TO DISSENT IS DEMOCRACY!'* She was slight and wiry, and might have been one of the oldest people in the crowd. Nancy had noticed that there were few young people here; most were middle-aged. Kim was probably the youngest person in the group.

Traffic had slowed to a stop for the light at the corner. A minivan with open windows landed in front of them, and a man in the passenger seat sneered at Elliot and the old woman with the sign. A boy of six or seven watched from between the front seats.

Abruptly, the woman driving leaned over and shouted, —You fucking traitors!

—My God! Nancy exclaimed.

Leo turned suddenly. —Who're you calling a traitor?! I got twenty-seven of military service...

The man in the car shouted over him, —Then you're the worst of all!

Leo started for the car, but the woman lurched forward and now the light changed. The man flipped the bird at Leo as they drove off. Leo spun around, looking for someone to vent his fury on and probably would have gone for the protester with the flag, AA friend or not, but the small woman with the sign stepped in front of him, and said sternly, —That's just what they want, people like that. This is a peaceful demonstration. You should try to talk to them next time.

—Talk?!

—That's right, talk to them.

—What good'll that do?

—Maybe none, she said. But if one person drives past here that wasn't thinking about the war and suddenly thinks about it, then we've done some good out here, don't you think? That's why we're here, after all. Look around. All you see are people going this way and that, out there in the park, in their cars, shopping, doing whatever. That's why there's a war, because no one gives a damn if we go to war or not. They just want to shop and keep shopping. That's all they care about.

—Whatever you think I am, lady, I ain't part of your cause.

— I have hope for you, she said, smiling.

Elliot laughed and said, —C'mon, Leo. Your head's smoking.

Leo marched ahead of them as they made their way across the park.

Nancy walked silently between Elliot and Kim and wondered how she'd managed to find yet another angry man.

APO

Always the same, seemed like. Never enough windows open and someone always getting a passport.

Jo could see across the parking lot, through the rain-drizzled front windows, Kimmy slouched in the front seat, wearing Flann's headphones, one of several endowments, which included various T-shirts, ballcaps, and posters, he conferred on her before he left.

Jo shifted her package from one arm to the other as the next customer stepped up to a window. A man on line chattered on a cell phone. A woman read a book, serene, resolved to her time in purgatory. Jo studied the ads for new postage stamps in the display cases: 'Birds of Finland,' 'Wright Brothers: First in Flight.'

She glanced over her customs form yet again, which listed the contents of her box: canned tuna, canned fruit, cocoa, snack bars, cookies, fruit juices, trail mix. Socks. He wanted socks, and not just any. She drove to three stores before she found the ones he wanted. She'd gift-wrapped the socks and several CDs for Christmas.

His deployment had dowsed her life in a weird cocktail of banality and terror. No matter what she was doing, it was always with her. The days here were quiet, ordinary, but who knew what was going on there, what he was doing, if he was even alive… or what he'd seen… and worse, what he might have to do. She wanted only to blot out everything that interfered with thinking and worrying about such things. She watched TV obsessively. She put on the TV in every guest room as she she cleaned and changed bedding. And she scoured the Web. There had to be something about him or his company if she looked, so she did, continually. An hour or more would slip away as she trolled news sites.

He'd called twice since he got there. Nick said that was something. Soldiers in Vietnam and WW II couldn't call home. Flann wouldn't write, she knew. He didn't like writing. Wringing two lines out of him for a birthday thank-you was worse than getting him to do homework. And all he said about email was they didn't have it where he was and there were long lines when he was somewhere they did. Despite his swagger about joining the Army, she knew it wasn't a good fit. His basic training photo, in his utilities and with his cap pulled low, betrayed a look that only she recognized, and it was fear. He had the same sour expression she saw on other soldiers' faces in similar photos, but also something more in the way he lifted his chin, in the squint of his eyes. You wouldn't know it without knowing him as she did, without knowing how he disguised it in a look of defiance, by trying to vacate his expression of any sense of warmth or joy, and so there it was. He was still thin, even after his training, so she knew he'd done what he always did as soon as something was required of him, which was as little as possible. He'd gotten through; they celebrated his success, praised his efforts, admired him in his uniform. But she knew how vulnerable he was, often because he just seemed oblivious to the world around him. She'd lay awake imagining him walking blithely into whatever awaited behind the shadowy doorways of dingy clay buildings she'd seen on TV. His calls came when she was least ready for them, once in the middle of the night, another time while she had a prospective guest on another line, and they spoke as if through a long tube, through the echoes of their own voices and delayed responses of the other's, for eight, maybe ten minutes, across eight thousand miles, from Kansas to Mesopotamia. Talking sounded as difficult as writing for him. He seemed impatient even with the ten minutes they gave him. He answered her questions in monosyllables and offered nothing more. She tried to think of questions that would get him to talk, but each one always came out the same as the others. *Are you getting enough to eat? Yeah. What's it like there? Hot. Where are you? Can't say.* He was somewhere west of Baghdad, they learned. Nick had pinned a map of Iraq inside the basement door, and she'd stare at the blank yellow-gray space to the left of Baghdad, so-colored to suggest sand, as if somewhere in the molecular density of the paper he and his company were to be found.

She lived as if anticipating something, as if each day's news would bring some sort of climax – the war ending? insurgents surrendering? Well, they said it was over last May, and that was before Flann even enlisted. 'Mission Accomplished!' the president proclaimed, but now, each day, things seemed worse and worse. Just this month, barely a week into it, 38 U.S. troops had been killed, almost 400 since the war began last March. How could the mission be 'accomplished,' she wondered, and darkly, too, what was the mission? She wondered. It no longer seemed clear. Every time the phone rang or a car pulled into the driveway, she thought something had happened, that the worst had happened. She imagined heavy footsteps on the front porch and opening the door to find soldiers standing there in dress uniforms. One time there was an insistent knock at the front door while she was upstairs in a back room, where she couldn't hear a car in the driveway. Not even the doorbell, just a repeated knocking at the door. She burst into tears when she opened it and saw guests standing there with their bags, who without doubt wondered what kind of place they'd just walked into.

Up ahead, on line, the next man to be waited on lifted his package off the floor, ready for his turn, and as he did so she noticed the familiar customs form, with its triplicate pages flapping loosely in his fingers, and saw the letters *APO* on the box. He looked back and forth between the two windows, wondering which would free up first. The passport people were nearly done, or so it seemed. Done was never done here. The clerk starting chatting with them about their travel plans as if the line of people behind them didn't exist. The man with the APO box shifted his feet impatiently. He was older than Jo, in his fifties, plainly dressed in a ball cap and jacket, indistinguishable really from anyone you might pass on the street, but that was the thing, wasn't it, about him, about her too? To see them, you wouldn't know how they lived. They were just on line, no different than the others here who talked on cell phones or read books or planned their travel. There was no war for them, so it felt to Jo, and for that man too, she thought. She didn't know any other parents of soldiers. She'd met several in South Carolina, when Flann finished his training at Fort Jackson, brief greetings in a chaotic and happy turmoil of families and soldiers, but now they lived wherever they lived, and she lived here, and it felt to her as if the world had gone to war — until she left her house, for beyond it there was no war, except for her, and now the man in the ball cap.

She became anxious, eager to meet him, exchange numbers, emails. The passport family left and he stepped up to the window, fumbling with his package and forms now, almost as if caught off guard after waiting so long. Jo couldn't catch his eye and was too reticent to call him, and he'd waited so long; she didn't want him to lose his turn. She watched him as she inched farther along toward the front of the line, and then watched him leave, following him with her gaze into the lot to see his car so she'd recognize it. Then he passed from sight, and several cars drove through the lot. His could've been any of them. He was gone. She mailed her package and returned to the car.

Kim wore the headphones but absent the rhythmic sizzling they usually emitted.

—Is it on? Jo asked.

—Unh-uh, doesn't work.

She sprung a finger at the CD player and shrugged.

—Aww, well, I don't think it worked for Flann all the time either.

—Doesn't matter.

Kim kept the headphones on as they drove home. Jo pondered whether to get a new set for her now or wait until Christmas, but that was so long.

Drywall Art and a Tow Down Main Street

AT NIGHT ONLY DOZE, never sleep sleep. Haven't slept two hours straight in twelve years. Just doze, twenty minutes, thirty most. Can't sleep with the noise, the howling, the grunts, the jacking off, the fucking, the thousand rattles and clanks and mutterings, footsteps coming this way, going that, then back again, the rustle of bodies on mattresses, the pissing and shitting and flushing, faucets splattering on and off, coughing and hacking, whispers, talk, and the endless grinding, rasping snores of a hundred open-mawed sleepers… can't… the dream loops and loops… not a dream… tatters of memory… shards of a day… voices, places… a feeling…

… how the road ahead unwound like a silvery strip of duct tape, brighter than the sky, which had darkened to swamp-water gray.

Two thin lanes straightaway, dipping and cresting and dipping again. He could see the far hill on the horizon, the road just a sliver, with dusk mingling the gray sky and the ridge of hedge trees that swallowed up the road so you couldn't tell where the trees ended and the sky began.

He drifted over the double yellow line as he came up on a pair of tail lights moving so slow the car might have been parked in the lane. Just swept past it without a thought about what might be on the other side of the hill. Driven these roads since he was thirteen-fourteen. There'd've been a glimmer of headlights on the ridge if something was there. Besides, what'd it matter now?

—What the fuck, he muttered into the wind and the engine's roar.

Right in my office! My fucking office!

She'd said it over and over, taunting him… taunting him.

He heard rustling out front when she got home, the screen door opening and closing, opening and closing, coupla times, her whispering to Kimmy. He was out on the back porch, feet up on the rail, enjoying the afternoon sun with a tall neck dangling from his fingers. Kimmy said she was hungry so he'd found a bag of Cheese Doodles and set her up with the TV in the front room.

Thing was, he was feeling good. Amped even, you could say.

New subdivision going up in Basehor… platted, roads and water lines and underground power and cable lines already in… well, he'd nailed the contract to do the taping, all the taping, every house, fifty houses to start. A year's work. Once the sheetrock was in, he'd tape them before the painters showed up. The contractor told Ross he'd heard about him from one of the painters. Said he was a drywall artist. Ross glowed. A drywall artist. He liked that. It was true, he thought. You get painters who try to do it themselves, then they fuck it up, rushing to cut tape while their mud dries… should have had the tape all cut and ready to go by then. Don't know how to thin the mud just right, or they leave dry spots under the tape so it bubbles up when the mud dries and wet paint hits it. You can't hide a mistake with drywall. The lightest speck'll show up. A drywall artist he was. Never find a seam in his walls once the paint's on. He didn't even clear twenty last year, and that was before taxes. Less than the rent once you took that out. But next year'd be different.

He felt good that day. Why'd she have to spoil it?

He was thinking maybe they'd get out of this dump soon. Place was like a mini-version of an actual house. He could cross the living room in two strides. In the bedroom he had to hobble along the wall like he was on a ledge just to climb in his side. Kimmy had more room in hers, just her in there.

He tallied the number of lots and his fee for each house as he scoped the field out back. The kids'd built some kind of fort or club-house or something from scrap lumber over on the edge of the woods. Couldn't see them out there now. Maybe do eighty-thousand or more from the Basehor job. Could be that much. Maybe they could even get into one of those places he'd be working on. *Farmstead Estates*. He liked that. Might get a deal from the developer. He was thinking they should go out tonight, celebrate, maybe down to the Legends by the speedway, or that roadhouse place. Texas Roadhouse, that was it. Have to check it out. He liked the sound of it.

Then he heard her out front. Hurried footsteps coming... and then going?

He found Anna in the front room by the door, holding Kimmy, and the kid's backpack too. And her bag by the sofa.

And now he saw the fear in her widening eyes and the tremor of her chin when he appeared.

She was leaving, she said, right now, taking Kimmy with her and going to her sister's. She couldn't do this any more. He'd humiliated her for the last time. She was going.

—What the fuck is this? he said.

—Don't use that language in front of her, she said.

Her voice trembled. Kimmy'd slipped down on her hip. She hoisted her up once more. She was defiant. She said look at yourself, drinking beer while your daughter is out here eating crap off the floor.

She took Kimmy outside and came back, now that he'd seen her, caught her in the act, so to speak, because she had a few more things to say before she left – like that was going to happen. And that bitch sister of hers – smug, superior, every little knick-knack in that museum dusted and set out just so, and that wimp she'd married, probably couldn't arm wrestle an old lady.

Anna lingered by the screen door, glancing out at Kimmy in the front yard with her toys, hovering by the door. He could see what she was doing, ready to dash out if he got closer. So he kept his distance on the other side of the room and drew her back inside, if she wanted to argue… even told her, mind your voice, they'll hear you up and down the street. The kids from across the way had just cut through the yard, probably going out to work on their fort. You want them to hear you? Pipe down. So how'd he humiliate her? he asked, stepping back into the kitchen, like he was reaching for his brew in there.

On and on she went. Almost funny how she couldn't stop herself – griping about Kimmy's nursery school and couldn't he have called to tell her he was picking her up. She'd rushed over there, thinking she was late again and they'd get hit with another fee, only to find out that he'd already got her. So now he understood. She'd already planned out her little exit, probably figured she'd just get Kimmy and go, not even show up here at all.

They were in the kitchen now. He'd backed up so she had to follow if she had more to say, and she did. Almost compulsive now. Couldn't zip her trap.

Right in my office – my fucking office! Like he just shows up there – announcing so everyone could hear it how we're sixty days over on the car. You were supposed to pay that! That was on you! You said you paid it, last month and this month too, but noooo… you didn't. So where'd that money go, Ross? Racing tickets? The casino? Beer? It was my money! Mine! I earned it! And you were supposed to make those payments! Do you have any idea how humiliating it was!? Right in my office, my fucking office! A collector standing there like a gorilla demanding money — cash! — two payments plus interest and late fees right that minute or they're gonna take the car right the fuck out of the parking lot, that minute, then! They had a fucking tow truck idling right outside the door. I had a half a dozen prospects to call — solid leads too — but what the fuck! I have to drop everything and go to the bank and get the cash — which, that money was supposed to be the rent, which I'd like to remind you is due in two days. Drove me up there too, they did, in the fucking tow truck with the car hitched to the back, right through the middle of town, and the truck rumbling away on Main Street while they waited and I got their money and they unhitched the car right in front of the bank. And then… and then I get home and you're parked on your ass drinking beer while Kimmy's out here eating crap off the floor…

As if she enjoyed the sound of her voice. And she didn't fail to remind him yet again how important she was, with that job, even now, dropping little bits of jargon in when she could. She did that all the time. She'd drop this shit when they were out with people, like for drinks at Buster & Dave's or whatever. Just out of nowhere she'd find some way to start with her office gibberish. *Loan deficiency payments. Put-thru charges. Up-limit. Down ticks. Coarse grain.* You don't hear other people talking like that with their office talk when they're out for drinks. Go out to forget all that.

Besides, he couldn't see the sense of paying for childcare just so she could work. Barely any margin at all. And when she got trained for sales and then got her own office, it was no bigger than a closet. Probably had been a closet. The whole place, from the manager's office in back to the tiny fake-walnut-made-in-China desk where she used to sit up front to answer phones, was packed into a pre-fab building with white siding and two green awnings like droopy eyelids, a rectangle no bigger, no, not even as big as a double-wide that was dwarfed by a six-pack of cement silos tall enough to shade the firehouse and ancient oak trees on the north side of the road. And she was gone a lot too, seeing farmers, getting contracts signed for the next harvest. Her looks helped, and that was another thing. Always bragging about how they looked at her, some of these old farmers out in hole-in-the-wall places like Humboldt and Ness City. She was gone three-four days some weeks, up to Nebraska and Iowa, sometimes down to Oklahoma, and he'd have to pick up Kimmy at nursery school – and if he was working, which hadn't been regular the last couple years, Kimmy'd go stay with his mother – so the schedule was always changing, and it was hard to keep track of who was picking her up when because Anna was gone so much. Be here one day then gone for two. Then she'd get home and brag about how all she did was park herself at a corner table in some lunch café in godknowswhere, and all she had to do was sit there for a few hours through the middle of the day and they'd come in, studying the chalk board for the special – five bucks for meatloaf and a buck for gooseberry pie – and before his food had come, some farmer with wheezy breath and a ConAgra cap would be sitting at her table, clutching the brochure she gave him while he gaped at her tits and thought she didn't notice. She wasn't movie-star magazine-cover good looking, either, like Meg Ryan or Julia Roberts. She had a kind of huskiness about her. Thick shoulders, pock-marks from teenage battles with acne. And her voice was coarse, like frayed hemp.

Right in my office! My fucking office! Right in my office! My fucking office!

Just couldn't stop saying it.

Like she enjoyed the sound of it, a kind of chant, a distilled version of the whole argument.

Finally he told her shut up. By now, she'd come fully into the kitchen, past the refrigerator, on the opposite corner of the table from him. He could get to the door as quickly as she could now, and when she realized she was trapped, she suddenly lunged for the door, and so did he, and caught her there and poked her in the chest with a stiff finger and said he'd had enough and shut up and no one was going nowheres tonight. And he told her too that she was so full of herself that she didn't even want to hear his news, which now she'd spoiled by bringing this load of shit home and dumping it on him.

She winced when he poked her, looking away as if to avoid the inevitable blow, but when he didn't swing, it almost seemed to encourage her, as if, maybe, if he'd just let her have a good smack right then… well, maybe that would have been the end of it. None of the rest would have happened.

He told her, he warned her, get off this shit about whatever.

But she was just plain reckless now, trying to push past him, telling him get the fuck out of her way, screaming now, calling for help, thinking anyone on this pissy street cared what happened in this house. No one was coming. No one gave a damn.

But still she screamed and pushed him, and he let her have a couple of shoves, even enjoyed the sport of it. He fended her off and cuffed her once, just a light one, playful almost, like play-fighting, but he'd left himself open, and now she suddenly screamed and flailed at his face with catlike quickness, and when he looked away, she caught him full across neck, scratching him sharply, painfully, and now he did smack her, for real this time – *whumpf!!* – so she flew across the room and stumbled to her knees in front of the sink. That's where she got hold of the carving knife in the sink, still wet and grimy. She turned and wiggled it at him so pathetically that he just advanced on her without a thought that she'd use it, and she didn't. Instead she darted around the table, but he grabbed her from behind, grabbed the arm with the knife, and pounded his closed fist into the side of her head. He shook the knife loose from her hand as she staggered from the blow, and then he swung again, this time a powerful uppercut with the back of his hand and the full force of his strength, which wasn't near enough to kill her, but her head ricocheted sharply into a corner of the cabinet, and that was. She wobbled and shook, a sudden momentary shiver, her eyes wide but staring at nothing, and she then collapsed at his feet. Blood muddied her hair. Her head fell back over her shoulder, and her unblinking eyes stared at the underside of a chair. Blood seeped onto the floor and puddled around the chair leg.

As he drove back to the house through the darkness an hour or so later, after leaving Kimmy at his mother's, her chant played over and over in his head like a jingle you can't get rid of, like some TV commercial or kiddie song.

Right in my office! My fucking office!

He picked up K-32 and headed west back to Sunburg, opening it up now that he had four lanes, pushing up behind a van in the passing lane until it moved over. Wind whipped through the cab, blowing papers around on the floor. They snapped and rattled and fluttered up and then flew out the window. The seat was smudged and sticky from Kimmy's ice cream. The highway wide and flat. The land stretched out in hilly pastures on each side of the road, with high-tensile fencing along places that kept livestock. Couldn't see much except the house lights from places back far off the road, separated by wide swaths of land and rows of hedge trees, just sprinklings of lights, dim yellow constellations in the distance; sometimes a sodium light glowed from the corner of an outbuilding.

The house was dark when he arrived. He went around to the garage, which was jammed to the door with every kind of detritus – furniture, yard tools, camping gear, the jet ski, stacks of paint cans, an engine hoist. He found the GoJo to wash off the blood from his hands from when he'd shaken her to see if she'd move, which she didn't. No mistaking death, even if you've never seen it before. He thought better before he opened the GoJo, putting it back on the shelf and shutting the door. He went up the back stairs to the kitchen, flipped on the light and stepped over her to pick up the carving knife from the floor in his right hand, and without hesitating long enough to think about it, he whacked the business edge twice quickly into his left shoulder and forearm, and wincing now, and groaning with the pain, but hurrying before his left arm weakened, he took the knife in his left hand and took one quick swipe at his right biceps. Then, as blood covered his arm and hands, he wrapped her fingers around the knife, grabbed the phone and dialed nine-one-one, saying nothing to the operator, whose crackly voice asked over and over with increasing urgency what the emergency was and was he still there, and he put the phone on the table with the line open, wrapped his arms with kitchen towels, and sat down to wait.

'Clouds of the west'

Aunt Jo said don't fuss with those dishes I'll get it but I knew she just wanted to be alone with the clean-up like she did most of the time but it wasn't good her being alone, so I gathered the plates and silver on the dining table anyway and brought them into the kitchen to rinse. One couple had gone back upstairs to pack and the other guests went out on the veranda, and Aunt Jo said you'll splatter something on your blouse with this mess, but so what I didn't care, almost hoped I would, but you could see how when I first came down wearing the slacks and print blouse Gammie brought for Christmas – first time I'd worn them ever was today – she checked me out up and down, but she didn't brighten or say a word about it but just made a little nod like that was the right thing to wear, like not so much pleased as she understood and that was all you needed to say about it. And Uncle Nick ditto, and we had one of those looks between us like where you both know the same thing and it was because Aunt Jo was going about her stuff, bustling around the kitchen like she always did, constantly in motion, like more steps and bending over and clatter than ten people would make doing the same thing, but just like she was a shell and nobody was inside her and that's the way she was most days, and he noticed the outfit too, which the blouse? it had half-sleeves and I'd buttoned it all the way to the throat which I wouldn't have but what Gammie said was dress modest-like and I just figured that's probably why she gave me this outfit in the first place so that's what I'd wear, even though she never said so, it wasn't hard to imagine that this was what she'd imagined when she picked it out from Dillard's. So enough about the clothes. Uncle Nick winked, like just between us, like we're carrying on, we're gonna help Aunt Jo best we can, like that, and I winked back but I could never do the one-eye wink like him and I could always feel the other eye blinking too, so now he grinned because of my wink, and we were all okay for the moment. So now Aunt Jo said anyone check on Elliot? and I said I would, and she said she'd brought him toast & tea earlier and see if he wanted fruit cause sometimes he wanted fruit too, and she said but what time was I leaving and I said wasn't for another half-hour or something, and she said Nancy'd probably come early, and I just shrugged like whatever and went up to Strang Line, which was the room down the end of the hallway on the second floor. Was the smallest room up there, which Aunt Jo said they didn't lose nothing having him there and saved a lot of steps for everyone, and I asked if I could have his room up in the attic and she said we'll see, which I knew what that meant, but Uncle Nick when she wasn't around? said if I moved up there it'd be like the third floor would be just them and why didn't I stay where I was for a while and then we'd see, so I said yeah. The TV was on in Uncle Elliot's room with a black and white movie, and every once in a while he'd speak up and say he knew this or that actor, or sometimes he'd start to say it, like he'd try to, and so I'd fill it in for him, like you were friends with him, weren't you? and he'd croak a husky uh-huh and his face'd light up with a story that was backed up inside him and couldn't get out and then we'd go back to watching the movie, but he wasn't watching now, just looking out the front window, where the cottonwood was filling in and seemed like we'd just had winter yesterday and today was spring, which was almost true because wasn't just maybe two weeks ago we had snow and the driveway had to be shoveled, and next day? if Uncle Nick hadn't done a thing? the snow would have melted anyway because it turned warm just like that, but so now the tree had a light green blush almost like a veil had fallen over it, and Uncle Elliot was watching it, like as if he could see the leaves growing, and he didn't know I'd come in even after I tapped on the door, and I said you want the TV on? and that was the first time he knew I was there, and I turned it off and I knew what happened was that Aunt Jo, she just puts it on, like thinking he wants it on, but he doesn't most of the time and then he has trouble with the remote and just gives up and ignores it, and I said you eat your breakfast? and he looked at me like he was waiting for me to say something else, but I knew he heard me, just that Uncle Nick said he'd looked it up on the Web? and what happened was that sometimes he couldn't use his face to make expressions, even when he talked, so he'd still be feeling something or thinking it or trying to say it but it would be trapped inside him, whatever he wanted to say, and he could still talk some, but his voice was flat and he couldn't always find enough words for what he wanted to say, but so we should just talk to him like we always had cause that would make him feel better, and but Aunt Jo? she knew all this too but she'd still put the TV on when he didn't want it or cover him with a blanket when he was already warm, but she was just trying to make him comfortable like how she thought it'd be comfortable for her, which it wasn't for him. But so his dishes were empty, sitting on the table by his chair, and I said oh good you ate everything, so how about some fruit or more tea? and he said no in a hoarse grunt that I wondered what else he might have wanted. Aunt Jo would ask him how about this or that or the other, but it just seemed like so much work for him to try to answer each question just to say no that's not what he wanted, but no one could bring him the things he really wanted which were already gone, or maybe yet to come, and so there wasn't much you could say about it. His head would sway suddenly, rocking about in a wide arc, and his eyes'd close briefly when that happened, so it looked like he was about to pass out, but he wasn't, and then he'd recover and blink once or twice like he'd landed someplace unfamiliar and had to get the lay of things. His chest was thin, almost concave, and his shirts hung like they'd been draped on him, and his belly drooped down over his belt like so much bread dough just hanging off the end of the rolling board. I said the leaves're coming in, you find any birds nesting out there? and he shook his head no, and I looked outside with him for a couple of minutes, studying the tree to see if I could find one he could watch until the leaves hid it but there wasn't one, so I went over to his nightstand and took up the book of poems he kept there but which he couldn't read cause his hands wobbled and the words jittered around, and I said I'm gonna read a poem now and he didn't answer or even look my way but just settled back in the chair like ready for a poem, and I started to read one he liked, that he used to read to me a long time ago and seemed like a good poem for looking out the window and imagining something more than just the tree and the street outside.

> *Flood-tide below me! I see you face to face!*
> *Clouds of the west - sun there half an hour high - I see you*
> > *also face to face.*

I read on, through the rushing crowds, the ferry gates, the river and sky, the ship masts and sunset. Uncle E had said it was like Walt was bear-hugging Manhattan and all the unborn ferry boat riders still a hundred years off in the future, like he was talking one-on-one to the clouds and the sun and the people in their usual costumes, and he'd say, Uncle E would, that it was us Walt was talking to, that we were the ones in our usual costumes, and he was talking directly to us from the past, knowing we'd be here one day, wasn't that something? he'd say, somebody from the past talking straight to you? But soon I heard a car slow and pull into the driveway and I knew there'd be footsteps on the hall in just a minute or three and it wasn't even that long cause Uncle Nick came up and said she's here and I said kay and told Uncle Elliot I'd finish the poem later cause that'd give him something to look forward to and he raised his arm slowly, like the gate at the railroad crossing, just lifted it up, bent at the elbow, and that was his wave and so I hugged him and said watch out the window cause I'll wave from out there too and be back later, and then Uncle Nick said Leo's coming by soon, and Uncle Elliot he looked over like he didn't know who Leo was but I knew he did but that's just what his face made it look like but Uncle Nick told him again anyway and said Leo's coming by to visit, and out in the hall Uncle Nick said you don't have to do this you know, and I shrugged like might as well cause I figured I'd have to sooner or later, it'd always be out there, a thing I'd still have to do, and Aunt Jo she probably would've tried to talk me out of it before Flann died in Iraq but that had just sucked the fight out of her and that's the way she'd been for almost a year, just settled into this numbness like, but her routines were so fixed, her baking and cooking and running the place, that they kept her alive on their own, like some back-up battery system that kicked on when the regular power went out, but you knew that sooner or later the battery'd run out, so we had to keep her going until the regular power came back again. One thing? was having the flag in a cherry-wood shadow box on the hearth and Flann's picture there too, well, if it was just us lived here you'd see it all the time for sure, but it'd be a fixture in the room and you wouldn't talk about it every time you passed through, but with guests it was like always like it just happened, like even now, as I went down to the kitchen, the couple that'd gone out on the veranda had come back inside and were looking at the picture and the clipping Aunt Jo had framed beside it from the newspaper describing how his camp got bombed with mortar rockets and they hit the ammo storage bunker and that went off and destroyed most of the camp and Flann and six others had died just cause of where their tents were, no other reason, just cause they were where they were and how to figure why it was them and not somebody else, but if it wasn't them it'd be some other family just like ours whose soldier got killed, and so I still wanted to go to the war protests and such like I used to with Uncle Elliot, but Aunt Jo put a stop to that when she found out, which Colonel Leo and Gammie didn't tell on us that one time a couple of years back, but she found out when she saw us on TV a few months later and that was something, and then after Flann died, I knew it'd hurt her and so I didn't go but I was still glad that other people did cause it just seemed like the war had no end, and so how you gonna stop it otherwise, cause too, like Aunt Jo would say, other people? it's like there is no war, so how else can you tell them about it because our soldier died and most people don't even know? First time it bothered me wearing these clothes was when Gammie said oh don't you look nice when I came into the kitchen because nice was something

I never want to look like but today I figured I'd just do what I had to cause for one, even though Aunt Jo had never wanted me to go there I was thinking maybe in some strange way it'd be good for her if I did and that'd put it behind all of us for good, and then a few hours from now, before it was even sunset, it'd be behind us and she wouldn't have to think about it again, and for the other, that was for Gammie, who I could see had carried this wish for so long and it seemed like it was the only thing that mattered to her now, and it was all she had, and so I decided that today I'd just leave myself here for a little while, for a few hours, and I'd let her take me up there and I'd see him and see what he had to say after all these years. I never told her what I knew. Thought about it, telling her, but then, having to say it out loud, to describe what I'd seen when I was only four years old, seemed like it would be so threadbare once it was aired that I'd just sound pathetic trying to bring it up now. Plus too, what was the point – just add more pain? for Gammie, for Aunt Jo? probably for me too, stirring it all up like that. Besides I remembered it better – it was all clearer to me – by not talking about it. And I think Gammie already knew the truth and always had – but how do you give up on your kid, your only kid, no matter what they do? So that's what the worst of this was for her, I was sure. To know what I knew the way I knew it, with that same certainty, would have turned him into someone she didn't recognize. Might just as well have picked a random convict to visit all these years as her own son. For my part, going there was more like unfinished business… seeing him, putting flesh on all that I'd imagined… and letting him see me too, take a good look and see that I was flesh too and not just a name he'd scribbled on an envelope or a picture Gammie showed him. Aunt Jo'd told me many times that I looked like Anna, which I thought was maybe true from the pictures, so I wondered what he'd think to see me, if that'd give him pause to reflect on what he'd done and how much worse he made it by writing a letter to try to put the blame on her. I had no plan to tell him what I knew either – but just to let him see that I knew he'd lied to me, to Gammie, and probably to himself. And too, to ask him just one question and see if he told the truth, which I'd know by how it felt when he answered, and that was this… I'd ask him this one thing… was she still alive when he left her? did he leave her there all alone, crumpled on the tiles of that kitchen floor which I'd seen a glimpse of myself to bleed away her life and breathe her last while I sat on a parking lot curb and licked strawberry ice cream? Did he leave her there… and leave me to know for my whole life that that's what I was doing while she died? He'd have to tell me that and tell me the truth. Only he could answer that one, no one else. No one else could know. It'd have to come from him – the truth – not from someone else showing it to him and leaving him with no other lies to tell. And I'd know if he was telling the truth. And I thought of this, too, that I didn't want Gammie to have to hear it, so maybe I'd just tell her wait outside, so it'd just be me and him, and he could lie to me or tell me the truth, and she would never have to hear what I asked him or what I knew, and what he'd say to that… so that's what I decided to do. But I didn't think he'd tell me the truth because all he knew was lies, or that he'd ask forgiveness, and I didn't believe for a minute that'd happen, and I wasn't going there expecting it, but on the one-in-ten-thousand chance that he did, he shouldn't be denied it, I decided. So that was it, too. This was his chance. His one chance. And that maybe worried me more than anything – because if he did, if he broke down and admitted the truth and begged forgiveness from me and everyone he'd hurt, I didn't know if I had it inside me to forgive him. Maybe I feared that most of all because maybe it was more than I could give. I didn't know if I could, but I'd have to find out, I supposed, and then that'd be one more thing I'd have done with. Downstairs Uncle Nick was at the hearth talking to the guests about Flann. I went into the kitchen and heard that I looked nice, and outside I waved up to Uncle E's room, and then Gammie and I got in her car to drive to the prison. Was a long ride too, about three hours. She asked where I might go to college, which I didn't know, but she said she wanted to help with that but didn't want me saying anything to Aunt Jo right now and she'd talk to her another time. And how sorry she was about Flann, too, but we should be proud of him. And she even told me that Colonel Leo had wanted to marry her but she didn't think she'd ever get married again and that she liked living on her own, but she got lonely too, and maybe I'd come up and stay with her overnight once in a while, which I said maybe I would. This much got us through Topeka, but we still had another couple of hours' drive, which was more quiet now and I enjoyed the fluid, rolling sweep of the Flint Hills as we passed through, and I thought of Flann when we passed Fort Riley off to the right, with its rows and rows of desert-camo trucks and tanks. He'd never been stationed here, but anything Army always made me think of him. Farther on Gammie told me what all we'd have to do with the gates and scanners and turnstiles and such, which I didn't worry about because I figured whatever the routine was I'd get through it because somebody'd figured out a long time ago how to get visitors in and out of the place so I didn't have to worry about it. Then she got quiet and stiff as we neared the place. Her apprehension just seemed to fill the car in the silence when she shut off the motor in the parking lot. She breathed in a stuttered sort of way, and then she said, which surprised me after all the years she'd been wanting me to come here, maybe this isn't right, after all, maybe we should leave. And she seemed to want me to decide, now that we were here, with these huge limestone walls looming over us and you could see guards moving around inside the tinted glass of the towers and prisoners in denim shirts working in the fields outside the fencing, and so now it hung over me whatever we were supposed to do. And I realized then how terrified I was at that moment, which I'd been able to keep down because I'd made myself believe I was doing this for her and not for me, that without her wanting me to be here I wouldn't have come, probably never would have come, and then I'd always have had to live, years from now, when he finally did get out, with wondering if one day he'd show up out of nowhere, and I'd live with a fear that would have me always searching faces in crowds and on streets to see if he was among them. But she hadn't actually asked me a question, and so I didn't have to say a word, which I didn't, and to fill the silence in the car, the silence inside myself, I listened hard with my inside ears for the comfort of a sound that hadn't come to me in a long time, seemed like, because everyone else had needed so much from me, with Flann getting killed and Aunt Jo just turning heartsick about it because she found ways you couldn't even imagine to blame herself, and I knew now in ways I never imagined before about all the men and women getting killed in this war because it was like she was feeling it the same way now for all the other mothers and fathers and wives and children and that was one reason that her grief stayed with her, and stayed with all of us too, because it was still happening every day, over and over again... and too, with Uncle Elliot getting sick and having to be brought his meals and needing someone to read to him, and there was so much to do around the house, and even now it didn't seem like Gammie wanted me to decide for her but that she wanted my help too, to relieve some of the burden of her guilt, about bringing me here maybe, but even more, about whatever it was that she did in her life before I was born, maybe even before he was born, that had, she believed, brought all of us to this place, to the lives we led, and the worst was, the emptiest part of what I felt right then was that there was no hum to shut out the silence of her expectations and guilt, or Aunt Jo's, or anyone's, nothing came to me then to shut it out, the silence of me not saying anything, not telling her what we should do, and not knowing, because so much of my life had been decided for me without me choosing it and seemed so random now, because how do you end up being one person and not another, and so maybe it was why I acted so random sometimes, like stealing and breaking dishes and fighting and doing other stuff for reasons that I didn't even know why. But while she waited and other cars pulled in and visitors crossed the lot to the gate, I realized that this was how it felt too when Aunt Jo took me to the cemetery where Mommy was, and I never knew how I was supposed to feel then either because trying to feel something for her made her seem farther away than when she just came to me when I wasn't expecting her, because what I'd feel then, as we stood in the grass at her grave where the marker said her name, was the sadness of emptiness, because she didn't come to me then, because trying to remember made her slip farther out of reach than when she'd come to me in the bedroom where we stayed at Aunt Jo's when I was little, which I could still remember, and Aunt Jo said I reminded her of Anna, and that's what she called her, was Anna, like I reminded her in how I'd accent a word in a sentence, she said, or how I walked and mostly, and she'd always said this, that I had my own will, and that Anna did too, she was willful, and stubborn, Aunt Jo'd say, but she wanted me to know it in a way like because I'd need to have that willfulness, that it was something good that Anna'd given me to survive, almost as if she knew I'd need it because she wouldn't be there, but she was still with me because she'd given me this part of herself and I would need it, so now I believed that how I remembered her wasn't by seeing her face or hearing her voice but because at just that moment I felt an impulse surge up from somewhere inside of me like you get when for no reason at all you suddenly feel like running instead of walking, and I knew I should share that impulse, that strength, with Gammie, who for the first time since I'd ever known her seemed so frail and weak, and when I took her hand and squeezed it, her skin just seemed to slide loosely over the bones, and I said, You didn't do anything wrong, and she seemed to know exactly what I meant by that and it wasn't about her bringing me here either, and she knew that too, and then she sniffed a breath as if inflating herself to sit up straight and we got out of the car and went inside…

> *… and our lives also passed,*
> *and the earth endured …*

Fomite

About Fomite

A fomite is a medium capable of transmitting infectious organisms from one individual to another.

"The activity of art is based on the capacity of people to be infected by the feelings of others." Tolstoy, *What Is Art?*

Writing a review on Amazon, Good Reads, Shelfari, Library Thing or other social media sites for readers will help the progress of independent publishing. To submit a review, go to the book page on any of the sites and follow the links for reviews. Books from independent presses rely on reader-to-reader communications.

For more information or to order any of our books, visit:
http://www.fomitepress.com/our-books.html

More Titles from Fomite...

Novels

Joshua Amses — *During This, Our Nadir*
Joshua Amses — *Ghatsr*
Joshua Amses — *Raven or Crow*
Joshua Amses — *The Moment Before an Injury*
Charles Bell — *The Married Land*
Charles Bell — *The Half Gods*
Jaysinh Birjepatel — *Nothing Beside Remains*
Jaysinh Birjepatel — *The Good Muslim of Jackson Heights*
David Brizer — *Victor Rand*
L. M Brown — *Hinterland*
Paula Closson Buck — *Summer on the Cold War Planet*
Dan Chodorkoff — *Loisaida*
Dan Chodorkoff — *Sugaring Down*
David Adams Cleveland — *Time's Betrayal*
Paul Cody— *Sphyxia*
Jaimee Wriston Colbert — *Vanishing Acts*
Roger Coleman — *Skywreck Afternoons*
Marc Estrin — *Hyde*
Marc Estrin — *Kafka's Roach*
Marc Estrin — *Speckled Vanities*
Marc Estrin — *The Annotated Nose*

Fomite

Zdravka Evtimova — *In the Town of Joy and Peace*
Zdravka Evtimova — *Sinfonia Bulgarica*
Zdravka Evtimova — *You Can Smile on Wednesdays*
Daniel Forbes — *Derail This Train Wreck*
Peter Fortunato — *Carnevale*
Greg Guma — *Dons of Time*
Richard Hawley — *The Three Lives of Jonathan Force*
Lamar Herrin — *Father Figure*
Michael Horner — *Damage Control*
Ron Jacobs — *All the Sinners Saints*
Ron Jacobs — *Short Order Frame Up*
Ron Jacobs — *The Co-conspirator's Tale*
Scott Archer Jones — *And Throw Away the Skins*
Scott Archer Jones — *A Rising Tide of People Swept Away*
Julie Justicz — *Degrees of Difficulty*
Maggie Kast — *A Free Unsullied Land*
Darrell Kastin — *Shadowboxing with Bukowski*
Coleen Kearon — *#triggerwarning*
Coleen Kearon — *Feminist on Fire*
Jan English Leary — *Thicker Than Blood*
Diane Lefer — *Confessions of a Carnivore*
Diane Lefer — *Out of Place*
Rob Lenihan — *Born Speaking Lies*
Colin McGinnis — *Roadman*
Douglas W. Milliken — *Our Shadows' Voice*
Ilan Mochari — *Zinsky the Obscure*
Peter Nash — *Parsimony*
Peter Nash — *The Perfection of Things*
George Ovitt — *Stillpoint*
George Ovitt — *Tribunal*
Gregory Papadoyiannis — *The Baby Jazz*
Pelham — *The Walking Poor*
Andy Potok — *My Father's Keeper*
Frederick Ramey — *Comes A Time*
Joseph Rathgeber — *Mixedbloods*
Kathryn Roberts — *Companion Plants*
Robert Rosenberg — *Isles of the Blind*
Fred Russell — *Rafi's World*
Ron Savage — *Voyeur in Tangier*
David Schein — *The Adoption*
Lynn Sloan — *Principles of Navigation*
L.E. Smith — *The Consequence of Gesture*

Fomite

L.E. Smith — *Travers' Inferno*
L.E. Smith — *Untimely RIPped*
Bob Sommer — *A Great Fullness*
Tom Walker — *A Day in the Life*
Susan V. Weiss —*My God, What Have We Done?*
Peter M. Wheelwright — *As It Is On Earth*
Suzie Wizowaty — *The Return of Jason Green*
Poetry
Anna Blackmer — *Hexagrams*
L. Brown — *Loopholes*
Sue D. Burton — *Little Steel*
David Cavanag*h*— *Cycling in Plato's Cave*
James Connolly — *Picking Up the Bodies*
Greg Delanty — *Loosestrife*
Mason Drukman — *Drawing on Life*
J. C. Ellefson — *Foreign Tales of Exemplum and Woe*
Tina Escaja/Mark Eisner — *Caida Libre/Free Fall*
Anna Faktorovich — *Improvisational Arguments*
Barry Goldensohn — *Snake in the Spine, Wolf in the Heart*
Barry Goldensohn — *The Hundred Yard Dash Man*
Barry Goldensohn — *The Listener Aspires to the Condition of Music*
R. L. Green — *When You Remember Deir Yassin*
Gail Holst-Warhaft — *Lucky Country*
Raymond Luczak — *A Babble of Objects*
Kate Magill — *Roadworthy Creature, Roadworthy Craft*
Tony Magistrale — *Entanglements*
Gary Mesick — *General Discharge*
Andreas Nolte — *Mascha: The Poems of Mascha Kaléko*
Sherry Olson — *Four-Way Stop*
Brett Ortler — *Lessons of the Dead*
David Polk — *Drinking the River*
Janice Miller Potter — *Meanwell*
Janice Miller Potter — *Thoreau's Umbrella*
Philip Ramp — *The Melancholy of a Life as the Joy of Living It Slowly Chills*
Joseph D. Reich — *A Case Study of Werewolves*
Joseph D. Reich — *Connecting the Dots to Shangrila*
Joseph D. Reich — *The Derivation of Cowboys and Indians*
Joseph D. Reich — *The Hole That Runs Through Utopia*
Joseph D. Reich — *The Housing Market*
Kenneth Rosen and Richard Wilson — *Gomorrah*
Fred Rosenblum — *Playing Chicken with an Iron Horse*
Fred Rosenblum — *Vietnumb* \

Fomite

David Schein — *My Murder and Other Local News*
Lawrence Schimel — *Desert Memory: Poems of Jeannette L. Clariond*
Harold Schweizer — *Miriam's Book*
Scott T. Starbuck — *Carbonfish Blues*
Scott T. Starbuck — *Hawk on Wire*
Scott T. Starbuck — *Industrial Oz*
Seth Steinzor — *Among the Lost*
Seth Steinzor — *To Join the Lost*
Susan Thomas — *In the Sadness Museum*
Susan Thomas — *The Empty Notebook Interrogates Itself*
Sharon Webster — *Everyone Lives Here*
Tony Whedon — *The Tres Riches Heures*
Tony Whedon — *The Falkland Quartet*
Claire Zoghb — *Dispatches from Everest*

Poetry - Dual Language
Vito Bonito/Alison Grimaldi Donahue — *Soffiata Via/Blown Away*
Antonello Borra/Blossom Kirschenbaum — *Alfabestiario*
Antonello Borra/Blossom Kirschenbaum — *AlphaBetaBestiaro*
Antonello Borra/Anis Memon — *Fabbrica delle idee/The Factory of Ideas*
Aristea Papalexandrou/Philip Ramp — *Μας προσπερνά/It's Overtaking Us*
Mikis Theodoraksi/Gail Holst-Warhaft — *The House with the Scorpions*
Paolo Valesio/Todd Portnowitz — *La Mezzanotte di Spoleto/Midnight in Spoleto*

Stories
MaryEllen Beveridge — *After the Hunger*
MaryEllen Beveridge — *Permeable Boundaries*
Jay Boyer — *Flight*
L. M Brown — *Treading the Uneven Road*
L. M Brown — *Were We Awake*
Michael Cocchiarale — *Here Is Ware*
Michael Cocchiarale — *Still Time*
Neil Connelly — *In the Wake of Our Vows*
Catherine Zobal Dent — *Unfinished Stories of Girls*
Zdravka Evtimova —*Carts and Other Stories*
John Michael Flynn — *Off to the Next Wherever*
Derek Furr — *Semitones*
Derek Furr — *Suite for Three Voices*
Elizabeth Genovise — *Where There Are Two or More*
Andrei Guriuanu — *Body of Work*
Zeke Jarvis — *In A Family Way*
Arya Jenkins — *Blue Songs in an Open Key*

Fomite

Jan English Leary — *Skating on the Vertical*
Marjorie Maddox — *What She Was Saying*
William Marquess — *Badtime Stories*
William Marquess — *Because Because Because Because Because*
William Marquess — *Boom-shacka-lacka*
William Marquess — *Things I Want You to Do*
Gary Miller — *Museum of the Americas*
Jennifer Anne Moses — *Visiting Hours*
Martin Ott — *Interrogations*
Christopher Peterson — *Amoebic Simulacra*
Christopher Peterson — *Scratch the Itchy Teeth*
Charles Phillips — *Dead South*
Jack Pulaski — *Love's Labours*
Charles Rafferty — *Saturday Night at Magellan's*
Ron Savage — *What We Do For Love*
Fred Skolnik— *Americans and Other Stories*
Lynn Sloan — *This Far Is Not Far Enough*
L.E. Smith — *Views Cost Extra*
Caitlin Hamilton Summie — *To Lay To Rest Our Ghosts*
Susan Thomas — *Among Angelic Orders*
Tom Walker — *Signed Confessions*
Silas Dent Zobal — *The Inconvenience of the Wings*

Odd Birds
Micheal Breiner — *the way none of this happened*
Bill Davis — *Cheap Gestures*
J. C. Ellefson — *Under the Influence: Shouting Out to Walt*
David Ross Gunn — *Cautionary Chronicles*
Andrei Guriuanu & Teknari — *The Darkest City*
Gail Holst-Warhaft — *The Fall of Athens*
Roger Lebovitz — *A Guide to the Western Slopes and the Outlying Area*
Roger Lebovitz — *Twenty-two Instructions for Near Survival*
dug Nap— *Artsy Fartsy*
Delia Bell Robinson — *A Shirtwaist Story*
Peter Schumann — *A Child's Deprimer*
Peter Schumann — *All*
Peter Schumann — *All, Nothing, Nothing At All*
Peter Schumann — *Belligerent & Not So Belligerent Slogans from the
                Possibilitarian Arsenal*
Peter Schumann — *Bread & Sentences*
Peter Schumann — *Charlotte Salomon*
Peter Schumann — *Diagonal Man Theory + Praxis, Volumes One and Two*

Fomite

Peter Schumann — *Faust 3*
Peter Schumann — *Planet Kasper, Volumes One and Two*
Peter Schumann — *We*

Plays
Stephen Goldberg — *Screwed and Other Plays*
Michele Markarian — *Unborn Children of America*

Essays
William Benton — *Eye Contact: Writing on Art*
Robert Sommer — *Losing Francis: Essays on the Wars at Home*
George Ovitt & Peter Nash — *Trotsky's Si*